Nate the Wyoming Story

Also by Mark Warren

The Westering Trail Travesties

A Last Serenade for Billy Bonney

Nate Champion Duology

Nate the Texas Story

Nate the Wyoming Story

Nate Champion Duology

Part Two

Mark Warren

WOLFPACK
PUBLISHING
— EST 2013 —

Nate the Wyoming Story
Paperback Edition
Copyright © 2024 Mark Warren

Wolfpack Publishing
1707 E. Diana Street
Tampa, FL 33610

wolfpackpublishing.com

Image of Nate Champion courtesy of the Jim Gatchell Memorial Museum

Paperback ISBN 978-1-63977-536-1
eBook ISBN 978-1-63977-535-4
LCCN 2024941071

To Nathan David Champion

Nate the Wyoming Story

Early Autumn 1885
Buffalo, Wyoming Territory

Chapter One

The Johnson County Agricultural Fair was the largest event to take place on the streets of Buffalo since the soldiers of Fort McKinney had paraded through town to celebrate the completion of their garrison in '79. A motley assortment of tables lined either side of Main Street where browsing customers sampled prize-winning cakes and pies, handled newly improved farming implements, and purchased crop seeds, colorful fabrics, and exotic teas from places as far away as China and India.

One of the most popular stations offered free sips of beer from six different countries. Another tested a man's strength in swinging a stout wooden mallet downward onto a thick slab of sycamore to send a twenty-pound weight up a fixed track to ring a bell. There, the only entrance fee was a man's willingness to embarrass himself if he failed. But nothing drew customers like the wild horse jump at the west end of town.

Shoulder to shoulder with strangers and friends alike, Nate Champion stood just outside the bare-bones arena that the fair committee had set up in the weedy lot beside the lumberyard. The tract of scrubby ground was marked off into the shape of a large oval by scores of iron cooking spits hammered into the ground. Each rod's upper end had been forged into a ring, and through each ring ran a coarse rope that completed the elliptical paddock. A strip of red cloth had been tied to each sagging span of rope between the rods. It wasn't much of a barrier as far as a horse was concerned, but the boundary might as well have been a stone wall by the way it held the spectators out of harm's way.

The crisp autumn air carried the savory scent of roasted corn and grilled beef, occasionally undercut by an acrid mix of tobacco smoke and horse manure. The sky was so blue that it seemed to enrich the colors of everything beneath it. The scrub brush. The knotty pine boards stacked in the lumberyard. The fine, handmade dresses that the womenfolk seldom wore unless it was to a dance or a church social. To the west, the shadowed Big Horns swelled like a giant, dark wave risen from the ground and then frozen in place as if Moses had commanded it to halt and forever hover over the Powder River Valley.

The afternoon was cool. So much so that Nate had dug out a blue flannel shirt from his store of winter clothes. It was the first time he had worn it since the roundup last spring. Considering he had soaped his boots and worn his new denim trousers with the copper rivets, Nate was about as gussied up as a cowhand dared to be.

"Let 'er rip!"

The terse call came from the chute—a voice Nate knew all too well. All heads turned to see the skinny livery boy from the Occidental Hotel throw open the chute gate and dodge under the rope, where the spectators opened a space and took him into the fold. From the chute, "Ranger" Jones burst into the arena on a spotted roan mare that bucked and twisted and lunged and spun as if fighting for her life. All the while, the horse squealed a kind of tormented growl that rose to a high-pitched shriek that made Nate clench his teeth and narrow his eyes.

Bareback on the roan, Ranger held a single rein in his left hand, his right flailing above his head as his lithe body whipped about with the gyrations of the horse. After a few seconds of impressive stick-to, he managed to turn the animal toward the jump bar and spur it into a wild charge. The crowd cheered and watched with keen anticipation.

One length from the bar, the horse lowered its left shoulder and cut hard like a well-trained cowpony. Ranger had seen it coming and leaned with the turn, but the roan braked and suddenly whirled around in a clockwise spin that sent the rider tumbling to the ground.

A collective groan rose from the audience, and then all became quiet as Ranger lay as still as a corpse. When, finally, he sat up and showed his crooked smile, everyone started clapping and talking at once. He stood, picked up his hat, and waved it once to the crowd before slapping the hat against his trousers, producing a cloud of dust that swirled around his legs before wafting away on the breeze. Limping across the makeshift paddock, he headed toward a table near the lumber office where three young women were selling hot cider. After pushing his fingers through his hair from front to back, he settled the hat on his head and began tucking in his blouse all the way around his slender waist. The closer he got to that table, the less his limp showed.

Over the last hour, nine cowhands had tried their luck on the same, spirited roan. Two had been unable to mount the animal and stay on long enough to signal to the gate-keeper. Of those who had made it into the arena, all had eaten dirt. Four had been bucked off within two seconds of leaving the chute. Three had clung to the bare back of the frightened horse long enough to run at the jump bar that had been set up in the center of the arena. But each time, the mare had cut hard left to avoid the obstruction, and, with that quick, jolting turn, she had jettisoned her load. Once, she sent a rider over the bar. That had brought a howl of laughter from everybody.

The challenge, of course, was to convince the horse to clear the bar with the rider perched on its back, and whoever could accomplish that first would take home the total sum collected for the entry fees. At four bits a try, the prize had swelled almost to five dollars. But Moreton Frewen—the owner of the Powder River Cattle Company —had promised to match the purse from his own pocket. With so much money at stake, it was a testimonial to the mare's penchant for battle that so few had signed up to ride her.

The bar was a narrow, eight-foot-long strip of wood laid across two barrels standing on end. It sagged only slightly to stand three feet above the ground at its midpoint and was fringed with the same red strips of cloth that hung from the ropes bordering the arena. These slender red banners gently waved and shimmered whenever the breeze picked up. There must have been twenty of them tied to the bar, giving it the look of an elongated, red-legged creature trying to escape but whose feet could not gain purchase with the ground.

Around the oval, the spectators had crowded in close to view the event. The smallest youngsters were perched upon their fathers' shoulders, but a host of older children had crawled through the maze of boots and legs and dresses and knelt or sat cross-legged under the rope. All the crowd jabbered among themselves, the sound as constant as a river shoal. They were excited—even jubilant—and they wanted to see a rider take that mustang over the bar.

In the boarded-up holding pen next to the entry chute,

three agitated mustangs were held in supply, in case one or two incurred an injury. They worried back and forth inside their confined space, the whites of their eyes burning bright with fear or defiance. From twenty yards away, Nate could feel their prickly apprehension like ants crawling across his skin. He knew just how they were thinking, too, facing the unknown and unsure how to tolerate such a gathering of people. Especially the noise. It must have been terrifying to animals just captured out on the prairie. None had ever been saddled, but someone had managed to fit a halter over each horse's head. On each halter a short lead rope was tied to the brass ring on the left side, offering a single, one-sided rein for the rider.

While three wranglers tried to capture the victorious roan that had thrown Ranger on his head, the mare pranced and snorted around the arena. One of these handlers finally threw a rope over the bobbing head, and the horse began backing away in a tug of war with its captor.

Jack Flagg—the official announcer—jogged toward the center of the oval with his rolled paper megaphone in one hand. As Flagg's coworker at the Bar C, Nate had grown to like the man for his ethics and the bold confidence he used to back up his principles. He was a good choice for this job at the fair. A handsome man with a robust personality, Jack held the respect of the people of Buffalo, for he had become the voice of both the small ranchers as well as the underpaid cowboys employed by the rich cattle barons. If anyone could quiet this crowd, that man would be Jack Flagg.

When he reached his destination, Jack spread his boots, propped his fists on his hips, and looked around at the animated crowd surrounding him. Applause started working its way around the periphery of the arena, until Jack raised an arm and made lowering gestures with his hand. When he brought up the megaphone, the crowd went quiet to hear him.

"Folks!" Jack yelled through the paper cone, "I'm beginnin' to think there ain't a man in Johnson Coun'y who can take this lively filly over that lil' jump!" He pointed to the decorated bar that had yet to be conquered. "Even on my worst day, I b'lieve I could jump over that bar in my boots with a saddle slung over my shoulder. I don't see why a mustang cain't do it, too. Do y'all?"

The crowd responded with so many different replies that none of them could be understood. Once again, Flagg motioned with his hand for quiet.

"You try 'er, Jack!" a man yelled, his booming voice filling the arena like the bray of a mule. "If *you* cain't make that mare fly, then maybe this deal is stacked ag'in us."

Jack laughed. "There is no stacked deck here, folks. Just wild mustangs. We were up front about the 'wild' part from the get-go."

"Come on, Jack!" someone else called out from the opposite side of the arena. "Show us how it's done!"

Jack's face turned serious, the way an actor on a stage turns his mood on a whim. "But what if I get myself killed on that she-devil?" Jack asked with feigned concern. "Who's gonna run this lil' contest then?"

As his audience laughed, he lowered the megaphone and studied it, turning it before him as if trying to understand how it had been constructed. When he raised it to his mouth again, he delivered the kick in the joke.

"It ain't ever'body can use one o' these new-fangled contraptions, you know."

More laughter. After a big, comical shrug, Jack leaned forward from the waist and squinted as he looked around the audience. When he spotted Nate, Jack straightened up.

"You know? I might'a spoke too soon. I guess if

anybody could sail over that bar on that wild beast, it'd be Nate Champion."

Like a wind pushing a green wave across a hillside of tall grass, hundreds of heads turned to see the man that Jack Flagg had chosen. Nate felt his face flush with warmth as if he had peered into the open door of a furnace.

A symphony of hoots and cackles rose from the far end of the oval, where most of the Bar C boys had gathered. The other spectators had trouble deciding where to look...at Nate or at his riotous coworkers. When it became clear that Jack was waiting for a response, Nate raised both hands before him and pushed his palms at the air. He shook his head and hoped that that would be the end of his involvement.

Jack cocked his head to one side. "No? Well, dang, Nate! I heard a story 'bout you mountin' a half-loco pronghorn and jumpin' the main fork o' the Powder from bank to bank! All that just to keep your boots dry."

The crowd laughed again. Nate smiled, lowered his eyes, and shook his head. When he looked up at Jack Flagg again, he hitched his head toward the holding pen.

"Don't see that you got any antelopes in there, Jack," Nate called out rather quietly.

Before Jack could respond, Nate heard a surprising voice speak up from the knot of people behind him. "Hell, I'll mount that sassy lady and give 'er a go!"

Nate turned to see a familiar Texas face. Though his old friend was now masked by a full beard and mustaches, Nate recognized Martin Tisdale smiling at him like a hairy jack-o'-lantern. "Tiz" wore a dusty, black Stetson tilted back off his forehead. His sunbaked skin made the collar of his white blouse shine like snow. A blue bandanna hung loosely around his neck. Tiz started laughing and raised his arms out to his sides, splaying his fingers wide as if to say, *well, here I am!* Both men began making their way toward each other through the crowd. When they met, they slapped their hands together in a firm handshake that tensed their arms into angle iron.

"Tiz!" Nate said, smiling. "What're you doin' in Wy—"

Before Nate could finish, Tisdale pulled him in for a bear hug. "*Tis* good to see you too, Nate." He said this loud enough to be heard by a dozen people around them. Putting his mouth close to Nate's ear, he whispered in a rush. "I ain't usin' my old name no more. You got to call me 'Al,' aw-right? Just 'Al'!"

When he stepped back and again plastered on his big smile, Tiz forked his hands on the sides of his hips, from which pose he studied Nate from hat to boots. "I guess you growed a coupla inches since I seen you. You look fit as a wildcat, son! You still outrunnin' horses in yore stockinged feet?"

Nate shook his head. "Ain't had no call to do that. Not since I raced you on that buckskin. You still got 'er?"

Tiz laughed. "Ain't seen her in ages." He pushed his bearded chin toward Nate. "What about you? Still ridin' that purty lil' paint?"

Nate shook his head. "She passed on the cattle drive when I come up here."

Tiz's smile snapped like an over-taut thread. "Passed?"

"Just two days into the Wyomin' Territory. She started foamin' from the nostrils...a yellow froth. Reckon it was her lungs. I tried hot compresses on 'er, but she only got worse. We were afraid she'd contaminate the cattle, so I had to put 'er down."

"Damn, Nate," Tiz whispered. He pulled in his lips and slowly shook his head. "I'm real sorry to hear that. I know she was special to you." He narrowed his eyes. "'Peaches' weren't it?"

"That's right," Nate said. He looked off toward the Big Horns long enough to swallow his emotions. "I'm ridin' a white mustang now. Bought her off a Shoshone down on the Medicine Bow River. Got me a pair o' soft, Ind'an moccasins in the deal."

From the arena, Jack Flagg's voice came at them through the megaphone. "How 'bout it, friend? You gonna step in here an' show us how to make a mustang jump?"

Tiz gave Nate a friendly slap on the shoulder and nodded toward the arena. "Lemme go out there an' make good on my word." He started sidling through the crowd until the spectators parted for him, each one gawking at him as if he were already some kind of celebrity. After dipping under the rope, Tiz looked back at Nate. "If I'm still alive after this, whattaya say we sit down with a coupla cold beers?" Without waiting for an answer, he plucked at the front of his hat brim, flashed the irrepressible smile that Nate knew so well, and then strutted toward the chute in typical cowboy fashion.

As Tiz crossed the lot, the crowd broke into a cheer, and the swell of voices put a little spring into his step. Whipping his hat off his head, he waved it high and turned his head left and right to spread his smile to all the citizens of Buffalo. When Tiz continued toward the chute, Jack Flagg hurried over and waylaid him to engage in quiet conversation.

Tiz listened, his hands resting on his hips, his elbows pointing north and south. When Flagg stopped talking, Tiz nodded once. Then Jack started in again, talking a mile a minute. This time, Tiz's reply was to lower his arms, raise them several inches from his sides, and let them fall back to slap against his trousers.

Jack Flagg turned to the crowd and raised the megaphone to his mouth. "Folks, our man here, Mister Allison, is game to ride but does not have any money on 'im. Will anybody stake 'im?"

The ring of onlookers went quiet, everyone waiting to see if someone would speak up. The scene was so motionless, it could have been a tintype. Then one of the Bar C boys broke the spell.

"I'm good for a quarter! That boy looks like a *rider*!"

Jack panned the crowd. "Anybody else? Who else will chip in?"

After a brief hesitation, two more voices chirped up, each contributing ten cents. Then five more men joined the cause. When the momentum stalled and it seemed that no one else would speak, Mr. Hall, who ran the Hole in the Wall Ranch, pledged the balance.

Nate moved closer to the holding pen and watched the wranglers wrestle the roan back into the chute. Tiz climbed up to stand on the bottom rail of the chute and watched as the horse banged against the boards and got the other horses in the holding pen agitated.

"Boys," Tiz called out to the wranglers, his eyes flashing with mischief as he pushed his hands into a pair of gloves, "it's only fair that this little mustang knows about me." He faced the mare but spoke loud and clear for the people around him to hear. "Fair warnin', lil' darlin'! I ain't never been throwed from a horse on a Sa'urday!"

The people standing close by broke into laughter. The wranglers quietly went about their business and readied the horse in the chute.

Tiz climbed to the top rails and stood above the chute, a boot planted on each side, balancing there as he waited for the wranglers to position the horse beneath him. Then, using his arms on the rails, he lowered himself onto the mustang's bare back. The horse stiffened, ears laid back, and her glassy eyes showed a lot of white. She stood as still as a stone. One of the wranglers handed up the single rope, and Tiz took it in his left hand, wrapped it just so, and held it before him at shoulder height. His right hand clutched a hank of dark mane at the withers.

"Aw-right!" Tiz called out in a dead-serious voice. "Let 'er go!"

When the gate swung open, the mustang leapt out of the chute, cut hard on a half turn, and tried to knock Tiz against the uprights at the chute entrance. Each time the roan spun and threw her weight against the boards, Tiz lifted his boot on that side. Once, when the horse looked back, Tiz thrust his leg forward, catching the heel of boot on the sharp angle of the roan's jawbone.

Giving up on the idea of crushing the rider, the roan took off at a gallop, stopped suddenly, and commenced to bucking, whipping Tiz's body forward and back like a switch of thin willow branch. He no longer held the mane. His right arm flailed above his head, angling its position to serve as a counterweight to all the lunging and lurching that this mustang was delivering.

"Where's that boy from?" one of the wranglers asked.

The tallest of the three shook his head. "I don' know, but this ain't his first time on the top side of a bone-headed cayuse."

The horse broke into a sprint and crossed the width of the oval, where it stopped again to buck with furious intent. Tiz tried to spur it into a run again, but the roan reared up so high that it sat down on its haunches and fell backward, twisting at the last moment to keep her spine off the ground.

Somehow, Tiz stayed on and rolled with the horse, even as the mare struggled to get her legs under her and stand. The crowd was loud and boisterous now. Everyone cheered Tiz on. The mustang bucked her way back toward the chute, and one of the wranglers hurriedly closed the gate. Then all motion stopped. The horse stood for a time, her chest heaving, sucking in air and blowing it out like a steam engine.

Tiz turned the head of the horse toward the jump bar. When he dug in with his spurs, the mare surprised him by crashing backward into the gate. Two of the boards cracked and a third one dropped an end to the ground. The roan reared up high, her front hooves churning in the air. When the horse tottered backward once again and began to fall, Tiz grabbed the top bar of the gate posts and remained hanging there as the mare collapsed backward into the chute. Scrambling against the boards to get her hooves on the ground, she made a racket like a team of carpenters gone mad banging their hammers. The sight of the rider hanging by his hands over the chute brought a swell of laughter from the crowd.

When the roan stood, Tiz pulled his knees almost to his chest, and the horse ran under him out into the arena. The other horses followed in a panicked escape. The crowd was laughing and clapping and shouting as Tiz lowered his legs and continued to dangle by his hands. There he swung slowly forward and back, as the specta-tors roared with renewed laughter.

Nate cracked a smile and shook his head. When Tiz craned his neck and met Nate's eyes, the two of them quietly chuckled.

Chapter Two

The crowd was wildly pleased with the performance—everyone shouting and cheering. Looking around at the riant faces, Nate saw all eyes were on Tiz as he continued to hang, his boots three feet off the ground. It was just the kind of moment that Tiz loved...and in time would be expanded into a grander story to be told over a beer or a campfire.

Turning back to the arena, Nate watched the liberated spare horses run in chaotic patterns inside the paddock, while the mare trotted a victory dance. Lifting her hooves high, she snorted and tossed her head up and down. Every ranch hand that Nate could see in the crowd was watching the horse. The townsfolk gawked at Tiz.

As the wranglers went after the horses, Jack Flagg jogged out to the arena and stopped shy of the jump bar. He raised the megaphone to his mouth and waved his other arm high above his head. Lowering his raised hand repeatedly, he tried to quiet the crowd, but to no avail.

"That's all for today, folks!" he yelled over the sea of voices. "We're gonna stop b'fore somebody gets hurt! The prize money will go to the Powder River Cattle Company for rounding up these wild mustangs and supplying them to us for the fair." Jack looked back at the cluster of big-money cattle barons who stood aloof from the rest of the crowd. Jack threw a lefthanded salute from his brow. "Thank you, Mister Frewen!"

Moreton Frewen graced the arena with a nod. Then he leaned to his foreman, Fred Hesse, and said something close to his ear. Both men chuckled to themselves as they watched Flagg yell through his megaphone and turn a full circle to address the crowd.

"Y'all have a good evenin' now," Jack called out. "And enjoy this cool weather for a change."

Dropping to the ground, Tiz stumbled on the broken boards of the gate but quickly got his legs. After straightening up, he arched his back, raised his bent arms to the level of his shoulders, and made two fists. Then he stretched, pushing his elbows behind him as far as they would go. After clapping his gloved hands together, he tugged upward on the waistband of his trousers and walked to Jack.

"Didn' make the jump, but I still ain't never been throwed on a Sa'urday." He pointed back at the broken gate. "That don't count as gittin' bucked. Am I right?"

Flagg smiled. "Whatever you say, friend." Jack extended his hand. "By God, you gave 'em a helluva show, that's for certain. You say your name is 'Allison'?"

They shook hands briefly, and then Tiz pulled up the waistband of his trousers again. "That's right...Al Allison." Tiz nodded toward the mustang that paced at the far end of the arena. "If you ask me, this deck *was* stacked. There ain't a horseman in this country could make that crazy roan jump over that damned bar."

Flagg smiled. "Well, it made it interesting, didn' it? People liked seein' you boys try." Jack's smile turned sly when he pointed at Al. "And it didn' cost *you* nothin'."

"Nothin'?" Tiz challenged. "If you was wearin' my backbone right now, you'd prob'ly change yore tune."

Flagg let his head sag for a moment as if in deep thought. His head bounced once with a private laugh, and then he looked up at Allison.

"Well," Jack chuckled, "ever'body admired your ride. I know I did. Your stick-to in the saddle is to be commended."

Now it was Tiz's turn to laugh. "Saddle! *What* saddle?"

Flagg lowered his head again and shook it several times. "Well, you got me there."

"Say," Al said and moved beside Jack as he rested his arm on Flagg's shoulders. "I could sure use some o' that prize money. I'm flat broke and ain't yet got a job."

Jack hitched his head toward the cattlemen elite. "I guess you'll need to talk to Moreton Frewen about the money."

Tiz turned his head and watched the group of well-dressed businessmen talking among themselves. The rest of the crowd streamed past them like cattle parting around a boulder.

"Maybe this Mister 'Frue-end' can offer me a job."

Jack raked his upper teeth over his lower lip. He took in a big breath and expelled it like a man blowing out a row of candles.

"You might wanna ask around some b'fore you try that." Flagg narrowed his eyes to give the stranger a shrewd look. "Just some friendly advice that might save you some troubles." He made a little wave with his free hand. "Good luck to you. Now I've got to go an' haul a wagonload o' firewood out to my bunkhouse." And with that, Jack Flagg hurried off with the megaphone still in his hand.

One of the wranglers coiled his rope into even loops as

he approached Tiz. "Where'd you learn how to ride like that?" he asked.

"Texas," Tiz replied. He snorted a rough laugh. "If you can call that a ride." He pointed at the rebellious mustang that still paraded around the paddock. "She's all yores now," Tiz laughed and started walking away.

"Williamson Coun'y?" the wrangler said behind him.

Tiz stopped and turned. The boy was already smiling at him like he knew the answer to his own question. Tiz studied the cowboy's face.

"Maybe."

The boy's smile widened. "*Maybe?*" he echoed. "How can you be from somewhere *maybe?*" He cocked his head to one side and raised both eyebrows. "I'm thinkin' *maybe* Round Rock in Williamson County?"

Tiz looked away quickly, as if someone had called him by name. When he turned back to the boy, he said nothing.

Nate, who had been watching Tiz from just outside the rope, now ducked under and strolled over with his arms crossed over his chest, his hands flattened in his armpits, and his thumbs pointing up in front of his shoulders. "Don't you remember my brother Dudley?" Nate said and draped an arm over the wrangler's shoulders. "Dud, this here is Mister Al Allison."

Dudley turned to frown at Nate and then leaned toward Allison to examine the man closer. "I thought you was a Tisdale." His head jerked back to Nate. "Don't he look like a Tisdale to you?"

Nate slid his arm around Dudley's neck and squeezed, bringing Dud's ear closer. "He *was* a Tisdale. *Now* he's Al Allison. *Comprendo?*"

Al's expression showed a mix of amusement and surprise. "This is yore little brother?"

"This is Dud," Nate said and pointed to the other

wranglers who were busy with the horses. "There's anoth-er'n right there. That's Ben on the left. An' the tall one... that's Billy Hill. You 'member him, don't you?"

Al squinted at the two wranglers, each with a lariat loop held out to his side as the the two of them cornered the mustang. "Yeah...reckon I do."

Dudley shook out his loop in his right hand. "Well, let me git over there an' help 'em."

They watched Dud stride off toward the roan, and as he got close, the three wranglers spread out evenly as if they had practiced this as a team. Letting their loops start to swing forward and back in a relaxed manner, they moved more slowly now and readied for their throws.

Al turned to Nate. "So, how many more Champions should I expect to run into in the Wyomin' Terr'tory?"

Nate smiled and hitched his head. "We're it." He patted Tiz on the shoulder. "I doubt Ben would remember you, but we'll tell 'im what he needs to know. We'll tell Billy too."

Tiz frowned. "I doubt Billy Hill will want to do me any favors. Prob'ly still holds a grudge 'bout me an' the Hildebrand girl." He shook his head. "Back then, I didn' even know he had feelin's for 'er. Lindy never said nothin' 'bout it."

Nate shrugged. "I doubt Billy will even remember. He's aw-ready courtin' two diff'rent girls here in town. B'sides, he ain't the kind inclined to feud with anyb'dy. Not for longer than a week, anyway. Don't worry 'bout him, Tiz."

They watched the wranglers start whirling their lassos over their heads. Ben threw first, a perfect throw. Dud followed with another "ringer," and then Billy completed the triangle on his second throw.

"You cain't be callin' me that no more, Nate. It's gotta be 'Al.' You understand?"

Nate looked down at the ground and nodded several times before looking up at his old friend. "Aw-right, *Al*. How 'bout that beer now? An', maybe you can catch me up on what this Allison feller has been up to?" Nate smiled, but Al shifted his gaze over Nate's shoulder. His eyes pinched, and his face hardened like a wood carving.

"What the hell is *he* doin' here?"

Nate turned to see Moreton Frewen and Fred Hesse talking to the sheriff. Frewen wore a light, buckskin-brown hunting coat that gathered at the waist and then flared over his hips to mid-thigh. The collar and lapels were made of soft velvet. Clamped in Frewen's teeth was a drooping, curve-stemmed pipe that bobbled as he talked. A stream of smoke jumped erratically from the bowl and then streamed off lazily into the air. Hesse nodded with fawning enthusiasm, agreeing with whatever spouted forth from Frewen's mouth.

"One with the pipe," Nate said, "that's Moreton Frewen. He runs the Powder River Comp'ny. The shorter one is his foreman, Hesse. Both are English. D'you know one o' 'em?"

Al Allison curled his lip into a sneer, and his light-blue eyes hardened to ice. "I'm talkin' 'bout that tall, beady-eyed sonovabitch smoking the cee-gar."

Nate turned again and frowned. When he looked back at Allison, he lowered his voice to a whisper.

"That's our coun'y sher'ff. His name is Frank Canton."

Al's head did not move, but his eyes cut to Nate and glowed like hot coals. "Frank Canton," he repeated under his breath. He snorted a quiet laugh through his nose and fixed his gaze on the sheriff. "*That* man got elected sheriff?"

"He did. D'you know 'im?"

Al snorted again. "I know 'im."

Nate watched his brothers and Billy Hill lead the roan mustang into the holding pen. They had some trouble loosening their lariats from the horse's neck. She fought the men's pull on the ropes and let go with a wrenching scream from deep in her throat. Ben caught the single rein and managed to take a two-handed grip on the halter. The mare lifted him off his feet and swung him around like a ragdoll, but he hung on. The distraction gave Dudley a chance to dart in, loosen a rope, and pull it off the horse's head. They repeated the technique twice more until all the lariats had been retrieved.

"Maybe we oughta go have that beer," Nate suggested. "Appears we got a lot to talk about."

But Al Allison was not listening. His eyes narrowed as he continued to look past Nate. Then Nate stood up a little straighter when he heard footsteps behind him. Two pairs of boots approached, crunching on the sandy hardpan in a slow and relaxed rhythm.

"Quite the show you put on out there, cowboy." The tight-jawed, English accent of Moreton Frewen cut the air like a sharp knife. "It is unfortunate you weren't able to commandeer that mustang over the bar."

Frewen's pipe smoke trespassed into their space with the scent of expensive tobacco. Nate turned to see the Englishman holding the bowl of his pipe as he sucked on the stem and puffed repetitive, miniature clouds from the side of his mouth. Hesse stood a little behind Frewen and looked at anything but Nate and Al. It was widely known that both Englishmen carried considerable disdain for the cowhands who worked for them. Nate had no use for either man.

"Nevertheless," Frewen went on, "you gave the audience quite a good show!" Without disturbing the pipe, the Englishman's mouth widened into a politician's smile.

"Well," Al said, "I reckon I'd rather take home the purse than give people somethin' to gawk at."

"And what might your name be?" Frewen asked.

"Allison," Al answered without hesitation.

Frewen removed the pipe, pursed his lips, and stared into the middle distance as though evaluating the worth of the name. He fingered a coin out of his vest pocket and thumbed it into the air in a shallow arc toward Al, who, though taken by surprise, caught it by cupping his hands into a bowl.

"There you are, sir," Frewen sang, as if he had solved all the problems of the world in one fell swoop. "I believe you have earned that."

Al raised the coin between thumb and finger. It was a gold, one-dollar piece, and it shone like the yellow eye of coyote staring at a man's campfire from out in the dark.

"I won't argue the point," Al laughed. He tossed the coin up, snatched it out of the air, and bent low to drop his reward into his boot.

Hesse hissed a haughty laugh through his teeth. "Is that where you keep all of your money?" he asked in his testy voice.

Al laughed again. "It is right now, 'cause that's all the money I got."

Frewen turned to Nate and lifted his chin so that he was looking down his nose at the cowhand. "Mister Champion," he sang melodically, as if he had just become aware of Nate's presence. "I was quite surprised to see you turn down a challenge to ride. I'm told you are a top-notch equestrian."

"Weren't a challenge," Nate said simply. "Just a invitation. An' I declined."

Frewen squinted through his pipe smoke. "Very likely a wise decision. Discretion, as it were. You might have lost that splendid reputation in front of quite a large audience." He shook his head regrettably. "A man's pride can be a fragile burden to carry, can it not?"

When Nate made no comment, Frewen nudged his foreman. Taken off guard, Hesse looked quickly at his employer and then recovered his cool demeanor. Taking the cue from his employer, Hesse cleared his throat and wormed his neck up through his shirt collar.

"Are you looking for work?" Hesse snapped and fixed hard eyes on Al Allison.

Al sniffed and briefly glanced at Nate. Nate kept his face expressionless but telegraphed a warning through his eyes. It took only a split second for Al to read the cryptic message. He grinned at the ground and scraped one boot in the dirt. When he looked up at Frewen, the grin had been replaced by a solemn look of regret.

"Well, I'll tell ya...I ain't lookin' right now," Al said and raised his boot high enough to pat the leather upper. "Think I'll take this stake to the faro table an' see what I can do with it." He nodded toward both Englishmen. "But I'll be sure to keep the offer in mind."

"It is not an open-ended offer," Hesse shot back. "You're lucky to be considered at all."

Al laughed. "'Lucky,' am I?" He spread his boots and hooked his thumbs into his waistband. "Well, I'll just have to use some o' that luck when I sit down at the green cloth."

Frewen removed the pipe from his mouth and poked the stem toward Al. "Be sure of your answer now, son." He lowered the pipe to point at Al's boot. "That coin in your shoe might represent half of a workday for you... assuming, of course, you have the proper skill set."

"I reckon you just seen my 'skill set,'" Al replied. "How many men you got could stay on that mustang long as I did?"

Frewen returned the stem of his pipe into his mouth

and smiled around it. "There are other skills we value at Powder River." He kept staring at Al as if he had said something clever.

"Can you handle a gun?" Hesse said, serving as translator.

Al took on a sly look and glanced at the ground. "I reckon anybody can handle one." He shrugged. "Far as the *shootin'* goes, I can knock the eye out of a jackrabbit at fifty yards."

Refusing to be impressed, Hesse mirrored Al's cunning smile. "What about with a pistol?"

Al cocked his head to one side as though taking a new perspective on the little English rooster. "I was talking 'bout 'with a pistol.'"

Hesse scowled, but Frewen allowed a modest chuckle at the boast. "Bravo," he laughed and flipped a hand at the wrist, "or should I say bravado?"

Al laughed. "Well, if I knew what the word meant, I might be able to narrow it down for you."

Dudley and Ben joined their parley, the two brothers standing on either side of Nate. The two of them remained quiet and listened.

"So, yo're offerin' two dollars a day?" Al said, squinting one eye at Frewen.

"Precisely," Frewen confirmed. "Plus, there are certain bonuses."

All ears, Al propped one hand on his hip. "Like what?"

"Five dollars for every maverick you bring in. And there are other special assignments."

"Why me?" Al asked. "You don't know me from Grover Cleveland."

"Hah!" Frewen said and rocked back on his heels to laugh at the sky. The smoke from his mouth swirled upward in little spurts of gray. "I have no use for that man Cleveland, but I might for you."

Al wrinkled his forehead and stared at the lumberyard as he pushed his tongue around the inside of one cheek. "Two dollars a day," he muttered. He looked back at Frewen and then at Hesse. Finally, he turned to Nate.

"That's bad luck, Al," Nate said, looking into his friend's questioning eyes. "Guess it's a good thing *we* got to you when we did."

Al's open mouth formed a small circle as if he were waiting for a word to form on his lips. Nate smiled at him and carried that smile to the pipe-smoking Englishman.

"Al's aw-ready joined up with the Bar C," Nate said and hitched his head to one side as if he had come across some bad news. "Won't git the kind o' pay yore offerin', but he'll be workin' with a good crew."

Frewen clamped the pipe in his jaws and forced a smile. Hesse pushed his eyebrows so low over his eyes, he took on the countenance of a hawk.

"Enough of this, Fred," Frewen said to his foreman. "I think our hounds are baying up the wrong tree." Turning, he removed the pipe and swept it upward as a final salute. "Good day to you, gentlemen."

Hesse hesitated long enough to glare at Al. Then, shaking his head in blatant disapproval, he turned to follow in Frewen's footsteps.

"What was *that* all about?" Dudley whispered. "An' whose hounds have got loose?"

Al took off his hat and pushed his fingers back through his hair. "Sounded like good money to me," he said. He arched his eyebrows and waited for an explanation from Nate.

"You may not know it," Nate said and put a hand on Al's shoulder. "But I just done you a big favor."

"Hell," Al laughed, "I guess I do know it. I didn' 'xpect

to git a job at the Bar C just like that." He snapped his fingers with a smart *pop!*

Nate offered a friendly wince. "Well, it ain't really 'just like that.' I ain't got the power to hire, but we'll see what Hank Devoe says about it."

Al settled his hat back on his head. "Who's Hank Devoe?"

"He's our foreman," Dudley volunteered. "An' don't worry. If Nate speaks for you, Hank'll hire you on the spot." He looked back at Nate with a question burning in his eyes. "You still ain't said whose dogs run off."

Ben spoke up for the first time. "I think that'd be those two high an' mighty English sonzabitches who just walked away."

Chapter Three

"Whattaya say we go git us that beer?" Nate suggested.

"Hold on now!" Al insisted. "First, I wanna see the famous Nate Champion take that crazy roan over that bar!" He pointed to the rail still balanced on top of the barrels. Its fringe of tied-on rags rippled in the breeze.

The clatter of lumber turned their attention to the chute, where Billy Hill wedged boards across the gap where the gate had been. "Hey, Billy!" Dudley yelled. "Can you bring out the roan? Nate's gonna have a go at 'er!"

Nate gave Dud a look. "No, Nate *ain't*."

"Yore announcer friend said you'd be the only one to do it," Al reminded. "I wanna see if he knew what he was talkin' 'bout...or if he was just blowin' hot air."

Billy began to dismantle the makeshift gate he had just improvised. When he entered the holding pen and took up the roan's lead rope, she backed against the fencing and went walleyed.

"Come on, Nate," Dud prodded. "Show 'em it can be done."

Nate watched Billy coax the frightened roan through the chute and out into the arena. There he held her in check and waited.

"Do it, Nate!" Ben said excitedly. "I wanna see this!"

Nate lowered his head and rubbed the back of his neck. After taking in a deep breath and slowly releasing it, he pointed toward the pen.

"Can you boys take those other mustangs away? Maybe behind the barn over there?"

"What for?" Ben asked.

Nate kept his eyes on the roan as he answered. "Might help this'n to focus on me."

"Sure thing!" Dud said and turned to his younger brother. "Ben, you and Billy go an' hide 'em like he said."

Ben frowned. "Why me?!"

Dud took on a solemn expression. "Well, yo're better lookin' than I am, an' so they'll be more likely to follow you."

Ben squinted one eye. "I guess that's kinda a sidewise way o' sayin' I look like a horse."

"Hell, Ben," Dud returned, "in the Champion family, that's a damned fine compliment."

When Ben walked toward the pen, Nate faced Dud and pointed at the jump bar. "Would you tear all them rags away for me? They flutter when the wind picks up."

"So what?" Dud laughed.

"A horse cain't tolerate that," Nate said. "Plus, that mare needs to see what's on the other side, and the rags are in the way."

Dud snapped his boot heels together and threw a comic salute from his hat brim. "Yes, sir, I'll go de-flutter that bar so that mare can see what she's gettin' into."

Al closed his eyes and shook his head. "Why the hell didn' I think o' that?"

When Ben and Billy had removed the other mustangs from sight, Nate walked toward the chute where the roan was tied to the gate post. He moved in a slow, careful fashion, keeping his boots from scuffing the ground. When he was a dozen paces from the mustang, she nickered, fixed her dark eyes on him, and pawed at the dirt with a front hoof.

"Hello, girl," Nate said in a low whisper, so quiet that his words could have been part of the wind. After untying the rope, he led the roan mare into the arena, where she began to balk at his pull. Each time she stopped, Nate talked to her with gentle words. As he soothed her with his voice, he worked a hand slowly up the rope until he could grip the halter. With his other hand, he stroked her neck. Whenever she backed away from him, he waited for her to settle and repeated the process of getting close enough to run his hand along the rounded muscle under her mane.

After twenty minutes of this, man and horse began walking the inside perimeter of the oval. Dud, Ben, and Al stood outside the rope barrier and watched. Behind them in the lumberyard, Billy Hill sat on a stack of boards and waited for the show, his arms folded over his chest and his long legs extended with his boots crossed at the ankles. The four of them remained absolutely still as Nate continued to bond with the mustang.

Whenever she stopped and put up a fight, he approached the mare and talked to her until she settled. Then, after one of those delays, Nate stood before her without speaking and let the animal examine him. She extended her muzzle toward his chin and took in his scent, her nostrils flaring and relaxing repeatedly, the rhythm as steady as a heartbeat. While she smelled him, Nate slowly bent at the knees and lowered himself until his face was level with the mare's muzzle. Holding that position, he breathed into her nose. When he rose back up to his full height, her head followed his, and then the two simply stared into one another's eyes.

After three stop-and-go revolutions around the arena, the mare began to match Nate's stride. Most of the lead rope was coiled in his left hand, while his right hand gripped the rope just a few inches from the horse's nose. Side by side they walked, and as they did, he praised her in that soft voice he had always used with horses. Gradually, he eased into a smooth jog, and the horse kept up with him at a fast walk. When Nate sped up again, the roan broke into a trot, and the two of them circled the paddock twice without interruption.

On the next time around, Nate picked up speed once again, and the horse responded with a canter. Then he slowed until the mare's withers came up beside him. Reaching to her back, he stroked the dip in her spine. She huffed and kicked out with her back hooves, but the protest was short-lived, and she sped up into a crisp canter.

They repeated this stimulus and response exercise for two more laps. Then, after about a dozen tries, when Nate flattened his hand on her back, she did not break stride. Snorting and whinnying, she threw her head up and down but stayed true to her gait.

"Whoa, girl," he said in a low hum and put tension on the rope as he slowed to a walk. The mare slowed with him, and the two stopped. Nate stepped in front of her again, gently gripped the sides of her halter, and bent at his knees. Leaning in close, he released the cheek straps, cupped his hands around his mouth, and exhaled a long, airy breath into her nostrils. She stood for it. The only parts of her that moved were her ears. They stiffened straight up like a wary jackrabbit.

She seemed a model of alertness, as though every fiber of her sensate being was focused on the man before her. A light, grumbling nicker issued from her throat, and, in that sound, Nate could hear the mustang's first hint of approval.

Nate straightened and rubbed both hands along the flats of her cheeks. The underlying bone felt like porcelain saucers inserted beneath her fine, stiff pelage. Moving slowly, he rubbed past the jawbone and down the neck, his boots light and quiet on the ground. When he had reached past her withers, he leaned into the mare and laid both his arms over the arch in her spine.

Making a nervous nicker, the mare sidestepped and tried to turn to face him. Nate took the rope again and pulled her through a tight circle until she was pointed in her original direction. Then he repeated the exercise. Stand before her, massage the jaws, slip down the neck, and softly drape himself over the ribs and spine. The mare circled again.

On the sixth try, Nate leaned over the horse, and she did not react. She seemed to be waiting for whatever he might do next.

Nate returned to his place in front of the mare, and she lowered her head in what looked like a cordial bow. He scratched the short, stiff hairs around her ears as he told her how well she was doing. Without turning his head or changing his tone, he surprised his brother Dudley with a request.

"Dud? Reckon you can find me a wooden bucket?"

Dud straightened and looked around, but it was Ben who replied. "There's a bucket inside the barn, Nate."

"Wood or metal?" Nate asked.

Ben hesitated in answering, but, when he did, there was certainty in his voice. "It's wood...but it's gotta metal bail."

Nate nodded. "Bring it to me where she can see you. Come at 'er from 'er front. Walk slow. No quick moves. Don't clank the bail or nothin' like that."

"Whatta you wont inside the bucket?" Ben asked in a whisper.

Nate continued scratching the mare's head. "Nothin'."

After retrieving the bucket, Ben walked outside the rope to the far end of the paddock and started toward Nate's back. The horse saw him, but Nate kept up a steady litany of reassuring words, whose meanings mattered little but whose tone communicated all he wanted to say.

"Here you go," Ben whispered, "I'm right behind you."

"I'm gonna move beside 'er now. You move with me. Stay at my back."

Nate stroked the horse as he quietly sidestepped to her ribs. "Ben, I want you to set that bucket upside down exactly where my right boot is." He raised his heel and pivoted his foot left and right on the toe. Then he moved the foot forward and resumed his monologue with the horse. He heard Ben set the bucket in the dirt with great care, barely making a sound.

Ben laid a hand on Nate's shoulder. "Okay, it's there."

Nate nodded once. "Now, walk back the same way you come...slow and quiet."

It took a full minute before Ben had rejoined Dudley and Al at the rope. All that while, Nate continued to hang his arms over the back of the roan, just as he kept up the soft murmur of a one-sided conversation.

Lifting his right foot high, he blindly searched for the bucket and quietly planted his boot on its flat surface. Pushing off from the bucket, he rose up and draped his torso over the sway of the roan's back, letting his full weight lie belly-down across the horse's spine.

The mare bucked once, and Nate deliberately slid to the ground, careful to straddle the bucket. When the horse sidestepped, Nate went with her and continued with the stroking and the talking. After circling the horse back to the bucket, he tried again. Same results.

Twice more he repeated the procedure, and neither time did Nate express impatience or disappointment. He expected the repetition of failure, but he saw each failed attempt as a step forward in the larger picture of the lesson.

On the fourth try, the roan stepped forward without bucking, and Nate remained jackknifed across her back. When she stopped, he slid down and praised her, stroked her, and combed her mane with his fingers. At this point, she seemed to be asking for compliments.

This time, instead of leading the horse to the bucket, Nate dropped the rope into the dirt, turned away from her, and walked to the bucket alone. With his back to the mare, he picked up the bucket and held it before him with both hands so that it rested against his belly. There he stood, as if he had nowhere else he needed to go other than the place where he was. He knew the roan's neck had hooked around, because he could hear her breathing in his direction. Nate knew the horse's dark eyes were fixed on him. He felt the attention like a hand gently pressed into his back.

The quiet in the paddock drew out. All present could hear wagons and harnesses and horses' hooves and people's voices drifting from the town, but those sounds served only to underscore the absolute silence in the arena. Nate waited. The four spectators dared not move. Then the mustang seemed to make a decision.

Clop...clop...clop...

She walked toward Nate's back and stopped behind him. Stretching her muzzle within an inch of his spine, she sniffed between his shoulder blades and then exhaled a long breath, that to Nate, felt like warm water poured down the back of his shirt. Turning slowly and shifting the bucket behind him, he stroked one hand down the long nasal bone to the soft velvet of her nose. Then he took the lead rope and recommenced his equine cooing. Moving beside her, he held both bucket and rope in one hand and with his other hand glided along her sleek neck to let her know where he was at all times.

When he stood beside her, he set down the bucket quietly, stepped up, and, again, went belly-down on the mare's back. For half a minute, she stood without moving. Then he made a *chick-chick* sound with his tongue against his teeth, and with his right hand he reached back and patted the mare's hindquarters. She started forward with her load as if she were being careful not to lose him.

Nate stayed on for half a lap. Then he slid to the ground and took up the lead position in front of her. His right hand still gripped the rope, but he applied no tension to it, letting the arc of the loose rein swing freely between man and horse.

Ramping up the speed, Nate brought the roan to an easy gallop. The consistent rhythm of the hooves made a sweet sound after so much stop-and-go action. After half a lap of this, Nate dropped back and took a handful of mane in his left hand. Then, in a smooth but deliberate effort, he threw his leg high, kept his head low, and swung onto the mare's back. Now astride her, he kept her running without interrupting her gait.

At the chute end of the paddock, he turned the roan with the rope until she was headed for the jump bar. Letting out the rope to its full length, he leaned forward and swept his right arm horizontally over the horse's ears, whipping the rope in front of the mare's face so that the rein now ran to him from the right side of the horse's neck.

"Hyah!" Nate called out. It was a sound not so much loud as it was commanding. Right away, the roan took the incentive and charged straight ahead. As they neared the bar, Nate could feel the mare gather herself for the left turn to avoid the barrier.

"Hyah!" he called again and began to pull on the single rein, enough pressure to let the animal feel his intention. When she resisted, he pulled harder and tapped her flanks with his heels. When she started her left turn in earnest, he pulled with all his strength to hold the mare straight. With another kick from his heels, the mustang put on a burst of speed.

"Up, now!" he yelled over the rumble of the hooves.

From ten feet out, the mustang sprang from the earth and gathered her forelegs beneath her. As she sailed over the bar, it was as if horse and rider had leapt through a vacuum where there was no air, no sound...no past, no future...only the truth of what a horse and a man could do together. Leaning forward on the rise of the jump, Nate touched his chest to the mare's mane. As they crested the bar, he leaned back a little and clamped his knees above the horse's shoulders to post. As they came down, Nate's hands splayed on the back of the mare's neck to brace, but the landing was smooth. Neither horse nor rider experienced a jolt. Then the sound of hooves returned, and with it came the cheers of the four men who had witnessed the feat.

Chapter Four

Ben chose the bar—the Gold Room on Laurel Avenue. It was in the cool gloaming of the evening when the five Texans stood outside on the boardwalk and stared through the window glass. Inside, the lighted oil lamps stationed along the walls revealed a shoulder-to-shoulder crowd milling about the bar and a room full of tables where men drank, played cards, and conversed. A collective din of male voices poured out onto the street through the open double-doors. Beneath this constant murmur, a tinny piano rattled a tune from the back of the room, while a lone fiddler supplied a scratchy accompaniment.

"You know this is a cathouse, right?" Nate said to his youngest brother.

"I know it!" Ben shot back in an irritated tone. "I like the place. Like the owner too. Red Angus is a helluva guy."

Nate nodded. "Yeah, I like 'im, too...but it's still a cathouse."

Dudley tapped the back of his fist against Nate's

upper arm. "The beer's cold, an' it don't know whether it's bein' served in a brothel or a church."

Nate turned and watched Dud strap his cartridge belt and pistol around his waist. Dud cinched the buckle and smiled.

"You plannin' on holdin' up the place for yore drink?" Ben quipped.

"Nah...no need, yo're buyin' the first round, ain't you?"

Ben's face squeezed down like a crushed hat. "I never said that!"

Dud feigned surprise. "You were 'bout to, weren't you?"

Ben set his jaw. "Why're you always sayin' things like that?"

"Simmer down," Nate said. "Ever' man'll pay for his own."

Ben led the way into the smoke-filled room, and the others followed. As four of the party took their place in line at the bar, Dud angled off to a table in the middle of the room, where he bent to Ranger Jones and spoke into his ear. Ranger's head came around so fast, Dudley had to straighten to avoid a collision of noggins. Frowning, Ranger stood and walked directly to Nate.

"You really jump that mustang over that bar?!" Ranger asked over the noise in the room. With his fists propped on his slender hips, he waited for an answer.

Ben Al, and Billy beamed at the question. Nate merely delivered an earnest nod. Ranger ballooned his cheeks, bowed his head, and blew a stream of air. Then his head came up quickly, his eyes as bright as polished coins.

"You win the prize money?"

When Nate shook his head, Ranger seemed to deflate like an empty water bag. Dudley reached up and tousled Ranger's crop of light-brown hair.

"He done it after the crowd left," Dud said through a smirk. "You know Nate!"

Ranger rubbed the back of his neck and stared at Nate. "Well, how come you didn' do it for the money?"

Nate shook his head. "Would'a took too long for people to sit through it. Only way I could see to do it was to take the time needed with the horse first."

Billy Hill had been quiet since they had left the lumberyard, but now he snorted a laugh. "Nate and that mare will prob'ly be exchangin' love letters now. We had to tear 'em apart there at the end." Billy backhanded Nate's shoulder. "You propose to 'er, Nate?"

Nate cracked just enough of a smile to show that he could take a joke.

"Only thing Nate proposed to her," Dud said, "was to jump over that bar, an' she complied willingly."

"Yeah," Billy chortled. "After 'bout a *hour.*"

Ben turned from the bar with a pitcher of beer in one hand and five, thick, glass mugs in the other. "Let's find a table, boys."

Billy led the way and claimed a vacant table against the back wall. There being only four chairs there, Dudley reached out to an unoccupied stool at a neighboring table, where four men were engaged in a poker game.

"You boys don't mind, do you?" Dud said and dragged the stool over without waiting for an answer.

One of the men at that table—a stocky young Irishman with reddish-brown hair—set down his cards and glared at Dud. He was thick in the chest, swelling the brown tweed vest he wore over a light-blue shirt. Nate had crossed paths with him out on the range, and each time the man's expression had seemed morose. His head was shaped like a breadbox, his lips thick, and his slate-gray eyes heavily lidded.

"That stool's for a friend o' mine," the Irishman

growled. Along with his raspy complaint came the reek of alcohol, so thick on his breath that Dudley retracted his head and laughed. A half-full whiskey bottle and shot glass sat beside the Irishman's cards. He was well on his way to being lit up proper for a Saturday night.

Dud pretended a concerned look for the absent rider of the stool. "Well, lemme know when he shows up, an' I'll loan it back to 'im."

The drunken Irishman scraped his chair around so that his knees were no longer under the table. He wore a cartridge belt with a heavy revolver holstered at his hip.

"Maybe I want it to be here a-waitin' on 'im!"

Dudley looked around the room. "Well, which one is he? I'll just ask 'im if he's plannin' on comin' back." He smiled at the surly man. "You just never know."

"Dud," Nate said in a low voice. "Leave off. He's drunk."

Dudley looked at Nate with the rebellious smile that had always accompanied trouble back at the Champion home in Texas. "What!" he laughed. "There's a principle involved here. A stool ain't a workin' proposition 'less somebody's a-settin' on it! Don't make no sense to let it stand idle. Hell, I doubt even the stool cares to waste time like *that*."

"Hey!" the Irishman growled. His bleary eyes tried to focus on Dudley. "You know what your mouth needs?"

With his mischievous smile stretched to the limit, Dud turned to the indignant man, sat on the stool, and widened his eyes like a child about to be let in on a secret. "Cain't wait to hear it," he whispered, adding some melody to the sarcasm.

A lean cowhand seated at the poker game tapped his closed hand of cards on the tabletop. "Hey! Shonsey! We gonna play cards here, or argue 'bout a empty stool? It's your play. You in or out?"

The drunken man named Shonsey sneered at his friend. "Shut up!" Taking the whiskey bottle by its neck, he popped the cork, and held the stopper in the palm of his hand as he turned back to Dudley.

"You need one o' these here," Shonsey said, "only bigger!" He narrowed one eye and pointed at Dud's mouth. "I'd plug it right there in that big pie hole o' yours."

Quick as a snake, Dud snatched the cork off the man's palm. "I think this one'll do just fine." He began licking the sides of the cork and making exaggerated sounds of satisfaction. "Hmm, hm! That's good! That's Irish whiskey, ain't it?" He inserted the cork into his mouth and rotated it using his thumb and fingers. "By God, that's gotta good bite to it!"

Shonsey started to get to his feet, but Dud was too quick for him. Standing up with the cork clamped in his front teeth, Dud bumped the disgruntled man with his body so hard that Shonsey fell back into his own chair and tottered backward into the lap of the man sitting next to him. Dud held the whiskey bottle firmly in place on the table, removed the wet cork from his lips, and rammed it into the neck of the bottle. Then, for good measure, he slapped the cork tight with the flat of his hand. Several men at a nearby table laughed, and Shonsey's face turned the color of a ripening prickly pear.

Pulling himself upright in his chair, Shonsey glared at the bottle. "You sonovabitch!" he spat. "I'll be damned if I'll drink after your slobber!" His hand fumbled for his pistol, but Dudley lurched forward and clamped his hand firmly on Shonsey's, pinning the gun in the Irishman's holster. Dud's other hand came up quickly, his forefinger stiffened just an inch from Shonsey's nose. The surprised man froze with his lidded eyes opened wide as he stared into Dud's face.

"You wanna die over a stool?" Dud said. Lowering his

free hand, he took a grip on his own Colt's, released Shonsey's gun hand, and straightened. Dud's thumb was hooked over the spur of the hammer. His body was slightly crouched, which made him appear like a steel trap set to spring. The room quieted by degrees, the silence spreading outward from the point of contention like the ripples from a stone lobbed into a pond. The musicians tapered off in the middle of a ballad, and now the silence was complete. It was as if a spell had fallen over the saloon.

Shonsey's breathing was shallow, and when he swallowed, a dry *tick* could be heard in his throat. The only movement in the room was the slow drift of tobacco smoke that hung in the air like a slowly opening curtain.

Shonsey's skin had lost all its color, and his face had gone slack. His eyes fixed on Dudley, stitching back and forth between Dud's hand on his gun and the iron-hard expression on his face. In answer to Dud's question, he began to shake his head slowly from side to side. Ben got up, walked around the table to Shonsey's back, and, without any resistance, slipped the man's pistol from its holster.

"Just so you don't decide to do somethin' stupid," Ben said, leaning to Shonsey's ear.

Dudley relaxed and checked the faces of the other card players. "Would you boys do me a big favor an' take him outta here so we don't have no trouble?" He met the eyes of the wiry man who sat next to Shonsey. "I'd be obliged. I'd hate to have to kill 'im over a damned stool."

When the man nodded, Ben set the gun on the table before the thin man. "Better hold on to that till he sobers up," Ben suggested. He nodded toward the cards on the table. "We're right sorry to interrupt yore game, boys."

As two of the men gathered the cards on the table, the amenable cowhand stuffed Shonsey's pistol into his waistband and then looked at his two friends. "Gimme a hand, boys. We don't wanna have to 'xplain to Mister Hord how Mike got kilt over a piece o' furniture."

As the three men helped Shonsey to his feet, the drunkard began to find his nerve. "Git your damn hands off me!" He thrust a forefinger at Dudley as if he were aiming over a pistol barrel. "I'm gonna send that sonovabitch to hell!" He struggled in vain as his companions escorted him out, but his tongue was well-oiled with whiskey, and he left the room cursing and insulting anyone who would dare to look at him.

As soon as Shonsey was hauled out the door, Dudley addressed the room. "Gentlemen, forgive the interruption, but I think you'll find the air in the room a little easier to breathe now that the stink has been drove out."

The musicians started up again, and the patrons in the saloon returned to their chatter and banter as if nothing had happened. The bartender, who had watched the scene of contention play out, turned his back to the room and began washing glassware in a tub of soapy water.

Nate felt a light hand grip his shoulder from behind. "Nate, can I talk to you in private?"

The familiar, whispery voice turned Nate in his chair. "Sumner! I ain't seen you since you left the Bar C! How're things down in Carbon Coun'y?"

The handsome, sun-browned cowhand was crouched with his hands on his knees. When he let his head sag, his longish, blond hair fell over his face. Streaks of sun-bleached amber and gold ran through his blond locks like veins of high-grade ore. He went down to one knee, looked up, and combed his hair out of his eyes with his fingers.

"Things have got right up to the edge down there, an' somethin's gotta pop soon." He looked Nate in the eye. "I come up here to see if I could talk some boys into goin' back with me. I reckon there's a fight a-comin', an' when it does, I'm gonna be sorely outnumbered."

He paused and looked to his left at Al Allison, who had been listening to his complaint. Sumner frowned and went quiet.

"This is a old friend o' mine," Nate said, gesturing with a hand toward Al. "You can talk in front o' him."

Sumner shrugged. "Well...any friend o' Nate's—" He offered his hand. "Sumner Beach," he said by way of introduction and gave Al a single, sharp nod as they shook hands.

"Al Allison," Al returned. "Pleased to meet you. I've knowed Nate since he was a kid."

Sumner studied Al's attire down to his boots. "So, yo're a Texan, too?"

"To the bone," Al replied with a smile.

Seemingly distracted, Sumner looked around the room. The conversations of the customers all but drowned out the piano and fiddle that kept up a lively beat. There was enough noise in the saloon to make the space around Nate and his friends feel like a bubble of privacy.

"You still working for the Major?" Nate asked.

"*Hell*, no!" Sumner spat. "That pompous, sonovabitch Wolcott will never hold sway over me again. I *quit* him an' took out a claim o' my own on Deer Creek. Me an' Tom Brannan. We partnered up. You know that section they call The Willows?"

"I do," Nate said. "That's a fine parcel."

"Well, that sonovabitch Wolcott has been houndin' us ever since." Sumner's eyes now began to blaze with the story bottled up inside him. "Called me a thief and a squatter. Claims *he* owns that land." He raised an eyebrow, and the skin on his face tightened like stretched canvas. "But he *don't*! He's *lyin'*. I took out a legal patent on that section. It's all recorded in the books at the courthouse."

Sumner took in a deep breath as though to quell his anger. Nate could see by the white-knuckled clinch of his friend's fist that there were more complaints to come.

"Once before, a feller tried the same thing out there at The Willows. Filed his claim an' built a cabin an' brought his family out there. Major Wolcott burned 'em out—cabin, hay, crops, an' even the privy. The law wouldn' help 'em, so they just moved on. Never saw 'em again."

Nate nodded. He had heard similar stories in the Powder River Basin.

"Wolcott won't find you to be a easy splinter to pull out," Nate said in a low tone.

"You're damned right!" Sumner said. "He's already sent over a coupla boys to threaten us, but I sent 'em packin'. Told 'em to git off my claim an' stay off. Them boys knowed I weren't just talkin'." He put on a hard smile and snorted a dry, humorless laugh through his nose. "Me and Tom cut the timbers we needed for a cabin, stripped the bark, sawed the logs to length, and notched a few to git started on the foundation. Had 'em curin' in the sun...laid out in the grass as neat as the pews in a church. Then, first time we leave camp to git supplies, we come back an' find our logs been dragged into the creek and sent downstream to who knows where."

Sumner's eyes showed some fire now, and Nate felt a spark of that fire jump to him, igniting his own sense of injustice. "You able to find any of 'em?"

"Some," Sumner replied. "Had to drag the damned things half a mile back to our building site. Hell, for all I know, the rest made it down to the Platte. Some cabin builder over in Casper prob'ly thinks he's got a angel upstream who's sendin' him logs for free."

"So you'll stick?" Al asked.

Sumner turned to Al. "Damned right I'll stick!"

Al kept his face expressionless as he stared at Sumner's show of defiance. Then he glanced at Nate.

"He'll stick," Nate assured Al and then turned back to Sumner. "Yore partner with you?"

Sumner pushed out his lower lip and closed his eyes long enough to shake his head. "He's at the claim. One o' us is always there now." Sumner took on a sour look. "We been seein' riders pass by the claim purty reg'lar. Now an' ag'in it'll be a man on foot. I just git a glimpse, an' by the time I saddle up an' git out to where I seen 'im, there ain't nobody there." He paused to let that sink into Nate's thinking. "I figure Wolcott has hired some assassins, who'll try to pick us off while we're out there workin'. But, if that don't pan out for 'im, I wouldn' put it past the pompous ol' windbag to organize his own army to drive us outta that valley."

Al leaned in closer. "A *army*!? To take on two men?"

Sumner snorted. "That prissy britches would like nothin' more than to be a major again."

"So, he was in the military?" Al pressed.

Sumner nodded. "Durin' the war. Fought for the North. Said he was a major, but I got my doubts. I wouldn' follow that man into a saloon offerin' free drinks."

Nate propped an elbow on the table, closed his eyes, and lowered his head into his hand. Pinching the bridge of his nose, he began to shake his head.

"If you raise yore *own* army, you'll have to be the aggressor."

Sumner frowned. "How do you mean?"

Nate pivoted in his chair and leaned into their huddle. "Say you take twen'y or thirty fightin' men to yore claim. Don't you think Wolcott will know 'bout it?"

Sumner's frown deepened. "I reckon he would."

"He'd know," Nate assured him. "Do you think he would round up all his hands and go up against such a force?"

Sumner stared at the floor and said nothing.

"Why should he risk all that," Nate went on, "when he can wait you out and come at you when yo're alone? You cain't keep a army there at yore place indefinitely. It would eat up every cent you have. You'd have to feed 'em on top o' payin' their wages." Nate spread his hands and offered a sympathetic smile. "You'd have to attack his ranch and his men, an' you know well as I do the Wyoming Stock Growers Assoc'ation would come down on you hard. They'd prob'ly lynch you on the spot and tell ever'body in Wyoming you'd been stealing their cattle. With the WSGA against you, there ain't a lawman in the territory who would have a problem with that."

The tendons in Sumner's jaws flexed, and the swell in his cheeks looked rock hard. "Well, whatta *you* think I oughta do?" he asked.

"For starters...git more partners."

A hopeful expression came over Sumner's chiseled face. "You int'rested?"

"I ain't saved up enough money to be nobody's partner, but I'm workin' on it. Just took a new job for better pay. So, I'm gittin' there." Nate leaned in closer and leveled his voice with certainty. "But you listen to me. See cain't you find a man in Wolcott's crew who can keep a ear out for you. You used to work for 'im. You prob'ly still got friends there willin' to spy for you. Then, when the time comes you need me there, I'll come. How's that sound?"

Sumner filled his lungs with the smokey air in the room, exhaled quickly, and got to his feet. Just as he had when he had arrived, he gripped Nate's shoulder and squeezed.

"You be listenin' out for me," he said. After acknowledging Al with a nod, he turned and made his way through the crowded room for the door.

Chapter Five

Carrying a heavy, wooden box pressed to his chest, Red Angus came out of the backroom of the saloon and closed the door with his boot. The stocky owner set down a crate of rattling bottles on the bar and spoke to his bartender, who pointed toward Nate's table. Amid the natural rhythms of conversations and laughter and the clink of glasses, Red looked over the room as if taking inventory of who was present and who was not. Then he took off his stained apron, draped it over the counter, and began to sidle his way toward the Champions, speaking to customers as he wove through the maze of tables. When he stood between Al and Nate, he groomed his rufous mustaches with two sweeps of a knuckle, put on his friendly smile, and propped his fists on his broad hips.

Raising his beer mug, Ben was first to acknowledge the owner's presence. "Well, hey there, Red! I've brought you some illustrious customers tonight. Best bunch o' cowhands in the territory."

Red frowned and laughed at the same time. "'Illustrious'? Where the hell'd you pick up a word like that?"

Ben raised his empty hand, striking the pose of a witness taking an oath in court. "I admit it. I finally broke down an' read a book. I thought I'd try out a new word on you."

Red nodded and shared his smile with all at the table. "Everything all right here, boys? I heard you mighta had a little trouble earlier."

"Red?" Dudley said in his play-acting voice. His head was cocked to one side, and his eyes were narrowed with a question. "Who cleans up here for you?"

Red poked a thumb over his shoulder at his bartender. "Burl does that. Why?"

Dud shrugged. "I just want to know who to talk to 'bout claimin' my share o' the pay. It so happens I have removed some trash for you in the form of Mike Shonsey."

The saloon man chuckled. "Well, good luck with that! I've never seen Burl part with his money without a fight." He broadened his smile. "Here, take this." He dug two fingers into his vest pocket and tossed a penny on the table. The coin rolled in a spiral and rattled to a stop right in front of Dudley. "I always pay according to the worth of the job. I figure that'll cover Mike Shonsey fair enough."

Dud picked up the penny. "Well, I guess I cain't argue that."

"Tell you what," Red continued, "I might add a big thank you to that. How's that sound?"

"Fair enough, Red," Dud agreed. "You go right ahead and thank me!"

"Thank you," Red said sweetly. Then he turned to Ben. "Maybe I ought to hire *you* now."

"What for?"

"I thought maybe you could try controlling your big brother when you're in here."

Ben spewed air as a laugh. "Who...Dud? *That's* a lost cause."

Red tapped Nate's shoulder with the back of his hand. "How 'bout you, Nate? Reckon you can control 'im?"

To answer, Nate met Dud's eyes. "Still a lost cause."

Red smiled and nodded. "Hey, I heard you tamed a wild mustang out there and jumped it over the lumber-yard office."

"*Noooo,*" Dudley said, "that's a flat-out lie. He jumped the barn! *Twice!*"

Red shook his head and started to turn. "You boys behave now, but don't forget to have a good time." He bumped Nate's shoulder again. "Hey, see if you can keep that one outta trouble, Nate." He nodded at Dud and then made his way back toward the bar.

Nate leaned over the table and lowered his voice. "Dudley, you know he's only half jokin', don't you?"

Before Dud could answer, Ranger was there spinning around one the empty chairs from the abandoned table. He set it down as close to Nate, sat, and frowned at the side of Nate's face.

"Say, Nate. If it took you a hour, you think the rest o' us got snookered on that mare?"

Nate shook his head. "Wouldn' call it that. Somebody might could'a done it."

"Like *who*?" Ranger pressed.

"Oh, you know!" Ben broke in. "Maybe Jesus...or some Shoshone medicine woman who can put a spell on a horse."

"Or maybe even Moreton Frewen," Dud added, "if he paid the horse enough."

The subtle laughter that ran through their group was swallowed up by the flood of voices around them, but, at a near table, a heavy-set young man turned in his chair and leaned toward Dudley. His curly, coal-black hair threw off glints of light from the oil lamps. Nate did not know him, but he knew that the men with him rode for the Powder River Company.

"If Frewen *was* to make that deal," the stout cowboy announced in a sly voice, "I guarantee you he'd pay it off with moldy wet hay that wouldn't be fit for a buzzard's roost."

When Fred Hesse appeared, one of the other Powder River boys nudged the curly-haired man's elbow. Standing over them, Hesse kept his spine board-stiff, as his dark eyes darted around the table. He reminded Nate of a hawk perched on a fencepost and searching for prey.

"You men finish your drinks!" Hesse ordered. "We're riding back now!" The cocky Englishman flaunted his accent like the snap of a whip. His roving eyes fixed on the cowboy who had made the crack about Frewen. "Tomorrow I'll need you in the saddle before sunrise. I have a few extra chores for you. We have a long day ahead of us, gentlemen."

When Hesse turned on his heel and walked for the door, three of the Powder River men threw back what was left of their drinks, pushed back their chairs, and started after their foreman. The heavy-set young man finished his drink slowly and leaned back to Nate's table.

"You notice how he says *we* and *us*?" The cowhand tried to inject an English accent into the two words, but he laughed at his failed effort. "We ain't likely to see his sorry ass in a saddle till almost time for the noon meal." He looked directly at Nate. "You really make it over that bar on that mustang?"

Nate nodded. "We made it together...me an' the horse."

The stout cowhand stood and picked up his slouch hat —a dingy, brown specimen with a blue feather of a jay pinched inside the band. Still looking at Nate, he shook his head with regret.

"I'd like to 'a seen *that*."

"I can tell you," Al said, "it was a sight to behold."

The young man leaned to Nate. "D'you git throwed after the jump?"

Nate shook his head. "We parted on good terms."

The cowboy closed his eyes and chuckled. "Well, damn!" he muttered and extended a hand. "Let me at least shake your hand. I'm Nick Ray."

Nate took the offered hand. "Nate Champion."

Nick gave a firm grip, but he stopped pumping at Nate's introduction. "Ser'ously? That's your name?"

"It is...goin' on twen'y-eight years now."

Nick huffed a laugh and gave Nate's hand one last pump. "Well, I reckon you're livin' up to that handle, all right."

"Say, Nick," Dudley said, "you workin' for Powder River?"

Nick shrugged. "'Bout a month now."

"I hope you got other possibilities lined up," Dud said. "I think you just made Fred Hesse's list o' vermin."

Nick grinned. "From what I hear from the other boys, that's a damned long list." He shrugged. "I just need the work." Nick pushed his slouch hat down on his head. "Speakin' o' which...reckon I better go an' see if I can smooth things over with Sir Hesse." He nodded a goodbye to the table of Texans and started for the door.

"Good luck!" Dudley called to his back.

Without looking back, Nick waved, and then he was gone.

The five Texans were quiet for a time as they sipped their drinks. Outside, the night was dark as tar, converting the windowglass into mirrors that reflected the room. Dudley set down his empty mug and looked straight at Billy Hill.

"You been mighty quiet. You sick or somethin'?"

Billy sniffed and curled his lip into a surly sneer. "I ain't sick!"

Al Allison leaned forward with his elbows on the table. "Could be he's sick o' bein' 'round me," Al said. He turned to face Billy. "You ain't still holdin' somethin' ag'in' me on account o' Lindy Hildebrand, are you?"

Billy's face flushed with color. He took a quick drink of his beer, set down the mug, and stared straight ahead at nothing.

"It was all her doin', you know," Al went on. "I never asked for nothin' from 'er."

The skin on Billy's face tightened, making his cheekbones appear as sharp as chips of broken stone. He looked directly at Al.

"But I bet you got it, didn' ya?"

Al huffed an airy laugh, as his face showed bewilderment. "Is that what's eatin' at you?"

Billy gripped his mug, looked into his beer, and sulked. "Yeah, maybe it is," he grumbled.

Al leaned over the table and tried to get his face into Billy's vision. "I didn' do nothin' I weren't asked to do. Hell, son, I didn' do nothin' *you* hadn' done, neither. Am I right?" He raised both eyebrows. "Even so, I ain't all twisted outta shape 'cause o' *you*." Al's face broke into bewilderment. "You didn' love 'er, did ya?"

Billy frowned. "Hell, no!" he replied. Then he seemed to think about his answer. "Least I don't think I did."

Surprised, Al sat up straighter, reached out, and clasped a hand to Billy's shoulder. "Billy, if I'd knowed she was spoke for, I would'a never horned in on you. I swear that on my daddy's grave." He shook Billy gently, and Billy's head bobbled as if he were riding in the back of a buckboard. "But she never tol' me nothin' 'bout bein' yore girl. In fact, she denied it."

With his hand still gripped on Billy's shoulder, Al took

on a serious expression. "You know it weren't just you an' me, don't ya? Lindy was seein' plenty o' others."

Billy blinked slowly and then nodded once. "I know it. It's just the way she was." He frowned at his mug on the table. "I just never sat down for a beer with any of 'em b'fore."

"Well, we ain't gotta be enemies," Al suggested. "Way I see it, we're like brothers o' the same lost cause."

Billy turned to Al and raised an eyebrow. "Yeah?"

Al nodded deeply. "It didn' surprise me none to learn she run off from that girls' school. That ain't no place for somebody o' her temper'ment. She prob'ly found some rich French man to be with. An' whoever he is, I bet he's a-sittin' in a bar 'bout right now ponderin' over his beer as to where she run off to."

"And who *with*," Billy added.

Al dropped his hand from Billy's shoulder and offered it as a truce. "No hard feelin's?"

Billy looked at the open hand before him and cracked a grin. "Guess not," he replied and shook with Al. Then they both clinked their beer mugs together and drank. The Champion brothers raised their mugs and drank, too.

"So, yo're ridin' for the Bar C with these fellers?" Al asked.

Billy shook his head. "Naw. I work for Mister Blair over to the Hoe Ranch."

"Hoe Ranch?" Al laughed. "Is that what I think it is?"

"Na-a-a-w," Billy groaned. "Ain't got nothin' to do with whores. Just a big cattle ranch."

Al nodded and lost his smile. He turned his beer mug by degrees in a full circle, cleared his throat, and put on a philosophical face.

"Well, I reckon Lindy'd be a growed woman 'bout now," Al allowed. "She's made 'er choices an' prob'ly learned to live with 'em. At least she's livin'. I was right sorry to hear 'bout 'er little sister. It was 'Dottie,' weren't it?"

"'Dory,'" Billy corrected. "She was four years younger than me, but I always had a lotta respect for 'er. She was real smart. Never tol' nothin' but the truth. Purty, too."

As Nate listened to Billy's assessment of Dory, he felt the old wound open inside his chest. His throat tightened like rawhide drying in the sun. Lifting his mug, he drank what was left of his beer.

Al shook his head at the memory. "I never did hear if they found out who killed 'er."

"'Killed 'er'?" Ranger butted in. "What happ'ned?"

As Billy talked about the mystery of Dory's death, Nate stared into his empty mug and slowly rotated the glass upon the ring of water beneath it. He could feel Dudley's eyes trained on him, while all the others, he knew, would be fixed on Billy's story.

"She was a damn good artist," Ben announced. "Nate's got a paintin' she done o' Peaches. Looks just like 'er, too."

"Who's 'Peaches'?" Ranger asked.

Ben glanced at Nate before answering. "That was Nate's horse. She was a pinto. Won a few races in 'er time."

When all heads turned to Nate, he managed a token smile and nodded. Before anyone else could speak, Dudley raised his mug and held it straight-armed over the center of the table.

"I say we drink to Dory and her memory," Dud proposed and waited for the others to raise their glasses. "Purtiest girl to come outta Round Rock, Texas, I'll wager." When the six mugs tapped one another, Dud spoke a little louder. "And to Peaches, by God. Never a better horse in all o' Texas."

While the others drained their glasses, Nate gathered

his boots beneath him, stood, and pushed his hat down on his head.

"You leavin'?" Ben asked and wiped his sleeve across his mouth.

"I wanna see Hank Devoe b'fore he heads back to the Bar C." He nodded toward Al. "See if I cain't convince 'im we could use another Texas cowhand."

"Hell," Dudley laughed, "Hank would hire a crippled ol' woman with the palsy if *you* was to recommended 'er."

"You want me to go with you?" Al asked.

Nate nodded. "Yeah, I do."

Chapter Six

Nate and Al walked the dark boardwalk to Main Street, where they turned toward the business district. Several stores were still open, the light from their lamps reaching dimly into the street.

"Hank should be at the bar in the hotel," Nate said, pointing up the street at the Occidental.

Al slowed Nate with a hand on his elbow. "Can we talk for a minute first?"

When they came upon Foote's Mercantile, Nate sat on the wooden bench that spanned a portion of the building's front wall. The store was dark, but across the street, the lights of the Occidental Hotel bar fanned across the thoroughfare and provided a faint glow for the two friends to see one another.

Setting his hat beside him on the bench, Nate crossed his arms over his chest and leaned back into the building. Stretching out his legs on the boards, he crossed his boots at the ankles. Al sat down next to him.

"B'fore you go riskin' yore reputation on me, I guess you'll be needin' to know why I go by Al Allison instead o' Martin Tisdale."

Nate shrugged. "I figured that was all 'bout you gittin' mixed with Sam Bass in Texas."

Al took in a deep breath. "Well," he began and laughed quietly to himself, "it was. But there's more to it, I reckon. I guess I got into a little more trouble in Texas after you left." He dipped his head to one side. "I won't go into all the details, but I got sent up to Huntsville for fifteen years." He paused as if he expected a scolding, but Nate said nothing.

"Some people said I was mixed up with some horse thieves, but it weren't true. Not entirely. I mean...I did know 'em an' hung out with 'em for a time, but that don't mean I rustled livestock with 'em, does it?"

"Did you?" Nate asked.

"Did I what?"

"Did you steal any livestock?"

Al clasped his hands to his knees and stiffened his arms. "Well, maybe a little." He frowned at his answer but then recovered with a look of hope. "But I didn' shoot nobody! That was *their* doin'. Them boys was mighty free with their lead."

"Fifteen years?" Nate said and gave Al a questioning look. "It ain't been but ten years since I last seen you."

Al removed his hat and leaned forward with his elbows propped on his knees. He rotated the hat brim by small increments and tightened his brow until the skin buckled in rounded folds.

"Well, see...that's the thing. I didn' see out my sentence."

Nate turned to check Al's face for a lie. "You git out on good behavior?"

Al pressed his lips together into a hard line. "Not 'xactly."

"You broke out?"

With a pained expression, Al bared his teeth and

looked straight ahead. "Well, I wouldn' say *broke out.* Broke is a hard word. I just sorta wandered off from a work detail."

Nate rested the back of his head against the store front and closed his eyes. "So, yo're a wanted man," he said, not bothering to pose the words as a question.

"Not me!" Al corrected. "They're looking Martin Tisdale."

Nate opened his eyes and checked his friend's face for the truth. "You didn' kill nobody?"

"Me?" Al chirped. "Hell, no! Didn' even pull out my gun! That's the God's truth!"

Nate stared out into the street. An old man wearing a tattered hat walked a gray-whiskered pack mule down the middle of the thoroughfare. The ragged animal's tongue hung out as it breathed in a labored rasp. Its pack frame was loaded with poles and canvas and a variety of supplies.

"Sir, there's a water trough one block over at the livery," Nate called out. When the old man stopped and turned, Nate pointed, showing the way.

The man took off his hat and held it high in a gesture of gratitude. "I thank you kindly," he said and returned the hat. When he reached the corner, he turned left for the stables.

"You know," Nate said quietly, "a lot o' the cowhands workin' 'round here hail from Texas."

"Hell, I know it!" Al admitted. "But Texas is a damned big place. I don't reckon there's anybody else would know me, an' I know *you* boys from Round Rock wouldn' turn me in." He pivoted his head quickly to Nate. "Would you?"

Nate shook his head. "Not me...an' not my brothers. I reckon you patched up things with Billy Hill aw-right. An' he ain't the kind to squeal, anyway."

Al smiled. "Well, there you go."

They sat for a while and watched a pair of freight wagons trundle down the street. The bearded driver in the second wagon saw Nate and smiled as he lifted his hat off his head.

"Still got it!" the man announced over the heavy rumble of the wheels.

Nate waved as the driver replaced his hat. "That's Old Ben Jones," Nate explained to Al. "One o' the last o' the old-time waddies. He does some trappin' in the Big Horns, too. Told me he met with a gypsy fortune lady who predicted he'd git scalped by a Ind'an b'fore he turns fifty." Nate huffed an airy laugh through his nose. "I ain't seen a hostile in the territory since I come here."

Al laughed. "Does ever'b'dy in the Wyomin' Territory take off his hat to you?"

Nate shook his head. "Not hardly. I don't think a man can live in Johnson Coun'y without he makes some enemies. I got my share."

Al narrowed one eye and retracted his head as if to get a better look at the whole of Nate. "Never knowed a man to dislike Nate Champion b'fore. 'Xcept, maybe, Dixie Brooks. But, o' course, that boy was mad at the world, weren't he?"

"What became o' him?"

Al settled back on the bench and coughed up a sarcastic laugh. "Prob'ly still in Texas tryin' to see what kinda trouble he can git his-self into. I guess bein' 'the Texas Kid' is a full-time occupation." Al chuckled. "That's what he started callin' his-self, you know."

When the wagons moved on and the quiet returned, Nate dismissed Dixie Brooks from his thinking and laced his fingers over his stomach. "Tell me 'bout yore brother. Where is he?"

"John?" Al seemed pleased at the change of subject.

"He's in the Dakota Territory, workin' as foreman at a ranch for some fancy-pants, New York politician. He's just got married, too. Not the politician...alkin' 'bout John."

"'Married,'" Nate repeated. "Does he know 'bout yore situation?"

"You mean 'bout prison an' changin' my name an' all? Yeah, he knows." Al's voice softened as he went on. "John used to write me regular when I was in prison. Even came to see me once."

Nate pointed up the street toward the county offices. "You worried 'bout the sheriff here figurin' out yore past?"

Al's face sobered like a preacher at a funeral. "It's you folks here who oughta be worried 'bout *that* man."

"Frank Canton? How do you mean?"

"Well, for one thing, that ain't his name. It was 'Joe Horner' when I knew 'im. I doubt he'd remember me. We were in Huntsville at the same time. He was servin' stretches for ever'thin' in the book: murder, bank robbery, stage and train holdups, horse theft...and for breakin' outta jail in San Antone. He was a genuine outlaw."

Nate thought about Canton's reputation as a relentless detective for the Wyoming Stock Growers before he became sheriff. "You sure this is the same man?"

"Hell, yeah, I'm sure," Al said. "That man's got the meanest eyes o' anybody I ever seen. I'd know him in a dark cave on the backside o' hell."

"People 'round here say he's a damned good sher'ff. Hard but efficient."

Al huffed. "He oughta be good. He knows just how a outlaw thinks."

"How'd he git outta Huntsville?"

Al laughed outright. "Same way I did. In fact, he inspired it in me. I knew who he was, 'cause most ever'body in prison was scared of 'im. I mean, he ain't all that big, but he's a tough sonovabitch. One day I was in a work detail next to his. We were all out there hoein' a cotton field that belonged to the warden. When I saw Horner skedaddle, it was like a fuse got lit inside me. I just took off, too. Didn' go with 'im. Went my own way. Didn' *wanna* go with *him!*"

Across the street, Jack Flagg came out of the Occidental Hotel. When he saw Nate, he waved and started toward him. Halfway across the street Jack called out.

"I just heard a crazy rumor about a man jumping a wild mustang over a bar down at the lumberyard." He smiled broadly, and his eyes twinkled like stars reflecting off the surface of rippling water at night. "Wouldn' know anything about that, would you?"

"Might," Nate said.

Al put a hand on Nate's shoulder. "I reckon the horse is more likely to tell you 'bout it than this here feller is. I was a witness to it myself."

Jack stopped at the edge of the street and placed one boot up on the boardwalk. "I wish the crowd could'a seen it." He shrugged. "Sorry if I put you on the spot out there, Nate. I was just trying to keep the show alive. You know what I mean?"

Nate waved at the air with the back of his hand. "They never would'a sat for it. It takes time to build up the first bit o' trust between a man an' a horse."

Jack leaned forward, his arms stiffened with both hands planted on his bent knee. His smile widened, so that his teeth shone like the keys of a new piano.

"Damn! I'd like to 'a seen that myself!" He motioned toward the hotel with a jerk of his head. "But I had to meet with some fellers from Hole in the Wall, the LX, and the Powder River. There's getting to be a lotta complaints from these boys working with the big outfits. Some of them are getting shorted on their wages." He interrupted his train of thought and pointed at Al. "You put on a good show yourself today. Did Frewen give you some of that prize money?"

Al put on his crooked grin. "He threw me a scrap. Offered me a job too."

Jack narrowed his eyes. "You take it?"

"We're hopin' Hank'll take 'im on to work with us," Nate explained. "Me an' Al been friends a long time." Nate looked Al squarely in the eye. "I think he'd be a good hand for us." He pointed across the street at the Occidental. "Is Hank at the hotel?"

Jack shook his head. "Hank's left...gone back to the ranch. But I reckon with you puttin' in a word for your friend, he'll have himself a job at the Bar C."

Al leaned back against the wall and smiled at Nate. "Well, that was easy," he said.

Nate cracked a grin. "Come winter, you might not be thankin' me. Might be wishin' for Texas again."

Al shrugged. "When do you think they'll want me to start?"

"Last week," Jack laughed. "But tomorrow will have to do. Ride back with us tonight, and we'll get you squared away in the bunkhouse." Jack took a step back and tugged up on the waistband of his trousers. "How long will it take you to pack up your gear?"

"I stay packed up," Al laughed. "I'm ready to go now."

Jack started to say more, but the sound of boots on the boardwalk across the street turned his head. Frank Canton and a deputy entered the front door of the Occidental. Al leaned to one side for a better view. Just as Canton reached the hotel door, the interior light carved out his profile in sharp detail. Then the two men disappeared into the hotel.

"That's him, by God," Al whispered to Nate. "I'll swear it on my mama's Bible."

Jack looked at Al and frowned, seeming to wait for an explanation, but Nate stood and spoke. "We'll ride back with you, Jack. Where's yore horse?"

"At Myers Livery." He pointed up the street.

Nate raised his chin toward the intersection from which he and Al had come. "Ours are back at the lumberyard. We'll wait for you there."

Chapter Seven

Retracing their steps to the lumberyard, Nate and Al walked in silence amid the celebratory sounds spilling from the saloons. As they came into view of the roped-off arena, the raucous voices of the town's nightlife faded behind them. In the small holding pen, the mustangs were quiet as they watched the two men approach in the dark. Nate untied his mare at the barn and walked her to the lumberyard fence, where Al adjusted the cinch on his buckskin.

When Al straightened up from behind his horse and looked over his saddle at Nate's mount, he whistled a down-sliding arc of notes. "Well, ain't she easy on the eye! 'Bout as white as the wings of a angel. What'd you name 'er?"

Nate turned and admired the fine lines of his mustang's physique. "Aw-ready had a name when I got 'er. *Dakah*. That's Shoshone for snow."

Leading their horses, they walked side by side into the street. As they waited for Flagg, Al rolled a cigarette and lipped it as he lifted his saddle rifle high enough out of its scabbard to scratch a wooden match against the receiver.

A yellow flame spurted and danced as it made a sound like tiny wind swirling in a canyon. When he lit the cigarette behind a cupped hand, his face shone pale in the night.

"So, how is it you got enemies here, Nate?"

Nate took in a deep breath for the long story he had to tell. "This country here is divided 'bout like oil an' water. It's all these rich men who dominate the land here just by the size o' their herds. Most are Englishmen, and they act like they're royalty. A man can legally own only so much acreage, but these land barons claim the free-range meadows for their own too. They even string fencin' 'round it. You heard Sumner's story. They won't let a man stake his rightful claim on a piece o' land they themselves want to graze their herds on."

"How can they do that?" Al asked.

"Money...an' pow'r," Nate said in a flat tone. "They're right free with their pocketbooks when it comes to bribin' newspapermen, sheriffs, judges, and any down-on-his-luck cowboy who's willin' to tell lies in a courtroom. They're even partnered up with the gov'nor. Hell, two o' the big ranch owners are senators in Washin'ton."

Al snorted a laugh. "Money talks purty loud, don't it?"

They stood in silence for a time. The night air was cool and comfortable. Stars now covered the dark sky from one horizon to the other. They were like sparks risen from a thousand bonfires.

"Al," Nate said in a gentle voice, "might be smart for you to keep ever'thin' you know about Frank Canton to yoreself. If he hears you been talkin' 'bout 'im...or if you should draw his attention in some way...he might be inclined to take a closer look at Al Allison."

Al had raised his cigarette for another draw but stopped when his hand was just inches from his mouth. The orange-red glow of the cigarette hovered in place.

"Yeah," Al whispered. "That's prob'ly some good

advice." When he drew on the cigarette, the ash brightened, and the paper sizzled. Then the glow dimmed behind a cloud of smoke. "I reckon I oughta forgit I ever saw him."

From up the street came the clopping rhythm of a horse moving toward them at a trot. As the rider approached, one of the mustangs in the holding pen whinnied. The trio of horses in the pen began to stir inside their confining quarters.

"Just don't do nothin' that would cause the law to come a-lookin' for you," Nate advised. "They say Frank Canton will follow a man to hell an' back to put 'im behind bars."

Al huffed a breathy laugh. "Well, I *been* to hell an' back aw-ready. It goes by the name o' Huntsville. I got no desire to return there...or any place like it."

Jack Flagg appeared as a dark silhouette astride his horse. He reined up and held his anxious bay gelding in check as he snorted and shuffled his hooves in the dirt.

"This ol' fuss bucket is ready to get back home," Jack said, leaning low to stroke his mount. "You boys 'bout ready?"

Al toed into his stirrup and mounted, but Nate hesitated. "What 'bout these mustangs here?" He pointed toward the pen. "Ain't somebody gonna see to 'em?"

Jack straightened in his saddle and focused his attention on the holding pen. "They're still in there? Fred Hesse was s'posed to collect 'em."

"They're in there," Nate said. "Think we oughta take 'em to Frewen's Ranch? We'll be goin' right by there."

Jack spewed air through his lips. "I ain't so anxious to be doin' any favors for Frewen or Hesse."

"Favor would be for the horses," Nate said. "They're bound to be due some feed and water. I didn' see nobody provide for 'em all day."

Jack said nothing. When his gelding made a quick step to the rear, Jack jerked on the reins, which elicited a grumbling nicker from the testy animal.

"Settle down, you ol' mule-headed outlaw!"

The horse stilled and blew twice. Now the mustangs got more vocal, and Jack seemed to be thoroughly irritated at anything with four legs.

"Well, go ahead an' give 'em some water, if you want to, but let's not take 'em with us. If we did and if we run across some o' the Powder River boys on the way, they'd prob'ly claim we were stealing the damned things."

Nate handed his reins up to Al. "Hold onto my horse for me. I'll be right back."

He found the bucket he had used earlier for mounting the mustang and made four trips from a rain barrel at the lumber office. After filling a metal washtub in the pen, he walked to the back of the yard where the mill-saw was housed inside the barn. There, he lighted a lantern that sat on a work bench, found pencil and paper, and wrote out a bill of sale, signing it with his name and the date.

Charge to Powder River Cattle Company: 1 bale of seasoned hay, it read. Nate laid the paper on the bench and anchored it with a pair of pliers.

He climbed to the loft, threw down a bale of hay, climbed back down to the bay of the barn, and blew out the flame on the lantern. After carrying the hay to the holding pen, he cut the baling twine with his knife and spread the hay. The feral horses nosed into the sweet smell of the dried grasses. When he started back to join Jack and Al, Nate saw that three more horsemen had joined their party, and two men stood on the ground talking to the five who were mounted.

Nate recognized Dudley and Ben by the way they sat their horses. Billy Hill showed his usual slump in the saddle. The two men on foot stood side by side, the shorter one with his thumbs hooked behind his cartridge belt. The taller one smoked a cigar and radiated a quiet confidence. Everyone turned at Nate's approach.

"Hey, Nate!" Dudley called out, "the sher'ff wants to know if yo're startin' up a notorious hay-rustlin' ring here in Johnson Coun'y." Dud pointed to the holding pen. "Startin' with that bale o' hay right there."

Nate said nothing. He stopped next to Al and took the reins of his horse before facing Sheriff Canton and his deputy.

"Evenin'," Nate murmured.

"He's caught you dead to rights, Nate," Dud said with a straight face. "May as well give yoreself up."

Canton was not a man known to smile. His posture remained relaxed, and he seemed in no hurry to explain his presence. After blowing a slow plume of smoke before him, he pointed his cigar in the general direction of Dudley.

"Seems your brother likes to stretch things a bit. Guess he believes himself to be entertaining."

Without moving his head, Nate glanced at Dudley and flashed a subtle warning through the intensity of his eyes. When he looked back at Canton, Nate nodded once.

"He's been known to suffer such delusions." Nate made an easy gesture with his hand toward the barn. "I left Mr. Trayner a note to send the bill to Powder River."

Frank Canton took another draw on his cigar and looked around the lumberyard. Then his eyes fixed on the barn, and, as he pondered it, a lazy string of smoke escaped his lips.

"So, you're making purchases for Moreton Frewen now?"

"Let's just say I'm takin' up the slack o' what his foreman forgot to do."

When Canton did not reply, Jack Flagg spoke up. "It's

a ten-cent bale of hay, Sheriff! Are we going before a judge over a dime's worth of seasoned grass?"

Canton stared into the dark arena. The holding pen was quiet now but for the hollow sound of molars grinding hay and the occasional nicker of satisfaction.

Dudley started chuckling. "I guess when an officer discovers a hay-thievin' gang startin' up in his coun'y, it's time to nip it in the bud. I'd say an arrest is imminent."

Looking up at Dud, Nate said not a word, but his deadpan expression carried its own message.

Never one to heed a warning, Dudley leaned and rested a forearm on the pommel of his saddle. "Well, Nate...guess you better find yoreself a good lawyer. Looks like the sher'ff has caught you hay-handed."

Canton ignored these comments and stared down at the ground between his boots. When he looked up at Nate, he spoke in a low, calm voice.

"I'll tell Fred Hesse about the favor you done for him."

"Didn' do it for *him*," Nate replied as he took his reins from Al. "Did it for the horses."

Canton shrugged. "Either way," he said. "It don't matter." He turned his head and eyed Ben, Dudley, and Billy. He seemed to pay no attention to Al. When he looked at Jack, he sucked on his cigar again, and the brightened ash revealed his dark, narrowed eyes that seemed to contemplate the man's destiny.

"Had a complaint about you stirring up trouble over at the Occidental," Canton said in a cold voice. He plugged his cigar into his mouth and waited for an answer.

"Trouble?!" Jack repeated. "It ain't me that's the source of the trouble around here."

"I'll disagree with you there, Mr. Flagg," the sheriff replied.

Jack Flagg sat up straighter in his saddle. "You can disagree all you want, Sheriff, but it don't change the truth of it. These cattle barons seem to make up their own laws. They're saying that no employee of any of the big outfits has the legal right to own any cattle. Not one!"

Canton held his cigar before him and studied the brick of red ash clinging to the end. "You'd do well to heed that advice," he said in a quiet tone of conviction. Then he flicked the ash from the cigar, and a constellation of orange-red sparks scattered on the ground and died.

Jack began to show some of the seething irritation he often fell into when discussing the rich cattle barons of the county. His upper lip curled like that of a snarling dog.

"Any common man has got the same rights as these arrogant cattle kings you like to associate with! You can't stop a man wanting to claim his own piece of land an' start up a herd for himself! He's got just as much right to it as any of these rich men!"

Throughout Jack's complaint, Canton did not blink. His reply came in a calm and collected monotone.

"Except for the fact that we all know how such a man collects the beginnings of his herd."

Jack bristled, and his voice took on the plaintive timbre of a wronged man. "If we find a maverick out on the range and give it a home, we're not doing anything different than what the barons are doing!"

Canton raised his cigar to his mouth, took a long draw, and then expelled the smoke in a slow, steady stream. "Except, now, it's against the law."

"Law?" Jack growled. "Hell, it ain't nothing but a piece of pie served out to all the rich men in the territory."

Canton's face showed nothing. "Still the law," he mumbled.

"Well, it's a crooked law!" Jack spat. "And it ought to be took off the books!"

Canton stood as relaxed as if he were waiting for his

change at the cash box in the mercantile. It seemed impossible to get him riled.

"Till it is," he warned, "it'll *be* the law and one that I will enforce. And you—" he pointed the cigar at Flagg, "you are inciting men to break the law. Do it again, and I'll throw you in a cell."

"Ha!" Jack huffed, the one-note laugh expressing equal measures of surprise and defiance. He stared at Canton as he spoke to the others.

"Apparently our sheriff is not familiar with the concept of free speech!"

Canton waved the cigar lazily before him, leaving a smoke trail hanging in the air like the stroke of an artist's brush. "Oh, you can talk all you want, Flagg. It's just that you'll be sitting in my jail, and your only audience will be my other prisoners."

Jack started to argue the point, but Canton pointed the cigar at him again. "Don't test me, Flagg," he commanded, his voice a hard monotone. "Any man who goes against me...who steals from any member of the Wyoming Stock Growers Association...that man will find Johnson County a damned difficult place to breathe."

Jack's eyes widened, and he almost laughed. "Is that a threat, Sheriff?"

Canton stuck the cigar into his mouth and spoke around it. "Anytime an officer warns a man about breaking the law, it ought to *be* considered a threat...a legal one."

Jack thrust out an arm and pointed at Canton. "Here's what I think about your—"

"I'm done talking to you, Flagg!" the sheriff interrupted, his voice now carrying more weight. "You'd do well to get out of my sight."

"Gladly!" Jack returned. "Bein' in sight of you is starting to ruin my evening!" He kicked his heels into his horse's flanks, and the animal responded with a series of quick stutter-steps. "Come on, boys!" he yelled amid the soft clap of hooves. "Let's go find some better scenery to look at!" He booted his horse again, and the bay broke into a trot.

At the sudden departure of Jack's gelding, all the horses reacted with snorts and nickers. They milled about in a nervous dance of uncertainty. Then, when Billy Hill started away to catch Jack, the other mounted men followed.

Still standing on the ground, Nate held his mare in check and waited for her to settle. After stroking her forehead, he stepped to the mustang's side, running his hand along her neck. There he paused and looked over his saddle into Frank Canton's steely eyes.

"Lie down with dogs, and you'll get up with fleas," Canton said to Nate in a no-nonsense voice.

Nate allowed a half smile. In no hurry, he took a grip on each end of his saddle, hopped up and toed into his stirrup. After swinging over his leg to sit his horse, he sorted the reins and then looked up, pursing his lips as he stared out into the night.

"Knew a Mexican horse trainer back in Texas," Nate said. "He had another version o' that old sayin'." Nate turned his head and faced the sheriff eye to eye. "From the dog's point o' view, I guess you'd say."

"Oh?" Canton replied without a trace of curiosity.

Nate closed his eyes as he recalled the words. "On a freezin' cold night, a man might pull his dog into his bed just to stay alive...fleas or not. But when the sun comes up, it's still the man who eats a meal first and the dog who laps up whatever scraps might be left over...if any."

Opening his eyes, Nate could see that the sheriff had not grasped the point, and he knew that Canton would not admit to that. The man simply made a noncommittal humming sound in his throat, as if he had heard an unamusing bit of gossip. Then he nodded down the street, in the direction where Nate's companions had ridden off.

"Who's your new friend?"

"New friend?"

"Bearded fellow on the buckskin."

"Al? He just got into town today."

"Al have a last name?" Canton pressed.

"Said his name was 'Allison.'"

The sheriff nodded once. "He working with you boys at the Bar C?"

"Just startin'."

Canton drew on his cigar again. Staring at Nate, he blew a cloud of smoke that hovered in the air between them. As the smoke cleared, one of the mustangs in the holding pen whinnied, and then two of the horses started at each other, snarling and biting, setting a up a racket as they banged against the boards. A loud hollow *clack* rang out, and the bucket rolled out of the pen and clattered along the hardpan. Soon after, the washtub banged against the boards, and water sloshed onto the ground. Then all was quiet in the pen.

When he faced Nate again, Canton seemed to have dropped all the hostility from his face. "I hear you jumped the bar on that wild mustang," he said, his voice almost friendly. "I'll tell Moreton Frewen. Maybe he'll fork over that prize money to you."

Nate shook his head. "Didn' do it for the money."

Canton narrowed his eyes. "What *did* you do it for, if it weren't the money?"

Nate let his eyebrows rise and then fall. "Hard to say. Don't know that I could explain it proper to you."

"Try me," Canton said.

Nate looked down at his hands stacked one over the other on top of the pommel, his reins woven loosely through his fingers. "Reckon it was a opportunity...to learn," he said.

"For the horse, you mean?"

Nate shrugged. "For both o' us."

Canton sniffed, looked back at the barn, and then nodded to Nate. "You have a good evenin', Champion," he mumbled. After plucking the front of his hat brim, he turned and walked slowly back toward the business section of town. The deputy, who had not spoken a word, followed two paces behind him, taking two steps for every one of Canton's.

When the two lawmen had rounded the corner of the nearest building, Nate eased his horse toward the arena and reined up at the side of the pen, where he could check on the level of water in the washtub. Backing his horse to the bucket, he gripped both pommel and reins in one hand and leaned below the horse's belly to snatch the bucket off the ground. With a *chick, chick* he walked his mustang to the rain barrel, filled the bucket, returned to the pen, and emptied the water into the tub. All this without leaving his saddle.

Then he set out south under the stars and coaxed his horse into a relaxed lope to overtake his friends.

Autumn 1885

Crazy Woman Creek Pastures, Wyoming Territory

Chapter Eight

Since dawn, Nate and Ranger Jones had been covering the pasturelands around Crazy Woman Creek, following the tracks of a few steers that had wandered off from the Bar C's main herd. The signs written in the dirt indicated a pack of coyotes had spooked the runaways. The sun was high now, and the cattle's trail should have been easy to follow through the dry, yellow grass, but the main herd had grazed this part of the valley the day before, and hoof marks were everywhere.

"Look yonder," Nate said and reined up as he extended an arm to point west toward the Big Horns. "'Bout three hun'erd yards out. What's that look like to you?"

Ranger halted his pony, stood in his stirrups, and squinted at the distant, dark object that stood out against the sun-bleached sea of grass. Ranger lowered himself to his saddle and held a frown on his face.

"I ain't sure. That a buffalo?"

They took their horses at an easy walk, but one hundred yards away, Nate held up his hand as a signal to stop. When their horses came to rest and began to settle, Nate whispered out of the side of his mouth.

"Grizzly."

Ranger went quiet as a church mouse. The hump in the bear's back stood several feet above a thick stand of dried buffalo grass. Its head remained unseen, working at ground level with occasional tugs and jerks.

"Damn!" Ranger breathed. "Looks 'bout as big as my horse!"

"Wind's shifted to our backs," Nate whispered. He pointed northwest, where the land dropped down into a grassy swale. "Let's git down yonder, swing west a ways, an' approach from the north."

"'Approach'?" Ranger repeated. He swallowed, and the lump in his throat bobbed up and down like a fishing cork. "Well, what're we gonna do once't we git there?"

"Could be he's got one o' our steers. If it is, then we'll know we're in the right area. But we got to be careful. If it's a sow and there's cubs with 'er, we'll give 'er a wide berth and just go our way. We'll look for the rest o' them runaways down the valley."

Ranger turned back to the feeding orgy and wrinkled his nose. "Why don't we just shoot the damn thing?" He leaned forward to pull his saddle rifle from its scabbard.

"Leave off on that," Nate said. "He's got as much right to eat as we do."

Ranger let his hand slide off the rifle stock and sighed. "Even if it's chewin' on Bar C livestock?"

Nate shrugged. "The Bar C ain't gonna go belly-up over one steer. B'sides, that bear don't know nothin' 'bout ownership o' animals. It's hungry, is all." He gave Ranger a nod. "Bear's gotta make a livin' too."

Circling the kill site, the two riders approached from the north, their horses already nickering with nervous protests. Forty yards away from the gore, they reined up again and watched the bear tear at the entrails of its prey. The shining, wet intestines uncoiled into the sunlight like a pink and blue snake writhing in the yellow grass. Each time the bruin tugged at the corpse, the bloody body moved in the grass as if it were trying to come back to life.

"Well, it ain't no antelope," Ranger whispered. "Look at them horns."

The flank of the dead steer showed a smooth coat of rust-red, which appeared dull compared to the grizzly's shaggy, silver-tipped pelage of walnut-brown. Nate pointed.

"Look at the shoulder where the bone juts out. That's the EK brand."

Ranger stood in his stirrups again. "Damn sure is!" he agreed, his voice cracking and then delivering a burst of dry coughing. He sat low and ducked his head as he clapped his hand over his mouth, but the muted coughing continued.

The grizzly straightened up and hooked its head around to show a muzzle glistening with fresh blood. When the beast stood on its rear legs to face the two intruders, it looked as big as the trunk of an old cotton-wood. Opening its mouth, it bared blood-pink teeth and bellowed a gargling growl as it slung its head from side to side in a wobbling figure-eight pattern.

The horses went into motion immediately, backing away and dredging up coarse screams from deep in their throats. The two cowhands worked to get their cowponies under control. When the grizz dropped down on all fours and charged, both riders wheeled their mounts and dug in with their heels.

"Head for that rise yonder!" Nate called out. "And, for God's sake, hang on!"

The two horsemen covered the hundred yards of grassland in a matter of seconds. When Nate looked back, he saw the bear returning to its kill in a relaxed, lumbering walk.

"He's quit on us!" Nate yelled and reined up his horse.

Atop the rise, they sat their horses and watched the bear resume its meal. Still jittery, the horses continuously moved their hooves in place, threw their heads up and down, and nickered. Nate leaned down and stroked the neck of his mustang.

"It's aw-right, girl," he murmured. "We just wandered into somebody's dinin' room uninvited." Straightening in his saddle, Nate saw the grizzly settle down in the grass and work on the steer. He chuckled quietly as he kept his eye on the bear. "He owns this valley, don't he?"

Ranger's head came around quickly. "I reckon the owner of the EK might argue that."

Nate smiled. "Not today, he won't." He nodded toward the bear. "Right now, this here valley is the territory of that grizz. Ever'thin' else—the steer, you, me, our horses—we're all just trespassers today."

Ranger took off his hat and, with the same arm, wiped his shirt sleeve across his brow. "You think free range applies to the needs of a grizz too?" He returned the hat to his head and waited for an answer.

"I reckon it's free to whoever is strong enough to take it," Nate said, nodding at the bear.

"It don't seem so free to me," Ranger argued. "Not among the cattlemen." He swept an arm across the valley. "All this grass is s'posed to be shared by anybody who keeps livestock, but these fancy-pants, English cattle barons act like they own it all."

Hissing air through his teeth, Ranger shook his head. "I knowed this one feller from Iowa who took out a patent for a hun'erd an' sixty acres right down there on the creek." He pointed east toward Crazy Woman. "Had a wife and boy. They's plannin' on raisin' beets an' taters. Didn' last there two weeks b'fore they was run off by Frewen's men."

He stared at the side of Nate's face and waited for a comment. Nate said nothing. He merely nodded with a barely perceptible movement of his head.

"'Nother feller I knew," Ranger went on, "he brought over a hun'erd head o' cattle over near the head o' Clear Creek. Took out *his* patent, too...a hun'erd an' sixty acres... all legal an' signed for. Started his herd grazin' in that little pocket o' land where the creek makes that horseshoe bend. The TA boys run 'im outta there inside of a month. You call that *free* range?"

The bear started dragging what was left of the carcass toward the foothills of the Big Horns. The steer's corpse must have weighed four hundred pounds, but the grizzly made the job appear effortless. Like a sixteen-hand horse pulling an Indian travois. Nate watched until the bear had climbed a low hill, topped the rise, and dropped out of sight on the other side.

"Like I said," Nate replied softly, "free to whoever is strong enough to take it."

Ranger's eyes narrowed. "So, you think that's fair?"

Nate shook his head. "'Fair' ain't got nothin' to do with it."

Ranger's troubled expression did not change. "So, we're just s'posed to accept it?"

"We ain't got much choice. It's the way it is. These rich Englishmen got the money an' the manpower an' the right connections. They got their hooks into whoever they need to control."

"What does that mean?" Ranger asked.

"I remember that Iowa family. After they got run off, the newspaper told it like they'd been rustling cattle from Frewen." Nate turned to Ranger. "There's the truth o' what happ'ned, and there's the truth accordin' to the Stock Growers Assoc'ation. Most people 'round here know not to b'lieve what they read in the papers, but when the newspapers in Cheyenne an' Casper an' Rawlins carry Frewen's version, well—" Nate hitched one shoulder as a shrug and left the rest unsaid.

"But you plan on startin' yore own herd one day, don't you?"

Nate nodded. "Soon's I save up enough money."

"Well?" Ranger said, getting a little worked up now. "What's to keep you from bein' run off?"

Nate ran his tongue across his teeth as he looked out on the valley sloping to the creek. "I plan on bein' the stronger one." He turned to Ranger to show the conviction in his face. "Ain't gonna let Frewen or nobody else run it over on me."

Ranger frowned as he studied Nate's face. Then his eyes flicked to one side as he looked off toward the creek.

"Rider comin'," he said quietly, his lips barely moving.

Nate turned in his saddle and saw a lone horseman approaching them from the northeast. In front of the man, a dog's head could be seen bobbing above the seed stalks of the grass and then disappearing, the movement repetitive and steady.

"Who *is* that?" Ranger whispered. "You know 'im?"

Nate eyed the horse more than he did the man. The chestnut mare showed a white blaze running down the center of her face, and her white socks flashed in the sun as she picked up her hooves and cantered behind a brindle dog.

"Looks like the foreman at the EK."

Ranger chuckled. "I guess we'll see what *he* has to say to this grizz."

The two men sat their horses and waited for the rider and his dog to approach. He was a middle-aged man, who had started to trade his lean frame for some extra padding around his midsection. He sat a little stiff in his saddle, but he handled his horse with practiced grace. Beneath his open gray jacket, a blue neckerchief hung loosely around his collar. Stuck in the brim of his dark hat and angled to the back was a brown hawk feather mottled with spots of white. His tanned face showed a web of creases, each one like a dark, bloodless incision sliced into his skin. When twenty yards away, the man threw a casual, two-fingered salute from the brim of his hat.

"Whattaya say, boys?" he called out in a lazy drawl. When he reined up, the muscular dog stood in the grass beside him and panted with its tongue waggling out one side of its mouth. "Ain't seen a stray steer out this way, have you? One carryin' a EK brand?" He turned his head long enough to nod at his canine companion. "Me an' Gyp been trailing it most of the morning." He looked straight into Nate's eyes. "You're Champion, right?"

Nate nodded. "Yes'r...Nate Champion."

"Name's Spaugh," the man said. "Foreman for the EK."

"Yes'r," Nate replied and pinched the front of his hat brim. "I know who you are." He lowered his hand and extended it toward Ranger. "This here is Orly Jones. We're out lookin' for some strays ourself...from the Bar C."

"Don't bother with 'Orly,' Mister Spaugh," Ranger laughed. "I go by Ranger." He pointed toward the kill site, where the grass was dark with blood and offal. "We run across your stray right there. 'Bout half et up. Grizzly bear kilt it." He swung his arm toward the Big Horns. "That grizz is hauling it off toward the trees yonder."

Spaugh frowned and scanned the grove of aspens on the higher ground. "You didn' kill it?"

Ranger puffed up a little. "I aw-ready tol' you. The bear kilt it."

"No, I mean...didn' you kill the bear?"

Ranger turned to Nate for an answer to that question. Spaugh leaned forward and stacked both hands over his pommel, seemingly interested in what Nate might say.

"Weren't no need," Nate advised. "The deed was done. Yore steer was long dead."

Spaugh narrowed one eye and studied Nate. "Most boys would'a kilt that bear anyway."

"Yes'r," Nate replied, "that's true enough."

Spaugh seemed mildly amused. He scanned the open grassland that rolled toward the mountains.

"Well, maybe that ol' grizz'll stay up in the high country for a while and leave us alone."

"He been a problem to you?" Nate asked.

Spaugh's lower lip pushed forward as he shook his head. "No more'n the occasional lightnin' bolt." He looked from Ranger to Nate. "So, how many did you boys lose?"

"Looks like, maybe, six," Nate answered. "They was run off by ki-yotes."

Spaugh nodded and looked down the long valley that curved with the creek. "Damned good grass here. Might run some of the EK herd through here." When he turned back to Nate, he wore a peculiar smile. "I was at that fair in Buffalo last month. I heard you jumped that mustang over that bar after ever'body left."

"He shore as hell did," Ranger cut in. "I've talked to four witnesses who saw it."

Spaugh kept his eyes on Nate. "Can I ask how much they pay you at the Bar C?"

"Enough," Nate said, not wanting to embarrass Ranger, whose wages were less than his.

The EK man lowered his head and rubbed the back of his neck. His eyes angled up to Nate as though he were uncertain of his words.

"Well, I'd guess standard pay there to be thirty dollars a month? That be about right?"

Nate nodded. "Mostly."

Ranger jumped in again. "I'd say you hit that right on the nose, Mr. Spaugh."

Ignoring Ranger, Spaugh leaned on his pommel again and held his gaze on Nate. "I'd like to offer you a foreman position at forty-five."

"Forty-five dollars a month?" Ranger said in a breathy voice.

Spaugh did not acknowledge the question. It was clear that the offer was meant exclusively for Nate. When Nate did not reply, Spaugh continued.

"Plus, there'll be some bonuses on any mavericks you bring in. Five dollars apiece. And a dollar for every ki-yote you kill." He nodded toward the Colt's on Nate's hip. "Can you hit somethin' with that pistol?"

Ranger started to butt in again, but Nate cut him off with a quick glance. "I can."

Spaugh smiled. "Would you mind if I asked for a demonstration?"

Nate looked down at his hands holding the reins. When his head came up, he saw that Spaugh was watching him carefully.

"Don't see no reason to shatter the peace and quiet out here."

Spaugh smiled again, straightened in his saddle, and crossed his arms over his chest. "Could you just humor me, son? I'd really like to see."

Nate shook his head. "Yo're gonna need to tell me why."

After a few moments of silence, Ranger could not hold himself back. "I seen Nate hit a playin'card—the queen o' clubs, it was—from twen'y yards out. An' he did it on the fly! Some o' us boys were makin' bets on who could shoot straight, an' we jammed that queen into the top of a fence-post. We was shootin' all around 'er, till Nate come up and tol' us to git to work."

Nate gave Ranger a look, but the boy only laughed, his eyes shining with admiration. Once he started a story, Nate knew, he was bound to see it through.

"Well," Ranger continued, "his brother, Dudley, who, himself, is a card—if you know what I mean—he says, 'We ain't movin' a foot from here till somebody puts a hole in that damned queen.'" Ranger shook his head in wonderment. "B'fore you could take a breath, Nate jerked his shooter an' plugged that queen right in her brisket. We still use that deck for poker at night, and when that holey card shows up in somebody's hand...well...the cat's outta the bag for that feller."

A silence fell over the three horsemen. Ranger looked back and forth from Nate to Spaugh, until the quiet seemed too much for him.

"Nate can damned well put that Winchester to good use, too. I seen 'im shoot the head off a turkey from fifty yards."

Again, Spaugh kept his eyes on Nate. "I lost my best man last month. Took off for Oregon to get married and got 'im a job with the new father-in-law to work with the railroad. I need a capable man I can depend on."

Nate crossed his wrists over his pommel and looked down at his idle hands. When he brought his eyes up to Spaugh, he offered just enough smile to keep the conversation friendly.

"Ain't sure I can work for Horace Plunkett, Mister Spaugh. Yore rich Englishman ain't no friend to the common cowhand." Nate hitched his head to one side and raised both eyebrows. "Way I hear it, he don't allow his crew to accumulate any cattle for theirselves. And like all the other barons—English or otherwise—he don't welcome any o' the small, independent ranchers to take part in a roundup."

Spaugh was nodding even before Nate had finished voicing his grievances. "You got *him* pegged all right. But he don't manage the roundups. I do." He shook his head. "Me and Plunkett...we don't see eye to eye on some things. He ain't fired me yet, but till he does, I will open up my roundups to any man who owns livestock. I don't care if he's got just two steers, a milk cow, and a cross-eyed goat. A man of little means has got the same rights as the owner of a cattle empire."

Ranger slapped a hand to his own thigh, leaned forward, and crooked his elbow out to his side. "You're damned right he does! Most o' us regular ol' hands got plans to settle here, too...make a livin' on our own...nob'dy tellin' us what to do! We shore as hell don' wanna be workin' the rest o' our lives for these damned far'ners who was born with a silver spoon stuck up their ass!"

Finally, Spaugh turned to Ranger Jones, produced a strained smile, and cocked his head to one side. "It ain't me you need to preach to, son. I'm in the same situation as you boys. But I'm willin' to take Plunkett's money to get me to where I wanna be."

When Ranger could think of no response to the foreman's declaration, Spaugh returned his attention to Nate. "Will you consider it?"

"Aw-ready have," Nate replied.

"And?"

Nate nodded once. "I'll take it, Mister Spaugh...on one condition."

Spaugh pushed up the brim of his hat from his face. "What would that be?"

Nate leaned and stroked the strong neck of his mustang. "I'd wanna bring along my best bronc rider with me."

Ed Spaugh looked toward the mountains and followed their undulating ridges with his eyes. Then he pulled in his lips, making his mouth but another thin line on his weathered face. He began nodding as he studied the Big Horns, and then he looked Nate in the eye.

"Done," he said. "What's this man's name?"

Nate kept his eyes on Spaugh, but he was aware of Ranger's unusual stillness as he sat his horse. "Orly Jones," Nate said quietly. "But he goes by Ranger." When Nate met Ranger's wide eyes, he could see that the boy was about to burst. "Would that suit you?" Nate asked.

Ranger cleared his throat and swallowed. He looked at Spaugh and then at Nate, as if he suspected he might be the brunt of a joke between them.

"You ser'ous?" he said, his voice cracking.

Nate hitched his head. "It's yore call."

Ranger raised an eyebrow at Spaugh. "Forty-five a month?"

Spaugh shook his head. "That's for foreman. I could make it thirty-five for you."

Ranger beamed. "Hell, yeah! I could call myself an EK man!"

Spaugh reached forward to Nate and offered his hand. "Reckon we got us a deal."

Nate gripped Spaugh's hand, and the two men shook, which sealed the deal as surely as if documents had been signed before a lawyer. Ranger nudged his horse forward to be a part of the proceedings. When he grabbed Spaugh's hand, he worked it like a pitcher pump.

"All right, all right!" Spaugh said laughing. When he got his hand back, he leaned on his pommel again. "You boys better call me Ed. When do you want to start?"

Nate pursed his lips and looked south across the bend of the creek. He tried to imagine Hank Devoe's face when Nate would tell him he and Ranger were quitting.

"We'll need a coupla weeks, till our foreman can find some hands to take our place."

"Hell, Nate!" Ranger huffed. "That'll be more'n two weeks. Cain't just anybody take *yore* place. Yo're practically the foreman as it is."

"Just like you'll be with me," Spaugh said with a determined look. "I'll be foreman in name only. You'll be the one out with the crew a-runnin' things. How's that sound to you?"

Nate nodded. "I'll let you know when we're comin'."

Late Summer 1886

EK Ranch, Upper Powder River Basin, Wyoming Territory

Chapter Nine

It was late on a Sunday when Nate was grooming his mustang, Dakah, in the EK barn. After months of dry weather, it had finally rained. All day long a series of powerful storms had swept over the land, until the yard outside the barn had mired to a mud slick. The downpour on the barn's metal roof resounded like the voices in a crowded saloon filling the air with too many conversations. Whenever the wind gusted and pushed hard against the barn, a high-pitched moaning sound sang through a crack in the loft boards, making a soft cry like a wounded animal.

As twilight faded to a starless night outside, the rain settled to a lighter assault, tapping the roof in changing patterns. With the barn in near dark, Nate put a match to the lantern that hung from the center post. As he blew out the match flame, hoofbeats rattled on the wood bridge down at the creek, announcing the arrival of a small group of riders.

When the party trotted into the yard, Nate was surprised to hear the familiar voice of his brother, Dudley, delivering the end of a story over the sloppy sound of the horses' shoes in the mud. When Dud finished off his tale in the falsetto voice of a woman, the other men laughed heartily, and Nate knew that, once again, his little brother had been the life of someone's party.

The quartet of horsemen dismounted outside the barn, and the three EK men, all bundled up in wet slickers, led their mounts inside from the weather, each nodding to Nate and heading for a stall where he would tend to his mount. Thick cakes of mud clung to the hooves of the animals, leaving a trail of fresh mud through the barn's breezeway.

Outside in the rain, Dudley tied his horse to the wheel of the hay wagon, as he softly whistled a Texas tune that Nate remembered from his childhood. When Dud walked into the lighted bay of the barn, he pulled off his hat and his wet slicker and hung both over the rounded end of a long-handled rake leaning against the wall. Moving to the tack room entrance, he kicked the mud from his boots against the single step at the doorway.

"I b'lieve I could ride in this rain all night," Dudley said. "This damned summer has been a scorcher. Hotter'n hell an' dry as a mouthful of desert sand!" He shook his head. "We'll pay for it this winter, for sure. Ever'body in the valley has overgrazed, and the grass that growed back ain't worth spittin' on."

Nate stopped brushing and studied his brother's face. "Has the Bar C stocked up on hay?"

Dud hissed a stream of air through his teeth. "Hell, no. There ain't no hay to be *had*! What about you boys?"

Nate shook his head. "We left plen'y o' free range pastures ungrazed for a winter supply for our cattle, but I cain't control what the other outfits do. They aw-ready run their herds right through ever' acre we tried to set aside." From deep in his chest, he hummed a sound of disapproval. "I been pushin' for us to stock up on hay, but Plunkett ain't put out a penny for it."

Dud ran his fingers through his wet hair. "What do these Englishmen expect to happen?"

"It ain't just the English," Nate assured him. "Seems like all the owners in the Stock Growers Assoc'ation don't think past their next meal. I guess they think that the world will look after 'em somehow." Nate started brushing the mustang again. "What're you doin' out this way?"

"Got some news," Dud said, his face uncharacteristically solemn. "Thought you'd wanna hear it sooner than later." He leaned a shoulder into the plank wall and watched Nate work the brush along the horse's flank.

After half a minute of silence, Nate looked up as he continued the rhythm of the grooming. "Well, right now would be sooner than later, wouldn' it? Or should I start guessin' at this news? Ain't nothin' wrong back at home, is there?"

Dud shook his head. "Far's I know, ever'thin's good in Texas." He hitched his head toward the back stalls, where the EK men were rubbing down their horses. Dud raised his forefinger to let his brother know that there would be a tacit silence between them until they were alone.

Sitting in the doorway of the tack room, Dudley settled in to wait. He seemed relaxed and patient, as if he had come all this way just to sit in the bay of the barn. Nate was always surprised to see how still and quiet his brother could be when he set his mind to it.

When the last cowboy trudged off to the bunkhouse, Dud stood and moved to the doorway to watch the man's dark shape cross the yard. When the man's boots could no longer be heard sloshing and sucking at the mud, Dud turned toward Nate.

"Sumner Beach has been indicted for first-degree

murder. He'll be goin' b'fore a jury that'll decide if he lives or dies."

Nate's hand stopped its motion, and he straightened to look over his horse's back. "What happ'ned? Who's he s'posed to a' kilt?"

"Oh, he kilt someb'dy aw-right," Dud assured his brother. "It's just the circumstances 'round it that are in question." He approached to stand opposite Nate, with just the white mustang between them. "Way I heard it, Wolcott's done ever'thin' he can to make life mis'rable for Sumner and his partner. Brought 'em up on charges of rustlin' an' on jumping Wolcott's claim at the Deer Creek pastures." Dud huffed a laugh. "When that didn' scare Sumner off, the Major started sendin' some tough-an'-uglies over there to threaten the boys. When none o' *that* worked, he hired a gunman out o' Utah to finish the bus'-ness. This man—name o' Locker—pretended to be a friend an' throwed in with Sumner, but word got out that this Locker was a killer an' had been hired by Wolcott."

"Locker," Nate repeated. "I know him. He worked for the Bar C b'fore you come up from Texas." Nate shook his head. "Guess I shouldn' say worked. He weren't worth his weight in cow dung." Nate leaned on his horse and gazed out the door. "Hell, Sumner knew 'im, too."

Dud placed a hand on the mustang's hip and stroked the smooth coat. "Prob'ly why Wolcott hired 'im. A familiar face, you know? So, then, Sumner finds out Locker is on Wolcott's payroll. But Sumner, bein' who he is—all polite-like—tells this feller Locker it would be best if he moved on." Dud laughed. "Anybody else would'a just shot 'im. But not Sumner." Dud laughed again. "Anyway, Locker comes back after a few days an' starts throwin' his weight 'round. I guess he throwed it one too many times, 'cause Sumner said he'd had enough o' him, an' he was to leave without delay. Locker took offense and went for his pistol, but Sumner got there first...plugged him with his Winchester. Shot 'im dead right there at The Willows. Then he turned his-self in to the sher'ff."

"Were there witnesses?" Nate asked.

Dud nodded deeply. "Yep. Sumner's partner, Brannan...he saw it all. But he's gone missin'."

Nate's brow lowered over his eyes. "Brannan wouldn' leave Sumner in the lurch."

"'Xactly," Dud agreed. "It's got to be Wolcott's doin'." Dud put on his crooked grin. "An' git this...Wolcott has made his-self the justice of the peace so he can be the one to oversee the trial. Rumor is...he'll create a new list o' witnesses...ones he'll pay for outta his pocket."

The rain had let up, and now there was only the dripping of water from the eaves of the building into the standing puddles below. When Nate spoke, his voice was so low and contained that Dudley stopped breathing to hear every word.

"Wolcott and the rest o' the Stock Growers Assoc'ation think they rule this territory. But there's still honest cowhands and small ranchers who know how to separate the truth from the lies. It's up to a jury...not to Wolcott."

Dudley huffed. "It ain't just witnesses that can be bribed. There's plenty o' skunks who'll take Wolcott's money an' sit in the jury box with their verdict aw-ready decided."

Nate gazed out the barn door at the blackness of the night. "When's the trial?"

Dudley shrugged. "It got postponed for a coupla months. Sumner asked for Hank Devoe to testify as a character witness. They'll reconvene when he can git down there."

Nate began brushing the mustang again, his strokes brisker and at a faster pace, as if trying to brush away the evils of the world.

"So, how're you an' Ranger likin' it here at the EK?"

Nate laid off the work and straightened. "Pay is good. I can work as a foreman and have nothin' to do with Horace Plunkett. Spaugh stays b'tween him and me."

"I thought Spaugh was foreman," Dud said.

Nate nodded. "He is...in name. But I do the work for 'im in the saddle." He tossed the brush into a wooden crate behind him and walked to the barn's entrance, where he leaned into the doorframe with his back to the bay. Just then the moon peeked through the clouds and touched each puddle of water in the yard with a rime of silver.

"You can stay here tonight if you wont, Dud. No sense in ridin' back alone in the dark. One o' our men is down at Fort Fetterman in the hospital, so we got a extra bunk you can use."

Dud shook his head. "I like ridin' at night...'specially a wet night like this'n. The moonlight 'bout lights up the trail like its cobbled with silver coins."

Dud took down his slicker and flapped it hard in the air, flinging droplets of water against the wall. Then he folded the slicker, rolled it up tightly, and slapped his hat on his head. Stepping beside Nate, he laid a hand on his brother's shoulder.

"Reckon I'll see you when I see you." Dud's hand slid away as he sloshed out into the shining maze of puddles in the yard.

"I 'preciate you ridin' out here to tell me," Nate said to his back.

Without turning, Dud delivered a jaunty wave of the hand. When he reached his horse, he tied down the rolled slicker behind the cantle of his saddle. Then, with the groan of leather, he mounted.

"What're you gonna do 'bout Sumner?" Dud asked.

Nate crossed his arms over his chest and stared into the yard. "I don' know. Somethin'."

Dud nodded as if that were answer enough. "Well, lemme know."

By the time Dudley's horse had clattered across the loose boards of the bridge, Nate had put Dakah in her stall and snuffed the lantern. As he followed the muddy path to the bunkhouse, the moon lost its argentine hue and now shone bone-white among a circle of clouds around it. Along with the white, a faint shade of blue streaked across some of the puddles.

These colors took Nate back to a time in Texas, when he had ridden into Round Rock on the night of the dance at the Masons' Hall. There he had seen Dory Hildebrand in a white dress with a blue lace collar. Against his better judgment, Nate had given in to her wishes and danced with her that night. He had done it within sight of a hundred people that he knew. Now, recalling the ordeal, he considered it to be one of his sweetest memories stored away in his mind. As he trudged through the mud on this wet night, he remembered how his feet had found the rhythm of the music and how Dory's strong but gentle hands had guided him through the unfamiliar gyrations necessary to fit in on the dance floor.

"Come on out o' that muck!" said a hoarse voice from the front of the bunkhouse.

The orange-red glow of a cigarette brightened in the dark just outside the bunkhouse door. As Nate got closer, he made out the familiar shape of Ed Spaugh sitting on the rough-hewn bench beside the wood pile. Hatless and in his shirt sleeves, Ed leaned back against the building and blew a plume of smoke that peeled away on the evening breeze and disappeared in the dark. He raised his free hand and stretched it toward the meadows west of the paddock. With his hand palm down, he splayed his fingers and made a sweeping motion as if he were smoothing out the terrain with a magician's touch.

"There's your show out yonder," he declared. "Look at those colors!"

Nate faced the open, wet grassland slathered with moonlight. Streaking through the eerie white of the grasses, a blue glow wove through the meadow like a caerulean thread. But there were also veins of gold and violet. It was something to look at, all right.

"Damned if it don't bring to mind a fine lady I once knew," Ed blurted out.

Allowing a look of surprise on his face, Nate turned and stared at Ed as if the older man had been privy to Nate's reminiscences about Dory.

"Yeah," Ed continued, "she favored those colors. Had a little blue and white tea set that looked just like that." He nodded toward the palette of hues that the moon and the wet grasses had conjured up together. When Nate sat down on the bench next to him, Spaugh turned to show his smile. "Can you picture that? Me holding one of those dainty little cups and trying to look like I was a proper candidate to court a young woman as pretty as she was."

Nate softened his voice. "Maybe it ain't too late for you. D'you stay in touch with 'er?"

Ed frowned, pushed out his lower lip, and shook his head. "Naaah. She's married and living in Saint Louis, so I'm told. Got three children and a husband who owns a two-story mercantile." Ed flipped the cigarette butt out into the mud and quietly laughed. "Loving a woman is kinda like trying to hold a little bird in your hand. You got to be gentle, but if you loosen up that grip, you know, she'll damned well fly." He turned to Nate. "What else would a bird do?"

Nate just nodded and kept his eyes on the colors in the pasture. He could smell the liquor on Ed's breath, but Nate knew that the whiskey took nothing away from what Ed was saying.

"You ever have a girl?" Spaugh asked.

Nate shrugged. "Reckon ever' man's had a lady turn his head."

"No, I mean that one special one. The one you know you're s'posed to be with."

Nate pulled his legs under the bench and leaned forward on stiffened arms, his hands cupped around the edge of the seat. "I did have someb'dy," Nate said quietly, "but I reckon I didn' know it at the time."

Spaugh seemed to be waiting for more, but Nate was not inclined to give it. "Well, Nate, I reckon I'll try the same line you tried on me. Might not be too late for you."

Nate felt his grip on the bench tighten. He wanted to tell his friend that Dory was dead, but there was no way to form words like those. Not in a casual conversation. He just clamped his teeth together and concentrated on holding back the tears that were trying to surface.

"Hey," Ed said and leaned close to Nate's ear. "Don't pay no attention to me. I tend to get melancholy when I drink. It's why I don't do it much."

Nate nodded and started to rise, but Ed gripped his elbow, and Nate eased back onto the seat. "I need you to ride down to Fort Fetterman this week. Can you do that?"

Nate frowned. "Fort Fetterman? What for?"

"Phil Montieth died."

Nate narrowed his eyes. "Who?"

"Montieth," Ed repeated. "You know...Monty. One we sent down to the hospital there. He's got family coming in from Indiana. They're coming to collect him from the undertaker, and we need to get his belongings down there before they arrive."

"What about the fall roundup?" Nate reminded.

"We'll handle the roundup," Ed said. "You ride for Fetterman tomorrow."

"Why me?" Nate argued. "Why don't you send somebody we can spare?"

Spaugh turned a solemn eye on Nate. "'Cause you'd be the one I'd want my family to meet under these circumstances. You can tell 'em a little about Monty and make 'em feel easy about the kind o' life he had here."

Nate sighed. "I didn' really know 'im that well. He mostly kept to his-self."

Spaugh shrugged that off. "None of us knew him well. But you'll know what to say." He pointed with his thumb over his shoulder. "I got his things all gathered together on his bunk. His saddle's in the barn. Pick you out a pack horse from the remuda and get started in the morning. All right?"

"Aw-right," Nate agreed.

"And while you're down that way, I need you to ride over to the Sweetwater and check out a herd o' cattle Mister Plunkett is considerin' to purchase from a man named Bothwell...Albert Bothwell. Just find out what grade o' beeves he's wantin' to sell."

"Anythin' else?"

"No," Ed replied. "But get on back here before the weather turns. They're sayin' this is going to be a bad winter."

Nate frowned at that. "Who's sayin' that?"

Ed shrugged. "Charlie Diggs. He's been pretty good at predictin'."

Nate smiled at his boss. "Rawhide Charlie? He gits all that from a gypsy woman who takes his money to tell 'im 'bout his future."

Ed hitched his head. "He's been right before. He's the one predicted the drought we had this summer." He turned to Nate with a dead-serious expression. "Just get back here safe, all right?"

Nate nodded. "I will," he promised. "But listen...long

as I'm headed south, I'd like to swing over to Rawlins. Friend o' mine has got his-self throwed into jail down there. Got hornswoggled by Frank Wolcott over his land patent."

"Wolcott?" Ed growled. He pushed a rush of air through his teeth and then spat into the mud. "That damned, arrogant sonovabitch! Thinks he owns every inch of Carbon County." Ed's face squeezed down with a question. "Who's he gone after now?"

"Sumner Beach."

Spaugh slumped back against the wall and stared straight ahead. His eyes were pinched with anger now.

"Wolcott is a chubby little tyrant who's got his hands into everything and everybody. I wouldn' work for him for no amount o' money." He turned to look into Nate's eyes. "You go see about your friend, but don't you get involved with Wolcott. Understand?"

Nate nodded, pushed himself up from the bench, and turned for the door.

Ed chuckled under his breath. "Never thought I'd miss the rain as much as I have this summer."

The opening in the clouds narrowed like a giant eye closing. All color was erased in that moment, leaving only shades of gray and the complete blackness in the distance. Nate started inside, but Ed wasn't finished.

"Hey, Nate? How many times you reckon we make the wrong turn and end up some place we weren't meant to be? Maybe without the person we're supposed to be with."

Nate turned and watched his friend stare out into the night. "We all got choices we got to make, Ed. I reckon we just do the best we can."

"Well, that's what I mean. I ain't so sure I did my best."

Nate looked down at the stone slab on which he stood,

and he nodded. "Well, you just learn from it. There'll be more choices to come. Maybe there's some other lady that's meant for you even more."

Ed turned sad eyes to Nate. "I wish I could believe that."

Nate went inside to the warmth of the bunkhouse. The room was humid and crisscrossed with ropes on which hung a motley array of wet trousers, blouses, socks, neckerchiefs, and union suits. The place was a mess, like an unkempt ship whose rigging had collapsed. Slickers and hats hung on the wall pegs, all of them dripping water onto the rough floorboards.

On the floor, at the middle of the room, a dozen pairs of muddy boots and soaked gloves crowded around the woodstove. The air was thick with the smell of wet leather. A few men were asleep on their beds, but the bulk of the crew played cards in the back of the room, where cigarette smoke hung in the air thick as a fog.

Nate walked to his bunk, and several of the boys spoke his name as he passed. He gave each one a friendly nod but showed no interest in conversation. Then he stood before his bed and began undressing, all the while keeping his eyes fixed on the painting that hung on the wall in his private space.

The scene was always the same: Peaches standing in an summer meadow...a grandaddy oak spreading its muscular limbs behind her. He had admired it countless times, but the picture never failed to impress him. It seemed to breathe with authenticity, and Nate marveled at how such a thing could be created with a brush dipped into paint. He could almost smell the sage-scented air of the Texas hill country.

When he slipped into his bedding and closed his eyes, Nate embarked on the secret journey that had become his ritual on most nights. He imagined God allowing him a privileged rendezvous with Dory, meeting on some neutral ground between heaven and earth. Each time she came to him, it was not the Dory of his memory but an invented version of her as he thought she ought to look as a woman. He gave her a more mature voice, too, but her old gestures remained true to form. Her attentiveness. Her smile. The gracefulness of her lithe body. The amber-brown eyes that could see into his soul. After a few minutes, he brought out the leather-bound book she had given him, opened it to the page where the pencil was tucked away, and wrote down his thoughts. He included every facet of his day—the good, the bad, the humorous, and the profane. He wanted to keep Dory apprised of everything in his life so that when they did meet again, there would be no surprises. She would have lived his life with him.

When the writing was done, he closed the book and held it to his chest. Before drifting into sleep, he reaffirmed the acknowledgment that there would never be another chance for him. No other person. Dory had been the one. And she always would be.

October 1886

Albany and Carbon Counties, Wyoming Territory

Chapter Ten

By the time the sun's rays had spread across the Powder River Valley, Nate had forded the South Fork and picked up the trail that skirted the Pumpkin Buttes and led toward Antelope Springs. Along the base of the mountains, the aspens caught the morning light and shimmered like yellow flames flickering atop white candles crowded on an altar. On the shoulders of the creek the tall, stout cottonwoods launched pale yellow leaves one at a time. Each sailing descent followed its own unique pattern to the water, where the leaves joined in a common, spread-out flotilla that hurried downstream.

The whisper of the wind and the murmur of the water comforted Nate, as though the two sounds combined into a common anthem of sanity for the world. Here, where there were no people or cattle to complicate the land with friction, there was a sense of balance. He felt this about all places that had not yet been axed, fenced, plowed, or overgrazed.

Relishing his solitude, he moved across the terrain as quietly as his mustang and pack horse would allow. He was by himself in this part of the territory, never seeing another human, but he never felt alone. Each new vista that he encountered begged the same question. *If Dory were traveling with him now, would she want to stop and paint this scene?*

Dory would be twenty-two. The maturity that he imagined for her was nothing like her mother's tight-lipped propensity to scorn. Dory was open and giving and possessed a rare beauty that was worthy of a painting itself.

"I wish I could know you now," Nate whispered, his words just loud enough to pivot Dakah's ears. He leaned forward and stroked the mare's neck. "Don't mind me, girl," he muttered. "I'm just talkin' to the wind."

———

On the afternoon of the fourth day, he rode into the small town that had survived the government's abandonment of Fort Fetterman. The scattering of buildings on the high bluff above the Platte looked nothing like a military facility now. All the structures had been converted to private homes and businesses. Nate reined up at the Over-land Hotel, a long, one-story building that had once been a barracks. There he secured a room and carried his gear inside. Then he walked the two horses to the old military livery and left them in the care of a stooped old man who had served as the farrier for the army and now ran a business for himself.

Returning to the hotel, Nate took a twenty-five-cent hot bath, shaved, and changed into his spare clothes. At the Red Rock Saloon, he found the main room empty of customers, tables and chairs positioned neatly, and a wood stove near the back wall pushing out heat. He walked to the bar and studied the scant inventory of liquors arrayed on a countertop beneath the mirror.

"Anybody here?" he called toward the back of the room.

A tall, wedge-shaped man with a shining, bald head appeared in the back doorway. He wore a black suit and a gray ascot with a pattern of evenly spaced black diamonds. He looked more like a banker than a barman.

"Reckon I could git some lunch here?" Nate asked.

A sly smile worked its way onto the man's face. "You must be new in town...to ask for a meal here," he said without moving into the room.

"I just need some food," Nate said plainly.

The man stared at Nate for a good five seconds. "Like what?"

"Anything you got."

The man frowned at the empty room and sighed. "Well, I got some bread and some cured ham and some cheese. How'll that do?"

"Add a beer to that, an' it oughta work just fine."

The saloon man pulled out of his coat and draped it over the closest chairback. Then he walked behind the counter, leaned down, and came up with a wadded apron. He flapped it open, hooked a strap over his neck, and then knotted the waist ties at his lower back.

"Where's all yore customers?" Nate asked.

"Douglas," he replied.

"Why 'Douglas'?"

The man sneered. "'Cause the railroad got there first and sucked this town dry. Everybody's headin' to Douglas. Without the fort, Fetterman is gonna blow away with the wind."

With his back to Nate, the man sliced bread and pork and cheese. Then he loaded the food onto a pie tin. This he set on the counter before Nate. After drawing beer from the tap, he set the mug on the bar without losing so much as a dribble of foam.

"Three bits!" he announced and stood there with his fists propped on his hips as if to say that he would not negotiate over the price.

Nate pulled his wallet from his boot and paid the man.

When the barman walked to the far end of the bar and sorted through a box of tools, Nate tore off a hunk of meat with his teeth and then did the same with the bread. The meat was tough and dry and the bread hard and stale. After chewing until his jaws threatened to cramp, he washed down the food with three big swallows of beer.

"What about the hospital?" Nate called out to the man. "Still in operation?"

The barman set down a pair of pliers he was using on the spout of a keg. "Yeah," he answered, "for little problems. If you get gunshot, you got to go into Douglas. The good doctors have already gone there." He laughed. "Thing about it is...a feller's more likely to get shot in Fetterman than he is in Douglas. That's what you call irony." His smile turned toothy. "You know what that means?"

Nate nodded. "I reckon so." He attacked the meat again, gave up, and tried the other end of the bread. It was just as disappointing. Biting off a corner of the cheese, he experienced an acrid assault to his nostrils as if he had inhaled smoke from a campfire. If it weren't for the beer, Nate figured he would have choked to death right there in the saloon, while the bartender ran outside to hitch up a wagon to haul him off to Douglas.

"You got a undertaker here in Fetterman?" Nate asked.

"Yeah, just down the street." The man glanced at the plate of rejected food. "You done?"

Nate ignored the question. "Does the undertaker have a cold room to store bodies?"

"Yeah, he does. But the price for storage is higher this time o' year. If you're plannin' on croakin', it's cheaper to get buried right away."

Nate pushed the tin of food away, finished off the beer, and set down the empty mug without a sound. "Can you wrap up the rest o' this food for me?"

Raising an eyebrow, the barman pulled out a newspaper from under the counter, slapped it on the bar, and tore off the front page. He emptied the pie tin onto the paper and folded the newsprint in a clever way that showed he had done this before. Crossing his arms, he leaned back against the counter where he had sliced up the portions of Nate's so-called "meal."

Nate nodded and picked up the package. "How come *you* ain't yet moved to Douglas?"

"Don't own the place," he said. "Long as the owner pays my salary, I'll be here."

"And what then?"

The man snorted and shook his head. "That's always the question, ain't it? 'What then?' Guess I'll go to Douglas, too. See if I can't find another place to sell dry pork and stale bread and cheese that would kill a rat."

Nate leaned on the bar, his forearms stacked crosswise, one beside the other. "You knew all that before you served this to me?"

The man pushed away from the wall with his ample hindquarters and leaned forward on the bar with stiffened arms. His impatient eyes bored into Nate's.

"Same damned thing I had for *my* lunch, son. Remember...you're in Fetterman."

———

The undertaker's office was a dreary room decorated with coffins of various styles. One was built of very dark wood and perched upon a wooden bier topped by a white cloth. On each of its outside corners, silver trim was inlaid flush with the wood. Its viewing hatch was propped open to expose a quilted, blue, satin interior that made Nate think of a cloud tinted by the color of the sky. He leaned in to see if the lining extended all the way to the foot of the casket. It did.

"May I help you with a selection, sir? My name is Matlow. I am the proprietor here as well as town coroner."

Nate straightened to see a tall, thin man shrugging into a black frock coat. His crow-black hair was neatly combed and glistened with oil. His face was narrow and bony, but his lips, nose, and ears were large. He raised both eyebrows in the manner of someone who wanted to be helpful.

Nate removed his hat and held it against his chest. "Are you holding a corpse here? A man named Phil Montieth?"

The man's eyebrows pushed low, and his big lips pulled inward as he frowned at the floor. Then his head came up quickly.

"Montieth. Yes. From Johnson County. We have him in cold storage. Are you a relative?"

"I worked with 'im. I just come down from Johnson Coun'y to bring his gear."

Matlow performed a partial bow from the waist. "I'm sorry for your loss, sir," he said quietly, offering his condolences with a surprising show of warmth.

Feeling uncomfortable on the receiving end of such a declaration, Nate shrugged a shoulder. "His kin is due to come in to collect 'im, an' I'm to hand over all his belongin's."

Matlow seemed to be familiar with the discomfitures that existed between the living and the dead. Smiling his understanding, he raised a long, bony index finger as a sign to wait. He walked across the creaky wood floor to the front of the room and stopped before a tall desk. There he leaned and pulled an assortment of papers from one of half a dozen wooden cubicles that stretched the width of the desk like a row of miniature horse stalls. Sorting through these papers, he lifted an envelope and held it up to catch the light coming through the front window.

"Yes...the Vanstory family...from Indiana." He opened the envelope and unfolded the paper inside. After reading silently, he began nodding and then folded the page and returned it to the envelope. "Yes, Mister Vanstory's wife is the sister of the deceased. They come into Douglas tomorrow by train. I suppose they will rent a wagon and team and come for him."

Nate lowered his hat and held it down by its brim. He looked around the shop again at the assortment of coffins and tapped the hat against his leg.

"Did they say which day they would come here to Fetterman?"

Matlow smiled his apology. "No, sir."

"How far is Douglas from here?"

"Seven miles."

Nate nodded, looked at the floor, and tapped the hat some more. "Do you know what time the train comes in over there?"

Matlow delivered a confident nod. "Eleven o'clock. Every Tuesday and Friday. You can hear the whistle here in Fetterman all the way from the depot."

Nate stilled his hat against his leg. "Would that be mornin' or night?"

"Morning, sir."

Nate nodded again. "Reckon you can git word to me over at the hotel when you find out when they're comin'?"

"Certainly, sir. Are you at the Overland?"

"That's right," Nate said. "Name's 'Champion.'" He

began reshaping the crease in the crown of his hat. When it seemed there was nothing more to be said, he started to turn for the door but hesitated and waved his hat toward the silver trimmed casket that looked fit for royalty.

"How much does somethin' like that cost?"

Matlow threaded his fingers together to make a double fist before his chest. When his elbows lifted even with his hands, he looked as if he might break into song.

"That's our finest model. It's called the Blue Chariot. It normally runs forty-eight dollars, but we are having a moving sale starting next week. We're relocating to Douglas. With the sale, I can let it go for forty-two."

Nate stared at the plush interior. He felt an urge to touch the lining but thought better of it.

"D'you reckon a man sleeps through his death any better in that git-up?" Nate turned to show the man that his curiosity was genuine.

For the first time since Nate had met the undertaker, Matlow smiled the way he might among friends. "Tell you the truth, Mr. Champion, a casket is more for the mourner than it is for the mourned." His smile widened. "Here's what I've learned about this business. One person might pay more on account of love, and another might do the same because of guilt."

Nate narrowed one eye and grinned as if he had heard a good joke. "I guess I see yore point." He settled his hat on his head, forked his hands on his hips, and grinned at the floor. When he looked up at Matlow, Nate grinned. "Sounds like some irony there, don't it?"

"Indeed, it does, sir," Matlow returned.

And with that, Nate pinched the front of his hat brim and turned for the door. When he opened it, he pivoted back to the undertaker and narrowed his eyes.

"You got a dog?"

Matlow's brow pushed low over his eyes. "You mean here at my business?"

"No," Nate said. "Just in general."

"I have a shepherd at home."

"Is he a big, healthy dog?"

Matlow nodded and held his curious expression. "I would say so."

Nate leaned just outside the door and picked up the package wrapped in newsprint. "Here you go. I couldn' finish my meal. Maybe yore dog will finish it for me."

Matlow stepped forward with a smile, but the smile waned when he raised the package to his nose. "You sure you don't want a coffin for this instead?" Matlow said with a straight face.

"Well," Nate laughed, "I guess the dog can decide if he wonts it."

Chapter Eleven

Nate was finishing up a plate of eggs, bacon, and biscuits in the Morning Star Café, when a young boy wearing a short-billed cap hurried through the front door and stood breathing like a race-horse. With eager eyes he inspected the customers dining in the room, until his gaze fixed on Nate. Leaving the door ajar, the boy approached at a fast walk, stopped at Nate's table, and pulled off his hat.

"Mister Champing?"

"I'm Champion," Nate said.

The boy held his hat pressed against his belly and lowered his head in a quick bow. "Sir, Mister Matlow says you're to come down to the funeral parlor now."

"I appreciate—"

Before Nate could complete his sentence, the boy turned and rushed out of the room, closing the door behind him. Nate looked at the other customers, but none seemed to have noticed the boy's abrupt behavior. He finished off his coffee and left two quarters stacked next to his plate. Then he left.

As soon as he entered the undertaker's shop, Nate

smelled a flowery scent that had not been present the day before. Mr. Matlow was engaged in deep conversation with a fleshy man in a gray suit and a square-shouldered woman carrying a folded parasol. The man had a thick head of hair that was dark brown and curly. The woman's pale-blonde locks fell as smooth as corn silk.

"Ah!" Matlow said, looking past his visitors. "There he is now!"

The couple turned and fixed their attention on Nate. While the man's eyes showed caution, the woman appeared warm and gracious, her eyes slanted as if she were already asking a question.

"Mister Champion," she breathed, as if Nate's presence somehow brought her some kind of relief. "I'm Irene," she declared. Now her face turned hopeful, as she seemed to wait for some kind of reaction to her name.

Nate removed his hat and nodded. "Yes, ma'am," he said. "I'm Nate Champion."

The husband approached with a bounce in his step that belied his weight. "Reynolds Vanstory," he announced in a voice too loud for the room. As he offered a right hand, his left hand slipped inside his coat at his breast and—slick as a magic trick—emerged holding a stiff white card between two fingers. "With Indiana Coal and Gas."

Nate shifted his hat to his left hand and shook the man's hand. "Pleased to meet you," he said, wondering if he was expected to name his employer too.

When Vanstory pressed the card onto Nate, Nate looked at it, nodded once, and handed it back.

"No, no!" Vanstory insisted as he pushed both palms at the air. "That's for you to keep."

Nate continued to hold the card out. "I cain't see how I'd be needin' it."

Vanstory smiled, took the card, and raised Nate's left

arm by the wrist so that he could drop the card into the hat. "You never know when you might need someone who is in position to do you a favor," he advised with a quick smile.

Nate narrowed his eyes at the man's persistence. "I cain't see how I'd ever need a favor from Indiana. Can you?"

Vanstory chuckled to himself. "Like I said...you never know."

The woman came up beside her husband and clasped both her hands lightly on Nate's forearm. "Phillip was very complimentary of you in his letters. He said you were the most competent and fairest person he had ever worked for."

Nate tried to keep any surprise off his face, but he was certain he had already failed at it. "Monty was a good hand. Never made no trouble. Carried out his duties just fine." Those were the words Nate had prepared, and now he was glad to have them on hand.

She smiled and her eyes moistened again. "Monty? That's what you called him?"

Nate nodded. "We all did."

She looked like a child as she soaked up this news. "He was only twenty-six, you know. I suppose he ended up doing what he wanted to do."

Nate pulled in his lips and nodded deeply. "Yes, ma'am, I believe he loved cowboyin'."

"So, he was good at it?" she asked.

Nate nodded again. "Sure...that's how he got a job with us."

Reynolds Vanstory brushed the length of one coat sleeve with two brisk strokes of his hand and then did the same to the other sleeve with the other hand. "What about any savings?" he said in a brusque tone. "Is there any money we need to claim?"

"I don't reckon so," Nate said quietly. "I brung all his gear. It's stored in my room at the hotel. There weren't no money among his things. I reckon all he had he was carryin' on 'im when he came down here to Fetterman."

Vanstory made a disapproving grunt. "He didn't use a bank for his savings?"

"Nos'r, don't none o' us do that. Most o' the boys don't save up enough coins each month to fill a snuff can."

Vanstory scowled. "Filthy habit...snuff!"

Irene Vanstory slid her hands from Nate's arm. "Did Phillip use snuff?"

Nate hardened his expression for the lie. "I don't believe so, ma'am." Nate looked away from her innocent eyes and found himself being appraised by her husband. "Did you bring a wagon, Mister Vanstory?"

"Yes," he said and pointed toward the front window. "We have a driver. He's gone to a blacksmith to see about a pin that came loose in the seats."

Matlow had stood by his desk all this time, exercising a patience that Nate assumed all undertakers possessed. Now he crossed the floor to be a part of the conversation.

"Shall we make a decision on the style of casket you would prefer for your dearly beloved?" He said this in a quiet, melodic voice, directing the question to the lady. Then he held a professional smile as he waited for her reply.

"We're not getting the blue one, Irene," Vanstory snapped. "It's overpriced, and—quite frankly—it's not what a young man of his station would prefer." He turned to Nate, surprising him by taking a grip on his shoulder. "Don't you agree, Champion?" He swept his other arm across the room. "Which one of these would you choose for yourself, if the need arose?"

"Reynolds!" the woman whispered forcefully. "What a thing to say!"

Vanstory waved away her reprimand. "We all come to the same end, don't we, Champion?" He shook Nate's shoulder the way a man playfully handles a young boy. "Come on. Tell me truthfully. Which of these boxes would you want?"

Nate met the woman's eyes for only a moment, for he could sense her pain at being dismissed. When he locked eyes with Matlow, he remembered what the undertaker had said about the coffin being more for the mourner.

"Well," Nate said and began appraising all the models in the room. "It's a man's last ride, I guess you'd say. I'd be proud to take it in that one." He pointed at the model called the Blue Chariot. In his peripheral vision, he saw Vanstory's face close down and darken to a maroon shade. The man's hand slid from Nate's shoulder, and he took a step back.

Irene Vanstory grasped Nate's arm again, and her face brightened like a sky whose clouds had blown away. "I think Phillip deserves that one. It's my choice, too."

Nate patted the backs of her hands and extricated himself from her grip. As he sidled toward the door, he spoke to the room for all to hear.

"I'll go down to the livery and tell your driver to stop by the hotel, an' him an' me will load up the gear together. Then I got to be movin' on."

"Oh, Mister Champion," Irene Vanstory said quickly, "can't we take you to supper tonight...to thank you for your journey? I would love to hear some stories about Phillip as a cowboy."

Nate picked the business card out of the crown of his hat and plopped the hat on his head as a sure sign that he was leaving. "Sorry, ma'am, but I've got to git over to Rawlins to help out a friend of mine. I'm 'fraid it cain't wait."

Matlow   stepped   around   the   Vanstorys   and

approached Nate. Holding out his hand, the funeral director moved in close to shake Nate's hand.

"It was a pleasure to meet you, Mister Champion," he said loud enough for all to hear. Then he lowered his voice to a private murmur. "I feel like I owe you a commission on the sale." He smiled and winked. "Thank you!"

Nate handed him Vanstory's card. "Here...in case you ever need some Indiana coal."

Matlow coughed to cover the laugh that bubbled up from inside him. "Do you suppose he knows this is coal country he's traveling through?"

Nate smiled and glanced at the floor. "Looks like we just run into some more o' that irony, don't it, Mister Matlow?"

Matlow's smile cut a wide swath across his narrow face. "You have safe travels, Mister Champion."

Nate nodded toward Irene Vanstory as he kept his eyes on the undertaker. "'Bout the blue casket," he whispered, "I did it for the woman, you know."

"Yes, I know," Matlow returned, altering his smile to a courteous one.

Nate looked over the man's shoulder at the Vanstorys and pulled at the front of his hat brim. Then he stepped outside and closed the door behind him.

———

A day and a half out from Fetterman City, after skirting the west end of the Laramie Mountains, Nate followed the Platte into the broad Deer Creek Valley and found himself riding through an impressive stand of old willow trees. The trees bordered a meadow of water-starved grass, and as Nate rode out into the open from the trees, a herd of six mule deer raised their heads to watch his approach. Slowly they began to move across the field, building speed until they seemed to pour down the slope into the creek bottoms, where they disappeared into the shadows of the trees.

He crested a rise and reined up when he spotted in the distance the low roof of a dugout and behind it a crude corral containing three horses. Just up from the corral, a lone figure swung an axe at a log lying on the ground. Each hack into the wood sent a report to Nate that lagged behind the cutter's stroke into the wood. Right away, the man stopped working and stood very still looking back at Nate. One-handedly, the man swung the axe one last time and left the tool perched at an angle in the log. He walked to the corral fence, leaned, and picked up a rifle.

Nate raised a hand in greeting, but the man offered no return gesture. With a light kick of his heels, Nate nudged his mustang into a walk, and the packhorse responded with its usual show of obedience.

When Nate was a hundred yards away from the humble settlement, the man worked the lever on his rifle, raised the barrel vertically, and fired off a round. The *crack* of the rifle was thin and trebly in the open space and was swallowed up by the sky without an echo.

"State your biz'ness!" the man called out clearly.

Nate reined up and turned his head slightly to cock one ear forward. He watched the man lever a new round into his rifle chamber and stand ready.

Nate cupped a hand beside his mouth and yelled. "Sumner? That you?"

The rancher lowered the rifle and took five steps closer. When he stopped, he spread his boots in the dry grass, removed his hat with his free hand, and held it high before him to shade his eyes from the sun.

"Nate?" he called back, letting the word rise in pitch. "Nate Champion?"

Nate lifted his own hat and held it high, letting the

sunshine light up his face. Laughing, he started forward again, and Sumner did the same.

When they met, Nate climbed down from the saddle, and the two old friends clasped hands with the iron grip of a vise. Sumner had lost some weight where there had been none to spare. His face was thinner. And pale. His blond hair lacked the streaks of gold that the summer usually bestowed upon him. But what he lacked in vigor, he made up for with his smile. His friendly eyes seemed to shine from within like a blue light.

"What the hell're you doin' down here in Carbon Coun'y?"

Nate laughed. "Well, I was on my way to Rawlins to see a friend o' mine in the jail down there. Guess I was misinformed."

"Hell, no...you weren't! But I got shed o' all that business."

"You didn' break out o' jail, did you?"

"Didn' have to. The jury set me free! Just like they should'a done. But things were not lookin' good for me for a while. Wolcott got his-self appointed judge, and he named one o' his kind from the Stock Growers Assoc'ation to be the jury foreman for my indictment. On top o' that, Tom Brannan—my partner—he was my prime witness, an' he just up an' disappeared." Sumner splayed his free hand on his hip and gazed across the valley toward the Medicine Bow Mountains. "There ain't no tellin'. Poor ol' Tom...he might be buried somewhere out there, where nobody will ever find him."

"Yo're thinkin' Wolcott did that?"

Sumner scowled. "Same thing he tried on *me*. Sent that damned Bill Locker out here to put me into the ground...only I put *him* there first."

"I remember Locker," Nate said. "It don't surprise me a lick 'bout him. Wasn't a good bone in his body."

"That day he threw down on me...he'd told Brannan just that mornin' that he felt like killin' somethin' that day. That spooked ol' Tom, and Tom wanted nothin' to do with 'im after that. I told Locker twice to git off our claim. I was ready for 'im when he pulled his pistol."

"You didn' have no other witnesses?"

Sumner shrugged. "There wasn't none to be had. Hank Devoe come down, but he was just a char'cter witness. He couldn' say what happened. It was just the three o' us out here that day." He huffed a humorless laugh. "But that didn' stop Wolcott from providin' his own witnesses, who swore they saw me kill Locker in cold blood."

"Where'd he find *them*?"

Sumner hocked up phlegm and spat into the grass. "Didn't find 'em. He *bought* 'em. They were his damned employees, an' they lied on the stand. Purged theirselves, as they say."

Nate removed his hat and pushed his fingers back through his hair. "Well, how the hell'd you git off?"

Sumner was already moving toward the dugout. "I'll show you."

After disappearing behind a blanket door for a few seconds, he emerged with the rifle still gripped in one hand and a rolled-up sheaf of papers in the other. He strode purposefully to Nate, propped the rifle against the corral fence, and thrust the papers toward him.

"Read that!"

Nate rocked his hat back in place on his head and unrolled a pamphlet with five words set in a printer's type on the front page: *Alias the Jack of Spades*. After thumbing through the half dozen or so pages, Nate frowned and looked up at Sumner.

"What *is* this?"

Sumner tapped his forefinger to the title page. "It's

what saved my life, I reckon. It got printed up an' spread all over the coun'y just before my trial. Don't nobody know who wrote it, but it exposes ever'thin' 'bout Frank Wolcott. 'Bout him bein' booted out o' the US Marshal's office for embezzling a hun'erd thousand dollars. 'Bout him cheatin' people out o' what he owes 'em...includin' his ranch crew. 'Bout him bein' in cahoots with the land commissioner an' fakin' claims he ain't got no right to. 'Bout how he's stole cattle from his neighbors an' how there ain't no one on this valley who trusts him, much less likes him." Sumner nodded at the pamphlet. "Time that information got into circulation, there weren't no way any jury was gonna find against me. It only took 'em ten minutes to agree on 'not guilty.'" He lifted his hands away from his sides. "So, here I am again, stakin' my claim, only I ain't got no partner."

Nate looked over the site, inventorying the sum total of his friend's belongings: an earth-and-log dugout spewing a thin stream of smoke from a metal stove pipe, a crude fencing for his horses, a well-worn saddle slung over the top rail, and eight hefty logs leveled out upon stacked slabs of stones as a foundation for a cabin. The land itself, nestled up against the creek as it was, stood out as the primary asset, despite the poor color of the grass.

"So, how do you feel safe out here?" Nate asked.

Sumner dredged up a hoarse laugh. "Anything happens to me now, there won't be no doubt at all who's behind it."

Nate wrinkled his brow. "An' that's enough to put yore mind at ease?"

Sumner spewed air from his tightened lips. "There ain't no *at ease* in my life, Nate." He picked up his rifle again and raised it before him as though he were intro-ducing a friend. "I just got to be on alert all the time."

"What about nighttime? How can you sleep?"

Sumner nodded toward the dugout. "I don't sleep in there." He poked the muzzle of the rifle toward a stand of aspen upslope beyond the meadow. "I sleep up there amongst the trees on the high ground ever' night. An' every mornin', b'fore dawn, I break camp an' cook my breakfast down here inside the dugout. I keep a string o' empty cans tied together out front while I'm in there. Soon's it's light enough, I scout the area each mornin' for any signs o' somebody snoopin' 'round."

They walked to the cabin site, where Sumner propped his rifle against the log where the axe stood at the angle he'd left it. A fire pit smoldered at the center of the rectangular frame, and a black enamel coffee pot sat balanced upon a triangle of stones at the center of the coals.

"I got coffee, if you wont," Sumner offered. "It ain't fresh, but it'll do."

Nate tied his two horses to a loop of drag rope still collared around one of the logs lying in the grass. "I got some fresh on the bay. Let me dig it out, an' we can start over." He opened one of the supply paniers on the pack-horse and pulled out a brown paper package, which he tossed to Sumner. When Sumner caught it, the bag made a quick, dry, percussive sound like a Mexican maraca.

"You keep that'n," Nate said. "I got plen'y more."

Without delay, Sumner tossed the contents of the coffee pot out into the pale grass. Then he jogged off for the creek to fetch fresh water.

As the coffee brewed, the two friends sat at one corner of the log foundation, each man on a different log, their knees almost touching.

"So," Sumner laughed, "did you come down to watch me hang?"

"I was on my way to Rawlins to see if I could help you somehow."

Sumner laughed. "What were you gonna do? Try to out-bribe Wolcott?"

Nate filled his cheeks with air and shook his head as he exhaled. "Reckon I would'a had to turn outlaw and break you out o' jail."

Sumner snorted a dry laugh. "Then I'da had to abandon all this, leave the territory, and change my name."

"All of which," Nate said, "would be preferable to swingin' from a rope."

Sumner tilted his head over to one side. "Well, I can't argue that." Then he sipped from his cup as he surveyed the sweep of the valley. "But I'd hate to walk away from this, Nate. 'Course it don't look so invitin' right now with this drought we've had, but, by God, when I first saw this place, it was so green and grassy, it made you wanna just lie down in it and take a nap. I knew I could finally sink roots into the ground an' live in one place till I died."

Nate took in the dry valley with an inspecting eye, from the bordering forest far up the hill down to the willows that were already covering the shoulders of the creek with a carpet of pale leaves. The open range of shriveled-up grass was mostly an anemic yellow, but it also showed patches of a dull, gray-brown color. It was the kind of sight that could make a non-believer pray for rain.

"Grass looks the same up where we are," Nate said. "Parched and stringy. But I can see how it might'a looked like a damned good place for cattle. Horses, too."

Nodding, Sumner plucked a dry sprig of grass and chewed on it. Working his jaws steadily, he stared at the Medicine Bows in the distance. Then he removed the grass from his mouth and studied it as he held it between his thumb and finger.

"Wouldn' consider partnerin' up with me, would you?"

Nate looked down at his boots and breathed out a

sigh. "I ain't ready to do that," he said with conviction." He brought up an earnest expression to soften his reply. "I need to save up some more money. Besides, I still got obligations with Ed Spaugh. He's been real fair with me, an' I ain't gonna let 'im down."

Sumner dropped the mangled blade of grass to the ground. "I figured as much."

Sumner laid out two cups, and Nate poured coffee into each. After he sipped from his cup, Nate pointed northwest toward the Seminoe Range.

"I got to ride over to the Sweetwater to inspect a herd the EK plans to purchase from a man named 'Bothwell.' You know 'im?"

As Sumner drank from his cup, he made a low, disapproving sound deep in his chest. When he set down the cup, his face was set with loathing.

"I know 'im."

Nate nodded to encourage more of an answer. "And?"

Sumner winced as if he'd detected a foul smell. "Hard man. I sure as hell wouldn' wanna work for 'im. I've knowed some boys who did. They say he's a cocky sonovabitch. His word is the law. Won't back down from nothin, even when ever'body else knows he's dead wrong."

Nate pursed his lips. "Sounds like yo're talkin' 'bout Wolcott."

"Might as well be," Sumner said. "I'd say they're cut from the same cloth. Both are in the Stock Growers Assoc'ation."

Nate nodded and twisted around left, then right. "Where's yore herd grazing at?"

Sumner's jaw flexed and put a bulge in his cheek. "I had a friend come out here an' check on things while I was in jail. He come back an' tol' me all my cattle was gone." He looked straight into Nate's eyes. "I reckon Wolcott took 'em an' burned his brand over mine."

"How many did you lose?"

Sumner closed his eyes and exhaled heavily. "Forty-four head o' cattle. Three horses."

"The law cain't help?" Nate asked.

Sumner shook his head. "Wolcott an' the Assoc'ation are all partnered up with the law." He stopped shaking his head but held a grim look on his face. "This territory's goin' to hell, Nate. There ain't no help for the little man. These rich cattle barons have got the game rigged."

The two friends looked out over the desiccated grassland where Sumner's cattle ought to be grazing on what little fodder there was. A cool breeze poured off the mountain like a harbinger of the season's change. Nate leaned forward and refilled his cup.

"There was this gypsy feller in the cell with me in Rawlins," Sumner began in his storytelling voice. "Indicted for stealing a sheep. He had this sister who came in to visit ever' day, an' she was a fortune teller, so she said. Tol' me it was gonna be a real bad winter."

Nate narrowed his eyes. "Yo're the second person to tell me a gypsy story like that." He kept staring at Sumner. "You believe in that stuff?"

Sumner raised his chin and squinted into the distance. "I don' know. But I'll tell you this. I'm gonna lay in five or six cords of firewood before winter. Wyomin' will kill a man who ain't ready for twenty or thirty below." He blew a whiff of air that made his lips flutter. "Man, I get cold just thinkin' 'bout it."

Nate studied the cabin foundation on which they sat. "Well, you won't finish this here cabin in time for winter. Reckon you'll make it in there?" He nodded toward the primitive dugout.

"It's my home," Sumner said. "It's all I got."

Nate looked around again. "You got a two-man crosscut?"

Sumner nodded. "In the dugout."

Nate finished his coffee and set down the cup on the log beside him. "I'll help you lay in a cord b'fore I leave. How 'bout that?"

Sumner nodded again, and his shy smile moved up into his gaunt eyes. "Yeah...that'd be real good."

Chapter Twelve

When Nate reached the Sweetwater River, he followed it upstream along the old Oregon Trail. The wide and dusty road was wheel-rutted, hoof-marked, and still littered with the occasional relic of jettisoned freight from wagons of decades past. At one point, where the riverbank was steep, he spotted the rusted remains of a metal axle angled into the water, its only wheel partially buried in silt and well on its way to rot. The metal wheel rim still held its shape, but only a few wood spokes remained intact.

After only a short ride upriver, as he approached the confluence of Horse Creek, two log buildings came into view, both newly built, the front one lying in the dappled shade of two giant cottonwoods that had shed some of their yellowed leaves. The trees spread their muscular branches into a joined canopy of intertwining arms, all sparsely dressed in pale yellow. Each time the wind picked up, a slew of shining leaves poured from the limbs and blinked in the sunlight like a spray of sparks escaping a sharpener's wheel. Beside the buildings a large square corral held a dozen cattle, all facing downwind and seemingly content to stand in the sunlight.

The cabin in front stood a good forty feet wide and was identified by a painted sign that hung above the door. Averell's Outpost was printed in dark green against a white background. Behind this building, in contrast to the dull-gray grass all around the compound, a large rectangular garden thrived with greenery. Red tomatoes and yellow peppers dotted a wall of staked vines that boasted all the good cheer of a Christmas wreath.

The farther cabin appeared quiet, while the closer of the two let spill the notes of a banjo in the hands of someone who knew how to play. Rhythmic handclaps accompanied the music. Above the juniper-shake roof, a steady stream of gray smoke rose from a well-built stone chimney. On the backside of the roof, a metal flue spewed another ribbon of gray woodsmoke.

The music stopped just as Nate dismounted in front of Averell's store. The steady cadence of handclaps that had supplied the beat of the song now broke into a modest applause and then quieted altogether. Beneath the chatter that followed, the banjo player began a series of redundant notes that bent and conformed to perfection as the instrument was tuned.

Through the front screened door, a young boy slipped outside onto the porch. Before him, he swung a short piece of rope tied to a three-foot-long stick. Each time he flipped the stick and whipped the rope into a dull *snap*, he made a whispery, percussive sound from his puckered lips. When the boy saw Nate, he lowered the stick and stood stock still, his eyes wide with curiosity.

"Howdy, son," Nate greeted and tried to put the boy at ease with a quick smile. "I've 'bout run out o' some o' my food supplies. Reckon I can purchase some here?"

"Yes'r, you can. An' you can set down to a meal here, if

you're of a mind. It costs three bits...but Mister Av'rell will sometimes trade if you got somethin' worth tradin' for."

Nate tied his mustang to the stout hitching rail that ran half the length of the porch. After he had tied the packhorse, he stood before the boy and cocked his head to one side.

"You sound like a pretty smart bus'nessman. D'you run this establishment?"

The boy squinted at Nate. "I'm only eight. Mister Av'rell runs the store." The homemade whip in his hand was forgotten now. All his attention was focused on Nate.

Nate nodded, as if he had received some good advice. "Where can I find this 'Av'rell?"

The boy pointed. "Inside."

Nate took off his hat and hung it over his pommel. "Well, in case he asks me who recommended his store, who should I say?"

"I'm Gene," the boy said in a shy voice.

"Aw-right, Gene," Nate said as he stepped up onto the porch. Stopping in front of the screened door, Nate looked back at his horses and hesitated. "Say, you wouldn' wanna do a little job for me, would you?"

Gene's eyes widened again. "What kind o' job?"

Nate swept a hand toward the horses. "'Bout ever'thing I own is packed right there on these two. Reckon you could keep a eye on 'em for me?"

"Yes, sir," the boy said and smiled. "I can look after 'em real good."

Backing to the wall, Nate leaned into the logs and pulled off his left boot. Reaching inside, he fingered the few loose coins he had and blindly singled out a nickel.

"Here ya go!" he signaled and tossed the coin in an easy arc.

Gene snatched it out of the air and studied it intently.

Then, clutching the coin tightly in his fist, he looked up at Nate with the fire of dedication in his eyes.

"I won't let nothin' happ'n to 'em," Gene promised, his tone so earnest that Nate was reminded of himself when he was that age.

Nate held out his hand, and they shook. "My name's Nate. If trouble shows up, just call out for me."

Now Gene looked as stern as a soldier. "Yes'r, I'll call you."

Inside the semi-dark of the store, three men sat on stools at a bar and talked over tall mugs of beer. A slender man with a neat mustache stood at the fireplace with one foot propped on the hearth. He wore a white, full-length apron over a white shirt and dark trousers. The skin on his face appeared as smooth as a woman's, and his cheeks showed a permanent blush of red. He seemed absorbed in conversation with a young man who sat on the hearth and tuned a banjo that was wedged into his lap. When Nate let the door close, the aproned man looked up.

"Help you?" the man said in a quiet voice somewhere between timid and polite.

"I was hopin' to buy some provisions, but I think yore business partner outside has convinced me to try out yore cookin' as well."

The man smiled, dropped his foot to the floor, and approached. "Gene been braggin' on Ella's apple pie, has he?"

"Apple pie?" Nate said with a chuckle. "Well, that seals the deal right there."

At the back of the store, a long table ran the width of the room. The table was empty, but just beyond it an ornate oven with white porcelain valve handles showed hot coals simmering through its open door. Just then, a short, plump woman with a pleasant face entered the room through a rear door. In the crook of her arm, she carried a basket of greens, which see set on a sideboard next to a large metal basin.

"Jimmy Averell," the man said and offered his hand. His grip was not much stronger than the boy's outside. "Ella?" he called to the woman. "Can we serve this man a meal?"

The woman dumped the greens into the basin and then leaned back from the counter to inspect her new clientele. "We've go' the last of the stoo, Jimmy. It's still wairm. But it may take me some time to cook up these greens." Her words were bolstered by a thick Scottish accent, but her voice carried an innate kindness that put Nate at ease.

"Stew will be just fine," Nate assured Averell. "What kind are we talkin' 'bout?"

The woman must have heard him, because she, herself, answered. "Come sit. It's venison stoo and no' bad, e'en if I do say so me-self."

"Heat up some pie for him too, Ella!" Averell added. Then he raised his chin to Nate and spoke in a friendly tone. "We'll get your provisions together after you eat."

The young fellow with the banjo finished his tuning, settled his instrument in his lap, and let go with a cascade of plucked notes that filled the room like a tinny question. When he finished and crossed his arms over the instrument, the last notes seemed to hang in the air for a moment as the men at the bar went silent. The banjo player smiled as if awaiting an answer.

One of the drinkers—a stunted man with bowed legs— slipped from his stool at the bar and, with a snappy dance step, clogged a dull response with his boots on the wood floor. Everyone laughed, but no one laughed more heartily than the woman.

"Ralphie, me boy?" she called out to the banjo player.

"Can we haire you play 'The Bonnie Banks of Loch Lomond?'"

As the player picked out the chords, the woman hummed along, providing a melody. When it seemed she could no longer resist, she traded the humming for words and proudly sang the lyrics as she stoked the stove with split sticks from a wood box.

> "'Twas there that we parted, in yon
> shady glen
> On the steep, steep side of Ben Lomond
> Where in soft purple hue, the highland
> hills we view
> And the moon coming out in the
> gloaming."

Her Scottish words contained many a hard angle, but her voice was sweet as an angel's. The banjo player muted his instrument by pressing his hand over the strings. Narrowing his eyes to slits, he smiled at Ella as she went about her work. The men at the bar seemed to be trapped in some kind of melancholic trance. They remained pivoted on their stools, as if they expected to be graced by another song. The room was quiet but for the woman bustling around in the kitchen. Jimmy Averell smiled, picked up a sorghum broom and began sweeping the floor, holding on to his smile as he worked.

When Nate sat down at the table, he watched Ella take a long-bladed knife and saw off the rounded, brown-crusted heel of an oblong loaf of bread on her countertop. After slathering the bread with butter, she ladled a generous portion of stew into a ceramic bowl. All this she carried to Nate, along with a cloth and spoon. Then she stepped back and propped her fists to be a witness to Nate's first bite.

After tucking a corner of the cloth into the front of his collar, Nate spooned up the stew and chewed. Closing his eyes, he began to nod. The meal was rich with the flavor of onions, potatoes, radishes, and salt. And there were spices he could not name. The meat proved tender without seeming overcooked.

The banjo music started up again with the same Scottish song, a stampede of finger picking that now included the melody embedded deep inside the rapid flow of notes. At the bar, the men who were drinking fell into conversation again. When Nate opened his eyes, Ella was there waiting for him with her eyebrows raised in a question.

"Ma'am, I ain't ate this good since my last Christmas in Texas."

Breaking into a robust smile, she nodded once smartly, dropped her hands from her hips, and sashayed back to the sideboard to sort the leafy greens.

Jimmy Averell stopped the rhythm of his sweeping and leaned on the long handle of his broom. "Where are you riding in from?" he asked Nate.

Nate nodded to the east. "Just come over from Deer Creek this mornin'. But I started out six days ago up around the Powder River...near Buffalo."

"I served at Fort McKinney a few years back," Averell volunteered. "Pretty country up there."

Nate tore off a chunk of bread with his teeth. The fresh-baked taste was more than he could have hoped for. Averell continued sweeping, but Ella turned at the waist and smiled.

"Soo, you're one of them, aire you?" She laughed. "I thoot all you Texas boys were a roowdy bunch!" she teased. "*You* seem to have picked up some manners somewhere along the whey." As she went on with her work, she gazed out the window above the wash basin, and the incoming light painted a fine edge of silver along her rounded cheek. She turned her head to speak over her shoulder. "And what brings you over this whey to the Swee'wa'er?"

Nate wiped his mouth with the cloth she had provided. "Came down to inspect some cattle that a man named Bothwell wants to sell us. That an' to check on a friend o' mine who'd got his-self into some trouble."

The banjo went quiet, and the woman's hands went still in the water. Averell's friendly demeanor gave way to a hard look of inspection. The boy with the banjo and the men at the bar all stared at Averell as if waiting to hear what he would say.

Averell walked slowly into the kitchen area and stood next to the woman. Facing Nate, he leaned his lower back into the sideboard and gripped both his hands to the edge of the counter behind him. Ella turned, too. Standing side by side, they made an odd couple. Though they stood almost the same height, he looked a decade older than she, while she had thirty pounds on him. Turning back around, she went back to her washing but now her hands moved quietly in the water.

"Did Bothwell send you here?" Averell asked, his voice now thin and wavering.

Nate felt the quiet in the room press down around him like water at the bottom of a deep pool. He pushed the half-full bowl away a few inches and then folded his arms on the table. Leaning forward, he smiled.

"Nos'r. Like I said...I come to look over his cattle. I ain't yet met the man."

Keeping his distance, Averell stared hard at Nate, studying his face the way one man looks for a lie in another's eyes. His brow was creased with lines, and each time after he swallowed, the tip of his tongue flicked around his mouth to moisten his lips.

"You know what kind o' man this Bothwell is?" Averell said, his voice taking on a sharp edge.

"Well," Nate said, "I have heard one opinion. Cain't say it was a fav'rable one."

No words were spoken for a quarter minute. Outside, in the corral, a calf registered a loud, abrasive complaint. Leaves tapped on the roof above them. The screened door squeaked open, and Gene stepped inside, stationing himself where he could still keep an eye on Nate's horses.

Averell—as if he had made some critical decision—pushed away from the sideboard, strode purposefully to the front of the store, and swept a newspaper off the bar. As he walked back to the kitchen, the banjo player laid his instrument aside and followed him for a better view of the goings-on in the back of the building.

Averell fanned through the pages of newsprint and folded back the crinkling paper to a chosen spot. "Read that," he said and dropped the newspaper on the table before Nate. After tapping his forefinger to an article at the bottom of the page, Averell backed away to stand beside the woman again. The banjo player took a position on her other side.

Nate pulled the paper closer and silently read the title of the piece. *The Fraud Pervading Carbon County.* In the second paragraph, a generic phrase in quotation marks began to dominate the article, "a certain cattleman on Horse Creek."

"Everybody in the Sweetwater Valley knows it's A. J. Bothwell who's the subject of that article," Averell informed Nate. "Just keep reading to see what kind of man you're planning to do business with."

Nate read. It was clear that whoever wrote the piece considered his subject to be a ruthless and dangerous rancher who brooked no ideas that opposed his own. The writer accused the "certain cattleman" of livestock theft, brand altering, cruelty to animals, and colluding with the land patent office in Cheyenne to support Bothwell's exaggerated claims of property ownership. Furthermore, Bothwell had fenced in a large amount of free-range acreage and threatened to protect his supposed boundaries by force.

"There's no one else it could be," Averell added, pleading his case.

Nate looked up at the beleaguered man, who seemed to be awaiting a reaction. "He from England?" Nate asked.

Averell frowned. "Iowa...I think."

Nate huffed a humorless laugh. "We got the same kind o' self-appointed royalty up in Johnson Coun'y. Most are English with fancy titles from their home country." He raised an index finger and pointed briefly at his host. "I'm bettin' this Bothwell is in thick with the Wyomin' Stock Growers Assoc'ation. Am I right?"

"Oh, yeah," Averell replied, his voice rising and falling with sarcasm. "Him and Wolcott think they rule the whole damned county. Bothwell has threatened us a number of times. He's tried to scare us off the Sweetwater both through the courts and by waving around a gun."

The woman, Ella, wiped her hands with a towel, turned to face Nate, and then crossed her arms beneath her ample bosom. "Boothwell is like a crazed animal, who thinks he must figh' any who dare to stake a claim on his boorders."

"We're in our rights here on these claims," Averell insisted. "They're filed proper at the courthouse...mine *and* Ella's. Bothwell doesn't have a legal leg to stand on, but he keeps on comin' at us."

"How big is Bothwell's operation?" Nate asked. "How many men does he have?"

Jimmy Averell looked out the back window and

rubbed the palm of his open hand across his mouth. When he turned back to Nate, he cleared his throat and squared his narrow shoulders.

"He has a herd of about fifteen hundred, I'd say. Six of his nephews work for him, each one a certified bully. They snarl at us like mad dogs, always pushing for trouble. Then there are drifters who sometimes join his crew, but few of them stay on. After most get their first wages, they usually disappear. He'd be a hard man to work for."

Ella was quick to back him up. "The Boothwells aire evil! The whoole clan o' them aire in league with the devil, if you ask me!" She huffed. "Some of that goovernment land that he fenced in was in my parcel. He still, to this dey, thinks of it as his oown!" She shook her head. "And noo that we rightfully oown it, Boothwell acts as if we stole it a-whey from him!"

One of the men at the bar left his stool and walked slowly to the dining area, scuffing the heels of his boots as he approached. He looked to be a few years younger than Nate, his eyes light-brown and his eyebrows lighter still. The sparse blond hairs trying to thicken above his upper lip looked to be hard won.

Stopping at the end of the long table where Nate sat, he leaned forward with the knuckles of his fists pressing into the tabletop. Overall, the young man's face showed a propensity for empathy, but he was doing his best to look like a hardcase.

"Mister, if we find out you're lyin'," he began in a rough whisper, "an' you're here workin' for Bothwell—"

"No threats, Frank!" Averell interrupted. "That's makes us no better than Bothwell."

The young man named Frank pivoted his head to meet Averell's reprimanding gaze. He straightened and backed away from the table and then watched Averell, as if awaiting further instructions. When Averell simply shook his head, Frank took in a deep breath through his nose, expanding his chest, and then he purged the air slowly. Leaning back against the log wall, he crossed his arms over his chest and let his head hang forward as if he were studying the floorboards.

"This is Frank Buchanan," Averell announced in a cordial tone. "He works for me."

Nate, expecting nothing neighborly from Buchanan, offered a cordial nod. "I'm Nate Champion."

Buchanan's head came up quickly, and the whites of his eyes burned like candleflames in a darkened room. "I know that name. You're a friend to Sumner Beach."

"I am," Nate assured him. "I just come from his place. Helped him lay in some firewood for the winter."

Buchanan narrowed his eyes and turned his head slightly as if to look at Nate from a new angle. "What part o' Texas are you from?" he asked, as if daring Nate to answer.

Nate took no offense to the grilling. In fact, he welcomed a solid proof that might settle everyone down.

"Round Rock...a little north o' Austin."

Frank glanced at Averell. "Sumner speaks well o' him."

Nate watched as Averell tried to make up his mind. "That's the friend I tol' you 'bout," Nate explained. "Sumner's the one I come down to see."

Averell seemed slow to come around, but Ella's round face softened with a smile as she approached and picked up Nate's bowl. "Let me wairm this up for you," she said sweetly and winked. "And the pie will be coomin' up soon."

"Thank you, Misses Averell."

She laughed. "Oh, Jimmy and I aire nae married...nae yet, any-whey."

Nate felt his face warm. "Beg yore pardon, ma'am."

Averell strolled toward the table. "It's just a formality. We'll get to it soon enough. We're keeping our names separate for a while. That way we could make two land claims. We'll be able to join the properties after we marry."

Nate nodded his understanding and then raised his chin to Buchanan. "How long you known Sumner?"

Frank sat down at the far end of the table. "I ran some supplies over to their cabin site a few times 'bout a year ago...for him and Tom Brannan. This was b'fore the trouble started. Sometimes I stayed over the night, and we played cards by the campfire. The three of us got to be pretty good friends." He laughed quietly. "Prob'ly 'cause we only played for pennies." Narrowing his eyes, Buchanan raised a hand and pointed at Nate. "Sumner says you're the best horse trainer he's come across. Says you can ride good as a Comanche."

"Well," Nate replied, "those are kind words, but far as the trainin' goes, you got to give half o' that credit to the horse. Right?"

Buchanan frowned and nodded with uncertainty.

"And as to the ridin'," Nate continued, "you gotta give *most* all o' the praise to the horse. It's the horse makin' all the impressive moves. Am I right?"

Ella laughed to herself and hung her damp towel on the edge of the sideboard. "Sounds to me, Mister Champion, that you aire one of thoose men who makes it haird to compliment."

Nate had to laugh. "Guess I heard that'n b'fore." He nodded and laughed again. "I reckon that's somethin' I could improve on. Maybe the years will help with that."

"Amen to that," Averell said. "Comes a time you're just too tired to work up some modesty. It takes some effort, you know."

Using a folded towel, Ella removed the bowl of stew

from the oven. She set it before Nate again and then stood a few feet away from him, as he dug into the meal again.

"Cdrivvens!" she laughed. "When was the last time you sat down for a meal, laddie?"

Working on a mouthful, Nate answered as he chewed. "Just this mornin', ma'am. It ain't a question 'bout when I last ate. It's 'bout when I last ate somethin' this good!"

Ella's smile lit up the room. She held up her forefinger before her and waggled it at Nate in a mock reprimand.

"Be shoor to leave room! The best is ye' to coome." Returning to the stove, she pulled from the oven a pan bearing a single slice of pie. By the time she set it before Nate, the smell of fresh-baked crust and cooked apples pierced him like an arrow from his childhood.

"Oh, Lord!" he chuckled and pushed aside his empty bowl. "I've gone to heaven an' I ain't even dead yet."

Ella raised an eyebrow. "See that you doon't burn yourself! That pie tin is blisterin'!"

Nate noticed that every man present was turned his way. Their focus was not on him but on the piece of pie. Even Gene had left his post to get a better view of the table. The other men, who had been so quiet at the bar, now joined the crowd of onlookers, their beer mugs in hand.

"Miss Ella," Nate said as gently as he could, "from the looks of it, seems to me you didn' set out enough slices o' pie for the occasion. I'm startin' to feel like a man dyin' in the desert as he looks up at the buzzards a-circlin'."

Ella looked around at the covetous eyes fixed on the pie. When she turned back to Nate, she leaned to whisper in his ear.

"If I were you, laddie, I'd gobble that up swith before we have us a cabble here."

Without looking up at his audience, Nate cut off a portion of the pie with his fork and began chewing. The sweet taste of the apples made a perfect complement to the buttery crust, and the result was something worthy of a blue ribbon at a state fair. Not wanting to telegraph any signs of pleasure or satisfaction, he was careful to maintain a neutral expression as he ate. The slice of pie was gone in four more mouthfuls, and Nate sat back in his chair to look each observer in the eye.

"Well, I reckon I can die happy now," he said.

"Nae," Ella laughed. "I doon't think it will coome to that!" She returned to the stove, refolded the towel, and bent to open the oven door. When she pulled out another pie intact, the room seemed to fall into a preternatural quietness. Like the still air on the prairie just after a lone coyote wails to the night.

"Come on, you boozards!" she announced. "Thair's soome for all o' you!"

Fall and Winter 1886–1887

Johnson County, Wyoming Territory

Chapter Thirteen

In early November, Nate returned to the Powder River Basin, traveling the last two days through the season's first snowfall. Already, a six-inch blanket covered the valley. The snow was pushed to an angle by the wind, big, poker-chip-sized flakes that tumbled and clung to his coat and trousers like a layer of downy feathers. Tufts of spindly grass still showed above the snow in places, and the scattered herds of cattle that he encountered seemed intent on finding every available blade of the inferior crop. Nate knew that once the grass was covered, the cattle would not know how to dig for it the way the buffalo had once done by swinging their heavy heads from side to side to expose the forage below.

From a distance, he passed four hay wagons cutting trails out to the herds, the drivers bundled up against the cold with blankets covering their legs. They presented a ludicrous image as their great, rounded loads of hay were covered in white, making it look as though these men were delivering more snow out onto the range.

When he reached the South Fork of Crazy Woman Creek, Nate spotted an outrider from the EK driving a couple of steers along the bottomland. The rider wore a heavy coat and sheepskin chaps. A long white scarf ran over the crown of his hat and was tied below his chin, pulling the soft hat brim down over his ears. Nate could not make out the man, but he did know the horse. It was Ranger Jones's palomino gelding.

When Ranger saw Nate, the young cowboy raised an arm high and kicked his heels into his gelding's flanks. The horse broke into a high-stepping trot through the drifts of snow, leaving the two steers behind to nose into a bristly clump of grass that crowded the base of a leafless chokecherry shrub. The chokecherry's branches were topped by an inch-tall column of snow.

"You just now gittin' back?" Ranger called out from ten yards away. When he reined up next to Nate's mustang, he reached for Nate's hand and shook, pumping the hand up and down repeatedly. "Pard, it's good to have you back."

"Everythin' go aw-right?" Nate asked.

"Purty fair. But I'm ready to stop tryin' to fill your boots as Spaugh's foreman. Some o' the boys older'n me don't take to bein' ordered around by a young'n, if you know what I mean."

Nate said nothing to that. Those same "boys" were older than Nate too.

"Hey!" Ranger chirped up, and his eyes brightened. "Al Allison is workin' for us now."

Nate nodded. "That's good. What else has happened 'round here?"

"Well, Jack Flagg's gone an' stirred up a ruckus...him an' a bunch from the Bar C."

"What happ'ned?"

Ranger hitched his head to one side and frowned. "With the price o' beef gone down like it has, Hank Devoe had to cut wages on his crew. Had to fire a few too.

Weren't Hank's decision, o' course, but he's the one had to d'liver the bad news. The orders came down from the owner. Jack weren't fired, but him an' about six other boys went on strike."

"'On strike,'" Nate repeated.

Ranger nodded. "Yeah...they just flat refused to work 'less their wages went back up to where they was." He flashed Nate a half smile of regret. "Same thing happened at a coupla other ranches. It was Jack talked *them* into strikin' too." Ranger shook his head and took on a worried expression. "Ed Spaugh says all the big owners in the Stock Grower's Assoc'ation plan to blacklist Jack an' ever'-body who followed his lead. They didn' let 'em take part in the fall roundup, an', come spring, ain't none o' the strikers'll be welcome to any WSGA roundup."

Nate chewed on the inside of his cheek for a time. "What did Ed say to that?"

"Didn' say nothin'. Like the rest o' us, I guess he's just glad to still have his job." Ranger shrugged off his bad news. "Say, how'd the cattle look down on the Sweetwater?"

Nate shook his head. "They ain't for us. Ain't up to our standards." When he sensed that Ranger was working up another question, Nate changed directions. "Sumner Beach got acquitted. Jury found 'im innocent, an' he's back on his claim at Deer Creek."

Ranger slapped his woolly thigh. "Damn! That's some good news! Maybe him an' his partner can finally git that cabin built."

Nate shook his head. "He ain't got a partner no more. Brannan's gone missin'."

Ranger's brow creased with three horizontal lines, and his mouth remained open in the shape of a small circle. "Gone missing'? What's that mean?"

"Don't know. Maybe he got bought off by Wolcott and

left the country. Or maybe he's buried up in the hills somewhere."

Ranger frowned at his gloved hands as he sorted his reins. "Well, let's hope Sumner can put up that cabin by his-self b'fore the winter gits ser'ous."

Nate nodded at Ranger's attire. "By the looks o' you, I'd say it's aw-ready got here."

Ranger's face reddened. "Well, ain't you cold?"

"Sure," Nate replied. "I'm cold."

Ranger leaned from the saddle and spat. "Hell, yesterday I spent the day lookin' for strays up in them hills, checking all them little creeks that head up in the Big Horns. There's a lotta shade up them canyons, an' I stayed so cold I thought my feet were gonna turn to ice an' snap off at the first brisk wind. I never seen it git so cold this early. Have you?"

"Guess not, but I ain't been up here in Wyomin' that long."

"Well, they're sayin' it's gonna be a bad 'un."

"They?" Nate said.

Ranger spat again and frowned as he shook his head. "One o' the boys in the other bunkhouse said he paid a dime an' a nickel to a ol' gypsy woman to hear 'bout his future. She said this winter is gonna hit hard. Said it'll be so cold that cattle will drop over like a plague has hit the land. She suggested we drive all our livestock to Mexico."

Nate leaned on his pommel and allowed a smile. "So... are you packin' up on the word o' a old woman who takes yore money to tell you things that cain't nob'dy know?"

Ranger squinted his eyes. "You don't b'lieve in such predictin'? She was a *real* gypsy!"

Nate shook his head. "I don' know nothin' 'bout predictin' *or* bein' a gypsy, real or not. I just know I ain't headin' for Mexico. I got plans up here in this country, an' I aim to see 'em through." The mustang nodded her head up and down, snorted, and stamped at the snow. Nate put a little tension on the reins and spoke to her quietly. "Whoa, now, girl." When the horse settled, Nate studied Ranger's troubled face. "Did Plunkett purchase any hay yet?"

Ranger scowled. "Not one damned straw. The barn's empty as a Monday mornin' church."

Nate gazed out across the valley, where all the sharp angles of the rocky terrain had been smoothed over by the gentle sculpting of the wind and snow. Pulling at his lower lip with his teeth, he inhaled deeply and then exhaled a cloudy plume of breath in the frigid air. From deep in his chest he made a low humming sound.

"What?" Ranger said.

Nate looked away, his face pinched with worry. "Just that it ain't the first time I heard about a gypsy prediction for the winter. If it's true, Plunkett's gonna need to buy a lot o' hay."

Ranger perked up at this. "So, you *do* believe in them fortune tellers?"

Without answering, Nate nodded toward the two steers that had strayed. "I can push these two back toward the herd, if you need to keep lookin' for more."

"Sure thing," Ranger said and pointed downstream. "We're roundin' 'em up 'bout a half mile down the creek near them sycamores. You'll see 'em."

Nate gathered his reins but hesitated. "Why is it yo're out here alone?"

"I ain't," Ranger replied and pointed up the South Fork. "Tom Gardner is with me. He's up in that canyon makin' a sweep."

Nate nodded. "Where's Ed Spaugh?"

"He was at Plunkett's house this mornin'. Been arguin' our case for us...tryin' to save us our jobs and our wages."

Ranger shrugged. "He's prob'ly back at the bunkhouse now."

Nate reined his mustang toward the two steers. "Aw-right, I'll see you back there. Don't lose yore feet to the cold."

"Hell, I can't afford to!" Ranger laughed. "These are my best boots."

———

When Nate entered the warmth of the east bunkhouse, he removed his coat and hat and hung them on a wall peg. Ed was bent over by the wood heater buckling up a pair of white woolies like the ones Ranger had worn out on the Crazy Woman Creek range. Ed straightened and jerked at the waist strap to center the chaps on his torso. Seeing Nate at the door, he craned his head forward an inch or two as if to verify what his eyes were telling him.

"Well...it's a good thing you got back when you did. We got cattle spread out all over the Powder Basin."

"You ain't thinkin' this is a early winter, are you?" Nate said.

Ed raised both eyebrows. "Well, if it ain't, it don't bode well for the one that's coming."

Nate grinned. "You been talkin' to ol' gypsy fortune tellers too?"

Ed frowned. "I just ain't never seen snow like this so early in November." His frown deepened. "You been talkin' to gypsies?"

Nate shook his head. "I hear you stole Al Allison from the Bar C."

Ed shrugged. "Didn't steal him. He came and asked. He's a good hand."

"Good to hear," Nate said. "Ranger says you been at

the boss's house today. We still gonna have jobs come spring? An' at the same wages?"

Ed shook his head slowly. "There ain't no tellin'."

"Well, what'd you two talk 'bout?"

Ed sat on his bunk, and his shoulders slumped. "Everybody in the Stock Grower's Association is gonna bar anybody who is not a member from taking part in the roundups. Which any rounded-up livestock that does not belong to a WSGA member will be turned over to whoever finds it." Ed tightened his jaws like a man wincing in pain. "Plus, they've got a long list of names... people they wanna force out of the cattle business...and out of the territory."

Nate sat on the bunk across from Ed. "How'll that play out with you, come spring?"

Ed sighed. "There ain't no tellin'."

Nate studied Spaugh's grim face for some sign of hope. "What I'm askin' is are you goin' along with all this blacklistin'?"

Ed huffed an airy laugh. "Plunkett seems to think I will."

"But *will* you?"

Spaugh shrugged. "There ain't no tellin'."

Nate cocked his head to one side. "Meanin'...you don't know yet? Or...you do know, but you ain't tellin'?"

Ed fixed his gaze on the window and pursed his lips as he thought. A log settled in the heater, the sound of it much like a boot crunching down through a foot of snow.

"If it's just you and me talking," Ed said quietly, "I'd say the latter." He pivoted his head and looked into Nate's eyes. "But if you're asking for my official foreman's position on the matter...well...there just ain't no tellin'." Ed stood and walked to the coat rack by the door. He took down his sheepskin coat and pushed his arms into the sleeves. "What about the Bothwell cattle?" Ed said. "How'd they look?"

"There ain't nothin' to recommend down there, Ed. I wouldn' pursue it."

Ed frowned as he buttoned up his coat. "Well, how much was he askin'?"

"Bothwell ain't much at askin'. He's more 'bout tellin'."

"How much?" Spaugh pressed, his usual patience starting to fray.

Nate pushed up from the bed and strolled to the front of the room. "Didn' matter how much," he explained in a quiet and logical tone of voice. "The deal was no good."

Ed looked long and hard at Nate, but he said no more. Nate pulled down his own coat, put it on, and fitted his hat to his head.

"So, where're you off to?" Nate asked.

Ed stepped before the window and gazed out at the weather. The snow was coming down harder now. The muted light from the gray sky seemed more like a day in February.

"You know," Ed began, his breath fogging the window before him, "all the outfits here in the Powder Basin—including us—we've overgrazed this range. Even without a bad winter, our livestock is going to have a hard time of it." He shook his head and turned to Nate. "I'm still having a helluva time convincing Plunkett to buy hay. The only ones cutting and selling are the farmers and the small-time ranchers who are not in the WSGA. The association won't allow purchasing from nonmembers. They say it's supporting the enemy."

Nate breathed out a long sigh. "It would take a heap o' hay to feed all the EK cattle through a winter."

"That's the problem. We got the barns for it, but it would be the most expensive purchase of the year. With beef prices down, Plunkett thinks it would break the back of the EK." Ed took down his hat and used it to point toward town. "I'm heading into Buffalo to wire some merchants in Nebraska and see what hay is selling for there."

"How'll you git it here, Ed?"

Spaugh carefully positioned his hat on his head. "By rail to Casper...and then by wagons to here. That's the only way it can happen. Both the railroad and the freighters are going to quote a steep price. And after this blazing hot summer, the hay won't be cheap."

"Sounds expensive, aw-right," Nate said.

Ed tightened his mouth into a false smile. "Not as expensive as losing all our stock."

Nate thought about that gypsy prediction again. "Well, good luck with Nebraska."

"Yeah," Ed agreed. "'Good luck' is right. What are you going to do?"

"Same as always," Nate said. "Ride from one crew to the other and prod those boys into earnin' their pay."

"I'll see you this evening," Ed said and opened the door. Pausing in the doorway, he turned back to Nate. "Why don't you eat something before you go out. There's some biscuits in the kitchen. A little bit of beef too. Coffee's hot."

"I ain't hungry," Nate said.

Ed smiled. "It's good to have you back, son."

"Good to be back," Nate said, and together they walked outside to see the snow so thick in the air that they could not see the other bunkhouse across the yard.

Spring 1887

Powder River Valley, Wyoming Territory

Chapter Fourteen

"I ain't never seen nothin' like this b'fore," Ranger said in a subdued whisper.

Even through the bandanna tied around the lower half of his face, his words pushed little puffs of gray fog into the wind. The white scarf tied tightly over the crown of his hat and knotted below his chin left only his eyes exposed to the weather. Like everyone else in the party, he was bundled up inside most of the clothes he owned.

"None o' us have," Nate assured him.

Spread out before the four horsemen, a log jam of icy bovine corpses clogged the frozen Powder River from one bank to the other. The ice must have been four inches thick on the water. No current could be seen. Hundreds of steers were locked in the ice, their rock-hard bodies and long, curved horns lending a horrific terrain to the water-scape. The sheer mass of dead animals was the stuff of nightmares, one so disturbing that it would stick to a man forever, like a festering wound that would not close.

The icy wind gusted, and Ed Spaugh raised a gloved

hand to his throat to cinch his coat collar tighter by gathering the material in his fist. Tears stood in his eyes as he slouched in his saddle, a still and grim figure of a man.

"Oh, dear God," he moaned. "How can a rancher recover from something like this?"

"They cain't," said Tom Gardner. "This is like somethin' from the Bible...a plague...or a flood. Hell, I cain't even—" He stopped in midsentence and raised an arm to point across the river. "Be damned! Look at that, would you? There's one that made it!"

The men peered across the macabre scene of frozen water and wasted meat. On the far bank a lone steer stood next to a large sycamore. The tree's trunk had burst open as if it had sustained cannon fire. The lone animal faced into the wind, its legs partially hidden beneath the snow. Even from that distance, Nate could see the dull, milky sheen of death on the poor creature's eyes.

"He *didn'* make it," Nate said. "He froze standin' up."

No one spoke as they all looked at the spectacle of a standing, dead steer. It was difficult to take in the enormity of all that lay around them. On the ride out to the river they had seen sporadic evidence of cold, cruel deaths. Maybe thirty or forty corpses. But here at the Powder, for as far as Nate could see up and down the floodplain of the river, dark mounds of death dotted the snowy landscape. Worst of all was the mass of ice-locked flesh frozen into a ghastly dam from bank to bank in the river.

"I heard o' men gittin' lost out in the cold," Tom Gardner said from behind his muffling scarf. Being the thinnest man of the four, Tom appeared to be unnaturally bloated with so many layers of clothing. "They git desp'rate an' slip into water to git outta the wind. The cold must make 'em crazy. I guess it's the same for the cattle."

The wind whipped up a flurry of snow, and each man turned his head downwind to take the icy blast on the back of his upturned collar. The sound was like a locomotive bearing down on them. When it had passed, they set their eyes again on the mass slaughter spread out before them.

"We won't have no job after this," Tom said. "A cowboy cain't work where there ain't no cattle. Jack Flagg had the right idea. It's time to quit workin' for these barons. This winter has prob'ly broke their backs. I've had my eye on a plot at Crazy Woman Creek, and, by God, I'm gonna stake my claim on it."

"Don't jump the gun, son," Ed counseled. "The EK is not going under." Ed had straightened in his saddle for this announcement, but his voice did not carry the steady timbre of authority that was his trademark.

Tom flung a hand toward the river. "It's aw-ready gone under! It's gonna be like this ever'where we look!"

Ed could not help but look again at the frozen bodies jammed together in the ice. "Maybe we'll find some that made it through," he mumbled, but the tone of his voice was more questioning than hopeful.

Dakah snorted and threw her head up and down, making the cold metal of her bridle tinkle like tiny bells. The other horses reacted by grumbling in their throats and shuffling their hooves in the snow. Ranger turned in his saddle and raised an arm to point north.

"Yonder comes somebody," he announced. "Looks like Allison."

Everyone turned to see Al Allison bundled up on his handsome buckskin, making his way along the trail that Nate's party had cut into the snow. Al's face was mostly covered by a gray scarf. Like Ranger, he had covered his ears with another scarf—this one light blue—that fastened over the crown of his hat and pressed the brim to his cheeks.

When Al was thirty yards out, Ranger called to him. "What the hell're you doin' out here by yourself, Al?"

As he approached with his eyes smiling at Nate, Allison shifted his gaze to the carnage in the frozen river. His eyes pinched and slowly scanned upstream and down. Between his hat brim and the gray scarf, the narrow band of exposed skin on his forehead turned as pale as the underbelly of a fish. He pulled down the scarf from the lower half of his face, as if he needed to breathe in the reality of what he was seeing. Slack-jawed and speechless, he sat his horse and stared as the color returned to his face.

"God, aw-mighty," he whispered into the cold air, his breath fogging before him. "I figured on losin' plenty o' cattle, but I never would'a believed somethin' like this could happ'n." Shaking his head, Al stood in his stirrups and squinted. "I can make out at least four brands out there. Ours...the CY...the Powder...and the TA."

"The winter don't pay no attention to brands," Tom said.

Ranger pushed a sibilant hiss through his teeth. "Amen to that!"

Al continued to shake his head. "Forty-five below, for eight days straight," he said to no one in particular. "Six feet o' snow in some o' the drifts. And a wind that blew like a blast o' dynamite comin' down outta Canada. Now we know what a Wyomin' winter can do."

"This is not normal," Ed Spaugh said. "Nothing like this has ever happened here before."

Al lowered himself into the seat of his saddle and leaned forward to look past Nate at Ed. "Tell that to the cattle...if you can find any to tell it to."

Al looked back at the frozen river. He seemed not to be able to tear his eyes away from the gruesome display in the ice. Slowly, he began chewing on a forgotten wad of tobacco he'd carried in his mouth. Leaning, he spat a thick, brown dollop into the snow.

"You ride out alone?" Nate asked.

Al shook his head. "I was with Lew Webb. But he turned back to git a second pair o' socks. I just come on an' followed yore tracks." For just a moment the tragedy in his eyes gave way to a flicker of excitement. He leaned in closer to Nate. "Got some news for you."

Nate nodded. "You wanna ride with me up to Hole in the Wall an' see if we cain't find some cattle that made it through?"

Al nodded. "Sure thing."

Nate turned to the EK men and spoke with his authority as Spaugh's right-hand man. "Me an' Al will search those canyons behind the Hall Ranch. Ranger, you and Tom cover that meadow west o' the TA." He put a gloved hand on Ed's shoulder. "Why don't you go back to the bunkhouse an' make assignments as to who's to cover what area."

"Yeah," Ed said and began backing his horse from the others. "You boys be sure to stay with your partner. If you find any of our stock alive, drive them back to the ranch. We've got a load of hay coming in today from Casper."

"Little late for that, ain't we?" Tom quipped.

"Couldn't be helped!" Ed snapped. "By the time Plunkett finally agreed to order hay, there was no way for a wagon to get through till now."

"Yeah, well, maybe Plunkett should'a thought about that back in October," Tom carped. "He's the owner, ain't he? An' yo're s'posed to be the man in charge o' runnin' things."

Above his scarf, Ed's eyes took on a pained expression. "I kept telling him to make the order. Must'a told him fifty times."

"Well, look what we got now!" Tom snapped.

Ed turned at that, his eyes as hard as glass. "Well, I don't like it any better than you do! He's the one with the money! We didn't have any credit last year! I can't go out and pay for it out of my pocket!"

"It's done," Nate said. "There ain't no use in talkin' 'bout what should'a been. Let's see if we cain't find some cattle that made it through all this."

———

As the two Texan friends headed upriver against the wind, Nate led the way through the untrodden white. Here at Hole in the Wall, the storm had dropped three feet of soft snow, hiding the terrain below. Nate knew that any man, who did not know this land intimately, could break a horse's leg by guiding it the wrong way. He held the mustang to a slow and cautious walk, with Al following in his trail. After a time, when they entered a broad pasture, Al nudged his buckskin into the deep snow and plowed his way up beside Nate's white mare, until they were breaking a wider trail together.

"Wanna hear my news?" he called out over the wind, his smiling eyes twinkling.

"Only if it's good," Nate replied.

"Oh, it's good, aw-right!"

Al watched Nate's eyes carefully, and it was clear that he was expecting a grand reaction. "John and his family are comin' here to live. Might be a year away, but he's comin'.'"

Nate turned. "John? Yore brother?"

Al was nodding even before the question was asked. "Damned right. Him an' his wife—Kate. They got a lil' boy now, and you ain't gonna believe what they named 'im." Al laughed, reached out, and clasped his gloved hand to Nate's shoulder. "Named 'im Martin! Martin Tisdale!" Al laughed again and shook Nate until his head bobbled. "I got a nephew named for me! Ain't that a hoot?" Al flashed his big smile. When he got only a mild reaction from Nate, he frowned. "What?!"

Nate tried for a smile. "Well, here you are with a nephew named for you, but now *you* got a diff'rent name. How're you gonna 'xplain *that* to 'im?"

They rode for a time without talking. Then Al spat into the snow.

"Maybe I'll take my old name back eventu'lly. You know? When he's old enough to understand."

Nate wondered how old a boy needed to be to hear that his uncle was an outlaw. "Maybe so," he said and gave Al a reassuring nod.

Al dropped back to follow in Dakah's tracks, and they traveled in silence up a gentle slope into a coppice of bare-limbed aspens. There, the winding trail was easily followed as it wound through the trees. The trunks were crowded on either side of the opening, like a mob of curious bystanders wanting to see who might pass through their domain. Their white bark rivaled the snow for brightness, but the old, blackened branch scars littered their trunks as if they had been singed with branding irons. The wind sliced through the trees and whistled in a thousand dissections.

"Hey, Nate?" Al called out. "Yore mustang has got somethin' treacherous lookin' tangled in 'er tail."

Nate reined up and twisted around in his saddle. "What is it?"

Al sidled his buckskin closer to Dakah's hindquarters. "Whatever it is, it's stuck purty good. Maybe a seed pod."

"Can you git it out?" Nate asked.

With his gloved hands, Al probed at the problem. "Gonna have to be cut out, Nate."

Nate leaned over his cantle to see. "My knife is in my left saddlebag."

Al coaxed the buckskin around to Dakah's flank and opened the bag. After digging through the pocket, he stilled his hands and whistled a little rising note of surprise.

"What we got here?" Al said in a curious tone. "Purty fancy!" He held Nate's leather-bound book in both hands and casually pried open the front cover.

Nate reached back and pulled the book from Al's grip. "You didn' find the knife?"

Al put on his amused smile. "No," he replied and kept his eyes on the book.

Nate twisted around and opened the bag on his right. When he turned back to Al, he held out his sheath knife. Al took it and slid the blade from its leather case.

"This is the knife you won at the Fourth of July races in Round Rock, ain't it?"

"Yep," Nate replied.

Al went to work slicing hairs to free up the tangle, but Nate could sense the wheels turning inside his friend's head. "I didn't know they made books outta leather," Al said casually. "Do I git to know what it is?"

Nate leaned back and stuffed the book back into his saddlebag. "Nothin' that would int'rest you."

Al brought his horse alongside Nate's and held out the sheathed knife and tangle of hair in the same hand. Nate stowed the knife away, and then he examined the hair-covered seed pod.

"Elk thistle," he said and tossed the hairy mass out into the trees.

"Now, Nate," Al began in a brotherly tone, "you've knowed me a long time...and you oughta realize by now that I got a pow'rful cur'ous nature. Kinda like a badger who don't know when to stop diggin'."

Nate felt Al's stare on the side of his face like heat coming off a stove. When Nate would not turn to look his friend in the eye, Al started to chuckle.

"Now, are you tellin' me I got to go the rest o' my life wonderin' why you carry 'round a shiny leather book that looks like it oughta b'long to the King o' China? And weren't that a paintin' o' yore ol' pinto on the cover? Peaches?"

"It's just somethin' I write in sometimes," Nate said.

Al nodded slowly. "You mean like letters that you post back home?"

Nate shook his head. "Naw, ever'thin' I write stays in the book."

Al tightened his brow. "Aw-right. So, who reads it?"

Nate breathed in deeply and let the air seep out slowly. "Nob'dy," he admitted.

Al's eyes pinched as if he were in pain. "If nob'dy reads it...why d'you write it?"

"Hard to 'xplain," Nate said softly.

Al pivoted his head slowly as if he were counting the trees. When he spoke, his voice was both casual and careful at the same time.

"This's got somethin' to do with the young Hildebrand girl, don't it?"

Right away, Nate felt the secret inside him flutter like a bird trying to escape its cage. "How'd you know that?"

Al shrugged. "I seen the paintin' over your bunk. I know who done that, 'cause her name's writ on it. I figure the picture on yore book might'a got done by 'er, too."

A wind gusted and carried a spray of dry snow swirling off the tree branches. Even after such a horrific winter, the world looked clean and uncomplicated to Nate. Up ahead where the aspens ended, the rolling white terrain was smooth and flowing without a single flaw on its surface. Nate could imagine angels shaping it by brushing their soft wings over the land...doing that in the dark of night, when no mortal was present to see it happen.

"She gave it to me b'fore she went to France with Lindy. I was to write in it when I felt like it."

Al made a humming sound in his chest. "You mean, like a di'ry?"

Nate shook his head. "More like...letters that don't git sent."

After a few moments, Al began to nod. "Letters to her, you mean."

Nate turned to let the expression on his face help to explain. "It's the only way I can talk to 'er now."

"Why cain't you just talk? You know, kind o' like a prayer?"

Nate met Al's eyes with his own. "Well, what if she ain't available at the time? I don't know how things work with the dead. I feel like if I write it down, the words'll be there for 'er whenever she can git to 'em."

Al closed his eyes just long enough to nod his understanding. The two friends continued to sit their horses without any indication that they would push on to Hole in the Wall. Far up in the mountains, a raven croaked several times, its husky voice echoing in an unseen canyon.

"So, you two got close, did ya?" Al asked.

Nate looked down at Dakah's mane and idly lifted a loose lock of hair from one side to the other. "I never really got to see 'er become a woman. Not on the outside. But I reckon she was ahead o' me all along. She knew somethin' 'bout us that I couldn' seem to learn until after she was gone."

The raven called again, and this time a reply came from somewhere more distant.

"So, you loved 'er?"

Nate felt his body go light with the revelations that

seemed willingly to pour out of him. "I love 'er still. I guess I always will."

Al laid a hand on Nate's shoulder. "Yo're a lucky man, Nate Champion."

Nate turned to his friend. "'Lucky'?"

Al nodded. "Most o' the boys I know working the Powder River country…they ain't never knowed such a thing as you got. They prob'ly never will."

When Nate made no response, Al leaned and rested a forearm on his pommel. "I never did hear 'bout what caused 'er to die. Was she sick?"

Nate set his gaze on the immaculate surface of the snow in the pasture ahead. When he spoke, his voice came out a notch higher than usual.

"Somebody kilt 'er. They never did find out who. The police figured it was a robb'ry."

Together they looked out at the mountains and the sky. Neither man spoke for the time it took a lone vulture to sail across the opening in the trees. It soared in a straight line toward the north. When it was gone from sight behind the aspens, Nate tapped his heels into Dakah's ribs and started forward. Al's buckskin kept up alongside the mustang.

"It's good you got somethin' to remember her by," Al said and pointed at Nate's saddlebag. "The book, I mean. And the paintin' in the bunkhouse too."

Nate turned to see what expression Al wore on his face. "You ain't gonna tell me I oughta leave the dead behind and move on with the livin'?"

"Nope," Al said without hesitation. "It's my b'lief you don't let go o' somethin' that close to yore heart." He pointed at Nate's saddlebag. "Same way you keep that book close. You always carry it with you?"

Nate hitched a shoulder. "Long as I'm livin' in a bunkhouse, the book goes with me." Nate narrowed his eyes at the profile of Al's face. "Sounds like maybe you've had someb'dy special too."

Al grinned, and his head bounced once as he laughed to himself. Then his smile relaxed, and his face took on a dead-earnest look of certainty.

"I wish."

Chapter Fifteen

W hen they reached the escarpment at Hole in the Wall, they scoured the snow-covered brush along the south face of the tall rock formations. It was there that precious sunlight had been most apt to reach into the canyons over the winter. After several hours of searching, they managed to gather eight steers, all of them more than half starved, their ribs as pronounced as the folds of a concertina. So weak were they, the cattle struggled to walk through the snow.

One of the depraved animals belonged to the Hall Ranch. Two were CY stock. One was from the Bar C. The rest wore the EK brand on the left shoulder.

On the return trip, they pushed the cattle with patience, moving slowly so that the pitiful animals could last the miles ahead. At a rise in the field, Nate pointed south toward a long string of bare trees that stood black and tangled against the white backdrop of snow. There, an angled plane of white marked the rooftop of a cabin. When the two horsemen stopped, the cattle did likewise.

"That's Mister Hall's cabin," Nate said. "I'll go see if we can leave his steer with him."

Al stood in his stirrups. "Don't see no smoke. If he's there, he's likely to be froze stiff."

Nate coaxed his horse off the trail and cut a new path to the one-room shack. There were no tracks around the building. The cap of the stove pipe that angled out of the window wore a two-foot-high cone of snow that pointed toward the gray sky. He reined up in front of the cabin and studied the undisturbed, four-foot drift of snow piled against the closed door.

"Anybody home?" Nate called out over the wind. "Mister Hall?"

The only reply was the wind slicing through the leafless branches of the trees. Nate dismounted and plodded his way to the side window. There, he rubbed the glass with his gloved hand and peered inside. Cattycornered in the limited space were two bunks, each topped by a rolled-up mattress. A five-foot-high stack of split logs stood against the back wall.

Returning to his horse, Nate spotted a small triangle of pasteboard sticking out from the pile of snow at the door. Wading in closer, he pulled out a playing card by its corner. The two of hearts. Across its white surface a faded message was scrawled in pencil.

> *Gone to town. This claim for rent or sale. Inquire at Occidental Hotel. — W. Hall*

Nate jammed the card into the door, mounted Dakah, and retraced his path back to Al and the cattle. Al waited with a question on his face.

"Nobody there," Nate reported.

"Good!" Al said. "Better an empty cabin than a cold coffin above ground."

Nate nodded. "Looks like he's put up his claim for sale. He left a note to that effect."

Nate began to rouse the cattle into walking again. Al took up the lead to give the animals something to follow. Once they were in motion, Al turned in his saddle and called back to Nate.

"Tom Gardner's right. It's a good time to buy. You oughta think on it."

They continued along the pockmarked trail for a full minute before Nate replied. "Are *you* thinkin' 'bout gittin' some land for yoreself?"

Al snorted a laugh and turned his head to answer. "Doin' more'n *thinkin'* 'bout it. I'm taking Jack Flagg's advice. Me an' Ranger...an' his brother...an' Billy Hill...an' a few others...we're taking out claims."

Nate frowned. "First I heard o' that."

Al shrugged. "Yeah, me an' Ranger are stakin' out claims on the Red Fork with Flagg. Our claims will be close enough so we can look out for each other. My brother will likely join us there. Tom's picked out a plot on Crazy Woman. An' Billy Hill is partnerin' up with a friend on the Middle Fork."

Nate fixed his eyes on the pitiful cluster of emaciated steers as they slogged across the snowy bottomlands. But he wasn't really seeing any of it. He was thinking about the money side of this devastating winter. He knew that plenty of ranchers would give up after losing so much of their stock. If these owners did sell, they might be desperate enough to sell their land at a loss. And they'd want to get rid of the few cattle—if any—that were left to them.

Nate made a *chick-chick* sound with his tongue against his teeth and coaxed his mustang through the deeper snow until he was stirrup to stirrup with Al. "How come you boys been keepin' me in the dark on this?"

Al shrugged. "Well, we been waitin' on the papers to

make it legal b'fore we quit on you. I guess we been dreadin' tellin' you...like we might be lettin' you down."

The soft sound of the animals' hooves pushing through the snow filled up the silence between the two men. Nate was surprised to feel a twinge of envy enter into his thoughts.

"You boys ain't lettin' me down. You got to do what's right for you."

Al quietly laughed. "I tol' 'em you'd say that."

Nate gave his friend a reassuring nod and reined his mare off the trail and pulled up. There he sat his horse as the cattle trudged by, their listless eyes dulled to the cold and their wobbly legs barely holding up their reduced body weight. When the last steer had passed by, Nate fell into place at the rear.

"Hey!" Al called out in a whisper. He was turned in his saddle, and his eyes appeared alert over his scarf. "We got comp'ny."

Nate looked up to see three men on horseback almost upon them. The riders were unrecognizable beneath their face scarves and heavy layering of clothes, but Nate knew the roan gelding in the lead. Frank Canton's quarter horse —Old Fred— was well known throughout the county.

When Al reined up, the cattle stopped too. Canton and one of his companions pulled up right in front of Al, while a shorter, third man on a white Arabian pushed his way forward to mingle with the skin-and-bones cattle. Ignoring Nate, he made a show of inspecting each animal. After a look at all eight, he turned in his saddle to call out to the sheriff.

"Two o' these are ours!" he reported in a hoarse voice.

When the interloper would not turn to show his face, Nate glared at the back of the man's head. "And who are you?"

Twisting in his saddle, the man showed hostile eyes

over his blood-red scarf. "I'm foreman at the CY," he barked. "Mike Shonsey." He pulled down the scarf and pointed at two of the steers. "Them two are clearly marked. They're Mr. Hord's." When his eyes cut away, Shonsey put on a pouting face that brought back Nate's memory of Dudley humiliating him in Red Angus's saloon.

For the time it took the wind to gust and then abate, Nate said nothing and waited to see if Shonsey would meet his eyes again. He would not.

"Yo're welcome," Nate said, his voice hard and flat.

Shonsey turned as though he might have been insulted, but, still, he could not look Nate in the eye for more than a few seconds. When Canton approached, Shonsey edged his horse aside to make room for the sheriff. The third man remained in front, blocking the trail.

"Looks like you're pushin' more'n one brand, Champion," Canton purred. He lowered his face scarf to show a smug grin. "You workin' for more'n one outfit now?"

"You know who I work for," Nate said plainly. "If these cattle don't come in now for some feed, they'll likely not make it. They're 'bout dead on their hooves as it is."

Canton's smile tightened. "But it ain't roundup time yet...is it?"

"I'm roundin' up whatever I can find. If you think I'd wanna steal these cattle, you need to take another look at 'em. There ain't enough meat on their bones to feed a ki-yote pup."

Shonsey edged his horse next to Canton's and puffed up like a sage grouse when he faced Nate. "And who asked you to do that?"

Nate felt his face harden as he made an effort to keep his voice even. "It's a common courtesy on the range to look out for your neighbor's livestock when the need is there."

Shonsey said nothing. He leaned and spat into the snow. When Al hissed a sibilant laugh through his teeth, Canton turned to him.

"Take that scarf off your face," he called up to Al.

Al's eyes pinched. "What for?"

The whites of Canton's eyes glowed like heated metal. "I want to see who you are."

Al sat up straighter in his saddle. "I'm Al Allison. I work with Nate for the EK."

Canton raised a gloved hand and pointed at Al. "The scarf!" he reminded.

Al jerked down the scarf to show a scowl etched upon his face. For ten seconds, the sheriff studied Al's features as if he were committing them to memory.

"You're a friend o' Flagg's," Canton purred. "I hear you plan to run your own outfit."

Al bristled. "So what?"

"So what!" Shonsey mocked. "All you squatters are takin' up claims along the rivers and creeks. Ain't none o' you got but a handful o' cattle, but you block access to the water for all the big herds!"

"Well, I plan to have a big herd, too!" Al countered. "Our claims are legal!"

While Shonsey's face remained hostile, the sheriff's stare was implacable. "What I wonder," Canton said in his razor-thin voice, "is how a fellow like you acquires his livestock." Without losing eye contact with Allison, Canton nodded toward the scrawny cattle. "Must be easy to find food scraps on the floor beneath a rich man's table."

Al gritted his teeth, and his jaws swelled beneath his beard. "Prob'ly would be if I was the kind to eat off the floor...but I ain't." Al glared at Canton. Neither man would blink.

"Got a smart mouth, don't he?" Shonsey murmured.

Al's gaze shifted to the CY man. "Most anybody would sound smart to yore ears."

Shonsey chuckled as if the insult did not bother him, but Nate could see that it did. Al sat as still as a rock. Only then did Nate notice that he had unbuttoned the lower part of his overcoat to allow access to the pistol strapped to his waist.

"Tell you what," Canton said, breaking the spell of tension. "I'll take note of these eight you've got here. Right now, I've got business to take care of on the Red Fork, but I'll check with the owners later to see where these eight cattle did or did not end up."

"Ain't got eight," Nate replied. "Not now."

Canton's beady eyes fixed on Nate. The wind gusted and picked up tiny crystals of ice that sprayed across the trail like scattershot. Shonsey pulled down on his hat brim and turned away, but the sheriff's face did not flinch.

Nate nodded toward Shonsey. "This CY man can take his two, and we'll drive the rest back with us."

Shonsey's thick lips turned down in an ugly frown. "I ain't got time for that now! I got bus'ness with the sher'ff, an' I need to—"

"I ain't gonna do yore work for you," Nate interrupted. "Not if yo're right here where you could do it yoreself." He turned to Canton. "Tell *you* what," Nate said, stealing Canton's line. "Ask Hank DeVoe an' Mister Hall if they trust Nate Champion to bring in some o' their strays?"

Canton's eyes took on a shine of amusement. "You think highly of yourself, do you?"

For the first time since the three riders had arrived, the man sitting his horse in the trail ahead of them spoke up. "Why don't you just arrest 'em, Frank, an' let the court sort it out?"

Nate recognized the tight-jawed, Midwestern accent of Joe Elliott, a hardcase inspector for the Stock Growers

Association. Elliot glared at Nate from under the wide brim of a new brown hat.

With his face still exposed to the cold, Al coaxed his horse closer to the man. "I've spoke my name," he stated in an irritated monotone. "Who the hell're you?"

Elliott fixed dead eyes on Al. "Range detective for the WSGA."

Al pulled up his scarf and hooked it over his nose, his movement as defiant as his eyes were challenging. A tension hummed in the air like a thin, taut wire stretched to its limit. The two men were careful not to move their hands, even as their horses began to nicker and shuffle their hooves in the slush.

"We'll be on our way," Canton announced. "I've said all that needs to be said here." He reined his horse around to take the trail that Nate's party had trampled into the snow to and from Hole in the Wall.

"What about me?" Shonsey called out, his voice carrying an irritating whine.

Canton turned his head enough to speak over his shoulder. "Take care of your bus'ness."

Mike Shonsey frowned and looked quickly at Nate. "You go ahead an' take 'em. I'll send somebody over to the EK tomorr'."

Nate shook his head. "They ain't my bus'ness no more. You'll have to take 'em."

Shonsey opened his mouth to speak, but no words came out. Finally, he twisted around to watch Frank Canton ride off.

"Frank!" he yelled. "Wait a damned minute!"

Canton reined up, turned his horse sideways in the trail, and ignored Shonsey. "Let's go, Joe!"

Up in front of the cattle, Joe Elliott tapped his heels into his horse's flanks, but when his mount tried to start off, Al slewed his buckskin around so that it stood crosswise in the trail. The two men sat their horses and eyed one another.

"You wanna move that hag outta my way?" Elliott hissed.

Al sat his horse and said nothing. He propped his right hand on his leg just below the hip.

"Joe!" Canton called again. "Let's go!"

Without another word, Elliott eased his horse into the soft snow beside the trail and plowed around Al's buckskin. When he reconnected with the stamped-out path, he kicked his horse into a trot and did not look back. When he passed Canton, the sheriff turned and took his roan at a slow walk to follow.

"Fra-ank!?" Shonsey yelled again, this time louder, his voice cracking on the word. When Canton rode on, Shonsey glared at his two steers and grumbled, "Goddammit!"

Nate eased Dakah in front of the CY steers, separating them from the other cattle. "Let's git 'em movin', Al," Nate instructed. "We've wasted enough time here."

After they had gotten back into their plodding rhythm, Al turned in his saddle and pulled down his scarf. Breaking into a wide smile, he began to chuckle, the bright flash of his teeth rivaling the white of the snow around them. He pulled up on his reins, and the buckskin stopped, which, in turn, signaled for the cattle to rest.

"What?" Nate said, reining his horse to a halt.

Al raised his chin to point. "Look behind you."

When Nate twisted around, he saw Shonsey, bare headed, his hair whipping wildly in the wind, as he kicked at his horse's ribs, trying to force it off the trail. Downwind about thirty yards away, Shonsey's hat tumbled across the snow like a wheel thrown from a wagon. As horse and rider went in pursuit of the hat, they encountered deeper drifts. Shonsey cursed loudly and kicked his heels harder, but the horse balked and bucked once, almost unseating the man.

"Who do you reckon is gonna win that race?" Al called out with a laugh. "I'll put my money on the hat!"

———

By the time the snow had melted in all but the most remote and narrow canyons at the foot of the Big Horns, the Johnson County ranchers had tallied up their losses from the killing winter. The estimate came to more than 170,000 cattle dead. It came to be known as "the Big Die-Up." For weeks the sky filled with swarms of circling vultures that spiraled down to feast on the endless heaps of wasting flesh. For as far as a man could see out on the prairie, the big, black birds formed dark mounds of flapping wings, like small wind-torn islands spread over a sea of grass. At dusk the coyotes took over and dismembered the remains.

"It's like watching money burn up," Ed Spaugh said.

Spaugh and Nate sat their horses on the little rise above Crazy Woman Creek, where they were afforded a long view of the tainted valley. The smell of death hung around them in a suffocating stench. Turning away from Nate, Ed pinched the bridge of his nose and then wiped his eyes with his kerchief. When he faced Nate again, he wore a grim expression.

"Plunkett's talking about selling out, but I think he'll hold on for another year."

Nate nodded. "So, we still got our jobs."

"For a while," Ed assured him, "but we'll need some new hands. Ranger, Gardner, and a few others have struck out on their own." Ed shook his head. "I hope they know what they're getting into. They're all on the blacklist now with Jack Flagg. It's them against the WSGA. They won't be allowed to attend the roundups anymore."

Nate kept his eyes on the carnage before them. "Don't mean *we* have to go along with ever'thin' the Assoc'ation says."

Ed snorted a dry laugh. "You starting a revolution, Nate?"

"Nope, but I ain't lettin' these cattle barons tell me how to treat my friends."

Spaugh turned and studied the profile of Nate's face. "Well, let's see what we can get away with, why don't we? If they show up at our roundup, we'll let 'em in."

The two men did not speak for a time. Then Nate nodded toward the bottomlands.

"New grass is comin' in. If the rain gits here, maybe we'll have a purty good crop."

Ed pinched the bridge of his nose again and spoke with his eyes closed. "Hell, it ought to be a bumper crop... with all this fertilizer." He opened his eyes and nodded at the closest rotting steer topped by two vultures.

"Yeah," Nate murmured.

Autumn 1888

Powder River Basin

Chapter Sixteen

When Horace Plunkett sold the EK to the American Cattle Trust, Ed Spaugh and Nate took up top jobs for "Dad" Hoskins on the Clear Creek range. But it was a short-lived employment. When Ed and Nate demonstrated that they would work fairly with the smaller ranchers, including all the blacklisters, Fred Hesse reported it to the association, which, in turn, came down heavily on Hoskins, who reluctantly fired his two new men in order to maintain good standing with the WSGA.

Spaugh, content to remove himself from being under the thumb of Johnson County "royalty," headed to Niobrara County. Nate stayed put. By being fired, he figured that a decision had been made for him. It was time to go it on his own. Breaking into his savings, he purchased 140 head of cattle from Hoskins with the agreement that Nate would not reveal the seller's name, unless, of course, a judge demanded it in court. Rounding out his venture into self-employment, Nate purchased a previously registered brand and rented Mr. Hall's claim at Hole in the Wall.

He had been settled in for weeks and erected a new horse shed when his first visitors arrived. Nate was finishing up the new shingling on the cabin when he spotted five riders approaching from the west.

"Climb down from there an' saddle up, cowboy! We're headed to a roundup!" Jack Flagg's robust greeting broke the morning quiet that had prevailed at the cabin.

Squatting on his heels, Nate laid down his hammer and took in the consensus of serious faces among Jack's companions. Al Allison, Ranger Jones, Tom Gardner, and Billy Hill all awaited Nate's reply.

"'Roundup'?" Nate said. "Ain't you boys all black-listed by the Assoc'ation?"

Al huffed a laugh. "We're gonna find out just how serious they wanna be 'bout that!"

Nate took the time to look each man in the eye. "You boys plannin' to barge in?"

"Abruptly!" Jack returned. "Want to join us?"

Nate pulled in his lips and squinted toward the Big Horns. "Well, I ain't blacklisted, far as I know, but I figured I didn' need to go to the roundup this year anyhow. My herd has stayed well-contained, an' it's small enough so I can keep a tally purty easy. So—" He shrugged.

"First o' all," Billy Hill said as he leaned forward, hands on his pommel, "you *are* on the list. An' second, if you miss this roundup, ain't that gonna make it harder for you to squeeze in there in the spring?" Billy swung an arm toward the others in his party. "Except for Jack, we ain't got enough cattle to have a dog in this fight neither, but we're goin' to help 'im out."

Nate nodded and dropped his hammer to the ground. "Lemme git my horse."

When the six horsemen reached the big meadow at Salt Creek, they saw only a small fraction of the number of cattle typical of a roundup in the county. As they approached, six riders came out at a gallop to meet them.

"You men are not welcome here!" Fred Hesse called out as the group reined up in a loose flank, barring the way for Jack Flagg and his friends. Nate recognized Joe Elliot, Mike Shonsey, and two others who worked for the WSGA —Fred Coates and Billy Lykins. These last two were hard men whom Nate suspected to be cold-blooded killers.

Flagg coaxed his horse closer to Hesse and stopped. "You own this land?"

Hesse, the only man present whose skin was not browned by the sun, was dressed like a businessman in his dark, three-piece suit. He raised his chin and curled his upper lip into a sneer.

"This is a private roundup!" he snapped.

Flagg leaned in, as if the man might be hard of hearing. "You didn' answer my question."

With his pallid face flushing to pink, Hesse glared at Flagg.

"I reckon this is all still free range," Jack bellowed, "Excuse me!" Wedging his way between Hesse's horse and Elliot's, he yelled back to his friends. "Come on, boys!"

Nate and his companions passed through Hesse's bluff of a barricade without any words spoken by either side. They were halfway down the slope when Hesse yelled to their backs.

"You men can't go down there! You're not allowed!"

Ignoring the Englishman, the outcasts took their horses at a trot toward the cattle. Nate saw Flagg working his way through the herd, his head pivoting in quick, angry jerks. Then Jack sidled his horse up against a cowhand on a gray gelding and said something to the man as he pointed at a steer.

The cowboy must have delivered an unsatisfactory

response, for Jack grabbed the man's shirtfront, and yelled into his face. The man clasped both his hands onto Jack's wrist, but he was shaken with such force that his hat fell to the ground.

Shonsey came down the hill at a full gallop, swinging wide of Nate's group and lashing at his horse's rump with a braided quirt. Cupping a hand beside his mouth, he yelled so loud that every man in the roundup turned to look at him.

"Git Flagg out o' them cattle, goddammit! He ain't allowed in there!"

When the hatless man pointed upslope toward Shonsey, Jack Flagg wheeled his horse around, barged his way through the cattle, and started back up the hill as fast as his horse could run. When he and Shonsey slowed their mounts and met, Jack grabbed Shonsey's reins and recommenced his yelling.

"I seen what you done, you sonovabitch! You blotched over my brand, didn' you?!"

"Let go o' my horse, you stinkin' squatter!" Shonsey ordered. He swung his quirt at Flagg, who took the blow on his hat and shoulder. "Let go, damn you!" Shonsey yelled louder. When he came down with the quirt again, Jack released the reins, grabbed Shonsey's arm with one hand, and used the other to punch him squarely in the nose. A fountain of blood streaked down over the CY foreman's mouth and chin.

Nate and his friends reined up shy of the confrontation. They watched Jack Flagg tear the quirt from Shonsey's hand and beat him over the head and shoulders with a series of savage blows. Hesse's group arrived and assembled like an extension of Nate's flank, and for several seconds, like a row of spectators at a boxing bout, they all watched Shonsey take his punishment.

Out of the corner of his eye, Nate saw Joe Elliot ease his hand toward the stock of his saddle rifle. When Nate's head turned that way, Elliot's head pivoted in mirror image, and his hand hovered motionless beside his mount's mane. The two men locked eyes. When Nate casually propped his right hand on his upper thigh just in front of his holstered pistol, Elliot's hand lowered to his pommel.

"Here now!" Hesse screeched in his high-pitched voice. He dared to prod his horse a few steps closer to the altercation. "Why are you assaulting this man?"

Jack flung the quirt into the grass and drove his fist into the side of Shonsey's head just in front of the ear. Shonsey's hat flew off, and the man tumbled out of his saddle to hit the ground heavily on his side. Then Flagg turned his wrath on Hesse.

"You've burned over my brand with a runnin' iron. No man is gonna steal from me!"

Hesse licked his lips, glanced back at Elliot, and turned back to Flagg. "You and these other men are not allowed at a sanctioned WSGA operation!" His face paled with uncertainty as he struggled for his words. "You are not allowed!" he repeated. "Do you hear me?"

Flagg brought his horse next to Hesse's and laughed in his face. "I'm takin' my cattle out o' your little tea party!" He turned to Nate and his other friends. "Give me a hand, boys!" He reined his horse around and approached Shonsey as the foreman sat up. "You'll think twice before you try an' blotch over my brand again, you little, fat-faced weasel."

When Flagg pried his way into the herd again, Ranger, Tom Gardner, and Billy Hill started down the hill at a leisurely pace. Shonsey sat in the grass, lowered his head into his hands, and, with gentle fingertips, probed at a swelling on the side of his head.

Al walked his horse closer to Nate. "You ain't goin' down there?" he asked quietly.

When Nate answered, his voice was relaxed but loud enough to be heard by Hesse and his men. "Thought maybe you an' me could set here awhile an' keep a eye on these boys." He nodded toward Hesse. "We'll give Jack time to sort out his livestock."

Al frowned and leaned in as if to whisper to Nate, but his voice was purposefully clear. "Well, this ain't hardly fair, Nate. There's five of them. Six, countin' Shonsey...if you consider 'im worth countin'. And there's two o' us!"

Nate kept his eyes on Joe Elliott and made no reply to Al. He knew where this was going.

Al conjured up a mask of regret. "Just don't seem fair, does it? Them six against two Texas boys. Maybe we oughta let 'em call up s'more o' their men. Even things out a bit."

Ignoring Al's jest, Nate raised his chin to Elliott. "Maybe you boys oughta see to yore friend there." He nodded toward Shonsey, who still had not gotten to his feet.

"Yeah," Al agreed. "Looks like he might'a suffered a crack in his pride."

Hesse turned to Elliot and gave a single sharp nod. As Elliott and Lykins dismounted to check on Shonsey, Hesse broke ranks and walked his horse to Nate.

"We know what you are!" he hissed with considerable venom. "All of you! You work for *us* long enough to steal our cattle and build up your own herds. Then you lay claim to your hundred and sixty acres of land, all of it fronting the rivers and creeks, keeping the large herds from water."

Al chuckled. "All you uppity English barons made yore claims, just like we're doin' now. You chose land with water just like us. Yore outfit is settin' on *seventy-five square miles* of prime pasture! Maybe you let yore herds grow so big they overgraze the valley." Al snorted a laugh. "You act like you own all the goddammed free range in the territory."

Hesse sniffed sharply and glanced back and forth between Nate and Al, his dark eyes seething with animosity. "The Wyoming Stock Growers Association regulates *all* of the cattle business, and to us you are nothing more than thieves and squatters." He sat up straighter in his saddle, parted the front of his fancy coat, and snapped his vest smartly against his thin torso. "We have the law on our side. Sheriff Canton knows about *all* of you. It's just a matter of time—"

"You mean *yore* law!" Nate interrupted. "Canton bends the law the way you tell 'im to." Nate nodded at the well-muscled quarter horse on which Hesse sat. "I know for a fact your men stole that sorrel and five more like it from George Harris over at Trabing."

Hesse puffed up. "This horse is part of a business negotiation. Who told you that?"

Nate almost smiled. "Harris tol' me. Tol' me all 'bout how you slickered 'im in that deal."

Hesse's face paled. He started to speak but swallowed instead.

Jack Flagg came thundering up the hill on his big bay. As he approached, Elliot and Lykins stood, leaving Shonsey to moan by himself. Both men faced Flagg, their hands free but careful not to hover near their holstered revolvers.

"The law is the law!" Hesse declared. "The territorial government legislates it; the sheriff enforces it!" He jabbed a finger in the air three times, pointing it at Nate. "Just because you find yourself on the wrong side of the law, doesn't mean the law is wrong. Our sheriff—"

"You won't be having that sheriff long," Jack Flagg

butted in. "Come November, there ain't no way in hell the good people of Johnson County will reelect that snake."

Hesse laughed outright. "Who do you think could defeat him?"

Flagg's broad smile stretched across his handsome face, showing a straight row of teeth. "You just wait an' see," he gloated. Then he turned to Nate. "I could use some help down there. I need you an' Al to hold some o' mine separate while we cut out the others."

Al and Jack started down the hill, but Nate walked his mustang around to face Hesse and his men. "I'd advise you boys not to try'n stop us from takin' what don't b'long to you."

When no one offered a reply, Nate reined Dakah around and trotted toward the herd.

Summer 1889

The Gold Room and Main Street, Buffalo, Wyoming Territory

Chapter Seventeen

S itting alone at a back table in Red Angus's saloon, Nate sipped a cold beer and read the current cattle prices in the *Big Horn Sentinel*. Three pairs of other cowhands were spread out through the room, talking, drinking beer, and playing cards. Burl, the barman, stood with his back to the room, counting money at the till. The front door swung open, and Nate looked up to see Angus walk to the bar, slap down his hat on the countertop, and talk to his bartender.

Returning to his newspaper, Nate began reading an article about a farmer in Natrona County who had plowed up a curved animal bone as long as the rib of a covered wagon and thick as a fence post. As yet, no one had been able to identify it. Even the coroner was called in, but he was no help.

"What're you doin' here without your cantankerous brother?"

Nate looked up into the smiling eyes of Red Angus. "You mean 'Dudley'?"

Red's drooping, rust-colored mustaches climbed on his face when he broke into a toothy grin. "Who else would I mean?" He laughed and pointed at an empty chair. "You mind?"

"Be my guest. How's the sher'ffin' business?"

Red pulled out the chair and sat. The silver star pinned to his dark-blue blouse shone like quicksilver. It was surprising, Nate thought, how a badge elevated a man's appearance.

"Oh, I reckon it's in better shape than when Canton held the office, don't you?"

Nate leaned on his elbows and crossed his arms at the wrists on top of the newspaper. "No doubt 'bout that," he said. "I reckon he didn't see you comin' a-tall in the election, did he?"

Angus shrugged. "Don't know and don't care. We don't talk no more." Red scowled and shook his head. "Not that we ever did." He waved at the air with the back of his hand. "Canton's a full-time detective now with the Stock Growers Association. Prob'ly still thinks he's a sheriff out on the range." He pointed at the newspaper. "Speaking o' snakes...you read about them cattlemen down in Carbon County...decided they'd hang a man and a woman?"

Nate frowned at the newspaper. "A woman?"

Red nodded. "Down on the Sweetwater." He pointed again. "Bottom o' the second page."

Folding the paper, Nate laid it flat on the table, leaned forward, and began to read.

"She cooked meals at her husband's way station," Red continued. "People say she was a kind one. Took in young boys who were orphaned or having trouble at home. The husband ran the store. Now they're both dead. Locals found 'em hangin' off the side of a gulch, rotted black."

Nate's body went cold as he read. His breathing became deeper and louder as he took in the printed words.

Stabbing his finger to a line in the article, he looked up at Red.

"I knew these folks! They were good people!" Nate tapped his finger twice to the paper. "Says here she was a prostitute!" Nate shook his head. "I don't b'lieve that for a second!"

Red huffed an angry grunt. "That's the WSGA talkin'. Tryin' to throw a reasonable light over this bus'ness." He nodded at the paper. "Says there she traded sexual favors for stolen cattle." Red shook his head. "Just a wagonload o' bullshit!"

Nate looked down at the article. "Do they know the names of the men who done it?"

Red raised a hand and spread four fingers. "Four witnesses saw it happen. Young fellows. Three of 'em disappeared, and one was poisoned."

Nate remembered the boy, Gene, who had stood guard over his horses at Averell's store. And the banjo player, Johnny. And the young man, Buchanan, who had stood up for Averell.

"It's all propaganda, pure and simple. I got the truth from the sher'ff down there."

Nate narrowed his eyes at Angus. "Did he mention the name Bothwell?"

Red nodded. "He was one o' them done the hanging. Sheriff said he's a hard rock to crack."

Nate stabbed his finger to the newspaper. "How do they git away with lies like this?"

Sheriff Angus propped his elbows on the table. "The WSGA controls a lot more than the range." He nodded at the newspaper. "That there shows what they can do. This article came out o' Cheyenne, but it's run in newspapers all over the territory and into Montana, Colorado, and Idaho. The WSGA can call any man—or *woman*—a rustler and make them disappear without answering to the law. They got connections all the way up the chain...even to Washington DC...with people who know the president."

Nate pushed away his unfinished beer, leaned back in his chair, and crossed his arms over his chest. "They're already callin' *me* 'a rustler' now. Hesse has been spreadin' that 'round for a year."

Angus nodded. "Yeah, they like to talk, but when it comes to the real pushin', they're startin' with the weak. And *you* ain't weak, Nate."

"I almost wish they *would* try somethin' with me. But if they did, I don't reckon I'd see Hesse's face among 'em."

"Lord, no," the sheriff laughed. "He'd be at home trimmin' the hairs in his nose and have six witnesses there to prove it." Angus leaned in closer. "But in time, they'll come for anybody who's in their way." He arched an eyebrow. "I hear you've gone on your own out at the old Hall Ranch? You got a crew workin' with you?"

"Just a stray cat that took up with me. Sometimes I'll hire a man if I got a project big enough." Nate shrugged. "But mostly it's just me."

Red pushed back from the table and stood. "You keep your eyes open out there, son. Every time the association gits away with somethin' like *that*—" he pointed at the paper, "they're gonna git a little braver the next time."

"I'll be watchin'," Nate assured him.

Red started to turn but hesitated. "Oh, by the way, Jack Flagg is in jail."

Nate felt his gut tighten. "What?!"

"It's Hesse's doin'. They seized hun'erds of cattle Flagg was shipping off for slaughter. Claimed he had to a' stole 'em. All on account o' he's on that blacklist."

"What can they do to 'im?" Nate said.

Red Angus shrugged. "The association has already got him indicted, but Flagg is lawyered up good, and there

ain't a jury that could be called up would convict 'im."
Red crossed his arms over his chest and frowned. "That
ain't the worst of it though. Got a telegram from the sheriff
in Weston County. You know Tom Waggoner?"

Nate narrowed his eyes. "He's that German horse
trader, ain't he?"

"Was," Red corrected, holding a grim expression on
his ruddy face. "Three so-called deputies showed up at his
place with a warrant sayin' he'd stole four horses. Took
him from his family, and they didn't hear a word for three
days. Finally found him in a gully...just like Jim Averell
and his wife...hanging from a tree. His flesh was black as
tar."

Nate closed his eyes long enough to let out a tired sigh.
"He wasn't a agreeable fellow, but he weren't no rustler."

Red shook his head. "He was in their way. They
wanted his land and its access to Cambria Creek. It's
common knowledge that Fred Hesse is behind this. Fred
Coates, Tom Elliot, and Billy Lykins are suspected of
doin' Hesse's dirty work." The sheriff scowled and shook
his head. "But nobody will be convicted. Not a damned
one of 'em. You mark my words."

The sheriff stepped back to the table and picked up
Nate's half-filled mug of beer. He walked back to the bar,
swept his hat off the counter, and set down the mug.

"Burl?" he said to his bartender, "give Nate a cold beer
on the house. I think I ruined that one for 'im." Then he
walked out of the room and into the light of the
summer day.

A dark-haired, husky fellow at a front table laughed in
a deep voice that sounded like it came from the bottom of
a barrel. Nate recognized the big man, Nick Ray, who had
worked for the Powder River outfit. He remembered Ray's
run-in with Hesse in this very saloon.

Rising, Nate walked to the front of the room and stood

back a courteous distance from Ray's table, waiting to be acknowledged. Both men turned to Nate at the same time.

"Nate Champion!" Nick greeted in a tone of good cheer. "Come sit with us! We're just jawin' away like a couple o' ol' biddies."

As soon as Nate took a chair, the bartender appeared at his side and set before him a fresh mug of beer. "Compliments of Red," Burl said in a lifeless monotone. Without waiting for a reply, he turned and lumbered back to his station behind the bar.

Nate sipped some of the foam off his beer and then wiped his mouth with his shirt sleeve. After nodding to the other man at the table, he turned his attention to Nick.

"Wouldn' be lookin' for work right now, would you?"

Nick's face filled with disappointment. "I would, 'xcept I gotta coupla more months I need to spend with a friend o' mine. We're raisin' a cabin on his claim at Crazy Woman Creek."

"Who'd that be?" Nate asked.

"Tom Gardener," Nick said. "B'lieve he worked for you at the EK."

Nate nodded. "But you ain't workin' today?"

Nick shrugged his head to one side. "I come into town for some nails, but I'm havin' to wait for the hardware man to pull 'em outta storage from a barn somewhere in town."

The lean man sitting to Nate's left was quiet. His clothes were patched and worn, but he presented a clean appearance. His face was freshly shaved and his hair parted arrow straight.

"I could use some work right now," the thin man offered in a high, wheezy voice. "I can do most anythin' needs doin' on a ranch. You got your own claim?"

Nate showed a friendly smile and looked the man in the eye, though peripherally he sized up the cowboy's slight physical build for work duties. "No claim," Nate said. "Not yet anyway. I'm rentin' the Hall' cabin out near Hole in the Wall. I've acquired a herd and a brand, and I need somebody to help me with the brandin'. That an' maybe cook up some meals an' lay in a good supply o' firewood. Cabin could use some repairs, too." Nate hitched his head with regret. "You wouldn' be workin' from a horse. I'd handle that part. How would that sit with you?"

"Just fine," the man assured Nate. "What would you be payin'?"

Nate nodded toward the cowboy's arms resting on the table. "Mind if I see yore hands?"

The man frowned and looked down at backs of his hands. Straightening in his chair, he turned his hands palms up on the tabletop. Nate leaned in to inspect them, and then he sat back.

"Pay is a dollar and ten cents a day. What's yore name?"

"Gilbertson...Ross Gilbertson." Each time he said his name, his voice climbed upward like a question. He looked down at his hands again as if he had never paid them any attention.

"I'm Nate Champion," Nate said and offered his hand. Gilbertson's grip was light, but the man's strength was less important to Nate than his dependability. "Can I ask where you've worked, Mister Gilbertson?"

"I'm new to Johnson County, but I worked a few o' the ranches around Lar'mie. The Triple K...the Bar Nine... and J. J. Afton's spread, the Rollin' F." Gilbertson smiled. "No need for the 'mister.' Just call me 'Ross.'"

Nick Ray made his deep-barrel laugh again. "I'll vouch for him, Nate. He's steady enough. He don't look strong, but I seen 'im throw a four hun'erd pound yearling on its side for brandin'. He knows how to do it."

"Just don't ask me to shoot nobody," Gilbertson insisted. "I ain't no gunman!"

Nate's smile turned curious. "Why would I ask you to do *that*?"

Gilbertson huffed a scratchy laugh that contained not a trace of humor. "I can see where this coun'y is headed. That's why I asked you if you took out a claim. A man does *that*...an' he's bound to go to war with these English kings and earls or whatever they are."

Nate watched the man hold back his anger and took this as a good sign. Not only because Gilbertson *could* get angry. But also because he could control his emotions.

Nate sat back and threaded his fingers together over his midsection. "I'd never ask a man to kill another on my account. But I wonder how you might handle a man who threatens yore life?"

Ross shrugged. "Any man can be pushed into killin'. Personally, I'd rather swallow my pride and move on. We all got to answer to God one day."

"Let's hope not!" Nick laughed, but his face sobered quickly when neither Nate nor Ross smiled at the joke. Nick picked up his half-full glass mug, threw back his head, and gulped his beer down in three swallows.

"What would you think about startin' first of next month?" Nate said to Ross.

Ross made a crisp nod and sharpened his eyes. "Yes'r! I can do that."

They shook again. This time Gilbertson's grip was firm.

"Tell you what," Nate said. "I'll drop the 'mister' an' you drop the 'sir.' I'll pay yore wages, but we'll run this more like a partnership. How 'bout that?"

Ross's face screwed up like he'd heard a riddle. "What do you mean when you say 'like a partnership'?"

"No kings and earls," Nate explained. "Just us commonfolk tryin' to make a livin'."

"All right," Ross said. "I'll come out first o' the month."

When Nate pulled his boots underneath him to stand, Nick reached toward him and flattened his hand on the tabletop. "After I finish up with Tom's cabin, I'll check with you."

"Aw-right," Nate said and pointed at his mug of beer. Before he could speak, the front door flung open, and Al Allison bustled in wearing a smile that lit up the semi-dark room. Grabbing Nate's upper arm, he lifted him from the chair and started pulling him toward the door.

"Pard, have I got a s'prise for you!"

Nate resisted. "Well, let me git my hat, would you?"

Al scanned the room with eager eyes and then hurried to the back of the room, picked up the hat, and returned to take another grip on Nate's arm. "Here!" he said and pushed the hat down on Nate's head.

Laughing at Al's antics, Nate called back through the door, "Someb'dy finish that beer for me! It appears I have been roped and rustled!"

All the way to Main Street, Al hustled Nate along with his grip on Nate's arm. "I can walk on my own, you know," Nate protested but to no avail. As they approached Foote's Mercantile, Al veered toward the side of a wagon parked close to the boardwalk. Two braces of horses were harnessed in front. The wagon bed was filled with all manner of household belongings: a desk, a wash basin, an inverted table, the disassembled iron frame of a bed, two black storage trunks with brass hinges and latches, sacks bulging with unknown contents, a canvas duffel stuffed with cookware, a long-handled shovel and a hoe, several wood crates packed with books of every color and thickness, and a finely crafted child's highchair painted sky-blue.

"Kate?" Al chirped as he positioned Nate beside the driver's box. "This here's Nate!"

Nate removed his hat and tried to lose the confused

expression he knew had taken over his face. The woman on the plank seat held an infant swaddled in a blanket. Next to her sat two very young boys aged three or four, both staring at Nate as if he were an unexpected messenger bearing questionable news.

The woman was short and compact, though very trim and neat. The modest swell of her belly suggested that she was with child. Her stoic face gave her a mannish look until she broke into a smile, and when she did that, her dark eyes sparkled with glints of light.

"Well," she said, as if Nate were ten minutes late for an appointment, "I have heard quite a lot about *you*, Nate Champion."

"Ma'am?" Nate said.

Al slapped Nate on the back and pointed to the taller child. "Nate, meet Martin Tisdale!"

At the sound of his name, the little boy formed a small circle with his mouth. His face darkened to burgundy. Just as it dawned on Nate who these people were, a short man wearing drooping mustaches and a dull-red work shirt appeared on the boardwalk on the other side of the wagon.

"Hello, Nate. I see you've met my family?" John Tisdale smiled and leaned forward to muss the hair of the two boys on the seat.

"Well, I'll be!" Nate said. "John Tisdale!" He started around the team of horses.

They met halfway and clasped hands with a strength that represented their mutual respect. Their friendship dated all the way back to Round Rock, Texas. John Tisdale slapped his free hand to Nate's upper arm and pulled him in for a bear hug.

"Bless my soul! It's good to see you, Nate!" John released Nate and stepped back two paces to examine his friend, letting his eyes rove up and down over Nate from hair to boot heels. "You're sure enough a man now!" He laughed. "Taller than I am! You look fit as a mountain lion, Nate. And the mustache suits you. I can see now you've got the look of your big brother William."

Nate blushed and tried to think of anything that could take the conversation in a different direction. He pushed his chin toward the driver's box.

"Looks like you're adding considerable weight to the Tisdale clan."

John pretended a secretive whisper. "Don't mention weight! Kate's carrying our next one as we speak. She might be a little touchy about losing her fine figure."

Nate's face went slack as he turned to the wife. "Ma'am, I didn' mean—"

"I know what you meant," she chuckled. "And so does John." She gave her husband a reprimanding glare, but the sparkling smile still showed in her eyes.

John slapped Nate's shoulder. "I hear you've got your own herd."

"More'n a hun'erd an' seven'y head. D'you know where Hole in the Wall is?"

John raised his hands, palms up, and shook his head. Then Al joined the reunion by coming around the horses with a nephew in each arm.

"Nate's southwest o' us, brother," Al said. "'Bout twelve miles." Al made a big grunt as he hitched the boys higher up on his torso. "John an' Kate are joinin' us on the Red Fork." Al bounced the two boys in his arms. "An' I guess these two monkeys will come along, too."

As the children giggled, John took a light grip on Nate's elbow and guided him to the driver's box. John stepped up on a wheel spoke and gently pulled the blanket away from the face of the infant in Kate's lap. "This is our little girl, Siggy." John's smiling face lit up like a lantern.

"And she's already got her daddy wrapped around her little finger," Kate added.

Gesturing wildly with his hand, John beckoned Nate to climb up. "Come look at her, Nate! She's just so beautiful!"

Nate had never seen John Tisdale so happy, so animated. He pulled his way up by the brake handle and stood with one foot in the driver's box. The little baby had a pink face and blue-water eyes and looked so small and delicate that it was hard to imagine her anywhere except in the arms of her mother. A wisp of dark-brown hair curled down over her rounded forehead. She looked like any other baby Nate had been asked to peek at, but he couldn't help but soak up some of John's paternal glow.

"She's a purty one, aw-right," Nate said and patted the blanket just below the baby's chin.

Al paraded the two boys right up to the driver's box. "Purty?! You wanna talk 'bout 'purty'? Just look at these two! Every girl in Wyomin' is gonna be after 'em!"

"What makes you say that?" Kate asked.

Al made a comical face, pretending to be taken aback. "Well, anyb'dy can see these two look just like me! An' I have to fight women off with a hot brandin' iron at least twice a week!"

Kate pretended a look of curiosity. "Oh-h-h," she mewled, "so we should expect to see burn marks on all the single women in the Wyoming Territory?"

Al didn't miss a beat. "No, no...you shouldn' oughta limit it to the single women. The married ones are the worst!"

John jumped down from the wagon and took the boys from Al. Al stood helpless with a silly grin on his face as his brother walked his sons to the back of the wagon and loaded them in over the tailgate. Then John walked to the driver's box, climbed up, and sat.

"Where're you headed off to?" Al asked.

"Anywhere out of the range of your mouth," John said. "I figure it would be good if I didn't corrupt my entire family on their first day in Johnson County." He looked at Nate and winked. "Now how do I find the Red Fork?"

Nate narrowed his eyes and rubbed at the whiskers on his chin. "Well, I can recommend a guide. He knows the country an' won't charge you nothin', but you got to listen to 'im try to entertain you for most o' the trip."

Kate held back a smile. "Anyone we know?"

Nate pointed with his hat toward Al, who stood by with his hands splayed on his hips.

"I was afraid of that," John grumbled as he unwrapped the reins from the brake handle. He sat up straight, sorted the reins, and then looked directly into his brother's amused eyes. "Well? Are you coming?"

When Al jogged off to get his horse, John pointed a finger at Nate. "Soon as we get settled in, you're coming over to sample some of Kate's cooking."

Nate slapped his hat onto his head. "That's the best news I've heard all day."

1891

Hole in the Wall, Middle Fork of
the Powder River, Johnson
County, W. T.

Chapter Eighteen

At mid-morning on a cool spring day, Nate and his brother, Dudley, rode through the north breach in the tall cliffs of red sandstone that comprised the east parapet at Hole in the Wall. Against a solid blue sky, the towering, flat-topped walls of red stone gave off a vibrant sheen as if an early sunset were slathering the cliffs with color. Leaving the opening in the wall behind them, the two riders entered the long, broad pasture that cowhands called "the Sweep," where the lush green grass grew as thick as the hairs on a grizzly bear's neck.

Yesterday, like so many other days, Nate had left his 172 head of cattle sequestered in the long canyon between the Big Horns and the east palisade. Today, however, he felt the potential of trouble. On the ride in, he and Dud had followed the fresh tracks of a herd that looked to be several hundred in number. The Sweep could accommodate a dozen such herds, but Nate knew that—in these days of conflict between the big and the small ranchers—the compatibility of grazing, neighboring herds depended upon who the owners were.

When they entered the natural, thirty-mile-long holding pen, Nate pointed to his herd grazing only a hundred yards from where he had left them yesterday. "There they are," he said.

But Dud was looking far to the south. "An' there's yore new neighbors."

When Nate turned that way, he could make out the larger herd that had passed through just hours ago. Eight cowhands sat their horses around the periphery of the cattle as the animals browsed on the rich grass.

When the Champion brothers approached Nate's herd, the cattle paid them little mind. Every animal seemed content to tear at the grass and chew, occasionally taking a lazy step or two to relocate and find a new source of untouched forage.

Sitting their horses on a small knoll, Nate and Dud counted, poking their fingers at the air to tally up the numbers. They did this twice, and both times they came up with 166. After checking a third time, the two brothers looked at one another and said nothing. As if by tacit agreement, they wheeled their horses around and started down the Sweep for a look at the interloping herd.

Fifty yards away from the herd, they reined up and studied the animals. "Looks like the CY outfit," Dud said.

Nate pointed to a steer turned in profile, showing its double-diamond brand on the hip. "Not that'n," he said. "He's one o' mine."

After a long inspection, he spotted another double-diamond steer and two white-faced cows, each accompanied by a spindly-legged calf that stuck close to its mother's flank.

One of the drovers on a fine bay mare approached Nate at a walk. The man wore thick mustaches and a green-and-black checkered shirt and a big, yellow neckerchief tied at his throat. His tan campaign hat was a relic, so tattered that it might have survived a number of wars. As he got within speaking distance, the rider pinched the front of his frayed hat brim.

"How you doin'?" he greeted amiably. "You're Champi'n, ain't you?"

Nate nodded. "That's right." The CY man offered his hand, and Nate took it.

"Charlie Padgett," the man said friendly enough. He acknowledged Dud with a nod.

"That's my brother Dudley," Nate said. "Would you be the one in charge here, Charlie?"

"Nope, not me." Padgett pointed down the valley at a stocky man on a white horse. "Right there," he said. "Mike Shonsey. He's foreman."

Nate nodded "'Preciate it."

"You bet," the man said and reined his bay around to return to his station.

Nate and Dud skirted the herd and reined up fifteen feet behind Shonsey, and there they waited as the foreman gave orders to one of his men. When the confab was over, Nate spoke up.

"Shonsey?"

Turning in his saddle, Mike Shonsey widened his lidded eyes as they stitched back and forth between the Champion brothers. His mouth hung open, but words failed him. Dropping the surprised expression from his face, he swung his horse around to face Nate, leaned to his side, and spat a brown dollop of tobacco into the grass.

"What do *you* want?" Shonsey said, looking directly at Nate.

"SIx head o' cattle," Nate said plainly. "Two steers, two cows, an' two unmarked calves."

The skin above Shonsey's nose buckled into folds when he smiled. "You mean 'to buy'?"

Nate would not play the game. "Must'a got mixed in with yores."

Shonsey squinted as he looked north toward Nate's herd. "Think so?" he said, pretending a concerned attitude. "Well, we'll just have to cut 'em out for you." Tilting his head to one side, he squinted again. "Four, you say?"

Nate kept his face neutral. "Six."

Shonsey smiled. "But you can't claim unbranded mavericks."

"Can if they're stickin' close to their mamas," Nate advised.

Shonsey made a quick shrug, twisted around, and yelled to a man on an Appaloosa. "Hey, Wick! See if you can cut out four beeves with a—" He turned to Nate with a confused look that did not quite hide the smirk on his face. "What's your brand? I forget."

Without changing his expression, Nate spoke quietly. "You know my brand."

Shonsey bowed his head, raised an index finger beside his ear, and waggled the finger. "Oh, yeah. I remember now." Turning back to the man on the Appaloosa, he cupped a hand beside his mouth. "It's a double-diamond brand!" He smiled at Nate. "We'll sort it out an' holler at you. How 'bout that?"

"And the two calves," Nate reminded.

"Well," Shonsey mewled, "you know the law 'bout mav'ricks. They go to whoever finds 'em."

Nate felt his eyes take on a hard focus as if he were aiming down the sights of a rifle. "Unless that man findin' 'em takes 'em from another man's herd."

Shonsey pushed up his hat brim, making his gloating face all the more visible. "But you ain't in the Stock Growers Association, and that makes you ineligible to claim 'em."

Dudley coaxed his horse beside Nate's, reined up, and

slapped his hand smartly against the leather of his holster. "We got other means o' bein' eligible," he announced in a hard voice.

Shonsey narrowed his eyes at Dudley. "There's eight o' us...an' only two o' you."

Dud feigned a look of surprise. "Well...you *can* count. That's good. Then you'll know how many double diamonds you need to cut out."

Shonsey leaned and spat off to one side again. Looking over the herd, he seemed not to know what to say.

Nate pointed with his thumb over his shoulder. "We'll be over there with my herd. I'll be expectin' six."

Nate reined his mustang around and headed back toward his cattle. "Dud?" he called over his shoulder, "let's go." When he had covered no more than twenty yards, Dudley appeared beside him and matched his horse's speed to Dakah's.

"That is one repulsive sonovabitch!" Dud said. "Looks like the offspring of a fat an' ugly whore and a warty toad."

"We'll give 'im an hour," Nate said.

———

A half hour passed, while the Champion brothers inspected the hoof of a steer that had developed a limp. When Nate mounted Dakah again, he spotted two steers far down the valley, wandering up the mountain on the other side of the river. With a tap of his heels, he coaxed Dakah into an easy gallop and followed the shoulder of the river upstream.

When he was squarely across the river from the two wandering cattle, he reined up and shaded his eyes with a hand. They were his steers. A third animal stood in the water almost a quarter mile away. On the sand flat beside it, a calf bawled. He could not identify the cow from that distance, but he knew there would be a double-diamond brand on that mama's hip. Scanning the river up and down he did not see any other strays.

By the time Nate reached the CY herd, Shonsey was seated on a four-foot-high boulder near the willows, taking a break and eating a biscuit stuffed with a slab of meat. He held a plaid yellow cloth under his chin and leaned forward each time he took a bite. Two other men sat in the grass nearby, each one busy with his own meal. One was Padgett, who wore the campaign hat. The other was the cowhand named "Wick." Their horses were tethered with Shonsey's in the shade of the trees.

Nate reined up and watched Shonsey chew on a mouthful that filled his cheeks. "Why are my cattle strayin' across the river?"

Shonsey smiled as he swallowed, wiped his sleeve across his mouth, and put on a puzzled expression. "Well, I don't know," he answered, his voice filled with wonder. "We cut 'em out, but I reckon they wandered off again. Did you ask 'em why they went over there?"

The two hands seated nearby stopped chewing and looked up. Nate glanced their way long enough to see that they were not amused at Shonsey's act.

"Said you'd holler for me," Nate reminded Shonsey, his voice like the purr of a cat.

Shonsey cocked his head to one side and wrinkled his brow. "Did I?" He narrowed his eyes and stared across the valley. "Guess I forgot." He took another bite of his biscuit.

Ignoring Nate, Shonsey chewed. The two hands seated on the ground did not move an inch. Nate dismounted and let his reins fall to the grass. He stood just outside the range of Shonsey's boots and hooked his thumbs behind his cartridge belt.

"Whyn't you climb down from there an' we can talk s'more 'bout this?"

Shonsey raised the remains of his biscuit nestled in the cloth. "I'm eatin'," he explained. "Don't like to be bothered when I'm eatin'."

Before Shonsey could lower his hand, Nate side-stepped closer to the rock, grabbed a loose corner of the cloth, and jerked it free, sending crust and crumbs and meat in an upward shower like a geyser. The food scraps sprayed into Shonsey's face, some of it landing on the brim of his hat. One of the seated men coughed up a single, rough laugh, and then the space around rock went quiet.

"Now yo're all done," Nate said, his voice as smooth as water parting around a stone.

It took a moment for Shonsey to realize what had happened. He seemed to struggle for an angry, indignant reaction, but mostly he seemed flustered.

"Goddammit! What the hell!"

Nate felt as if he were looking at a caged animal, who had just come to realize that its own safety was defined by that cage.

"You gonna climb down?" Nate said.

Shonsey stayed put and flung out a hand toward the creek. "Go an' git your own damned cattle! You're the one lost 'em!"

"No," Nate said calmly. "I'm gonna hold you to yore promise. Maybe help you learn somethin' 'bout the common courtesies that one rancher extends to another."

Shonsey's thick lips turned down, and his lidded eyes showed both resentment and fear. "I ain't got no need to learn *nothin'* from you!"

The cowhand named Padgett put away his food and stood up. "I'll help you, Mister Champi'n." He turned at the waist and nodded to his friend. "So will Wick, here."

When the second man stood up, Shonsey's face

contorted into the likeness of a demon. "You men work for me! I'll tell you what to—"

"No, Mike," Wick interrupted. "He's right. It's a common courtesy an' ever'body affords it to the next man."

Shonsey pointed at Nate. "He's a goddammed rustler! You don't afford him *nothin'*!"

Nate stepped in front of Shonsey's boots and now hoped that the loudmouthed foreman *would* try to kick him. "You wanna stand down here an' back that up?"

Shonsey glared at his men. "Git him outta here!" he ordered. "We got work to do!"

Wick forked his hands on his hips. "How d'you propose we do that, Mike?"

Before Shonsey could think up a proper reply, Padgett spoke up. "We'll work cattle for you, Mike, but we ain't gonna fight your pers'nal fights for you."

Nate waited for Shonsey to look him in the eye. "Now that we got that straightened out, why don't you climb down here an' call me a rustler again."

Shonsey wet his lips with quick darts of his tongue. "We cut out your damned cattle! Now take 'em an' git outta here so we can tend to our own!"

A memory floated up from the depths of Nate's mind. A day at the schoolyard in Round Rock, Texas. Sitting on top of the lunch rock, Henry Kirkpatrick had taunted Nate with insults. Nate had been the younger of the two and was outweighed by Henry by sixty or seventy pounds. But Nate had been in the right, and that had made all the difference. He had pulled the older boy off the rock by his booted foot and watched as Henry hit the ground like a poleaxed steer.

"So, I guess you ain't gittin' down, are you?" Nate said calmly.

Shonsey flattened his hands on the rock as if nothing

could budge him from his perch. He wouldn't look at Nate. Instead, he sacrificed one grip on the rock to brush at the food scraps littered across his lap.

"Me an' Wick'll help you round up your cattle, Mister Champi'n," said Padgett.

Shonsey's head jerked up, and he glowered at his men. "The hell you will!" he growled.

"The hell we *won't!*" Wick said. "That's the way it is, Mike."

The foreman leveled a stiff finger at his cowhands. "I'll fire the both o' you!"

Wick bowed his head for a moment, and his hat brim covered his face. When he looked up, he wore a calm but subtle smile.

"You could...but then we might have to tell Mister Carey and Mister Hesse 'bout those so-called lost steers you sold to that Mennonite farmer. I don't reckon that cash went any farther than your pocket, did it?"

Shonsey's face reddened. He could not help but glance at Nate, but then he quickly turned toward the Big Horns and pouted.

Nate tossed the yellow cloth back at Shonsey, hitting him in the chest. Too late, the man flinched and brought up a shielding forearm before him, but the cloth now lay in his lap.

"Guess we know now who among us is the rustler, don't we?" Nate kept staring, but Shonsey would not look at him. "Same one who's the cow'rd here."

The skin on Shonsey's face darkened, and his lower lip pushed forward. "Go git his damned cattle then, an' git back here quick!" Shonsey snapped at his two men. He brushed at his trousers again with three brisk sweeps of his hand. "I wanna move this herd south today. There's better grass down there."

Nate gave the man fifteen more seconds to take up his

challenge, but Shonsey still would not look at him. The foreman was not game.

Nate walked to his horse, took a grip on pommel and cantle, and leapt lightly off the ground. Deftly, he slipped his boot into the stirrup. Watching Shonsey all the time, he slowly scissored his leg over and eased into his saddle. Without a word, he reined Dakah around and started for the river. The two CY hands untied their horses, mounted, and followed him, leaving Shonsey alone on his rock like a man stranded during a flood.

Chapter Nineteen

One month later, Nate enlisted Al Allison, Ranger Jones, Billy Hill, Ross Gilbertson, Nate's brothers Dudley and Ben, and a man named Willcox to help move his herd south six miles down the Sweep. His destination was Shoshone Canyon, one of the prime, free-range meadows at Hole in the Wall, where Nate had grazed the Bar C cattle many times in years past. The summer morning was pleasant and made even more satisfying to Nate, because today he was driving his own cattle to one of his favorite grazing grounds.

After four or five miles from his position riding point, Nate could make out a large mass of cattle spread across the flats. Though disappointed, he was not concerned, for here there was room to spare for other outfits. What he spotted closer, however, struck him like a slap in the face. Raising his arm as a signal to halt, he turned his horse and called out to all behind him.

"Hold 'em up!"

The swing riders closed in at the front, and the flankers came up to take their places. When the cattle in front started to turn in upon the herd, the momentum of the journey began to founder until the only movement was the intermingling of the animals in place. A chorus of bleating and baying marked the herd's confusion and discontent. Al Allison and Dudley rode to the front and circled until their horses stood on either side of Nate's mustang.

"What is it?" Al asked.

"Look yonder," Nate said and pointed down the valley.

Al and Dud twisted in their saddles and then went still as they eyed the long stretch of wire fence strung across the width of the valley floor. "What the hell?" Dud mumbled.

"First I knowed of it," Nate said.

Al squinted. "Ain't this still free range?"

"It is," Nate said.

Dud filled his cheeks with air and exhaled in a rush. "What're we gonna do?"

Nate leaned back and opened one of his saddlebags. Pulling out a set of wire cutters, he held the tool before him as an answer. Al reached into his own bag and produced an identical tool. Then Dud did the same.

They cut the wire away from its crude posts for a forty-yard-wide swath and moved the cattle through the gap without incident. When they were less than half a mile from the larger herd, a trio of horsemen broke off from the other outfit and rode three abreast toward Nate's party. These riders came in at a gallop and reined their lathered mounts to a dramatic halt ten yards in front of Nate, their horses snorting, slewing in place, and breathing hard.

Nate recognized two of the cowhands, men who had ridden for the Powder River Company. The third rider was a plump, red-faced man who glared at Nate from under the brim of a brand-new hat as white as Dakah's coat. This one appeared unaccustomed to hard work, as he carried a lot of weight around his midsection and hips, but he presented the bearing of one in charge. He sat astride a stout, dapple-gray mare with high, dark socks.

"How did you get through my fence?" the fleshy man demanded.

"So, that was yours?" Nate said and continued toward them. "I cut it. You cain't put up fencin' on free range."

The man looked ready to spit. The steady advance of Nate's cattle forced the three intruders to back their horses in reverse and move with the herd's momentum. Their mounts nickered and tossed their heads in protest as they were forced to march backward.

"Turn your herd around!" the man ordered. "This pasture is taken!"

Nate said nothing as he continued at his regular pace as point man. Coming in at a trot, Al Allison took up a position on Nate's right. Then Billy Hill fell in at his left. Dudley and Ben arrived and took up positions on the wings. Willcox came in last and reined up a little behind the others. Gilbertson remained at drag behind the herd. Walking their horses in a flank, the five Texans kept their eyes on the three men backing up before them.

Nate kept a friendly tone to his voice and looked the talker in the eye. "I reckon *you'd* better be the one to turn around. I don't b'lieve yore horses take to walkin' tail-first."

"I insist you turn this herd around now!" the plump man commanded. "And you can wire that fence back together as you leave!"

Nate spoke in the most genial tone he could muster. "Mister, I don't know who you are, but it appears you have been misinformed about how things go on the open range."

"I am J. N. Adstile, and I have two thousand head of cattle that I am keeping here for the next two months!"

"Well, that's fine," Nate said, "but you cain't fence this land off." He nodded toward the vast grassland ahead of them. "This spot can handle a lot more than what you an' me can graze here together. I got less than two hundred head."

Adstile's face flushed with color beneath a generous sheen of sweat. His gray kept trying to turn on him, and each time it did he jerked the reins hard enough to make the bit *click* against the horse's teeth. As he wrestled with the horse, Adstile constantly pulled his lips in and then pushed them out as if he were sucking up water through a hollow reed.

"You can't just barge in on another man's grazing land!" he blustered.

"Ain't bargin'," Nate replied. "Yore cattle can graze right alongside mine. I don't intend to mix 'em together." Nate turned to acknowledge one of Adstile's workers. "You boys didn' apprise yore boss on how the free range works?"

"I know exactly what I'm doing!" Adstile insisted. "And you can go to hell!"

Nate continued forward, his body swaying with the rhythm of his horse. "That a threat? Or are you just bein' rude?"

Adstile sniffed and wormed his neck up through his collar. "Take it how you want to!"

Al laughed. "Mister, yo're gonna need more men if you wanna talk that way."

Adstile snorted. "I've got twenty men back there to back me up!"

Al smiled. "I can see that. I figured them into my assessment. Yo're gonna need more."

Adstile sneered at Al but directed his outraged glare at

Nate. "We'll see about that!" He spun the gray around, kicked it into a gallop, and raced off toward the larger herd. "Come with me!" he called back to his men.

The two cowhands who had accompanied Adstile held their horses at a walk and watched their boss ride away.

"You boys oughta educate your employer on the law," Nate suggested.

Dudley laughed. "You don't wanna git into a fight just 'cause you work for a jackass."

One of Adstile's men made an airy laugh. "He don't listen to nobody but Fred Hesse." He spat tobacco off to one side. "None o' us wanted to string that fence. We just do what we're tol'."

"Well," Billy said, "that ain't the kind o' man I'd be willin' to die for. How 'bout you?"

Glancing at Billy, Nate made a subtle sign with his right hand, as if he were smoothing out a wrinkle on a blanket. Then he addressed the two men of Adstile's.

"See if you cain't talk some sense into 'im. I rather not see any blood spilt here."

Without a reply, the two men rode off in tandem to catch their employer. Al started to chuckle as he watched the two cowhands race across the grass.

"They move purty fast when they're in retreat, don't they?"

Nate turned to Al. "I meant what I said 'bout spillin' blood. We ain't lookin' for a fight."

Al snorted. "Well, it looks like a fight might be lookin' for *us*! *I* ain't turnin' tail!"

"Didn' say nothin' 'bout 'turnin' tail,'" Nate replied in an even voice. He pointed to a swale in the land where the grass showed a darker shade of green fifty yards from a stand of cottonwoods. "We'll graze our herd over there, an' we'll keep our eyes open. If the ball opens, we'll make a stand in them trees. I don't wanna see any o' my cattle shot up."

"I don't know the fat man, but I know them two other boys," Billy said. "They worked for Moreton Frewen before he quit the country. Those are Powder River boys."

"Frewen sold out?" Nate asked.

Billy nodded. "Him an' Plunkett an' a few other fat cats in the Assoc'ation. I reckon they're all sippin' tea with the Queen o' England 'bout now."

Al laughed. "If that's so, I just lost all regard for that woman."

"How 'bout you boys drop back to yore positions," Nate interrupted, "an' let's git these cattle over to that bottomland."

As soon as Nate's crew had settled the cattle in the swale, Ross Gilbertson rode toward Nate, checking over his shoulder as he did. "Look yonder, Nate. They're pushin' some o' their cattle our way."

Nate looked toward Adstile's herd and saw ten riders driving about four hundred head of cattle his way. There was no question about their intent.

Nate yelled across the swale to Ranger, Ben and Willcox, who were closest to the oncoming herd. "Hey, boys!" He pointed. "Let's push back on that before they can mix theirs with ours!" The three horsemen wheeled around their mounts and started off to intercept.

"There ain't gonna be no fight, is there?" Gilbertson asked in his whiny voice. "I ain't never had to shoot at a man b'fore."

Nate reined his horse closer. "Well, I ain't neither, Ross, but let's don't let these fellows know that. Come on!" He put his heels to Dakah and raced around the herd to follow Ranger, Ben, and Willcox. Al, Billy, and Dudley did the same.

Gilbertson yelled to their backs. "Somebody's got to watch this herd! Guess it'll be me!"

By the time Nate's men came together at the front of the encroaching herd, Adstile's men had dropped back and formed a flank at the rear. These men were slapping coils of rope against their chaps and keeping up a constant barking of commands to keep the animals moving. Nate and his men, despite their efforts to shunt the beeves away, could not turn the headstrong march of hooves, and they watched helplessly as the two herds intermingled.

Al called out to Nate. "That's what I call 'startin' a fight'!"

When Nate saw Dudley checking his pistol loads, he cupped a hand beside his mouth and yelled to all his men, "Don't start nothin'. I'll do the talkin'."

Adstile and his men reined up ten yards away. Nate walked his horse forward, and Billy Hill came alongside him. Nate stopped when Dakah was nose to nose with Adstile's gray.

"What're you playin' at?" Nate said.

Adstile put on an innocent smile beneath his sly eyes. "Didn't you say this strip was big enough for both of us?"

"Git yore cattle outta my herd," Nate ordered.

"Why, sure," Adstile replied, a twinkle of amusement showing in his eyes. He looked to either side at his crew. "Let's go, boys! Move 'em back to the main herd!"

Adstile's cowhands hesitated, some looking at one another and others staring down at their hands. That was when Nate recognized Nick Ray sitting his big bay among Adstile's men. Nick removed his hat and scratched the top of his curly-haired head with the same hand.

"Mister Adstile," Nick said in a subservient drawl, "this ain't hardly right to—"

"Do what I told you!" Adstile snapped.

The drovers went into motion—all but Nick Ray—and

positioned themselves around the mixed herd. But instead of weaving into the cattle to separate brands, they remained on the periphery and pointed their horses south as they whooped and whistled and slapped their ropes against leather. When they got the animals moving, the entire mass started away from the swale toward Adstile's main herd.

Nate drew his carbine from its scabbard and raced Dakah to the front. Billy pulled his rifle and followed. Then came Al and Dudley, each with a Winchester in hand. When Nate spun his mustang around to face the leaders of the herd, he raised his rifle, muzzle to the sky, and called out to Adstile's men in a loud and commanding voice.

"Turn 'em back!"

Billy came at the leaders from the side and forced them into a veer that quickly spiraled into itself. Ben and Willcox assisted at the flanks. Adstile's men reined up and did nothing.

Al walked his horse next to Adstile's with his rifle propped across the bow of his saddle and loosely aimed in the cattleman's direction. The Winchester and the expression on Al's face had a numbing effect on Adstile's mouth. He simply glared at Nate and quietly fumed.

Nate called out to Adstile's idle cowhands. "I'd be obliged if you boys would help us cut out my cattle!" Nate pointed to the lush, low ground behind the herd. "We're gonna drive mine back into that swale yonder."

Nate's crew pushed into the herd and began singling out every steer, cow, and calf with a double-diamond brand seared into its hide. They began a chorus of roundup calls and whistles, nudging Nate's cattle back toward the swale. Needing both their hands for reins and ropes, none of Nate's working crew wielded a weapon, but each man's holstered pistol was close at hand. Nick Ray nosed his bay into the crowd of beeves and began helping. Willcox and Gilbertson lingered at the periphery of the herd and watched.

Adstile was like a pot trying not to boil over. "Get the hell out of there!" he yelled to Ray. "I gave you an order!" he barked. "Now I expect—"

Abruptly, he quieted and glanced down at the rifle muzzle pressing into his ribs. He turned to Al but could not form a word on his lips. Closing his mouth, he swallowed as his color transformed from ruddy-pink to a sickly pale.

"You'd best keep yore mouth shut, while we sort out Nate's stock," Al said. When Adstile started to reply, Al jabbed the rifle barrel harder into the man's side. "Just shut up!"

Adstile's other men sat their horses and pretended not to see the altercation. Most simply looked out toward the Big Horns and waited out the time. No one other than Ray offered to help, but neither did anyone try to object. Gilbertson and Willcox began to work the herd with the others but kept their distance from the Adstile crew.

Half an hour later, when Nate's herd was up to the proper count and left to graze in the swale, Al backed his buckskin away from Adstile and rejoined his crew. Nate took his horse in a direct line toward the flustered cattleman, who was ordering his men to take up their positions around the splinter herd to drive them back to the south. When Nate pulled up so close that their knees were touching, Adstile stopped talking in midsentence and went still.

"You can take yore cattle back now," Nate said, his voice as pleasant as if they were packing up after a picnic.

Adstile sneered. "And you can keep that one!" he spat and pointed at Nick Ray. He kicked his gray into motion and started around his herd. When he was far enough from Nate to muster some courage, he twisted around awkwardly in his saddle and screamed with such force that his voice screeched like a woman's. "Frank Canton will hear about this! You'll regret this day, Champion!"

Nate turned Dakah for the swale and took her at a walk toward his friends. The cattle tore at the grass and chewed peacefully. Nick Ray was talking and laughing with the boys—all but Ross, who walked his horse toward Nate and reined up, his face as pale as pasteboard.

"Damn, Nate...I thought for sure we were gonna git into it!" Gilbertson's wide-open eyes darted back and forth, as if he could not decide which of Nate's eyes to look at.

"Tell me, Ross," Nate said quietly, "did you feel like we were in the wrong?"

"No!" Gilbertson insisted. "It's just that I ain't never been in a gunfight b'fore."

Nate nodded. "Well, if ever you do, just make sure yo're in the right."

Chapter Twenty

It was the last night of October and the end of the six workdays that Ross Gilbertson had promised Nate for the fall branding. Both men were tired after putting in extra hours to finish the job. Too worn out to cook a proper meal, they had settled for jerky and coffee and the last of the buttermilk pie that Kate Tisdale had sent out by Al the day before. Ross sat on his bunk and wrestled off his boots in the cramped cabin.

"I should'a rode back into town this evenin'," Ross announced in his usual plaintive tone of voice. "First cold night we've had this season." Pursing his lips, he looked around the small, low-ceiled room with a scowl creasing the skin around his eyes. "I'm wonderin' how old man Hall lived out here in this little pea pod of a shack all by his-self. There ain't hardly enough room in here for a man to stretch his arms." He shook his head and huffed. "An' two men! Lord! I ain't so sure we oughta try an' take in a breath at the same time."

Dressed in his light union suit, Nate lay on top of his bunk, his back propped against the wall, as he scratched with a pencil inside his leather book. Tucked into his ribs, the cat purred, its faint ticking as steady as a clock. Nate laid the pencil inside the book and closed it.

"If yo're gonna suggest we take turns breathin'," Nate said, "I reckon you'll need to sleep out with the horses."

Ross pushed his boots under his bed. In the stark glow of the oil lamp, he looked to Nate like an old man with his new crop of whiskers creeping all over the lower part of his face. Ross frowned as Nate set his book next to the oil lamp on top of the cold wood heater.

"Nate, what is that you're writin' ever' night?"

"Letter," Nate said as he plumped his pillow. Then he stretched out on his back.

"Must be a long one," Ross guessed. When Nate made no reply, Ross stared at the metal stove with a longing slant to his eyes. "Ain't we gonna have a fire?"

Nate crossed his legs at the ankles, angled his elbows north and south, and laced his fingers behind his head. "We will if yo're the one to build it," Nate said. "I'm too tired."

Ross seemed to consider this option for a time, but Nate knew that it was just for show.

"Well, cain't we at least close the door for once't?"

"That's a two-man job," Nate explained. "One to lift up the foot o' my bed an' the other'n to shut the door."

"I'm game if you are," Ross said.

Nate rolled out of his bunk and levered his bed up so high that the cat made a graceful leap to Ross's bunk. Ross forced the door on its hinges as it scraped across the floor.

"There ain't no latch!" Ross complained.

Nate lowered the bed and returned to the warm indentation he had left in the mattress. "Just lift up and push it," Nate said. "The floor will hold it shut."

The scrape of the door produced a little chirp of friction as the boards squeezed into the jamb. Ross sidled between the beds, sat on his mattress, and stripped down for sleep.

"Whatta you call this cat, Nate? If she's gonna sleep with me, I oughta know 'er name."

"'Dory,'" Nate said quietly.

Ross's face wrinkled like a balled-up rag. "You named 'er for the door?"

Nate shook his head. "Short for Dorothy."

After crawling under his blanket, Ross wiggled around endlessly to get comfortable. When, finally, he got quiet, Nate looked at the hunch in Ross's back under his bed cover.

"You gonna blow out that lamp?" Nate asked.

Ross's only reply was a soft snore. Sitting up to snuff the light, Nate noticed that, when he had lifted the bed, his pistol belt had slid off the corner of the bedframe. Reaching down, he hooked the belt in place again, but it fell to the floor. Yawning, he pulled his Colt's from its holster and slipped it under the edge of his pillow. Then, leaning over the cold wood heater, he cupped a hand behind the top of the lamp shield and blew down to the flame. The room went dark as tar.

After peeling back his blanket, Nate settled in and covered himself. Outside the cabin, the trickle of the creek could barely be heard, and a few sluggish cricket chirrs announced the coming of the cooler weather. From the other bed, Ross's snore and the cat's purr wove together in an odd duet of strange bedfellows.

Reaching out for the top of the heater, Nate felt his way to the book and rested his hand upon its cover. "G'night," he breathed, his voice as soft as a downy feather floating on a breeze.

———

It was still dark when Nate awoke. The cat lay curled up against his thigh. Ross's quiet snoring was regular now, but rather than being intrusive, his breathing was dry and airy like a pulsing wind trying to pry through a crack in the wall. Gently placing his hand on the cat's spine, Nate stroked her silky fur and felt the fragile bone structure beneath her skin. Closing his eyes, Nate allowed for a little more time in bed, sinking just below the surface of sleep, like a fishing float bobbing at the top of a lake.

When Nate's eyes opened again, the cat was on the floor, standing alert between the beds and staring at the door. He assumed the movement of the cat had dredged him up from sleep. There was just enough light coming through the window to define the individual objects in the room. Ross slept, oblivious to the world. Nate stared and listened. From outside came the subtle crunch of weeds in front of the cabin. The sounds were close and stealthy.

The boards of the door strained as if a powerful wind were trying to push inside, but there was no wind. When the door squeaked on the jamb, Ross woke up with a start and mumbled, "What?" The door squealed as it flew open and banged against the foot of Nate's bed so forcefully that a crack in one of the boards could be heard.

The dark silhouettes of two men filled the doorway, one behind the other, their shapes carved out from the pale lavender sky of the nascent dawn. Behind them, a third man tried to peer over their shoulders.

"We got you now, boys!" someone yelled. "May as well give it up!"

Nate squinted, trying to identify a face, but all he could make out was the glint of gunmetal. "Who are you?!" he demanded. "What the hell do you wont!"

With the light from the window creeping in, Nate felt like a fish in a barrel. Pretending to stretch his arms, he reached under the pillow and gripped the wooden handle of his Colt's. Before he could pull it out, two gunshots exploded from the doorway. Despite the magnified sound in the tiny room, Nate heard the bullets whine through the air and slap into the wall behind him. The left side of his face stung from powder burn. The cat leapt up onto the other bed, and Ross made a high-pitched yelp that cut through the echo of the gunfire like the scream of a hawk.

Cocking the hammer, Nate brought up the Colt's in a smooth fashion and leveled the barrel at the midsection of the black outlines crowded in the doorway. When he fired, he heard a wheezing sound like a man taking a solid punch to the abdomen. Then it was all scraping boots and flying elbows as the intruders scrambled to retreat. Nate fired again out the door.

Gilbertson was balled up at the head of his bed trying to squeeze into the corner of the cabin. Gun in hand, Nate stepped up on of Ross's bed and peered out the window. In the growing light he saw a man bent over, hobbling away as he held both hands to his stomach.

Easing to the doorway, Nate peeked around the frame but saw no one out in the brush. A Winchester rifle lay in the weeds just two yards away, and Nate made an instant decision to use it for its better accuracy over his pistol. Hurrying outside, he picked up the rifle, and right away a man jumped out from behind the corner of the cabin and swung a shotgun to his shoulder. There was enough light for Nate to see the man's face but not enough time to work the lever on the Winchester, not with so much scattershot about to come his way. He sprang for the door and made it to safety, surprised that the would-be assassin did not fire.

"What the hell's goin' on?" Ross whispered.

Nate ignored the question and listened for sounds outside. The man with the shotgun was moving away from the cabin, crashing through the brush, arguing with someone ahead of him.

"Git yore boots on!" Nate whispered to Ross. Setting down the rifle, he pulled on his trousers, sat on his bed, and tugged on his boots. Then he sat on the bed and tugged on his boots.

"Who the hell *are* they?" Ross whined.

Nate pointed beneath Ross's bed. "Git yore boots on! Now!"

Ross sat and began fumbling with his boots. His face was as pale as chalk.

"What're we 'bout to do, Nate?"

Thinking about the light color of his long johns, Nate donned his plaid blouse. He stuffed his Colt's into the waistband of his trousers and picked up the Winchester. Then he snatched up the box of matches from the top of the wood stove.

"I hit one o' them buzzards. We're goin' after the others!"

"The others?" Ross echoed. "How many was there?"

"Three that I know of...maybe more," Nate said. "Come on! Git yore pistol an' let's go!"

They followed the worn path that led down to the creek, and there among the bare-limbed willows they found a pile of overcoats stacked on a trunk-sized boulder. Nate went through them one by one, checking pockets, and then throwing each to the ground.

"Four of 'em," he whispered. After listening for a several seconds, Nate knelt to one knee and struck a match against the receiver plate of the rifle. Holding the flame to hover six inches above the ground, he studied the fresh signs of boot heels and rocks displaced from their natural depressions in the earth. He pointed to a gully across the creek. "That way!"

As Nate rose up, Ross grabbed Nate's shirt sleeve at the elbow. "Should we be doin' this?" Ross whispered, his voice raspy and desperate. "Four o' them an' only two o' us?"

Feeling Ross's hand quivering, Nate knew that, in reality, the odds were closer to four against *one*. "I wont you to ride to the Red Fork an' tell Al Allison and John Tisdale what's happ'ned. See if you can find Ranger Jones too...an' Jack Flagg."

Ross shook his head. "I ain't goin' nowhere without you!"

Nate took Ross by the arm and squeezed to get his attention. "You can do this, Ross."

Ross began shaking his head. "It ain't me I'm worried about. It's *you*...out here alone...amongst there-ain't-no-tellin' how many killers. You got to come with me, Nate."

"I hit one with my pistol," Nate returned. "That's gonna slow 'em down. I wanna git to 'em b'fore they can disappear."

Ross grabbed both of Nate's arms and shook him once. "Listen to me! You an' me both know I ain't no fighter, but you ain't thinkin' straight about this, Nate! You'll be the one to disappear! You don't know what's out there a-waitin' on you!"

When Nate turned his head to glare at the gully, the fire in his belly told him to follow those men now. Ross tightened his grip on Nate and shook him again.

"Think about why they come out here in the night like this, Nate! They come for *you*! You go up that gully, an' you might be playin' right into their hands."

Nate took a deep breath of the brisk morning air, and it was like throwing water onto a campfire. "Yo're right," he conceded. "We'll ride together an' git some help."

Inside the cabin, the acrid scent of spent gunpowder still hung in the air. As Ross pulled on his clothes, he looked around the small room.

"Where's your cat?"

Nate strapped on his gun belt. "Prob'ly hidin' out in the grass somewhere."

Ross stared at the wall above the head of Nate's bed. "I'll be damned!" he said. "Your paintin' got shot up!"

Nate turned to see two holes punched into Dory's painting. One had gouged the canopy of the oak tree, and the other had plowed into the grass just below Peaches.

"Come on!" Nate ordered. "Let's go!"

When they left the cabin, there was enough light to show large dollops of fresh blood on the ground. "Some-b'dy was sure 'nough hit purty bad," Ross said. "It's a miracle you ain't hit, Nate. You kept a cool head, son."

Nate led the way to the horse shed, where they saddled up and mounted. Ross pointed to one of the rafters.

"Yonder's your cat," he said. "She don't look hurt."

Nate turned to see a ball of gray fur wedged above a rafter in the corner of the shed. He spun Dakah around to point northeast.

"You ready?"

Ross pushed his hat down tightly on his head. "I'm ready."

The two horsemen started north and broke out into the open country that was shedding its gray darkness for the colors of a new day.

Chapter Twenty-One

W hen the two riders reached the Red Fork, Ross agreed to ride on to Buffalo and report the attack to Sheriff Angus, while Nate turned upstream for the Tisdale place. Along the way, he stopped at Ranger Jones's homestead and then at Jack Flagg's ranch, lingering at each place only long enough to raise the alarm about assassins in the area.

Riding hard into the Tisdale yard, he found the windows of the house lit up as well as a soft, yellow light shining from inside the barn. Nate swung down from his saddle even before Dakah had come to a halt. Leading the mustang by the reins, he jogged to the barn entrance just as Al Allison emerged carrying a pitchfork.

"What're you in such a hurry 'bout?" Al asked, his eyes already bracing for bad news.

"Four men attacked my place at dawn. Busted in through the door and started shootin'. I'm gonna need some men to go after 'em with me. Is John at the house?"

Al propped the pitchfork against the barn. "Yeah, come on."

As they hurried to the house, Al asked, "Who were they?"

Nate shook his head. "It was purty dark, but I recognized Joe Elliott well enough."

On the porch, before going inside, Al looked up and down along the length of Nate. "You didn't git hit, did you?"

"I was lucky, but one o' them boys is carrying my bullet in his gut."

As soon as they entered the house, Nate smelled salt pork cooking and heard the voices of children and the *clink* and *clack* of silverware and plates. Stepping into the kitchen, Nate saw Kate standing at the stove, while the rest of the Tisdale family was gathered at the table. All eyes turned his way, and Nate took off his hat and nodded.

"Some men tried to kill Nate this mornin'," Al announced as he came into the room.

John removed the napkin tucked into his collar and dropped it on the white linen tablecloth. "Are you hurt?" he said, rising from his chair.

"No," Nate replied, "I'm aw-right."

"Nate plugged one of 'em in the brisket," Al said, his voice taking on a ring of pride.

Moving behind a wicker bassinet nestled in a chair at the table, Kate cleared her throat and gave Al what appeared to be a practiced look of censure. "Perhaps you three should talk outside while the children have their breakfast."

"Oh, yeah," Al mumbled and looked down at the toes of his boots.

John leaned to her. "Sorry, hon," he murmured and kissed his wife on her cheek. "Let me just talk to Nate a few minutes."

Taking Nate by the arm, John led him into the front

room. Al followed. Standing before a bed of dying embers in the hearth, they faced one another in a close triangle.

"Who were they?" John asked quietly.

"Cain't say for sure 'bout three of 'em," Nate admitted, "but one was Joe Elliott. He's a stock detective for the WSGA. An' I figure Mike Shonsey has got his hands in this somewhere." He pointed back in the direction from which he had ridden. "I wanna git after 'em while the tracks are still fresh. One o' them back-shooters is losin' blood, which ought to work in our favor, both in leavin' a trail an' in slowin' 'em down."

John pushed his palms toward Nate. "Just start at the beginning and tell me what happened?"

After Nate finished relating the events of the morning, Al was first to speak. "Yo're damned right we'll go! We'll git Jack Flagg...an' Ranger an' his brother...an' maybe—"

"No!" came a firm voice from the doorway. The three men turned to see Kate Tisdale standing just inside the room. John walked to her and stood before her like a schoolboy getting a scolding from his teacher. The two of them exchanged whispery words, and there was no doubt as to who was holding sway over the hushed conversation.

When Kate spun around and returned to the kitchen, John walked slowly back to Nate and Al and shook his head. "She's right. I can't be leaving my family here alone with unknown assassins in the area. Not after what happened with that WSGA detective yesterday."

"Whatta you mean?" Nate said.

"A man named Cannon came out to where I was checking on the cattle at the river. He was very clear about his threats to all of us here on the Red Fork. It didn't seem to matter to him one bit that I have a legal patent to this land, just like everyone else does on the Red."

Al's face hardened as he stared at his brother. "You didn' tell me nothin' 'bout that!"

John turned sober eyes on Al. "I didn't want you running off half-cocked. This man was dead serious, and I didn't doubt his ultimatum. I've never seen such danger in a man's eyes."

Al's face was livid. "That was that damned Frank Canton! Prob'ly one o' them that tried to ambush Nate this mornin'." Al glared out the front window, the tendons in his jaw flexing rock-hard. "God...dam...Canton!" Al hissed. "He's throwed his weight 'round here too long to suit me. He just plain needs killin'!"

John poked a finger at his half brother. "See there! That's why I didn't want to tell you."

"Canton was sher'ff b'fore you moved here," Nate explained to John. "Now he works for the WSGA an' carries 'bout the same legal standin' as he did wearin' the county badge."

"He was a damned outlaw in Texas!" Al added. "Was in Huntsville the same time I was there! He was doin' time for ev'ry crime in the books." Al swung away from John to clasp Nate's shoulder. "I'll go with you right now! Just let me round up my arsenal."

When Al started away, Nate stopped him with a word. "No!"

Al twisted at the waist and showed the hurt in his eyes. "What?"

"Kate's right," Nate said in an even voice. "The both o' you need to be here. This family needs protectin'." Nate nodded to Al. "It's yore family too. We don't know what else might be in the works today."

Al turned and frowned at the floor. "Well, hell-fire! Maybe yo're right."

"What are you going to do?" John asked Nate.

Nate moved to the front window and peered out at Dakah waiting at the barn. "Gilbertson rode into town to fetch Red Angus. I'll go out an' meet 'im. If he's brought some help with 'im, we'll ride out to where them bushwhackers took off from my place. See if we cain't catch up to 'em." Nate raised the hat in his hand and fanned it toward the kitchen doorway. "Tell Kate I'm real sorry I barged in like this. I hope I didn' upset yore children."

John waved the notion away. "You just be careful out there, Nate. No matter what happens, don't go after those men by yourself. You've got to promise me."

"Aw-right," Nate said and fitted his hat to his head. "There's a reason Canton came out to see you in particular, John. Yo're smart. Good with words. That's somethin' he prob'ly fears if you was to git a article into the newspaper. People tend to listen to smart folks."

John started to speak, but Nate went on.

"My point is...we're gonna need you not just for yore words...but also for yore strategies. It's pow'rful men we're up against. We're gonna need to outmaneuver 'em somehow."

"Two of the cattle barons in the WSGA are United States senators," John warned. "That means they have the ear of the president."

Al leaned toward John and tapped a finger on his brother's shirtfront. "What 'bout that Easterner you worked for in the Dakotas? He's in the gov'ment, ain't he?"

"Mister Roosevelt?" John said and shook his head. "He has only a minor position."

Al pulled up on the waistband of his trousers and grabbed his hat off the table by the front door. "I'm gonna saddle up an' ride down to Ranger's spread. I'll git him an' Johnny to come up here. Then I'll go down to Flagg's an' talk him into joinin' us. We'll have us a war council."

"I'll do that," Nate said. "I'm goin' right by there anyway. You stay here with yore brother. I'll let the both o' you know how things go."

———

When Nate left the Red Fork, he rode northeast across trackless country, forded the North Fork of the Powder at Three Willows, and cut the road to Buffalo just below the Carey Ranch. Expecting to intercept Sheriff Angus's posse at any time, he kept a sharp eye out to the north, but at the same time he kept up his guard in all directions.

Two miles north of the TA Ranch, a lone rider came into view on the road up ahead. The man came to a halt four hundred yards away. Sitting his horse on the rise in the road, the rider and his mount were silhouetted against the gray-blue sky. Where the man's long dark coat parted in front, a vertical strip of white shirt showed. Nothing else about the man could be discerned, but the horse appeared to have white socks on its rear legs only.

As Nate came on at an easy lope, the distant horseman turned around and disappeared behind the swell of the rise. When Nate reached the spot where the man had reversed directions, he saw no one on the open, rolling land before him. The road was dry and, like all well-traveled thoroughfares, was difficult to read for tracks. Nate slid his rifle from its scabbard and carried it across the bow of his saddle just behind the horn. For the next few miles, he saw only grazing cattle in the grasslands and idly soaring vultures in the sky.

As he entered the edge of town, Nate pushed his Winchester down into its leather sheath and walked Dakah down the middle of Main Street. Moving his head left and then right in a slow, methodical arc, he eyed the boardwalks and checked each shop and building that comprised the business district of Buffalo. The moderate foot traffic on the sidewalks gave the impression of citizens going about their daily routines, oblivious to the crimes that were committed out on the range.

When he came abreast of Hertzman's Tailor Shop, Nate saw Frank Canton smoking a cigar and leaning a shoulder into the front window frame. Canton was dressed in a long overcoat over a white shirt and broad string tie. His hat was in his hand. Standing next to Canton, Joe Elliott hunched a shoulder as he pushed a hand into a leather glove, then reversed the maneuver to pull on the other glove. Elliott wore canvas work pants and a heavy wool vest over a light-gray blouse. Strapped around his waist was a cartridge belt heavily laden with ammunition. The butt of his pistol rode high on his hip. As he usually did, Joe Elliott presented the brooding face of a killer. From the shade of the awning, both men followed Nate's progress with their eyes as they continued to converse in low tones.

Nate pulled up and reined Dakah around to face the two men. With the slightest movement of his hips, he coaxed the mustang forward three staggered steps. Lowering his right arm to hang loosely by his side, he sat his horse and eyed the two range detectives.

"New coat?" Nate said, looking directly at Canton.

Frank Canton donned his hat and turned to face Nate. He raised his cigar to his mouth and sucked in his cheeks. The brick of ash brightened to red, and Nate noticed that, though Canton had brought up the cigar with his right hand, he now removed it with his left. Taking two steps toward Nate, the tall detective crossed the width of the boardwalk and stood in full light. When he stopped and spread his boots, his eyes remained as dead as nail heads hammered into seasoned oak.

"That's right," Canton replied.

"Looks so new, you might'a bought it this mornin'."

Canton never blinked. "Might have."

Nate nodded. "Cost you a pretty penny, I'll wager." When Canton made no reply, Nate put a little edge into his voice. "Too bad you didn' check with me. I recently come into a pile o' overcoats I got no use for."

Canton reached forward and flicked the ash from his cigar into the street. His right hand came up and loosely gripped the front of his open coat.

"Why should I check with you about anything?"

Still standing by the door of the tailor shop, Elliott laughed quietly. Nate turned his attention to him and raised his chin to the man.

"How 'bout you, Elliott. You needin' a new coat too?"

Joe Elliott's morose glare crystallized as if he had been challenged, but he remained in the shade, seemingly content to glare at Nate from a distance.

Nate nodded to the south. "What happ'ned back there, Joe? D'you lose yore nerve with that scattergun when I wouldn' give you my back?"

Nate could feel the animosity radiating from Elliott's face. The man appeared to be wound up so tightly that he had trouble forming a word on his tongue.

"You boys must'a got up mighty early this mornin'," Nate said in a flat monotone.

Canton took another draw on his cigar and let the smoke creep lazily from his mouth. "Early bird gets the worm," he said with a sputter of smoke.

Nate's face showed nothing. "Except when it don't."

Canton pushed the cigar forward as if conceding the point. With the movement, a trail of smoke curled from his cigar like a gray snake that slithered up through the air.

"What's your herd count up to now, Champion?" Canton said.

Nate held Canton's gaze. "Don't see how my numbers concern you."

Canton flicked ashes again. "And that's where you'd be wrong."

"How do you figure that?" Nate said.

"We know how all you small ranchers acquire your stock."

Nate slowly straightened in his saddle and flattened his right hand upon his thigh just in front of his holstered Colt's. "If yo're callin' me a thief, say it outright 'stead o' coming at me from 'round the corner..." He nodded toward Elliott. "...Like yore friend there does."

Canton could not be ruffled. "From what I hear...all these squatters who play at being cattlemen...they hold you in high esteem. They seem to look to you for leadership." His eyes darkened to onyx. "Guess that makes you the king of rustlers in Johnson County." He pointed the cigar at Nate. "Is that direct enough for you?"

"Who put those words in yore mouth? Fred Hesse? Or one of the other WSGA royalty who pays yore wages."

Frank Canton raised the cigar to his mouth and brought the ash to a searing red glow. Lowering the cigar, he blew a steady stream of smoke toward Nate.

Nate heard half a dozen horses come trotting up the street and slow to a stop behind him. Canton fixed his beady eyes on the party just arrived. Nate kept his attention on the two men standing before him and resigned himself to a plan. If this standoff went over the edge, he would kill Canton first and then Elliott.

"Nate?" said a familiar voice. "Gilbertson told me what happened. You all right?"

"I'm finc, Sher'ff," Nate replied without turning. "Not a scratch on me. It appears the cowards who came after me got a little rattled an' were off their game."

Red Angus coaxed his horse forward beside Nate and addressed the two men on the boardwalk. "Where were you two this morning just before dawn?"

Canton clamped the cigar in his teeth and began buttoning his new overcoat. "We were down at George Hobson's Saloon all morning, Sheriff...goin' over a list of complaints from some of the big outfits. Seems there's been a rise in rustling lately in Johnson County."

Angus made a nondescript humming sound in his chest. "What about you, Elliott?"

"What *about* me? Frank just told you."

"'Except that was a lie," Nate said calmly. "You were skulkin' 'round my place near Hole in the Wall at dawn. We were standin' 'bout as close as you an' me are right now."

Elliott huffed a laugh. "It's dark at dawn. Maybe you saw somebody who might'a looked like me." He turned his smirk to Angus. "I been in town with Frank all mornin'."

"Can anybody else verify that?"

Frank Canton gazed down the street. "Oh, I s'pose six or seven men can vouch for us. Why don't you go down and ask George. He was there."

Red turned in his saddle and spoke to his deputy. "Roles, go down to Hobson's and check on that." When he turned back to Canton and Elliott, the sheriff spoke with the melody of sarcasm. "We'll just all wait right here and waste our time together."

Nate kept his eyes on Canton as he spoke. "Sher'ff, the men who attacked me left in a hurry...left a pile o' over-coats down by the creek." He pointed with his chin toward Canton. "Looks like Canton here has been shop-pin' for new clothes this mornin'."

Red Angus studied Canton's coat and made a humming sound in his throat. "I'd like to see those coats, Nate. We'll ride out there with you and see what else we can find. I hear you put a hole in one of your visitors. Gilbertson told me there's a lot o' blood out in the brush."

Angus eyed Canton. "Any of your assistants got a new hole in 'im, Frank?"

"Wouldn't know," Canton said.

"What about Billy Lykins and Fred Coates? Seen them this mornin'?"

Canton sucked on his cigar and exhaled, staring at Angus through a skein of smoke. "Can't say I have, Sheriff."

"'Can't' or 'won't'?"

Canton pursed his lips. "Pretty much the same, ain't they?"

"Found this too," Nate said, patting the stock of the rifle in his saddle scabbard. "Thirty-six caliber Winchester." He watched Canton's face carefully. "Looks a lot like the one I seen you carry in yore saddle boot."

Staring into Nate's eyes, Canton would not look at his lost rifle.

"Where'd you put up your horse, Frank?" the sheriff asked.

Canton remained as cool as a banker turning down a man for a loan. "Well, if you mean Old Fred," he said, "he's at my place south of town."

Angus frowned. "You mean to say you walked in?"

Canton shook his head. "My wagon is down at Hobson's."

Angus nodded to Elliott. "What about *your* horse?"

Elliott scuffed forward to stand beside Canton. "Right there," he said and extended an arm to point across the street. "That bay gelding. Been there since last night."

Angus twisted around in his saddle and studied the horse before turning back to Elliott. "You keep that horse well-groomed, do you?"

Joe Elliott bristled at the question. "'Course I do. I been around horses all my life."

Angus nodded. "When's the last time you brushed that'n down?"

Elliott squinted at the sky. "Last night after I got in from my range duties. Why?"

"Bud?" Angus said to one of his men, "go and check out the bay."

The deputy looked across the street for several seconds, frowned, and then turned back to the sheriff. "What am I lookin' for, Red?"

Angus narrowed his eyes. "See if he's been lathered up recent. Check under the saddle and under the cinch. And comb through the tail to look for pieces of dried brush and seeds and broke stalks and such. Have a look at the hooves too. There's no soft ground here in town on the streets, but a horse fordin' streams is gonna pack some mud around the frog."

Elliott snorted. "Be sure to check up his ass too. See what he had for supper last night."

Canton threw his cigar into the street. "I think we're done here," he announced. "If you wanna talk to us some more, we'll be down at Hobson's."

Canton started north up the street in a slow and confident stride. Elliott crossed the thoroughfare, untied his horse, and led it as he walked up the street. The deputy named Bud hurried back to report to Sheriff Angus.

"Sher'ff, that bay might as well a' slept in the hotel last night and then visited the tonsorial parlor this mornin'. There ain't a drop o' sweat or a speck o' mud on that animal. Looks like he got all dressed up just to stand on the street and be admired by folks passin' by."

Angus narrowed his eyes at the two detectives disappearing up the street. "They didn't use their regular mounts," he growled out of the side of his mouth." He turned solemn eyes to Nate. "They planned this thing down to the finest detail. Only thing they didn't plan on was you being hard to kill."

Then Deputy Roles returned and reined up his horse before the sheriff. "George Hobson and six other men swear that Canton and Elliott come into the saloon well before dawn and spent hours goin' over some papers together. Said they never left the room till about a half hour ago."

"You know these men, Howard?"

Howard Roles allowed a smirk. "Two of 'em work for Hesse and two others for the CY. I didn' know the others. Just a coupla saddlers fillin' up on free beer."

Red Angus turned to Nate. "Let's go out to your place and see what we can find."

"Where's Ross Gilbertson?" Nate asked.

As an answer, Angus just shook his head, but Roles supplied the information. "He was a might shook up. Said he was gonna head up to the sutler's store at Fort McKinney. But I think he was gonna try an' get a bed at the infirmary. He did look a bit peaked."

Sheriff Angus reined his horse to point south. "Let's go, boys," he called out, and he and Nate led the posse down the street at a gallop.

Chapter Twenty-Two

Back at Hall's cabin, Nate walked the posse men through the events of the morning's ambush and led the way down to the rock where the overcoats still lay in a heap on the ground. Not far from the creek, they found the tracks of four horses, where the attackers had left their mounts behind a shield of large boulders.

Next to a crate-sized rock, Nate spotted three cigarette stubs pressed into the dirt by the heel of a boot. All over the area, the sparse tufts of grass had been trampled like a dirty woven mat. Dismounting, Nate picked up what was left of one of the cigarettes, studied the singed paper, and then held it out to the sheriff.

"I reckon this is where somebody held the horses," Nate said and pointed at the base of the largest boulder. "Whoever it was I shot...he sat right there. That's blood on the rock."

Angus nodded and then turned to his deputy. "Lotta rocky ground out here. Howard, circle around and see if you can cut their trail."

After ten minutes of circling the boulders on an increasingly wider radius, Deputy Roles called out for the others. By the time the posse had joined him, Roles was crouching in the grass, his head low and turned on its side. "They came right through here. Looks like they've bound leather to their horses' hooves." He pointed west toward the headwaters of Beaver Creek. "The ground gets to be solid rock over that way. If I was on the run an' wantin' to leave no trail, that's the way I'd go."

They followed the creek for a quarter mile, with Roles out front looking for signs. Where the canyon narrowed to a span of twenty feet, they pulled together to talk strategy.

"There's no outlet where this canyon heads up," Roles informed the group. "The creek springs up from the rocks at the base of the slopes. To climb outta there with a horse would be near to impossible." He pointed north. "We know they got back to town, so they're bound to a' chose that d'rection."

For three miles they moved along the east side of the east palisade of Hole in the Wall, until the presence of grazing herds around the North Fork of the Powder made tracking too difficult. After another mile, the riders relaxed their vigil with the tacit understanding that nothing was going to come of this initial search.

"Red?" Nate said as he dropped back to join the sheriff in the rear. He pulled the .38 Winchester from his saddle scabbard and held it out to Angus. "D'you think you can trace this to Canton?" He kept holding out the rifle, but the sheriff just shook his head.

"No way in hell. I might can find out when and to where the company shipped it off to, but storekeepers don't keep records of their customer sales. You keep that'n. You earned it."

Nate pushed the rifle back into his scabbard. "I'll be headin' back to my place now."

Angus frowned. "Why don't you stay in town tonight?"

Nate shook his head. "I'll be aw-right."

When Nate reined his horse around, Angus called to his back, "Stay sharp, son."

———

As night fell over the Hole in the Wall pastures, the thin arc of the moon hung low over the Big Horns. When Nate dismounted at the horse shed, the cat mewled from the rafters. She jumped down to the saddle rail and waited as Nate tended to Dakah in the dying light.

Inside the cabin, Nate lighted a fire in the wood stove and prepared a meal. The cat curled up on Gilbertson's bed and quickly fell asleep. As Nate sat on his own bed and ate, he considered the ploy used by Sumner Beach down on the Sweetwater, keeping a fire inside the cabin but sleeping outside in the trees behind a blind of brush. It was either that or ride over to John Tisdale's house and let the midnight assassins waste their time stalking up on a cat in an otherwise empty shack.

In the end he followed the streak of defiance that burned inside him and decided to remain in the cabin. After sawing three boards, each to a three-foot length, he tacked them to the window frame with hammer and nails. Then he slid his bedframe against the door and laid out his weapons where they were easily accessible. By the time he had arranged his defenses, he almost welcomed the idea of the cowards returning.

After lighting the oil lamp, he pulled off his boots, stretched out on his mattress, and wrote to Dory of all that had happened that day. He wrote it as if she were still alive, and so he took care to phrase the words in such a way that she would not worry about him.

An hour passed as he sipped coffee and chronicled the day. Then he set the book aside and thought about finding another claim to rent, one with a cabin more suited to staving off the cold of winter as well as the approaches of unwanted visitors. He had heard that the Nolan cabin at the KC Ranch was available. It was four times larger and had windows on all sides.

As he downed the last of his coffee, Nate stilled himself and listened to the sound of hoofbeats out on the prairie. Two horses coming from the northeast. There was nothing stealthy about the approach. The horses came to a halt out front, snorting and jangling their bridles. Nate set down his cup, picked up the new Winchester, and quietly levered a round into the chamber. Putting his back to the wall, he aimed at the door and waited.

"Nate! It's me! Billy Hill! Me and Nick Ray need to talk to you. Are you in there?"

Nate lowered the hammer to the safety click and set the rifle on the bed. "I got the door barricaded," he called out. "Gimme a minute!"

By the time he wrestled the bed aside and opened the door, the cat had retreated under Ross's bed. Billy stooped through the doorway and bustled inside, bringing the cool of the night with him. He took off his hat, looked around at the tiny room, and tossed the hat on Nate's bed. Then he pulled out of his coat and threw it next to the hat.

"Watch yore head, Nick," Billy warned, but Nick thumped his forehead against the low head jamb. His hat fell behind him and rolled outside. When he retrieved it and ducked through a second time, he bumped his head again, this time without the buffer of his hat.

"Damn, Nate!" Nick laughed as he looked around the room. "Who built this place? Leprechauns?" He dropped his hat on Ross's bed.

Nate pushed the door shut, and the three men fairly filled the floor as they stood in the only available space between the beds. Nick Ray—burly fellow that he was—

looked like a bull squeezed into the passenger box of a stagecoach. He carried a set of saddlebags in one hand. After he set these beside his hat, he pulled out of his coat, forcing Nate and Billy to lean away to avoid a fist or an elbow.

"I hear ya gave 'em hell this mornin', Nate," Nick said. "Wish to God I'd been here to lend you a hand."

"Well, I could'a used the help. That's for sure."

Billy cackled at the array of firearms cached around the room and then started talking nonstop like an auctioneer. "Nick's got some information yo're gonna wanna hear, Nate. He's still got friends in the big outfits, and they keep their ears open. He knows the names o' those snakes who came after you this mornin'. There was—"

Nick splayed a hand on Billy's chest, pushing him back a few inches, and the flood of words spewing out of Billy's mouth shut off like a valve had been closed. "I didn' ride all the way out here to listen to you tell it," Nick grumbled. He turned back to Nate, his eyes glowing with excitement. "You know Frank Wolcott? The one they call the Major?"

"Know *of* 'im," Nate said. "He's the one that give Sumner Beach a hard time down on the Sweetwater."

Nick began nodding and licking his lips. "Well, he's just about top dog in the WSGA, an' he sure as hell knows who *you* are. It ain't just Fred Hesse who's out to git you. Both o' them are the ones who put out the order to have you kilt. They put Frank Canton on that job, an' Canton picked out four others to help 'im." Nick held up a finger for each man he named. "Joe Elliott...Billy Lykins...Fred Coates...and Mike Shonsey." Awaiting a reaction, Nick stared at Nate with his four fingers still held out between them.

"Those are the ones I figured for it," Nate said.

"It was Lykins that you gut-shot," Billy added. "He's holed up somewhere...dyin'."

Nate inhaled deeply and let out the air in a rush. Looking at the intensity in Nick's face, Nate knew that there was more news.

"'Member that feller Willcox you had with you that day you put it over on Adstile? He weren't workin' for you, Nate, even though you thought he was. He was spyin' for Hesse! He was s'posed to report back 'bout any rustlin' you might be doin'. It just about burned Hesse up to find out you didn't steal nothin' from nobody."

Nate nodded. "Do you think Willcox—or anybody else—would be willin' to testify in court about Canton and his crew o' assassins?"

Nick pursed his lips and shook his head. "Most o' the hired hands are scare't o' Frank Canton. Scare't o' Hesse too." Nick propped his big hands on his hips and looked down at the floor for a moment. When his head came up, he wore the solemn expression of a preacher. "Hell, I'd testify...only it'd be just what I heard from someb'dy else. 'Heresy' I think they call it."

"Heresay," Billy corrected. "Wouldn' be worth a cow patty in court."

"Well, for what it's worth," Nick went on, "Willcox come to me today in Red Angus's saloon. Said he was ashamed about spyin' on ya like he done. Said 'If you wanna find out about the men who attacked you, go up in the Beaver Creek Canyon.' That's all he said."

No one spoke for a time, as each man weighed the veracity of the tip. Then the cat made a wailing whine from under the bed, and Billy grabbed for the pistol in his holster. Nate laid a hand on Billy's wrist, and the three men stood like mannequins in a store window as the cat stalked out from under the bed.

"Don't kill my cat," Nate said quietly.

Embarrassed, Billy straightened and pushed his fingers back through his hair. "Damn!"

Nick laughed. "This cabin got you spooked, boy?"

Billy eyed the interior of the cramped room. "This here is tight livin', Nate. Too tight!"

Nate leaned, picked up the cat, and set her on his bunk. "I may not stay here much longer. I need a place closer to the river."

Nick picked up the saddlebags off the bed, opened a pouch, and pulled out three rattling boxes of cartridges. "From Red Angus. Said you can pay 'im back later." Nick squinted as he read the label. "Winchester, thirty-eight caliber." He set the ammo on the bed.

"That's for the rifle I acquired this mornin'," Nate explained.

Nick closed the pouch and shouldered the saddlebag. "I heard the posse that rode out here today came up empty. Did they go up Beaver Creek?"

"Not all the way," Nate replied. "Did Willcox say anything else 'bout the creek?"

Nick shook his head. "Just to get up there soon as you can."

Billy huffed a warning. "Willcox tricked you once," he argued. "Might be a trap?"

"I'll take some men with me," Nate said.

"When do you wanna go?" Nick asked. "I'll ride with ya!"

Nate nodded his thanks. "My brother, Dudley, is coming out in the mornin'," he said. "He'll bring a few men with 'im. You can stay here tonight, if yo're of a mind."

Nick looked around the cabin. "I'll ride to the KC. It's *you* who oughta stay with *me!*"

The three men were quiet as the fire crackled and the cat purred. Outside, one of the horses nickered and shook its head. Nate was careful not to look at Billy, who had not volunteered to ride with them up Beaver Creek.

"We got to go," Billy announced. "I gotta a lotta work lined up for tomorr'." He grabbed his hat off the bed and slapped it down on his head. Then he put on his coat. "You take care, Nate." He pulled on the crippled door. "Come on, Nick. I got to git up early." The more he pulled on the door, the more it bent and crackled under the strain.

"You got to lift up on it," Nate advised.

While Billy continued to bow the door, Nick stepped next to him and with one hand gripped the edge of the door and lifted. Billy almost fell backward when door swung open. They grabbed their coats and ducked out of the door into the cool night.

"Hey?" Nate called out from the doorway. "I 'preciate you fellows ridin' out here."

Billy mounted his horse and sorted his reins. "You stay sharp, now, Nate."

Nick stepped back to the doorway and lightly slapped Nate's upper arm. "I'll see you in the mornin'."

When the two men rode off into the night, Nate stepped outside to the corner of the cabin where Joe Elliott had thrown down on him with a shotgun. The grasslands were quiet. The moon had sunk beneath the Big Horns, and the sky had opened up to a spectacle of stars that glittered like countless beads of ice clinging to a black buffalo robe.

From inside the cabin, the cat sang out a short, mewling phrase that rose in pitch like a question. Nate went back inside, wrestled with the door, and began arranging the beds again to fort up against the possibility of another attack.

Chapter Twenty-Three

The five horsemen took their mounts at a walk single file along the narrowing trail. They had followed Beaver Creek upstream for half a mile, where a man could stand over the stream and comfortably straddle it with one boot on either side. Due to the ledges of rock protruding from the canyon wall about six or seven feet off the ground, the trail had become problematic for the riders. In some places, the men had to flatten out over their horses' withers and lower their heads beside their animals' necks.

"Just how far are we going up this little crack of a canyon, Nate?" Ranger asked.

Before answering, Nate reined up and waited for all to gather: John Tisdale, Nick Ray, Ranger, and Dudley. "The canyon opens up into a circular room 'bout fifty yards ahead. If we don't find nothin' there, we'll turn around."

"How do you know about this place?" John asked.

"The winter o' the Big Die-Up," Nate said, "I found eleven steers, two cows, an' two calves back here. All of 'em froze up as hard as marble tombstones."

"Hey!" Nick whispered. "You smell that?"

All eyes fixed on the bend of the trail ahead.

"That's smoke!" Ranger said quietly and eased his pistol from the scabbard on his hip. The others did the same.

Nate turned slowly back to his friends, careful not to let the leather of his saddle creak. "Roastin' meat too," he whispered. "Let's go quiet now...on foot."

Nate dismounted and tied his mustang to a small juniper tree growing from a crack in the canyon wall. The others tied their horses to whatever they could find. Nate led the way around a curve in the trail. He could sense the open space ahead where light seemed to gather in the air. Now the woodsmoke could be seen as it climbed the canyon wall.

Inching forward, Nate saw the hindquarters of Mike Shonsey's white mare outfitted with a bedroll behind the saddle. Turning back to Ranger, Nate held up a hand, palm out.

"Wait here," he whispered. "I wanna see how many there are."

With his back to the rock wall, Nate sidled through the shade of a ledge until he could lean forward and peer into the open space ahead. Next to Shonsey's Arab, four bays were picketed to a rope. A canvas tarpaulin—wadded and wrinkled—was stuffed into a crevice in the rock wall. Dressed in a dark wool coat, Shonsey squatted before a campfire with his back to Nate, mumbling something to himself as he ate like a man who had not seen food for days.

Turning back to his friends, Nate leaned past Ranger and whispered to Dudley. "I need you to stay with the horses in case someone comes up behind us."

Indignant, Dudley recoiled his head and glared at his brother. "Like hell I will!"

Nate gripped Dud's upper arm. "Shhh! Quiet down, will you?"

Dudley jerked his arm free. "I ain't stayin' behind! That's all there is to it, Nate!"

Nick Ray butted into their staring contest. "I'll stay with the horses," he said. "Whatta you want me to do if I see riders?"

"Fire off a warnin' shot up into the air, and we'll come a-runnin'."

When Nick started back, Nate slid his Colt's from its holster and edged toward Shonsey. When he stepped into the light of the circular space, he saw that Shonsey was alone. Even after Ranger, John, and Dud had joined Nate, Shonsey was still unaware that he had company. As he babbled to himself, he held up a wooden cooking spit with both hands and sank his teeth into a chunk of skewered meat. His head wagged from side to side, and it became clear that he was trying to eat and sing a song at the same time.

Dudley laughed, and Shonsey spun around quickly, losing his footing. Still holding the spit in his hands, he fell but spared the meat from dropping to the dirt by landing heavily on a shoulder. Sprawled on his belly, he strained to look up to see who had walked up on him.

"Never heard nobody eat an' sing at the same time!" Dudley crowed. "I weren't all that sure it was poss'ble."

Shonsey's face flashed through a number of emotions: first, embarrassment, then anger, and, last, fear. His eyes panned across the group and held fast on Nate.

"Whatta *you* want?" he snarled.

Nate holstered his pistol and walked to Shonsey. He tore the skewer from Shonsey's hands and dropped the meat into the fire. Then he nodded toward Shonsey's hip.

"I want yore gun, for starters," Nate said quietly.

"What?" Shonsey's fleshy face squeezed down into a

web of wrinkles. "You can't take a man's gun like that! Who do you think you are? *You* ain't the law!"

Nate almost smiled. "Well, you *could* try an' stop me... but I don't think you will." He gripped the front of Shonsey's wool coat and jerked hard enough to pop two buttons and expose a fully packed cartridge belt. From Shonsey's holster Nate lifted a Colt's revolver. Turning at the waist, he tossed the gun to Dudley. When he faced Shonsey again, the man got to his feet.

"What're you doin' back here in this canyon?" Nate said.

Tugging up the waistband of his trousers, Shonsey curled his lip into a scowl. "What goddammed bus'ness is it o' yours?"

Nate turned his head and studied the four horses. Each was shod in crude, leather stockings lashed with rawhide strips just above the pastern. One bay was of particular interest for the crusty texture of its mane at the withers. Nate crossed the canyon floor and felt of it with his fingers. Then he leaned in and smelled it.

"Dried blood," Nate said and looked back at Shonsey.

When Shonsey made no reply, Nate moved to the crack in the rock where the tarpaulin was stuffed. Pulling it out, he whipped open the canvas to reveal a dark blood stain as big as a Mexican sombrero.

"I reckon that's where you laid out Billy Lykins."

Shonsey swallowed and stared at the tarp, the tip of his tongue flitting across his big lips. "I kilt a antelope an' dragged it back here on that. I ain't seen Billy Lykins."

"Yo're a liar," Nate said in an even voice. He pointed at the bays. "Those are the horses you boys used to git up near my cabin. An' this here canvas is what you laid Lykins out on after I shot 'im." Nate dragged the tarpaulin by one corner as he walked toward Shonsey. Surprising the man, Nate flung the canvas forward, causing Shonsey to throw his forearms in front of his face. The tarp slapped against him and folded back on itself as a cloud of dust was swept up from the ground and hung around him.

"You were one o' the crowd that tried to kill me." Nate's voice was cold and hard as steel.

"I ain't tried to kill *nobody*!" Shonsey shot back.

Dudley laughed at Shonsey's pitiful act. "Betcha I could beat it out of 'im, Nate."

"If there's any beatin' to be done here, I'll be the one to do it," Nate said over his shoulder. When he glanced back at his brother, he noticed that John Tisdale held a worried expression on his face. Nate spoke up to Dud again. "Keep that gun trained on this duck. If he tries to make a run for it, don't kill 'im. Shoot 'im in the leg. I still got some talkin' I need to do with 'im."

Nate walked to where John stood alone, but before Nate could speak, John started up. "I thought we were going to let the law handle this."

Nate kept his voice low. "We are, but I don't wont Shonsey to know that. I wanna scare 'im so bad he loosens up his tongue. Ain't nobody gonna git kilt here today, understand?"

John frowned at their prisoner. Then he looked Nate in the eye and nodded.

"All right," he whispered. "I've always trusted you. No need to stop now."

Returning to Shonsey, Nate stopped in front of the man and widened his stance. "Talk," Nate said plainly.

Shonsey turned down the corners of his plump lips. "About what?"

For five heartbeats, Nate remained absolutely still. Then he slapped Shonsey's face, the *smack* echoing off the walls of the canyon before Shonsey knew what happened. Reeling backward, the insolent man cupped a hand to his cheek. His face darkened to a deep red.

"What'd you do *that* for?!" Shonsey growled.

Nate waited long enough for the man's breathing to settle. The men behind him remained quiet as church-goers during a silent prayer.

"Talk," Nate said again.

Shonsey raised open hands before him like a shield. "About *what*?!" he yelled.

Nate slapped him again. Then, quick as the strike of a rattler, he drove his fist into Shonsey's belly and heard a rush of air escape the man's open mouth.

Shonsey doubled over and held both hands to his abdomen. His eyes were clamped shut so tightly that wrinkles spread across his temples. When he looked up at Nate with spiteful eyes, Nate slapped him again, this time with such power that Shonsey stumbled back into the shallow fire pit and fell against the sloped wall of the canyon.

Nate stepped around the fire, grabbed Shonsey by the lapels of his coat, and jerked him upright. Shonsey pressed his bent arms against his body with his fists knotted under his chin.

"*Talk!*" Nate said more forcefully.

Shonsey got louder, too. "*I don't know what—*"

Nate slapped his face again. And then again. Shonsey yelped and tried to cover his head.

Dudley laughed. "Nate, maybe he's gonna need more convincing than a few pats on the cheek an' a tickle to the belly. I bet if you sat 'im down in that fire he'd do some talkin'." Dud made a gagging sound. "Forgit I said that! I got no desire to smell that skunk's ass cookin'."

Shonsey leaned back against the rock. "I don't know what you want me to say!"

Nate spoke quietly. "I wont the names of ev'ry man who attacked me in my cabin."

"It wasn't *me*! I swear it!"

Nate pulled his Colt's from his holster. "I've give you all the chances I'm gonna." He cocked the gun. "You give me the names," Nate demanded, "or I'll finish yore career right here."

"Now wait a minute!" Shonsey whimpered.

Nate held his gun low before him, the barrel pointed in front of Shonsey's boots. "I'll give you three seconds." Nate held his poker face. "One!"

Shonsey's eyes widened. "Now wait! Just wait!"

"Two."

"If I tell you, you got to swear you won't tell nobody it was me who did the namin'."

"Bye-bye, Shonsey," Dudley teased.

Shonsey's panicked eyes fixed on the gun. "Will you let me go if I tell?"

"Three," Nate said and brought the gun up to sight down the barrel.

"All right! All right!" Shonsey yelled. "But I didn't come at you with the others. I just kept the horses down at the creek. I swear it!"

Nate held dispassionate eyes on the sniveler. "Names," he said.

When Shonsey swallowed, the lump in his throat bobbed up above the collar of his shirt. "You got to swear you won't say it was me!" he insisted. "And you got to let me go!" He stared at Nate with pleading eyes, as he flattened his hands before him as if they might deflect a bullet.

Ranger came forward to stand beside Nate. "Looks like that's the only way he's gonna tell us, Nate. Might be worth the deal."

Nate shook his head. "I cain't promise that. I aim to take this into court, an' when I do, I'm gonna need to name my source."

"Nate?" It was John Tisdale's voice. Nate heard him

approach across the rocky soil until he appeared at Nate's side. "You've got the three of us as witnesses to what he says. We can testify in court even if he doesn't." He laid a hand gently on Nate's gun arm. "But if you kill him, we'll be witnesses to that, too."

It took Nate a few seconds to realize that John was playing an impromptu part in this scheme. "Maybe I *need* to kill 'im," Nate said in that cold voice that he rarely used. "Take yore hand away, John."

John removed his hand. "What if you gave him your word that you won't name him except in court." Tisdale turned to Shonsey. "Would that satisfy you?"

Shonsey's forehead creased like a freshly plowed field. "I reckon so," he mumbled.

John turned his attention back to Nate. "Nate?" he said in earnest.

Nate felt his light touch on the trigger and thought about how the fate of a man can rest on the slightest pressure of a finger. At the same time, he knew that he could never bring himself to shoot an unarmed man.

"Aw-right...you got my word," Nate promised.

He held his gun beside his thigh but left the hammer cocked. Shonsey looked down at the ground and wet his lips with flicks of his tongue.

"Canton was in charge. Joe Elliott was with 'im. Fred Coates and Billy Lykins too." His head came up quickly. "But I swear to you...I stayed with the horses!"

Nate lowered the hammer on his Colt's, stuffed the pistol into his holster, and pointed at the horses.

"Why are these horses here now?"

"It was part of Canton's plan. He wanted fresh mounts waitin' here in case trouble came up. Which it did. So, they took the rested horses an' left *these* here. I was told to come fetch 'em today, but I was to wait till dark to drive 'em back to Canton's ranch."

"What about the tarpaulin?" Ranger said.

Shonsey exhaled a heavy sigh. "Yeah, it was Lykins. He bled like a sonovabitch."

Everyone was quiet, digesting the information, until Dudley strode up laughing. He stood right before Shonsey and propped his hands on his hips. Shonsey looked at him warily.

"Now don't it feel good to git all that off yore chest?" He reached up and patted Shonsey's cheek twice. Then all the humor drained from Dud's face. "Yo're a damned, snivelin' cow'rd. D'you know that?"

Nate put a hand on Dud's upper arm and eased him back out of Shonsey's face. Then he spoke to Shonsey in a voice that brooked no debate.

"Now git outta here! Git on that Arab and ride!"

Shonsey frowned and flung an arm toward the four bays. "What about these horses?"

Ranger spoke up, "Looks like you lost 'em. I bet you'll think up a dandy story to tell Frank Canton."

John Tisdale turned a concerned face on Nate. "You're keeping them?"

"I don't care nothin' 'bout 'em," Nate said. "If Ranger wonts 'em, that's his bus'ness."

"I want 'em!" Ranger broke in. He laughed. "Hell, I'd be proud to own some o' Frank Canton's horses."

"'Less Canton catches you," Shonsey said.

"Well, he ain't here to catch me, is he?" Ranger spat. "To hell with 'im! To hell with all of 'em. Damned back-shooters who skulk around in the night!" He pointed a finger two inches from Shonsey's bloated face. "I ever see you or any o' your crowd on my claim, I will shoot you dead without a word o' warnin'."

"I ain't got no claim," Dudley said, "but if I see any of o' you out on the range, you can expect the same from me!" He started away but stopped and pointed again. "If it was my call, I'd kill you right now an' leave you out here for the buzzards and ki-yotes."

Nate stepped closer to Shonsey and spoke so quietly that the frightened man stopped breathing to hear what Nate had to say. "You better turn tail an' run now, while you still can."

Shonsey checked the faces around him and then gave Nate a sheepish look as he nodded. When he started for his horse, Dudley sidestepped into his path and widened his stance. Smiling, he presented a silent challenge that stopped Shonsey just out of arm's reach.

Turning at the waist, Shonsey spoke to Nate in a subdued voice. "Can I go now, or not."

"Go on!" Nate said.

Facing Dudley again, Shonsey spoke with a shaky voice. "He said I could go."

"That's right," Dud agreed. "You'll just have to walk around me." He smiled.

Mike Shonsey lowered his head and detoured around Dudley only to find Ranger now in his path. Without a word he veered again and wasted no time getting to his horse. There he fumbled with the reins, trying to untie them.

Nate walked back down the trail about ten yards and cupped a hand beside his mouth, "Nick?" he called. "Shonsey's comin' out! Let 'im pass!" When he returned, Shonsey was mounted. Nate pulled a carbine out of Shonsey's saddle scabbard and stepped back.

"What about my guns? Do I git 'em back?"

For several seconds, Nate stared up at Shonsey's pleading eyes. "No," Nate said. He walked to the rear of the mare and gave it smart slap with the flat of his hand, setting man and horse into motion.

John Tisdale stepped beside Nate, and together they watched Shonsey retreat down the canyon trail. "I see why you didn't want my brother here today," John said. "His temper might have changed the outcome considerably." He hitched his head back toward the canyon room, where Dud and Ranger roped the leather-shod horses for travel. "And yet you invited Dudley," John added with a question on his face.

Nate huffed an airy laugh through his nose. "Wasn't no in-vite. I couldn' stop 'im." He turned to John. "How do you think we should go about the legal process now?"

"Do you know if the county prosecutor is in the pocket of the WSGA?"

Nate shook his head. "Cain't say for sure, but the Assoc'ation controls most ever'body in the gov'ment... judges, too."

John pursed his lips. "What about Sheriff Angus? Do you trust him?"

"I do," Nate said without hesitation. "He's a fair man."

"All right," John said. "You talk to the sheriff...and I'll get with the lawyer who helped me with my land patent. He is no friend of the cattle barons. That's how we'll start."

Nate swept a hand toward the four horses now lined up nose to tail on the same rope. "Might leave out this part here 'bout where these horses are headed."

"Let's not lie," John insisted. "We don't want to look like we've got anything to hide."

"I won't lie," Nate said, "but I ain't gonna bring it up 'less the sheriff asks. I don't wont to bring any trouble down on Ranger if I can help it."

"The way things are going in this county," John said, "I'd say we're already in trouble up to our necks."

Chapter Twenty-Four

Over the next couple of weeks, Nate packed his belongings and moved his herd of cattle and string of horses east to the KC Ranch, where Nick Ray had been living as a squatter in the old Nolan cabin. The new place had a barn, stables, and split-rail fencing with double posts for paddock and corral. The living quarters were downright spacious compared to the Hall cabin at Hole in the Wall.

The cabin consisted of one square room with a stone hearth and chimney in back. Behind it, a storage room had been added on, with one door for access from the main room and another that led outside. Centered in the front room was a plank table with bench seats, which could accommodate eight men at a time for meals. Bunk frames of bare wood lined the walls on three sides, each topped by a rolled-up mattress. Above each bed on the wall was an empty shelf supported by metal brackets, strong enough to hold clothing and personal gear.

The northeast corner of the room served as a kitchen. The front wall's only window illuminated this area. On either side of this window, someone had hung crude burlap curtains that were tied back to ten-penny nails tapped into the wall. A short sideboard ran across the east wall, and at its end stood a white porcelain basin propped up on a wooden frame. Two windows looked out onto the cottonwoods that lined the river. Below the first window's sill stood a wood stove with a bent flue that angled out the window and then rose above the roof.

In the small storage room in back, a window afforded a view of a brushy plain that rose up to a rocky ridge south of the cabin. A rear door provided the cabin's only other entry and exit. Back in the main room, a lone window provided light on the west wall as well as a view of the Big Horns. This window was nestled between the bunk attached to the wall.

The exterior walls of the cabin were adequately fortified with thick slabs of lumber all the way around. With windows on all sides, the building had no large blind spots for those who were inside looking out. The wood floor was as level as a billiards table, with no give or warping so that the front door swung freely without resistance.

Nick's bedroll was laid out on the bunk in the southeast corner, next to the entrance of the larder. Nate took a bunk in the northwest corner. After unrolling the mattress, he pressed into it with his hands, testing the filling of alternating layers of hay and wool blankets sewn up inside a ticking cover. After laying out his personals on the shelf, he hung Dory's painting just below it, putting her artwork at eye level when he lay in the bed.

Dakah enjoyed better quarters too, having a snug stall in the barn. The cat lasted only a day before disappearing, and Nate figured she had rejected the new cabin and returned to the familiar, tighter quarters at Hole in the Wall. He understood the cat well enough to know that if he tried bringing her to the KC a second time, she would run off again.

On a cold Saturday night in the first week of December, Nick Ray had ridden to the Cross H Ranch to take part in a poker game. Nate sat at the table, his back to the fire, his stockinged feet propped beneath him, toes to the floor so that the soles of his feet received some radiant heat from the hearth. Leaning on the table with a lighted oil lamp before him, he wrote in his leather-bound book, scratching away with his lead pencil like a man of letters.

Listening to the crackle of the fire, he wrote to Dory, letting her know about his plans to take out a claim nearby, where the Middle Fork and the South Fork came together in a rich pastureland. In his writing, he described the terrain down to the last hillock and gully. And he also painted a word picture of the streams, stressing their importance to him as a cattleman.

After half an hour, when he changed course to write about his feelings, to admit that he sometimes wondered how *she* would react to one thing or another—if she were somehow here with him—he heard horses coming in at a gallop from the north. Setting the book and pencil aside, he crept to the front of the room and peered out the window to see two riders coming down the main road from Buffalo. They clattered across the bridge of the Middle Fork and turned into the main yard, bringing their mounts down from a gallop to a smart canter.

When the horsemen slowed in front of the cabin, Nate walked to his bunk and picked up his Colt's revolver. Then he blew out the flame in the lamp and moved lightly to the front wall next to the door. The fire burning in the hearth made the room flicker with shadow and teasing light. When he heard voices, Nate peeked out the windowglass again and recognized his younger brothers, Dudley and Ben, as they dismounted in the dim light of the sickle moon.

Laying the gun on the table, Nate tripped the latch,

opened the door, and stood in the doorway facing out into the cold evening. "Ever'thin' aw-right?" Nate asked.

Dudley tugged his horse toward the tie-rail. "Hell, no! There ain't nothin' 'aw-right' about nothin'!"

Wearing a grim expression, Ben stepped beside Dud, and both lashed their reins to the rail.

"What's happ'ned?" Nate said, but neither of his brothers spoke they marched past him into the cabin.

By the time Nate had latched the door, Dudley—still dressed in his wool coat and hat—had added a log to the fire and now squatted before the hearth, stabbing at the coals with the iron poker. Ben set his hat on the table, took off his fleece-lined jacket, and dropped it on the bench. Nate relit the oil lamp and remained standing by the table.

"We got bad news," Ben said quietly. "I'm sorry to be the one to tell you."

Nate waited, his mind like a dry bucket as he readied himself for whatever misery was about to be poured into it. Ben took a deep breath, looked down at the floor, and let the air seep from his lips. When he looked up, Nate could see the dread in his eyes.

"John Tisdale and Ranger Jones are dead."

Nate stared at his little brother and forced the words to repeat themselves inside his head. Then, as if seeking corroboration, he looked to Dudley, but Dud continued to thrust the poker into the coals like a man trying to kill something in its burrow. Nate walked to the hearth and sat, letting the heat of the flames balance out the chill that had spread down his spine.

"'Dead,'" Nate repeated. "Are you sure?" He looked at the side of Dudley's face and saw nothing but anger. When Nate looked up at Ben, his youngest brother affirmed the news with a single nod.

"Ever'body in the valley is mighty stirred up 'bout it," Ben reported. "Red Angus is so mad he cain't stand still.

He's lookin' for answers, but there ain't no mystery to it. Not after what just happ'ned to you at Hole in the Wall."

"Frank Canton is in this somewhere!" Dudley growled. "Him an' those other so-called range detectives that do his dirty work!"

Nate closed his eyes and lowered his forehead into his hands. He could still hear John Tisdale's voice in his head, advising him about the legal proceedings that they planned. And Ranger's easy smile was as indelible in his memory as the boy's uncanny grace on a wild horse. When Nate's head came up, he stared across the room at the wall rack where, just a week ago, John Tisdale's hat and gray winter coat had hung next to Nate's.

Then an image formed in Nate's mind. An old Somerset saddle was, at that moment, perched on a sawhorse in the barn, where Nate had been cleaning and soaping the leather. He had bought it used and was restoring it as a wedding gift for Ranger's bride. They were to have been married in the spring.

"Kate Tisdale is mighty tore up," Ben said. "And Ranger's bride-to-be has took ill. Seems like the both o' them just got their hearts broke."

"How did it happen?" Nate asked.

Ben turned to Dudley as if he might answer, but when Dud continued to stab at the logs, Ben sat on the table bench and settled in for the telling. "Both of 'em got shot... at diff'rent times, I mean...ambushed in a coupla lonely stretches along the road to town."

"Each of 'em was alone?"

Ben nodded. "John took his wagon into town. Wasn't nob'dy with 'im but 'is dog. He drove in for supplies and for some Christmas presents for his family. Kate says she begged 'im to take his brother with 'im, but John didn' wont his family to be at home without a man there to look after 'em."

Ben shook his head with regret. "Turns out, soon's he come into town, he had a run-in with Frank Canton and Joe Elliott in an alleyway. Later, John talked to Red Angus an' found out he'd been put on that death list that the WSGA made up. So, John said he didn't wont to drive home alone. Said he'd wait in town until he could arrange for a friend or two to ride back with 'im." Ben shrugged. "Only nobody showed up."

Ben looked down and rubbed his hands together before continuing his story. "John got a room at the Occidental. He bought a twelve-gauge double-barrel an' a coupla boxes o' shells, and then—" Ben spread his hands and shook his head. "Now, here's the part I don't git. For four days runnin' it rained, an' John spent his afternoons down at Jensen's Saloon drinkin' whiskey. People said he got purty liquored up."

Nate frowned at the floor and shook his head. "John wasn't a drinker. Not like that."

Ben spread his hands again and shrugged. "Well, the rain let up, and he fin'lly set out for home, but the road was so muddy he only made it as far as the Cross H that night. He slept in the bunkhouse, and the crew sleepin' there said John insisted on closing up all the curtains on the windows. Said he was afraid o' bein' assass'nated."

Gripping his right fist with his left hand, Nate squeezed so hard that his fingers paled to white. "I've knowed John all my life, an' I ain't never seen 'im worried like that."

"Next day," Ben went on, "him an' his dog started off again, an' a few miles down the road at a gulch, somebody ambushed 'im. Shot 'im dead."

Dud snorted, leaned the poker against the rock hearth, and stood up. He pulled off his coat and hat and dropped both on a nearby bunk.

"Might as well tell it *all* if yo're gonna tell it!" Dud

snapped. "Angus figures he was shot from behind at fifteen feet. John never got to use that shotgun. The sonovabitch back-shooter drove the wagon down the gully a ways, shot the horses, an' shot the dog, an' left John there to rot with his dead animals."

"An' git this," Ben added. "You 'member Charlie Basch? Feller you loaned out a horse to last year? He happ'ned to ride by that gulch that mornin' an' saw those wagon tracks cut into the soft mud. He looked down the gully an' saw a man on foot leading a team of horses hitched to a wagon. Not thinkin' much of it, Charlie kept on goin', but when he reached some high ground, he heard two gunshots go off. Then a third shot, and a dog squealed. Looking back, he watched a man mount a horse and ride away. Said that horse looked a lot like Canton's bay with the white socks in back—the one he calls Fred."

Listening to the crackling of the fire, the three Champions were quiet for a time. Dud turned his back to the fire and sat on the hearth beside Nate.

"What about Ranger?" Nate asked.

Both Ben and Dudley started talking at the same time, stopped, and looked at one another. Dud flipped his hand at the wrist, signaling Ben to do the talking.

"Ranger left for town two days before John did. He was to pick up lumber for the floorin' of his new cabin— the one he's building for after he gits hitched—but he never got to Buffalo. They didn' find his body till day b'fore yesterday. Down at the Muddy Creek bridge. They say he was shot through the side and through the chest. Looks like two or three men hid under the bridge and popped up an' shot 'im as he crossed. Just like with Tisdale, they drove the wagon down the gulch an' left it hid, but the tracks gave it away."

Dudley snorted a laugh. "Guess who came to Red

Angus an' asked to be put into jail for protection?" He curled his upper lip in a scowl. "Frank Canton!"

"There'll be a hearing this week," Ben informed Nate.

Nate closed his eyes long enough to get a grip on his emotions. "They got anythin' more on Canton than 'it might'a been his horse'?"

Ben shook his head. "Nope. That's all they got."

"An' that'll never hold up in court!" Dudley added. "Which is why Canton needs stringin' up on a telegraph pole, courtesy of the citizens of Buffalo. I will gladly supply the rope."

The three brothers dropped into a tacit quiet. The fire sizzled and popped like meat frying in a skillet. When the heat began to feel suffocating, Nate stood and walked to the door. Without grabbing hat or coat, he stepped out into the cold, closed the door behind him, and walked into the yard to stand under the stars.

Bringing up a picture in his mind, he studied the face of John Tisdale. Nate's older brother, William, had once said that John was the smartest person in Williamson County, Texas. That included all the teachers, rich businessmen, and preachers. When Nate was a boy of ten, John, though two years older, had treated him like an equal. Their mutual respect for one another had spawned a lasting friendship that Nate had always considered a prized possession.

In the last weeks, John had pushed the county prosecutor, Alvin Bennett, into action against the men who had attacked Nate at Hole in the Wall. But he had done more than initiate a hearing. John had helped Bennett with strategies that could be used to convict Canton and his "detectives." John's strength was his intelligence, and this was the very thing that Canton would fear. It would have been an easy task to eliminate John Tisdale, Nate knew. He had never known John to fight another man—not physically. That was not John's way. John's only weapons were his sound reasoning and his sharp mind. It was for these qualities that he had been killed.

Ranger Jones was the flip side of John Tisdale. Ranger was more like Nate—a horseman and cowman who was good with his hands. As a skilled laborer with a self-made work ethic, Ranger had earned the respect of everyone who knew him. He didn't have the education that John had accrued, but Ranger was smart about animals and tack and tools. His easygoing manner and good humor had won him many friends in the Powder River Basin. Nate could not picture Ranger's face without a smile and sparkling eyes.

The door to the cabin opened and closed, and footsteps crunched through the sandy soil until Ben appeared at Nate's side. "Here," Ben said and held out Nate's coat. "Ain't gonna help things if you freeze yoreself to death."

Nate pushed his arms through the sleeves of the coat and buttoned up the front. The warmth that gathered around him seemed like a cruel reminder that the dead had to settle for the cold dark embrace of the earth. Six feet under and gone forever. Death was immutable.

Ben rested a hand on Nate's shoulder. "I know you an' John were friends for a long time. He thought mighty highly of you. And there ain't nobody admired you more'n Ranger."

Nate gritted his teeth and shook his head with a quick jerk. "I cain't make sense o' how some men can take away another man's life as easy as blowin' out a candle." Nate said this so quietly that Ben had to lean in to hear.

Ben straightened up and stuffed both his hands into his overcoat pockets. "Red Angus told me it's like a pois'-nous worm that bores into a man's head. Once it's in there, it ain't never comin' out. He saw it take hold o' many a soldier durin' the war an' change 'em forever. It meant they could shoot a man's brains out as easy as grinding a scorpion under their boot."

"Red was in the war?" Nate said and turned to his brother.

Ben nodded. "Drummer boy. He was twelve years old. Fifteen when he mustered out." Ben pursed his lips and looked toward the black outline of the Big Horns to the west. "Red says he can look in a man's eye and tell whether or not that man is carryin' that worm in his head. A man like that—so Red says—don't even need a *reason* to kill. He just kills 'cause he *can*."

They looked toward the mountains and listened to the cold wind slice through the bare branches of the cottonwoods that lined the river. Along with that airy sound came the low burbling of the water pushing its way toward its confluence with the South Fork.

"There *was* a reason that John and Ranger was kilt," Nate said quietly. "It was the one thing they had in common."

Ben narrowed his eyes. "What would that be?"

Nate filled his lungs with the cold night air and exhaled a long plume of gray fog. Staring out into the darkness, he spoke with the restrained timidity of a confessor confiding in his priest.

"Both o' them heard Mike Shonsey name the men who attacked me in my cabin."

Ben frowned. "Well, Dud was there with you, too!"

Nate nodded. "Yep. Him an' me. Nick was with the horses."

Ben cocked his head. "So yo're expectin' 'em to come after you again? You an' Dud?"

Nate pivoted his head to look his brother squarely in the eye. "Makes sense, don't it?"

Eventually, Ben nodded.

"I'm thinkin' the smart move might be to strike first,"

Nate said. "I reckon the people o' Buffalo would thank me for it."

Ben reached out and took Nate by the arm. "You'd better come back inside. There's somethin' you need to see."

When they entered the cabin, Dudley was tending to the fire again, jabbing the poker at a burning log. Ben and Nate pulled out of their coats and sat on the table bench facing Dud.

"Dud?" Ben said. "You still got that Cheyenne newspaper?"

Dudley dropped the poker with a loud *clank* on the hearthstones, stood, and walked to his coat. Pulling out a rolled-up newspaper, he unfurled the paper and held it out to Nate.

"I don't care to hear what the Cheyenne papers are sayin'," Nate said. "They just print what the cattle barons tells 'em to."

"Yo're gonna wont to read this, Nate," Dud insisted. "This story has gone out to Casper an' Rawlins an' Sheridan an' Lar'mie an' all the way over to Omaha an' up to Butte."

Nate shook his head. "Still don't wonna read it."

Dud exchanged a glance with Ben and then snapped the paper flat. "Aw-right, then I'll read it to you...just some of the highlights." Dud held the article closer to his eyes. "'There are more rustlers in Johnson County than fleas on a stray dog'...'thanks to the efficient work of the Wyoming Stock Growers Association's range detectives'...'Frank Canton's unsurpassed record'...'the big cattle companies' devastating losses to the so-called settlers'...'Johnson County commissioners would do well to investigate their sheriff's ties to the small-time rustlers who infest his county...'none more so than Nate Champion, said to be the leader of the rustler element'..."

Nate had been staring at the floor, but at this last item, he looked up at Dudley.

"Hey," Dud growled. "I don' enjoy readin' this stuff any more'n you like hearin' it, but you need to know 'bout the lies they're spreadin', Nate. Hell, when you take your case to court, Frank Canton might have the territorial gov'nor as a character witness! Or God His-self!" Tossing the paper on the table, Dud sat down on the hearth.

"Yo're gonna have to be lookin' over yore shoulder now, Nate," Ben said. Then he pointed at Dudley. "And you, too!"

Dudley laughed. "They got me on that blacklist now?"

Nate leaned forward and propped his forearms on his knees, putting his face closer to Dudley's. "We're the last two witnesses to hear Shonsey's confession."

Dud hissed a laugh through his teeth. "Even if we go to court, Shonsey will deny ever'thing. It'll be our word against his, and ever'body knows that you and me had run-ins with him. A lawyer is gonna use that to discredit us."

Nate laced his fingers together and rubbed the tips of his thumbs in a circular motion as he thought through the problem. Then, abruptly, he stopped the movement.

"I got one thing nobody can take away from me," Nate proclaimed. "On that mornin' they attacked me an' Gilbertson, I stood nine feet away from Joe Elliott right outside the cabin. I looked 'im in the face as he leveled a scattergun at me."

"Did Gilbertson see 'im, too?" Dud said.

Nate shook his head. "He was inside the cabin."

Dudley frowned. "It's the same thing! Yore word against Elliott's!"

Ben stood up and propped a boot on the hearth. "Dammit, ever'body knows Nate's word means somethin'! You sure as hell cain't say that 'bout Joe Elliott."

"No, I cain't," Dud agreed, "but twelve men paid off

by the Wyomin' Stock Growers Assoc'ation can say that Joe Elliott is the Saint of the Powder River Basin."

"Nobody is gonna b'lieve that!" Ben said.

Dud showed his tolerant smile. "Money can buy its own truth, brother. Don't you know that?"

Nate was no longer listening to the argument. He was thinking about John Tisdale and Ranger Jones...and their women, who would never see their men again. And in John's case, children who would never hear their father's voice. Nate knew that it was the worst kind of emptiness. A hole that—no matter what people said—time could not fill. He closed his eyes, and the shining image of Dory Hildebrand blossomed like a flower in his mind.

"Nate?" Ben said. "Ain't that right?"

Nate gazed at the flames and spoke in a voice that sounded, to him, like something detached and distant. "I reckon we'll see." Then he turned to Ben. "When're their burials?"

"Tomorrow," Ben said, "Willow Grove Cemetery. Me an' Dud thought we'd stay here tonight an' ride in with you tomorrow. How's that sound?"

Nate nodded. "Yeah...we'll go in together."

Late Winter and Early Spring 1892

Buffalo, Wyoming

Chapter Twenty-Five

I t was mid-February before the preliminary hearing against Joe Elliott came up on the court docket. The room was packed with people from all over the county, most of those being business owners who worked in town and the ranchers who ran small outfits throughout the Powder River Valley. Only two of the WSGA barons showed their faces.

The spectators seemed anxious for a ruling against Elliott and were vocal about it, jeering the defense lawyer at outlandish claims and cheering on the prosecutor during his questioning of a witness. The judge had to warn the citizens three times about their conduct. But all that changed when Nate Champion took the stand—which, in reality, was a simple, wooden, straight-back chair set beside the judge's table.

When Nate answered the introductory questions about name, age, and occupation, his voice was confident and direct but as quiet as the frayed edges of an owl's feather. To hear every word, the spectators leaned forward in their seats and seemed to collectively hold their breaths.

But for the smoke rising from Joe Elliott's cigar, the court-room was as still as a painting.

As Nate related the story of the attack on Gilbertson and himself at Hole in the Wall, his audience was rapt. A newspaperman scratched notes on paper but struggled to hear Nate's words over the sound of his busy pencil.

Keeping his eyes on Joe Elliott, Nate finished his narration with a comment about the kind of coward who would shoot a man in his own bed while he slept. Still, Elliott's head remained bowed, his face set in a dispassionate expression. Now and again, he leaned down to tap cigar ash into a small ceramic dish that sat on the floor next to him.

The prosecutor, Alvin Bennett, turned his back to the judge's table and faced the crowd. "And do you see in this room today, Mister Champion, anyone who was a part of that group that attacked you?"

With his gaze still fixed on Elliott, Nate nodded once. "Yes, that man right there smoking a cigar...Joe Elliott." He said this as calmly as a man pointing out a landmark on the horizon.

At the mention of his name, Elliott lifted his head to lock eyes with Nate. The reporter stopped writing, and the silence of the courthouse became absolute. The air in the room seemed charged with some kind of static energy, like the prairie just before a lightning bolt splits open the sky to slash at the land like a brightly polished sword.

After a dozen heartbeats of suspended tension, someone in the audience coughed, and the spell was broken. A murmur of voices began to build until the judge banged his gavel and scowled his displeasure to the spectators.

"Let's have quiet!" the judge ordered. Then he raised his chin to look down his nose at Elliott's lawyer. "Anything else from you?" he asked.

The lawyer stood, tugged down on the vest of his expensive suit, and fastened one of the buttons on his coat as if it were a requirement for rising from his chair. "No, Your Honor."

The judge turned to the prosecutor. "And you?"

Bennett half stood. "Nothing more, Your Honor."

The judge turned to Nate and nodded once. "You may return to your seat, Mister Champion."

Nate stood and crossed the small open space between the witness chair and the spectators. Sitting next to the county prosecutor, he leaned to whisper into the man's ear.

"Gilbertson didn't show up?"

Keeping his eyes on the judge, Bennett shook his head. "Couldn't find him."

"You reckon he run off...or *got* run off...or *worse*?"

Bennett sighed. "Don't know. But he's not the only one. Apparently, Canton and Hesse have left the territory too."

The judge pointed his gavel at the prisoner. "Joseph Elliott, you are to be bound over to the district court for trial. A date will be set to determine bail—if any—within the next two weeks. Meanwhile, you will remain in the custody of Sheriff Angus at the county jail." He turned smartly to Red Angus. "Sheriff, take custody of the prisoner." Then he smacked the gavel on the table. "This court is adjourned!"

While the rest of the audience shuffled toward the door amid a sea of conversations, Nate and the prosecutor remained in their seats and watched the sheriff clamp manacles on Joe Elliott's wrists. Elliott showed no signs of concern on his stoic face, but his skin had taken on a grayish cast.

When Red Angus and his deputy started the prisoner for the front door, Nate watched his brother Dudley stand up from his chair and block the aisle. The trio of exiting men stopped, and Nate hurried over to head off any trouble that Dud might make with the sheriff. Dud spread his boots and crossed his arms over his chest as if settling in for a conversation.

"I figure yore options are not lookin' too good, Elliott?" Dud said, putting on the rueful mask of an actor. He freed up a hand and extended his forefinger straight up. "One... you rot in prison for fifteen years for attempted murder." He flipped up a second finger. "Two...you git tied to the murder of Tisdale and Jones and git yore neck snapped on a gallows." A third finger went up. "Three...you git hauled outta jail in the middle o' the night by a mob of mad-as-hell citizens an' they string you up to strangle and squirm around like a frog on a gig."

The sheriff stepped in front of his prisoner. "Dudley, I don't want any trouble from you. Move aside, or I'll have to arrest you."

Dud showed a concerned frown. "Hang on, Red! Just one more!" He raised a fourth finger. "And four," he continued, "maybe these fat polecats in the Assoc'ation will worry 'bout what you might say to the sheriff. Could be they wanna keep you quiet...permanent-like!"

Red Angus arched a bushy eyebrow and fixed Dudley with a hard stare. "I don't want to hear any threats!"

Dud held up both hands before him, palms out, and became a picture of innocence. "These ain't threats from me, Sheriff. I'm just stating the possibilities."

Nate worked his way past the sheriff and tried to usher Dudley toward the door. But Dud was not finished.

"You know...a lot o' people are damned upset 'bout John Tisdale and Ranger Jones. And now this attack on my brother, too." Dud canted his head to one side. "It don't take much figurin' to see that all three ambushes could'a been done by the same cow'rds."

For the first time since Dudley had blocked the prisoner's exit, Elliott broke off his baleful glare at Dud and looked at the sheriff. "Do I gotta listen to this?"

"Better post some extra guards 'round the jail, Red," Dud advised. "This boy's prospects do not look good."

Elliott's morose face soured, and he grabbed at Dud, the chains of his manacles jangling. The sheriff jerked his prisoner back by the arm, and the deputy put Elliott in a chokehold. Dudley did not move, but now a radiant smile stretched across his face.

"If you're takin' me to jail, then *take* me, goddammit!" Elliott demanded. "I don't have to listen to this shit, do I?"

"Are you gittin' a little bit scared, Joe? That somebody might try an' shoot you while yo're in yore bunk at the jailhouse?" Dud cocked his head toward one shoulder and pulled at the sides of his chin with one hand. "Sounds kinda familiar, don't it?"

"Dudley!" the sheriff said with iron in his voice. "Would you kindly step out of our way? I don't want to have to arrest you."

Dudley bowed his head once and smiled at Red. "Why, of course, I will...since you asked so nice." He sidled between the rows of chairs and freed up the aisle. Sheriff Angus and the deputy escorted Elliott out of the building and down the boardwalk. When Dud started to follow them, Nate took a firm grip on the waistband at the back of his brother's britches.

Leaning out the door, Dud yelled a parting line to the prisoner. "You be sure an' sleep with one eye open, Elliott! You never know what's comin!"

Nate spun his brother by the arm and got into his face. "Leave off on that! You hear me?!"

Dud put on the sly smile that reminded Nate there was no way to control his brother. It was the one thing Dudley was stubborn about: saying whatever he wanted to say to whoever he wanted to say it to and whenever he felt like it.

Dud chuckled. "I'm just tryin' to put the fear of God into that sonovabitch an' help 'im be as mis'rable as possible." He looked down at Nate's grip on his arm. "You can remove that now."

Nate relaxed and lowered his arm. "You have a habit o' pushin' things right up to the edge, Dud."

Dudley chuckled. "If yo're gonna push, it oughta be right up to the edge, don't you think? Otherwise, it don't mean nothin'."

Nate shook his head and sidled into the main aisle. "Let's go git us some hot coffee?"

Dud smiled. "How 'bout we go where *you* can git hot coffee and I can git a cold beer?"

Nate took his overcoat off the wall rack and pushed his arms through the sleeves. "It's nineteen degrees out there, an' you wont a cold beer?"

"Couldn'a said it better myself, big brother."

———

They settled on the Occidental Hotel, where they stood at the bar to order. Nate dropped three coins on the bar, and they carried their drinks to a table at the back of the room, where the wood stove pushed out a steady halo of heat. Only one other table was occupied—three men playing cards. Nate knew each one by name and nodded to them when they looked his way.

Once seated, Nate sipped from his coffee. Dudley took a big gulp of beer that coated his mustaches with foam. With a hardy exhalation, he hummed his approval of the beer and wiped a shirt sleeve across his mouth.

"Well," Dud said, "I guess Joe Elliott is freezin' his ass

off in Red's jail 'bout now." He smiled with a satisfied look.

"This was a big win for us today," Nate said. "I didn't know nothin' 'bout that judge...whether he had ties to the WSGA or not. He could'a dismissed Elliott with just a word. Now Elliott will have to face a jury, an' that's to our advantage. All we got to do is make sure none of the chosen twelve gits paid off by the WSGA."

Dudley lost his smile, rested a forearm on the table, and leaned forward. "How the hell do we do that?"

Nate looked around at the men gambling, each of them frowning at his hand of cards. Nate leaned toward his brother and lowered his voice.

"First, we'll need to find out who they are. Then I figure to have a little talk with each one...an' make sure they all understand the penalty for takin' a bribe."

Dud raised an eyebrow. "Does that mean the legal penalty or the Champion penalty?"

Nate drank from his cup and then set it down without a sound. "Whatever works. I just wanna see the law carried out for once in Johnson County."

Dud raised his mug like a toast and drank half the contents. "So, who's next for a preliminary hearin'?"

"Coates first...then Shonsey. Looks like Frank Canton has left the territory. Nobody knows where Billy Lykins is."

Dud finished his beer and pushed the mug away. Then he stacked both forearms on the table—hands cupping elbows—and stared long and hard into Nate's eyes.

"I heard Lykins is in Missouri where he's takin' up space in a graveyard. Got that from one o' the CY boys I used to ride with."

Nate made no reply. He looked out the window at the

front of the room and saw snow flurries swirling in the air above the street. As he drank from his cup, a lanky man, bundled up inside a sheepskin coat, came through the door, brushing flakes of snow from his shoulders and sleeves. When the man took off his hat and slapped it against his trouser leg, a burst of white crystals showered to the floor. He hung his coat and hat next to the Champions' apparel.

"Ranger's brother," Nate said quietly.

Dud finished his beer and banged it down on the table. "Hey, Johnny!" he called. "Come an' join us!"

Johnny Jones paid for a shot of whiskey and carried it to Nate's table. Stepping over the chairback, he sat and managed to work his long legs under the table.

"That sonovabitch Joe Elliott is gonna git his," Johnny announced for anyone in the room to hear.

"You were at the courthouse?" Nate asked.

"Damned right I was!" Johnny said, still speaking louder than necessary. "Ever'body in Buffalo knows the four men that just about got you are the same ones who kilt my brother and John Tisdale." He pointed a bony finger at Nate. "You agree with that?"

Nate nodded once. "I do."

"Hang the lot of 'em!" called out one of the cowhands at the other table, and his two companions nodded their agreement.

Johnny threw back his drink with a toss of his head and slapped the empty shot glass onto the table. As he stared at the glass, his eyes shone with a film of moisture that could have formed from rage or heartbreak. Nate reached over and cupped his hand over Johnny's wrist.

"Those boys will answer for their crimes, Johnny," Nate said gently.

Johnny turned his head quickly to face Nate. *"Will they?"*

Nate nodded. "One at a time."

"That ain't what I heard," Johnny said. He stared down at his empty glass, and his jaws tightened, making the tendons in his hollow cheeks knot.

Nate looked Johnny in the eye. "Who's sayin' that?"

Frowning, Johnny looked down at his glass again as he turned it in circles on the tabletop. He seemed to draw air deeper into his lungs as he began shaking his head slowly.

"I didn't know what I was s'posed to do about Janey. I ain't sure what's expected o' me."

Dudley sat back in his chair and folded his arms over his chest. "Who's Janey?"

"Ranger's girl," Nate said quietly. He released Johnny's arm. "The one he was to marry."

"That cabin was for her," Johnny went on. "I didn't know if I was s'posed to finish it an' give it to 'er...or maybe even offer to marry 'er! I mean, she ain't got no family or friends here."

He looked up at Nate and then Dudley. Then he studied the empty glass again.

"I had to talk to *some*body, so I went to where that gypsy woman has set up a tent outside the fort. I paid 'er to give me some advice on that, but I got more'n I bargained for when she told me 'bout these men that kilt my brother. She said they'll all gonna wiggle outta this. All except Lykins. He's dead. She guaranteed me that much."

Nate kept his voice as gentle as he could. "You cain't b'lieve what the gypsies tell you. They're like faro dealers. Just bankin' on the odds an' tryin' to make some money off it."

Johnny was shaking his head even before Nate had finished. "No, this is that woman that knew 'bout the Big Die-Up. You 'member? Ranger told me 'bout 'er right b'fore that killin' winter hit us."

Nate nodded to show that he remembered. "Still, Johnny...I wouldn't put much stock in it. I don't see how a gypsy has any more grasp on what will happen than you an' I do."

Johnny narrowed his eyes and shook his head as if in regret. "But, Nate, you ain't talked to this woman." There was a tone of awe quieting his voice.

Nate just smiled and nodded. "We'll help with the cabin, Johnny, but I think you oughta give Janey some time b'fore you talk to 'er 'bout what she plans to do. An' just forget ever'thin' 'bout any obligation to marry 'er. That ain't the way it works."

Johnny looked beseechingly at Dudley. "You go along with all that?"

Dud smiled. "I never knowed Nate to deliver nothin' but sound advice."

Johnny rotated the shot glass some more, and then, abruptly, he stopped and nodded. "I got to git back to the cabin an put in that floorin'." He stood but hesitated. Leaning to Nate, he offered his hand. "At least you kilt one o' them bastards. I'm obliged to you for that."

They shook hands. Then Johnny strode to the wall rack, donned coat and hat, and walked out of the bar.

"Hey!" Dud said, tapping Nate's shoulder with the back of his fist. "Somebody I wont you to meet. You got time right now?"

"Yeah," Nate said with the rising pitch of curiosity. "Do I git to know who it is?"

Dudley winked and turned on his charm. "Let's make it a surprise."

Chapter Twenty-Six

The tent was made of gray canvas mottled with dark stains and draped over a cylindrical framework of poles and one stout center pole to support a pointed roof. A border of red paint circumscribed the bottom of the, and another band of red marked the transition from wall to roof. The structure was reminiscent of a small circus tent set up on the outskirts of town. It stood close to the bank of Clear Creek, a good fifty yards from the loose cluster of buildings comprising Fort McKinney. The snow had stopped falling, but the wind swept hard through the leafless branches of the trees by the creek.

Next to the tent, a boxy, gypsy wagon stood idle, its tongue angled to the ground and its wheels chocked by blocky stones. Behind this, four aging draft horses were picketed among the cottonwoods and sycamores.

Over a small pit fire that flapped in the wind like an orange flag, an iron pot heated on a blackened, metal grate. Two gypsy women, an old man, a young girl, and a black and gray brindle mutt sat beside the fire and watched the two riders approach.

Forty yards away, Nate reined up and sat his horse, staring at the tiny settlement of nomads. "This is why you brought me here?" he whispered to his brother.

Dudley turned with a smile and leaned his forearm on his pommel. "I'm buyin', big brother. It won't cost you nothin' but a little time." He gave Nate a wink. "Come on! What can it hurt?"

Nate watched the gypsy man feed the fire with broken dead branches. One of the women stirred the pot, while the other seemed content to watch the flames lick through the grate.

"It's just a lot of foolishness," Nate said. "And a waste o' yore money."

"Well, it's *my* money, ain't it? If I wont to, I can throw it in the Powder River." Dud gripped Nate's upper arm and jostled him. "Come on! Let's go see what she can tell us."

When they dismounted, Dudley walked directly to the man, who slowly stood up and easily engaged Dud in conversation. He appeared to be knocking on the door of old age, his skin starting to crack and wrinkle like old leather. He had been strong once. His chest was thick, and his hands showed a history of physical labor, but he stooped a little as he talked with Dudley. Each time he moved, he did so carefully, as if some fragile part of him might break.

The woman working with the pot was fleshy and industrious and gave off the appearance of someone who knew how to survive whatever ills befell her. Her dull black hair was tied in back by a red ribbon and hung down her spine all the way to her hips. Over her hefty body she wore a gray wool blanket pinned at the throat by a bone button.

The other woman was thin as a willow wand and ancient, her ash-gray hair loose and uncombed as if she had let the wind decide her appearance. Her swarthy skin was marked with creases like an old map that had been incorrectly folded and opened countless times. She wore an old buffalo robe cinched at her tiny waist by a thong of leather. From one ear lobe hung a small silver trinket that threw off bright glints of reflected light with such regularity that it resembled a twinkling star.

The little girl was dressed in a black, woolen vest worn over a crude, burlap tunic and wool trousers. She sat on her heels with her arms wrapped around her shins, her small feet bound in deerskin moccasins. Staring at the fire she remained as unmoving as the dog.

Dudley brought out a leather purse from his coat pocket, dug out a few coins, and counted them out into the man's waiting hand. The gypsy man dropped the coins into a cloth pouch and began helping the older woman to her feet. As he led her into the tent, Dud swaggered back to Nate with a big smile stretched across his face.

"Aw-right!" he said, rubbing his palms together briskly. "We're in bus'ness!"

After tying their horses to a wheel rim on the wagon, the Champion brothers started for the tent, Dudley moving with a brisk, enthusiastic stride while Nate followed behind with his hands buried in his coat pockets.

"Should we come in?" Dud called to the closed flap over the door.

No one answered. Beneath the rush of the wind, Nate could hear the man inside mumbling to the woman. Then came the scratch of a lucifer across a stone, followed by the airy sound of a flame coming to life. After another fifteen seconds, the man pushed through the flap, his face as somber as a pallbearer carrying the corpse of his best friend.

"She ready now," he said grimly. Pulling the flap to

one side, he stepped back and held the door as Nate and Dud removed their hats and stooped through the entry.

In the semi-dark of the tent, three candles burned, each one waxed upright to a stone and forming a perfect triangle that evenly divided a two-foot-wide circle of smooth river stones. At the center of the circle lay a different kind of stone—a crystal the size of a ball of twine. The tent's center pole stood at an angle so as not to interfere with the ring of rocks. Around the periphery of the tent walls, the family's personal belongings had been hastily swept to the edge and covered with blankets and various pieces of clothing.

The woman extended both arms and opened her spindly fingers to indicate where her visitors should sit. A red blanket had been laid out on the door-side of the circle of stones, and there the brothers sat shoulder to shoulder. Nate set has hat on the ground next to him and remained quiet and still as he watched the old gypsy woman mutter to herself with her eyes closed.

She no longer wore the buffalo robe. Now a colorful garment of bright blues and reds and yellows wrapped around her thin body, held in place by a number of leather thongs, one at the waist, one at each upper arm, and one at each wrist. Once Dud finally settled in, she produced a small bundle of dry twigs from her lap and held one end over a candleflame. Smoke wafted upward from the smoldering twigs and a strong herbal scent like camphor filled the tent.

Behind him, Nate heard the door flap rustle, and the three candle flames wavered. The little girl entered and moved as light as a bird to the woman's side. There she sat cross-legged, wrapped a gray wool blanket around herself, and stared mutely at the ring of rocks.

The woman opened her eyes and pointed a crooked

finger at Dudley. "You holdt da rock in da center...holdt wit' bote hands."

Dud laughed and held both palms out to her. "No, ma'am, this ain't for me." He swept a hand toward Nate. "We come for you to talk to my brother."

When the girl spoke to the woman in a choppy language, the crone turned her obsidian eyes on Nate. "You holdt," she said and nodded at the rock.

Nate pointed at the many-faceted, central stone that looked like a chunk of cloudy glass. "This'n?"

She made no response except to stare at the stone. Nate picked it up in his right hand and bobbed it up and down in a weighing gesture.

"Bote hands," she said and raised both her knobby hands in a bowl-shape as if she were holding the stone.

"She's sayin' to hold it in both yore hands," Dud advised.

Nate held the rock in his lap, cradling it in his right hand and covering it with his left. The old woman nodded and closed her eyes. A long minute passed in silence, until Dudley came to the end of his patience.

"How long are we—"

The woman broke in with a rapid chain of complicated words that fell easily off her tongue but to Nate sounded like the meaningless, clickety-clack percussion of a stick raked across a picket fence. It was a language he had never before heard, but he likened it to the sound of the Lipan Apache wrangler who had worked for his Uncle George in Texas.

The little girl spoke up in a shy voice. "She say you be quiet." Her large, dark eyes fixed on Dudley with the innocence of her age.

Dud went through the motions of pretending to sew his lips together with imaginary needle and thread. Once sutured, he held a tight smirk on his face, but he had no audience. No one so much as smiled at his performance.

Once again, the woman closed her eyes, and a heavy silence returned. Nate could hear the roar of the wind outside...and the water folding around the boulders that were scattered along this section of the creek. No noise at all came from the people outside by the pit fire.

Finally, the woman opened her eyes and leaned across the circle of rocks with her arms extended and her hands cupped into the shape of a bowl.

"Giff," she said, and the scent of garlic and onions accompanied the word.

Nate placed the heavy crystal in her hands and watched those hands retreat to her side of the circle. There she held the rock to her breast and closed her eyes once again.

Dudley leaned to Nate and whispered, "I'm startin' to think I paid for the priv'lege o' watchin' her catch up on 'er sleep."

The girl frowned at Dudley and pressed a thin forefinger vertically to her lips. "Shhh!"

The longer the old woman remained in her inert pose, the more troubled her face grew, the skin on her forehead tightening with new crease lines that stacked up above the bridge of her nose. When her eyes opened to Nate, they were filled with pity.

"You know great loss. It stay wit' you. Make empty place in heart."

She waited as if she expected Nate to verify her words. But Nate said nothing.

"You reckon she's talkin' 'bout our mama?" Dud said.

The woman narrowed her eyes at Dud. "Leaf brutta to hear alone."

Dud's face wrinkled up in a rare portrait of complete confusion.

"She say you go out," the young girl explained.

Dud laughed a single note of surprise. "I'm the one paid for this!"

The old woman shook her head and rattled off another rapid sentence in her own tongue. Then she closed her mouth and glared at Dudley.

"Does not matter," the girl said. "She say you go."

Dudley looked at Nate, then at the gypsy woman, and finally at the girl translator. Laughing, he slapped his hands to his thighs, stood up, and exited the tent. The candleflames danced from the movement of the door flap, but they soon settled back into their steady, teardrop shapes. Once Dud's footsteps faded toward the creek, the old woman raised her chin to Nate.

"Da golten light leaf you long ago. It make empty droom dat never fill."

Nate frowned and looked to the girl for an explanation.

"She say a golden light fall away from your life some-time in da past. She say it leave a empty space inside you and it never fill."

"What kind o' golden light?" Nate asked the girl.

As an answer, the little girl lifted a strand of her dark hair away from the side of her head and let it fall back.

Looking back at the woman, Nate felt his curiosity dredge up more questions. "Are you talkin' 'bout a person?"

The woman nodded. "Wit' da golten hair. Wit' da hand can pain' the pitchus. She got took 'way by evil hand." She gestured toward the girl. "She yung and smot like Nadia."

The little girl seemed to look right through Nate as she recited from memory. "Her hair was yellow. She could paint pictures. She was young and smart."

"Who's Nadia?" Nate asked.

The girl blushed. "I am Nadia."

The woman pointed her aged finger at Nate. "You goot. I see da goot in you. Da golten girl tell me dis is true. But goot not enough in dis land, where da rich man haff all da power." She made a pained expression. "Rich man iss enemy to you."

The girl cleared her throat and began to translate, but Nate held up his hand to her. "I think I got all that." He smiled at the old woman. "I reckon I can take care o' myself."

The woman sagged a little and tilted her head to one side as if it were too heavy to hold upright. She stared at Nate with somber eyes, and he felt the first stirrings in his gut that she just might have some kind of preternatural vantage point from which to see distances that other people could not.

"You leaf dis place...now!"

He frowned. "You mean our time is up? You want me to leave your camp?"

The girl answered for the woman. "She mean Wyoming."

Nate made a halfhearted laugh. "I been workin' for years to build up what I got...almost two hun'erd head of cattle...and my own brand. Come spring, I'll take out a claim on a hun'erd an' sixty acres, an' I'm gonna have the kind o' ranch I've always dreamed 'bout."

The woman was shaking her head even before he had finished. They looked each other in the eye, and not once did she blink.

"Go!" she whispered forcefully.

Nate shook his head in protest. "I cain't be walkin' away from ever'thin' I've started."

"Go!" she said again, this time louder. "Go while you can. If you wait too long, dere iss nowhere to run."

Nate breathed out a long sigh, straightened his arms,

and clasped his hands to his knees. "How is it you know 'bout Dory?"

Her eyes pinched, and the tip of her tongue curled to touch her upper lip. "Dor-dree?"

"The golden girl," he explained. "The one you been talkin' 'bout."

The woman looked back at him, and her eyebrows slanted to a peak like the slopes of a symmetrical hill. "She speak to me now."

Nate felt his body go light as air. "She's here right now? In this tent?"

The gypsy nodded.

Nate swallowed. "How do you know?"

Now the woman's eyebrows arched high on her forehead. "She speak to me," she said, as if the answer were obvious.

Nate watched her face for a long time, trying to read the woman's hold on sanity. "If she's here," he said softly, "can you tell 'er somethin' for me?"

The woman waited. The little girl drew herself into a ball, her arms wrapped around her legs and her chin resting on her knees. It was as if she were trying to disappear to give Nate the privacy he deserved.

"*You* tell," the woman said.

Nate frowned and looked around the interior of the tent. Then he licked his lips and cleared his throat.

"Do I just say it out loud?"

The gypsy set down the crystal very gently and nodded.

Embarrassed, Nate fixed his gaze on the milky stone. "I'll just say it to you, if you don't care." He glanced at her to see if she might object. When she did not, he looked back at the stone. "Tell 'er I should'a held on to 'er an' kept her safe. I should'a never let 'er go off to that school." After a time of silence, he brought up his head and looked into the woman's eyes. "Can you tell 'er that?"

The woman shrugged. "She hear you."

Nate studied the woman's face for a lie. "You sure 'bout that?"

The woman nodded to the space on the floor next to Nate, just behind one of the lighted candles. "She iss dere now...wit' us. She come to deliver *her* message."

A chill climbed up Nate's spine. "What message?"

The gypsy woman's eyes filled with a warmth that changed her face from stranger to friend. "You loose two friends. Bote was goot men." Leaning forward with her hands pressed to the earth inside the circle of stones, she blew out the flame on the candle to Nate's left. A ribbon of smoke rippled and then rose straight up, climbing to the top of the tent. Then she leaned to the candle at Nate's right. When she blew out the flame, another stream of smoke ascended.

"Dos goot men gone like dat."

Nate frowned at the two dead candles and then studied the woman's face. "Yo're talkin' 'bout John an' Ranger," he whispered. "How do you know 'bout them?"

The woman held up a hand, palm out to Nate, and closed her eyes. She was like one of those wood-carved Indians set outside a tobacco store.

"Da golten girl say you go 'way from dis valley."

The woman sat upright and fixed her gaze on the lighted candle before Nate's shins. He looked down at it, too. No one moved, but Nate sensed something inside the tent besides the woman, the girl, and himself. He wondered if the old man had entered the tent behind him, but Nate could not take his eyes off the still-lit candle. The flame was gradually pushed to one side, flapping like a small yellow rag caught in a brisk wind. But there was no wind. The air inside the tent was calm and still. And yet, as he watched, the agitated flame angled sharply from the candlestick. Yet it refused to die.

Nate looked at the two faces across from him, searching each for some expression that might better explain what was happening, but neither the woman nor the girl displayed any emotion whatsoever. He turned to see that the door was still closed. No one had entered. When he turned back to the candle, its flame had converted back to a serene teardrop shape that seemed to float before him. It surprised him when a hot bubble of anger rose up from inside him and hardened his voice.

"This's some kind o' trick, ain't it?"

The woman's humble eyes lowered to the ground, and she said nothing. The young girl hugged herself tighter and remained quiet.

"She made a paintin' for me!" he blurted out in an accusatory tone. "What was on it?"

The old woman kept her eyes lowered when she spoke. "Paint," she said clearly.

Nate pushed himself up to one knee and glared at the woman. "Well, I reckon any paintin' is gonna have paint on it, don't you figure?!" When he got no response, he picked up his hat. "I'll be goin' now."

Pivoting around, he pushed through the door flap and straightened up to face the cold wind that blew from the northwest. Dudley leaned against the wagon where the horses were tied. Smoking a cigarette, Dud gazed out over the prairie of withered grass that stretched beyond the fort and into the foothills of the Big Horns. Nate slapped his hat onto his head and started toward his brother but stopped when the tent flap buckled open. The little girl, still wrapped up in her blanket, emerged with a look of urgency on her young face.

"She mean da horse," the girl said quickly.

"What?"

"The paint horse."

Nate stared at her for ten heartbeats. Then he knelt down on one knee before her. Very gently, he took each of her shoulders in his hands.

"What're you sayin'?"

"The paint horse...in the picture."

Feeling his eyes start to burn, Nate looked through the tent door and saw the last candle still burning. He tried to swallow, but his mouth was too dry.

"How could she know that?" he said in a raspy whisper.

"She beg you to leave dis valley. What should I tell her?"

He couldn't see the old woman's face inside the tent. She sat with her head bowed exactly as he had left her. The candle burned as steadily as the north star.

"I can't turn back on my plans now. I've worked too hard to git what I got. Tell 'er I thank 'er for all her concerns."

Inside the tent, the candleflame flared for a moment and then snuffed out as quickly as the snap of two fingers. The girl slipped from his hands and went inside, pulling the flap shut behind her. Nate stood and listened for any words he might hear through the canvas, but there was only silence inside and the wind roaring through the trees above him.

When Nate turned and walked to the horses, Dud plugged the cigarette into the corner of his smile and pushed away from the wagon. "Well?" he said in a cheery voice, "was it worth the trip?"

Nate untied Dakah's reins and led her a few paces away from Dud's horse. He stood facing his saddle, his left hand on the pommel and right on the cantle. Looking over the bow of the saddle at his brother, he spoke in a quiet voice that was almost lost in the whispery shoals of the creek.

"I reckon I'll have to think on it for a while."

They mounted and rode in silence toward town. Snow began to fall again, and the low ceiling of gray clouds had softened to charred cotton with the promise of more snow to come. Dudley rode a little ahead, giving Nate the space he needed, but Nate hardly knew what to do with the privacy. He had a lot to think about and miles to go in which to do just that.

Early Spring 1892

KC Ranch, Johnson County, Wyoming

Chapter Twenty-Seven

April brought harsh weather—the kind that sent men home at the end of a workday with their beards and mustaches frozen solid and their feet stumps of cold iron. The pasturelands of the Powder River Basin were blanketed in a foot and a half of snow. Wind blasted across the white landscape with unforgiving force, delivering an icy bite to any exposed skin, especially when a gust carried tiny pellets of ice that stung the face like a nest of angry hornets.

Nate and Nick Ray—both dressed in wool sweaters, heavy coats, and oilskin slickers—prodded their horses toward the KC with their firewood harvest in tow. It took two ropes and both horses to drag the dead cottonwood they had axed to the ground near the Red Fork, and they were determined to sled it intact to their cabin, where they would saw it into stove-length sections.

Nick leaned toward Nate and yelled over the howl of the wind. "You ever hear that ol' sayin' 'Injun keep warm with small fire.'" He bent forward over his pommel to show Nate his smile. "'White man keep warm *swingin'* a axe an' *gatherin'* up wood an' *haulin'* it back to camp for a blazin' fire big enough to roast a elephant."

Nate nodded. "I reckon our horses oughta fit into that sayin' somewhere. They're doin' all the work now."

Nick laughed. "You're right. I reckon if it was you an' me on foot a-draggin' this tree, someb'dy would find us froze out here like a stone-carved memorial to the fools o' the world."

After a dozen rest stops to spell the horses, it was late afternoon when they came in sight of the bridge over the Middle Fork. Nate tapped the back of his gloved hand against Nick's shoulder and then pointed across the river at the KC's low barn that stood between the cabin and the river.

"Looks like we got comp'ny," Nate called out.

All over the yard, fresh tracks had been punched into the snow, both hoofprints and boot prints. Five horses were crowded into the bay of the small barn. Nate thought he recognized Old Ben Jones's saddle horse and pack horse among them. He knew that Ben was trapping with a new partner, so it was a safe bet that two of the remaining horses belonged to Ben's companion. But the fifth horse troubled Nate. It was a white Arabian like the one Mike Shonsey rode.

Dismounting in the yard, Nate approached the front door, leaving Nick to untie their ropes from the tree. The jaunty picking of a banjo and the lively scratching of a fiddle came through the door, causing Nate to hesitate, bow his head, and smile. When he opened the door, a peculiar, rank odor met him at the threshold. He saw Old Ben sitting on a corner bunk, sawing away at his old, scarred-up fiddle. On the adjoining, angled bed, a tall young fellow with a full beard leaned over a banjo tucked into his lap and coaxed a flowing stream of rising and falling notes from the instrument. His fingers moved like a spider dancing on its web. The oil lamp had been moved to the end of the long table so that its glow lit up the two musicians as if they had set up an impromptu stage.

In their stockinged feet and long johns, both men were absorbed in the music they played and oblivious to the closing of the door. But a third man knelt before the fire, feeding split sticks to the flames, and he spun around so quickly that he lost his balance and almost fell. Mike Shonsey steadied himself with a hand on the floor and stood up fully clothed, except for his pale, bare feet. Those feet looked like a couple of dazed fish left stranded on land. His pistol was strapped to his waist and his cartridge bristled with ammunition.

Three pairs of boots stood upright on the hearth, as if three men who had been warming themselves unexplainably vanished, leaving their footwear behind. A rope had been strung across the southeast corner of the room, and draped over it was an assortment of damp clothes from which the smell in the room originated.

When Nate took off his hat and slapped it against his leg, the music stopped, and Old Ben smiled at Nate as he lowered the fiddle and bow to his lap. Ben reached up and held a hank of his graying hair away from his head and stretched it taut. It was the same gesture the young gypsy girl had used to show Nate that her grandmother knew who Dory was.

"Still got it!" Ben crowed.

"So I see," Nate replied as he hung his hat on a wall peg.

Ben bumped his fist against his friend's knee. "I tol' Nate 'bout that gypsy woman," he explained. "The one who tol' me 'bout me losin' my scalp." The young man narrowed his eyes and nodded, his mouth forming a perfect circle of understanding. "Nate, this here is Billy

Walker," Ben introduced. "We been trappin' together this winter."

Billy laid the banjo on the bed and stood to shake Nate's hand. "Hope you don't mind us elbowin' in like this. Ben figured it was okay. Said you two went back a ways."

Nate nodded to set the young man at ease. "Git too cold for you boys out there?"

Ben waved away that idea. "We was on our way into Buffalo for supplies, but we got started too late. Figured we'd better bunk here than push on to the CY, where we might not be welcome."

The remark was an obvious jab at Shonsey, who had yet to speak. Ben flung a hand from the wrist in Shonsey's direction.

"This'n here just showed up 'bout a half 'our ago. Bein' as it ain't my cabin, I didn' figure it was my place to say yes or no to 'im."

When Nate turned to look at Mike Shonsey, the room became quiet but for the crackle of the fire. At first, Shonsey pretended not to notice that all eyes were upon him. Then he lowered his eyebrows and exhaled a heavy sigh.

"My horse threw me fordin' the Red Fork," Shonsey mumbled. "Landed upright but took on water in my boots. My feet are like are bricks." He shrugged. "Didn't have much choice, but I'll go if you want me to."

Nate pulled off his gloves and slicker and hung them on the wall beside his hat. Then he walked toward Shonsey, who began shifting his stance like a man uncertain of his balance. When Nate stopped one stride away from him, Shonsey stilled himself like a clock's pendulum come to rest.

"I know you ain't brave," Nate said, "so that only leaves bein' stupid."

Shonsey shrugged again. "I figured since I gave up the names o' those men to you, we might be square."

"You figured dead wrong," Nate said in a quiet voice.

Shonsey's face paled to the color of his pitiable feet. "But I—"

"But nothin'!" Nate interrupted. "Don't you git it, you damned coward? You were part o' the den of snakes that tried to kill me while I was in my bed."

Shonsey lowered his head and swung it back and forth as he recommenced shifting his weight from leg to leg. "My feet are bad off," he mewled. He stopped moving and raised pleading eyes. "You ain't gonna throw me out, are you?"

Nate knotted his hands into fists and thought about poleaxing the sniveling whiner and knocking him onto the fireplace. He decided if Shonsey looked away from him again, he would do just that. But the miserable man pulled out some gumption from somewhere and held his pleading eyes on Nate's.

"Can you at least let me git my feet workin' again? That an' git my socks dry?"

The door flung open, and Nick bustled in with two sets of saddlebags slung over a shoulder and a rifle in each hand. After closing the door with his boot, he stood looking around at the crowded room, his face pinched with confusion like a man who had walked into the wrong residence. He let the bags slide off his shoulder onto the floor and propped the rifles against the front wall.

"Well, damn! Looks like we're runnin' a hotel now!" Nick's big smile broke off when he caught sight of Shonsey. Watching Nick's face was like seeing a dark cloud cover the sun. Frowning, he whipped off his hat and slapped it against his leg, sending a shower of snow and ice crystals to the floor. After pulling out of his slicker and hanging it on the wall, he strode to the hearth and, ignoring Shonsey, rubbed his hands together briskly and held them out to the fire.

"I brushed down the horses, Nate," Nick said. "Put 'em away in the stalls and hooked on their blankets. Doled out some hay an' grain for 'em too."

"'Preciate it, Nick." Nate patted Nick on the back as he moved toward his bunk and began unbuttoning his coat.

"You boys stayin' the night?" Nick said loudly, throwing out the question to all.

The room went dead quiet for a few seconds. Outside the wind wailed and pushed against the front door like a wild beast trying to force its way inside.

"We'd shore appreciate it," Old Ben said in his kind, melodic voice. "This here is Billy Walker, Nick." Ben slapped his partner's knee. "We're obliged to you for your hospitality."

"Yes, sir," Billy spoke up, "we damned sure are."

Nick swept a hand toward the line of clothes hanging behind the stove. "I guess this stink is all part o' the package, huh?"

Ben laughed. "We didn't know. I guess we're so used to it, we don't hardly notice it."

Nick turned to face Shonsey. "And what about you?"

Shonsey's forehead rippled with lines. "What *about* me?"

"I don't remember invitin' you out here," Nick growled.

Shonsey frowned at Nick and then fixed his eyes on the flames. "I just figured it was common courtesy out on the range. Always has been. A roof and a meal...that ain't too much to ask, is it?"

Nick stared at Shonsey the way one man looks at another's onset of gangrene. "So, you ain't gonna show some o' that courtesy by askin'?"

Shonsey breathed out a long sigh. "I'd appreciate a roof for the night."

Nick laughed, but there was no joy in it. "Hell, the *barn's* gotta roof!"

Shonsey glanced down at his feet. "I might'a got frostbit out there. I'd 'preciate it if you let me stay here."

In the awkward silence that followed, Nick looked to Nate to see if he wanted to provide some input to the problem. But Nate said nothing and started pulling out of his sweater.

Nick turned back to Shonsey. "Well, here's another old tradition o' common courtesy. You believe in barter?"

Shonsey narrowed his eyes and studied Nick from an angle. "Whatta you mean?"

Nick leaned toward Shonsey, as if the man were hard of hearing. "Tradin' one thing for another? Barter? You know? It ain't a difficult concept."

Shonsey frowned. "I ain't really carryin' nothin' o' value."

Nick's mouth tightened to a spiteful smile. "How're your arms workin'?" He pointed at the door. "We got a dead cottonwood outside needs sawin' into stove lengths." Nick shifted the aim of his finger to the crosscut saw hanging on the wall behind the woodpile. "Right there is the saw."

Shonsey's frown turned to misery. "Takes two to handle one o' them, don't it?"

Nick turned to the two trappers, as if waiting for a volunteer, but Nate spoke up in a quiet and deliberate voice. "We got enough wood for the night. Why don't we hold off on that till tomorr'?" He nodded toward Shonsey's bare feet. "He ain't in no shape to go back out tonight."

"Hell," Billy Walker spoke up, "I can help with sawin' tomorr'. Me and Ben can cut firewood for you all day!"

Old Ben laughed. "If we can find that tree. There ain't no tellin' how much it'll snow tonight."

Nick folded his arms and nodded. "All right, you two will work the saw." He pivoted his head to Shonsey. "We got a axe, too." He freed up a hand to point at Shonsey. "You'll do your part with that! If that ain't agreeable to you, you can ride out right now!"

Shonsey took on his well-used pouting look and lowered his eyes. "I can swing a axe."

"You boys hungry?" Nate asked.

"I could eat the south end of a mule!" Ben returned.

"We got a little salt pork we can donate to a meal," Billy offered.

Nick turned to scowl at Shonsey. "How 'bout you, Mister CY foreman. What can you volunteer for supper?"

Shonsey lifted his arms from his sides and let them fall back. "Not much to offer. Got a three-day-old, stale biscuit that's prob'ly froze harder'n a cue ball."

"'Not much to offer,'" Nick mimicked. "'Bout the story o' your life, ain't it?"

With all of Nick's abrasive attitude wearing Shonsey down, the beleaguered man turned his plea to where Nate sat on his bunk. "Ever'body says you're a fair man, Champion. Just let me stay the night...git my feet workin'...then I'll git outta your hair."

Nate clenched his teeth and glared at the man. "What would you know 'bout 'fair'?"

"Well, I know this new cattle assoc'ation has voted you top foreman for their roundup this spring."

That turned every head in the room toward Nate. "What assoc'ation?" Nate said.

"They're callin' it the Northern Wyomin' Farmers' and Stockgrowers' Assoc'ation."

Nate shook his head. "I heard of it, but I ain't connected to it."

"Well, it appears they thought highly o' you, 'cause they voted you in as head foreman."

"I wasn't in on any votin'," Nate insisted. "I don't care to be joinin' up with any organization. I just wonna run my ranch an' take care o' my own affairs an' let others do the same." Nate felt an anger rise inside him like a flame climbing a rope. He had started to pull off a boot, but he stood and stamped back into the boot and strode to the hearth with his heels making solid contact with the floor. In three strides he was right in Shonsey's face.

"You tell me this," Nate began in a forceful whisper. He pressed a stiff forefinger into Shonsey's chest and held it there firmly. "An' you better tell it straight! If you lie to me, I *will* find out, an' I *will* pay you a visit you will regret." Nate pulled back his finger and poked it again right over Shonsey's heart. "Were you in on the killin's of John Tisdale or Ranger Jones? Or both?!"

Shonsey's face went slack as he raised his right hand to make an oath. "I swear to God and to you right now that I had nothin' to do with them killin's. I swear it on my mother's eyes. I'm tellin' you the truth, Champion, and, if I ain't, I hope to be struck down by the hand o' God."

Nate held his finger in place and listened to Shonsey's heavy breathing. When the frightened man's eyes covered with a film of moisture that reflected the firelight in bright flashes, Nate looked down at Shonsey's bare feet. Now they had turned the bright red of raw meat. When his head came up, Nate removed his finger from the man's breast and looked him in the eye.

"If the tables were turned...an' I was knockin' on yore door on a night like this...d'you reckon you'd let me in?"

Shonsey winced as if he'd been caught in a lie. He bit his lower lip and pushed his brow low over his eyes.

"I'd like to think I would," he murmured. "But you're

prob'ly a better neighbor than I am...so, I can't say for sure."

Nate nodded at the first truthful thing he had heard come out of Shonsey's mouth. "I never yet turned away a man in need," Nate said quietly and moved past Shonsey to take a wide stance before the hearth. He held out his hands to the radiant heat and casually turned his head to Shonsey. "Unless I figure a man is a danger to me," Nate added.

Shonsey shook his head. "I ain't no danger to nob'dy here tonight. I'll just stay till I git some life back into my feet and dry my socks. If you'll allow me that, then I'll push on."

A long minute of silence passed as everyone in the room awaited Nate's judgment. Nick stood with his elbows angled out to either side, his fists on his hips. Nate turned his back to the fire. Keeping his eyes on the painting above his bunk, he tried to imagine Dory being here and what she would think of all this.

"Till yore feet thaw out," Nate said in a firm decree. "Then I wont you gone." He pointed to the front wall pegs. "Rack yore gun over there till yo're ready to leave."

Shonsey bowed his head and nodded. "I'm obliged," he whispered.

"What?!" Nick barked from six feet away. "Couldn't hear that!"

Shonsey frowned, but he would not look at Nick. "Said *I'm obliged*," he repeated, loud enough to be heard by everyone.

When Shonsey unbuckled his cartridge belt and carried it to the front wall, Nate sat down on the corner of the hearth facing the trappers. "Reckon you boys could whip up another song for us. It's startin' to git purty ripe in here. Maybe some music will help."

"Shore!" Old Ben chirped. But he pointed his fiddle

bow at the place where Nate had been staring at the wall over his bed. "Hey, Nate? Where'd you git that purty picture? Looks like a tree I know down on the Sweetwater."

Nate shook his head. "That's Texas...down in Williamson County."

"I didn' know Texas was that green," Ben said.

Nate nodded. "Yeah, it's green. Not like here, but...in some places."

"So, who painted it?" Ben pressed.

Nate pulled off his boots and set them on the hearth next to the others. Then he walked to his bunk, sat, and slipped on the Shoshone moccasins for which he had traded on the day he had acquired Dakah.

"She was a friend o' mine," Nate said quietly. He stood and walked to the kitchen area, his feet silent on the floor. There he knelt and fed kindling into the stove. Taking a long serving spoon from the sideboard, he moved to the hearth and scooped up a healthy red coal. Walking it back to the stove, he noticed that Old Ben was leaning in closer to admire the artwork.

"And she painted this for you?" Ben asked in breathy awe.

Nate set the coal in the bed of sticks, added a few larger pieces, and turned at the waist to point the spoon at Dory's painting. "That's my paint horse there...Peaches."

Ben kept staring at the painting as he shook his head and blew a silent stream of air like a man learning to whistle. "That's a mighty fine gift, Nate. You tell 'er when you see 'er, Old Ben Jones admires her work."

Nate nodded. "I'll do that."

Chapter Twenty-Eight

When the first light of dawn crept in through the east window, Nate propped up on an elbow and studied the dimly defined shapes in the room. There was a gap in the flank of boots on the hearth. The drying line was bare for a third of its length. And several of the pegs on the front wall were freed up. Nate checked the bunk in the back of the room. Shonsey was gone.

Donning his moccasins, Nate crossed the floor to the front window and saw fresh tracks leading from the cabin. The snow was coming down at a slant with the wind, but the tracks were still well-defined. They veered around the dead, snow-capped cottonwood lying in the yard and then continued to the barn. Coming out of the barn and curving around the yard to cross the bridge, the prints of a single horse led out to the main road. Nate flattened his hand to a snow-framed pane of windowglass. It felt like a sheet of ice.

With Shonsey departed, the cabin seemed to breathe out a sigh of relief. Nate stoked the stove with fresh sticks and put on yesterday's coffee to heat up. When he turned to add a log to the fireplace, he saw Nick sitting up in his bed, one big leg bent across the other as he tried to pick at something on the bottom of his foot.

"That polecat gone without doin' a lick o' work on that cottonwood?" Nick growled.

Nate nodded. "Looks like it."

"Figures!" Nick said, and then he snorted. "Hell, it's a wonder we didn't wake up dead."

Nate smiled, thinking that this was just the kind of thing Dudley would say.

"Whatta you say we go git that other dead tree we saw yesterday?" Nate said. He waved an arm toward the corner of the room where the trappers had not yet stirred. "Maybe these boys here could work the crosscut together while we're gone."

Billy Walker sat up in bed and stretched. "Hell, yeah!" he said through a yawn. "Me an' Ben will put in a whole day, if you don't mind us stayin' another night. Tomorr's Sa'urday, an' I'd rather wait till then to go into town. There's s'posed to be some kind o' dance tomorr' night, an' I wanna be there for that!"

"Lookin' for a female, are you?" Nick laughed.

"Well, the only face I've seen for the last coupla weeks is Old Ben's there. I figure it might be a dose o' good medicine to meet me a purty girl."

There was movement under Ben's blanket, and his head emerged from the covers. His gray hair was wildly disheveled, and his eyes raw and vulnerable, full of sleep.

"If you think you can find a girl purtier than me at that dance, son, you'll be mighty disappointed."

Billy laughed and pointed at Ben. "You're goin' with me, by God, an' we're gonna find a woman for you, too. D'you know how to dance, you ol' skunk?"

Old Ben winced and gave the boy a hurt look. "Do I know how to *dance*? Son, I was swingin' free-spirited girls around the dance floor b'fore you knew how to pull on your britches all by yourself."

As the two trappers bantered, Nate ladled water from a bucket into the kettle and set it on the stove. Then he sat at the hearth and let the heat cover his back. Staring at Dory's painting, he felt a twinge of guilt that last night he had neglected to write in his book. It was the first night in months that he had missed the ritual.

When the kettle began to boil, Nate made coffee and returned to the hearth. Nick poured for himself into a metal cup, wrapped a bandanna around the handle, and then carried it to the table, where he sat across from Nate, who continued to stare at Dory's painting.

"I'll bet she was a purty one," Nick said.

Nate snapped out of his reverie. "What?"

Nick turned at the waist and raised his cup to the painting. "The girl who gave you such a gift as that."

"She was," Nate whispered. "Outside and inside." Before Nick could ask another question, Nate turned to him. "Yore week for cookin, you know."

Nick took a swallow of coffee and nodded deeply. "So, we're goin' after that other tree today?"

"We are," Nate said. "We git back early enough, maybe these two will saw it up for us."

"*We'll* saw it!" Billy assured them. "Hell, we'll saw up both of 'em!"

Old Ben stood up in his long johns and checked his clothes on the drying line. "I see that CY buzzard took off early to avoid any labor." Ben shook his head and curled his lip. "Ever' time I run across that man, I feel like sticking my head down in a cold river just to clear my thoughts. Somethin' about him makes my skin crawl. It's like a nest o' ants has gone to war b'neath my shirt." Ben squinted at Nate. "Did I do wrong by lettin' 'im in."

Nate shook his head. "Might be you taught 'im somethin'."

Ben frowned. "I doubt that. I ain't sure he's the kind that can be taught *anythin'*!"

Nick stood and finished his coffee. "I don't trust the sonovabitch. I'll tell you what...I slept with my pistol in my hand last night...an' I kept my back against the wall."

The two trappers stared at Nick in silence, both of them lost in thought, no doubt weighing the possibilities of what could have happened in the night. Nate set down his empty cup. Leaning forward, he flattened both hands on the stone hearth and let his head sag so that his chin almost touched his chest.

"How 'bout we spend the rest o' this day without bringin' up the name o' Mike Shonsey," he announced to the room. "I'm purty tired o' thinkin' 'bout 'im."

"Yeah," Nick agreed, "we done our good deed for the year bringin' *him* outta the cold." He picked up Nate's cup and started for the basin. "I'll get crackin' on breakfast.

"You need some help?" Billy called out.

Nick stopped and turned. "You know how to make biscuits, son?"

"Yes, sirree. My mama's recipe."

Nick smiled. "You're hired, young man. Git over here an' help me."

———

It was late afternoon when Nate and Nick dragged in the second tree behind their horses. Old Ben and Billy had finished sawing and stacking the wood from the first tree, and now they went to work on the new arrival.

After tending to the horses, Nate carried a metal bucket to the river and, using an oblong stone, broke up the shelf of ice at the shoreline. He scooped up a full pail of gelid water and hauled it to the cabin, where he set it upon the wood stove to heat.

By the time the sawyers had come in, the bucket of water was more than warm. Nate ladled heated water into the white porcelain wash basin. After placing a rag and chunk of lye soap in the basin, he stripped down and hung his clothes on the drying line that the trappers had set up. Then he commenced scrubbing his body with the soaped rag from ears to toes. Naked and wet, Nate wrapped the soap in its waxed paper, wrung out the rag, and carried the basin to the backdoor, where he stepped out and flung the cloudy water into the yard. It cut through the snow like a sharp knife through soft butter.

Back at the stove, he repeated the ladling and scrubbing but this time without the soap. Then he carried the bucket out back, stepped out into the snow in his bare feet, and emptied what was left of the water onto his upturned face, letting the runoff rinse his body. He stood naked, steaming in the frosty air, feeling the bite of the cold on his skin like a burn.

When he came back inside to stand before the fire, Old Ben chuckled as he tugged off his boots. "I swear, Nate, I always thought o' you as a small feller—you know, kinda lean and not as tall as most—but what there is o' you is built 'bout as compact as a locomotive."

"He runs like one too," Nick said. "Outran every soldier at the fort that day they held that footrace. Take my advice an' don't never bet against Nate Champion."

Old Ben chuckled a little louder. "That sounds like the voice o' experience talkin'. You bet ag'in Nate?"

"Just the one time," Nick admitted. "But you should'a seen that soldier ever'body said would win. Long legs and built like a antelope. Strong-lookin', too."

"Nate whipped 'im, huh?" Old Ben asked.

Nick sneered. "Weren't even close. Soldier boy didn't see nothin' but Nate's back. Ran in his bare feet, too."

Billy watched Nate cross the room with his towel wrapped at his waist. "How'd you git so fast, Nate?"

"Ain't you heard Nate's story, son?" Nick crowed. "Why, he was lost on the prairie as a baby, and a herd o' Texas mustangs found 'im, raised 'im, and taught 'im ever'thin' he knows. When they ran, he ran with 'em. When they ate grass, Nate ate grass. That's why he's easy to cook for. Sometimes I just feed 'im some buffalo grass with a few oats scattered in."

Nate finished dressing and tied on his moccasins. "Well, I hope we're havin' somethin' better'n grass tonight. An' I hope the cook gits started purty soon."

Grinning, Nick made a little bow from the waist, turned, and lumbered into the cooking corner. Nate pulled out his leather book and sat on his bed with his back to the wall next to Dory's painting.

"Would you two boys consider strikin' up some more music for us?" Nate asked.

Billy laughed. "Nob'dy ever has to ask us twice for that."

As they tuned up their instruments, Nate settled in to write, explaining to Dory about the way he thought of her now...about the love that had grown inside him since she had died...about how he ought to have told her his feelings all those years ago, when they were young and learning to trust each other with their secrets.

When the two trappers began a soulful tune that seemed to wrap around his heart, Nate aligned the rhythm of his writing with the moving passages of the music. For the first time, he wrote the three words that he had never said to Dory. Or written them, for that matter. Then he closed the book and listened to the song, until Billy quietly strummed his strings a final time and Ben delivered the last sustained note of the melody, letting it fade and disappear like a dying breath.

After their meal, with the cleanup complete, Ben and Billy picked up their instruments again and delivered a lively tune, the banjo notes running together faster than a woodpecker chiseling into a tree and the fiddle bow bouncing on the strings, giving the song a sense of frolicking and gamboling like a frisky colt in a pasture.

Nate readied for bed, slipped under his covers, and watched the musicians put a fine touch to their tuning pegs. "Hey, fellahs...would you play that first song again? The one you played before supper?"

Billy beamed. "Be proud to!"

Even Old Ben grinned. "Can't turn down a encore."

"What's the name of it?" Nate asked.

Ben's face scrunched up, but he couldn't hide his smile. "It's just somethin' we worked up together. It ain't really got a name yet."

Nate closed his eyes for several seconds, and when he opened them, Ben and Billy were still staring at him. "I figure it's 'bout feelin's for a woman," Nate said. "Am I right on that?"

Old Ben smiled at the floor before answering. "Well, it is for me, but I can't speak for Billy." He turned to his companion and raised his eyebrows like a question.

Billy blushed. "Yeah...but it ain't nobody in particular. I guess for me it's just moonin' over what might be down the road."

"You mean '*who* might be,'" Ben countered. "Don't you?"

Billy blushed again and turned his attention back to tuning his banjo.

Nate propped up on an elbow. "Hey...can I make a suggestion for the namin' of it?"

"Shore," Ben said without hesitation. "Fine by me." He looked to Billy for agreement.

Billy swallowed and widened his eyes at Nate. "We'd be honored, Nate."

Nate nodded and closed his eyes again. "How 'bout 'The Purtiest Girl in Texas,'" he whispered.

When he opened his eyes, Nate found both men staring at him with their eyes asking the same question.

"Sounds good to me!" Ben said.

"Yeah! That's just right!" Billy agreed.

Nate lay back on his mattress, closed his eyes, and eased out a long breath. "Good," he said. "Now I'll know how to ask for it."

Chapter Twenty-Nine

After a sound sleep, Nate woke to the light touch of someone's fingertips on his shoulder.

"Hey, Nate?" Billy Walker whispered. "Sorry to wake you, but Ben an' me want to git a early start into town. Would you care if we borrowed your method o' bathin' by the stove. We got our own soap an' rags." He made an embarrassed laugh. "If we're goin' to that dance, we're gonna need to scrub off some of this 'trapper's scent.'"

Nate sat up and wiped the sleep from his eyes. The little room was starting to define itself by the first rays of dawn. Billy stood there in his long johns, waiting for an answer. Nick was stoking the stove, and the coffee pot sat on top.

"Sure you can," Nate said. "But what 'bout yore clothes?"

Billy hitched his head to one side. "We each got another set that's purty clean."

"When you fetch yore water...take somethin' with you to break through the ice," Nate suggested. "There's a old pickaxe in the barn."

When Billy turned, Old Ben stood at the door looking at him. Ben was fully dressed and wrapped up inside his heavy coat. In his gloved hand hung the metal bucket.

"I'll git it!" Ben said. "Why don't you start packin' your gear."

"Did you hear the part about gittin' the pickaxe?" Billy asked.

Ben closed his eyes and nodded once. "I ain't deaf yet! I heard it!"

"Say, Ben?" Nate said hoarsely. "While yo're out there, would you break up the ice in the water troughs at the barn?"

"Shore will!" Ben said and pulled open the door to a blast of cold wind. When he shut the door behind him, the cold moved through the room like the ghost of winter prowling through the cabin.

Needing to empty his bladder, Nate started to pull on his boots to visit the privy, but he decided to use the chamber pot instead. Then he pulled down his clothes from the drying line and dressed in yesterday's work outfit. Sitting on the hearth, he checked his boots and found them dry enough to pull on over his best wool socks.

After pouring a cup of coffee, Nate sat at the table with Nick and Billy. Nick had brought last week's newspaper from the kindling box and now spread it before him to read, even though he and Nate had taken turns reading every article out loud to one another.

"How far d'you two have to ride to cut down that tree?" Billy asked.

Nate set down his cup and pushed his lower lip forward. "Less than a mile, I'd say."

Nick spoke up without taking his eyes from the paper. "But it's twice that far on the drag back home...I can tell you that!"

Nate smiled down into his coffee. "Nick gits confused sometimes an' thinks he's the horse a-haulin' the load."

Nick sighed as he shook his head. He gave Billy a tired look.

"Nate's thought process always starts with a horse somehow. Prob'ly got somethin' to do with that upbringin' amongst mustangs I tol' you 'bout."

Billy smiled but then lost that smile when his gaze fell on the door. "Wonder what the hell's keeping the old fiddler?"

Nick rustled the newspaper, folded it once, and held one of the articles closer to his eyes. "Prob'ly seein' to the horses," he mumbled.

Billy stood and pulled down his laundry from the rope. "I better go see if he's fell through the ice at the river." He dressed quickly, pulled on his boots, and bundled up in his coat. Then he pushed his hat down firmly on his head.

When he went outside, Nate had a view of the barn through the open doorway. He saw movement in the bay and called out to Billy.

"Looks like he's in the barn! Check there, Billy!"

When Billy closed the door, the room seemed to fall back into a state of normalcy with the fire crackling, the wood stove quietly inhaling, and the wind shearing around the corners of the little cabin.

Twenty minutes later, Nick set a large skillet on the tabletop, balancing it on the three stones they used as a trivet. A mass of scrambled eggs sizzled in one half of the pan, while the rest of the available space was taken up by stacks of flatbread. He sat and served his plate and stuffed into his mouth a mound of eggs wrapped inside a folded slice of bread.

"What the hell you think is keepin' those boys?" Nick mumbled around a mouthful.

Nate spooned eggs onto his plate and chose two pieces of bread. "Don't know," he said.

Still chewing, Nick extracted his long legs from the bench seat and opened the front door. He stood in the doorway for several seconds, as the cold air moved into the room like a river.

"Don't stand there like that in full view, Nick," Nate advised. "I ain't sure what I saw movin' in the barn."

"I don't see either one of 'em or nobody else," Nick growled. He stepped over the threshold, closed the door within a few inches of being shut, and yelled out into the yard. *"Ben!"*

Nate stopped chewing to listen for a reply. There was none.

"Billy!" Nick called out. After five more seconds of silence, he closed the door, and Nate heard Nick's boots crunch in the snow as he moved out into the yard. *"Ben!"* Nick called louder.

Another spell of silence passed, and then the peace of the morning was shattered by the sharp report of a rifle. The unexpected sound was like an icicle sliding down Nate's spine. Dropping his fork, he spun on the bench seat and lunged for his bunk, where his Colt's pistol lay next to his pillow. As he grabbed it, three more guns exploded outside. Then five, six...ten more shots followed.

With gun in hand, Nate threw open the door and scoured the perimeter of the yard with his eyes, his Colt's extended before him. He saw a number of heads peek out from behind the barn and in the brush beyond the fence and among the cottonwoods at the river. In his peripheral vision, he saw Nick, motionless, sprawled out in the snow.

The first man to show his upper body leaned out from the back corner of the barn, his head tilted over the sights of his rifle while aiming at Nate. He wore a shiny hat band that caught the sun and threw out a bright reflection of silvery lights. Nate cocked his revolver on the rise, bringing it up in a smooth arc, and took aim. When he fired, the gun kicked up and sent a plume of gray smoke into the cold air, but the wind cleared it away as quickly as it had appeared, and Nate recognized the hatless man who grabbed his face and howled like a kicked dog. His blond hair fell to his shoulders, and his fancy hat sat upright on the snow six or seven feet from the corner of the barn.

What the hell are you doing here? Nate thought.

A barrage of gunshots rang out from the cottonwoods, and the bullets slapped into the front of the cabin, the sound like a crew of rail workers hammering spikes into a cherrywood tie. Nate leveled the Colt's and shot at a man who stepped out from one of the trees. Jerking around a quarter turn, the man fell back into the branches of a leafless shrub. Nate rotated his arm and fired at a movement in the doorway of the barn, and right away, a man yelped in a high-pitched voice.

With bullets flying around him, Nate high-stepped through the snow, grabbed one of Nick's wrists, and began tugging him back toward the open cabin door. A thunderous barrage of gunfire exploded from the trees, kicking up wisps of snow and ice all around him. An ominous circle of bright-red snow emerged where Nick's body had lain, and a smeared trail followed his boots as he was dragged. Nick was deadweight, but he was still alive. He groaned each time Nate pulled. Twice, Nate stopped and crouched to fire at someone who showed himself at the barn. The gunfire would not let up, and the front of the cabin was riddled by bullets.

With a desperate burst of strength, Nate heaved himself and Nick through the doorway, falling as he did. Lying on his back, with lead flying into the cabin and crashing into the table, hearth, and the wall behind him, he kicked the door shut, and right away a dozen bullets banged into the door front. Rolling to his side, Nate latched the door and then knelt over Nick. He pulled his friend behind the wood stove and began assessing the damage done.

The wound in Nick's chest pumped out blood to the rhythm of a heartbeat. Nate stuffed his Colt's into the waistband of his trousers, reached to the table, and swept away the rag that had been wrapped around the skillet handle. Folding it three times, Nate pressed it to the well-spring of blood and then picked up Nick's limp arms to cross his hands over the rag.

"Hold that there, Nick!"

Running back to his bunk, he snatched up the rifle and hurried back to the door. As soon as he peeked out the front window, a flurry of rifle fire shattered the glass in all the panes. Ducking low, Nate worked the lever on the rifle, and eased his bare head up cautiously. Three men were moving from the brush beside the front gate and heading for the barn. Staying low, Nate took a wide stance beneath the window frame, popped up, and pushed the muzzle of his rifle through an empty pane. He fired almost immediately, and one of the runners went down. Just as Nate ducked out of sight, the window above him exploded in a shower of splinters and shards of glass. It seemed like twenty guns going off at once.

From the north wall, he dashed to the closer of the east windows and saw four men getting to their feet in the brush. Using the same technique as before, Nate popped up from below and quickly got off two shots, shattering the glass before him. One man's leg jerked as if he had come to the end of a tether, and he went down. Another man's hat flew off and was carried by the wind back into the brush. He flattened himself on the ground and started crawling backward on his belly as the others around him dove for cover.

Running in a crouch, Nate darted to the other east window. Coming from the river, two men approached at a slow run toward a stand of sagebrush. Nate broke through a windowpane and opened up on them. They retreated in an all-out sprint, one man limping severely and the other holding his wrist against his chest.

Hurrying into the storage room on the south side, he peered out the window and saw a group of men gathered on the ridge. They stood about seventy yards away half-hidden by a cluster of spruces. No one was shooting. To his left was a brushy ravine. It was a mere stone's throw away from the cabin and offered the attackers a close position from which to shoot, but Nate could see no activity there. He checked the latch on the backdoor and hurried back into the front room.

At the west window, he knelt between two bunks and studied the thick brush and wispy clusters of winter-bleached grasses that stood above the snow. Two dark shapes huddled together behind a maze of branches. Nate eased the barrel of his rifle out through a broken pane and fired once. The two men scurried away from there in opposite directions. Then came the fusillade from hell.

Outside, the air filled with the sound of exploding gunpowder. Nate dropped flat on the floor as bullets buzzed through the interior of the cabin from every direction, tearing into bunks, the table, the skillet, the oil lamp, and the hearth stones. Every interior wall was chewed up by gunfire and pockmarked like a wasp's nest. Over at the sideboard, a tan cloud of wheat flower hung in the air over the punctured bag. Dory's painting was riddled with so many holes that Peaches was no longer recognizable.

Nate feared that the barrage was a signal for attack, so he made the circuit again, covering all sides. To his surprise, no one tried to advance. Returning to Nick, he saw that his friend's hands had fallen away from the compress, which was now so soaked with blood as to be useless.

Staying low, Nate snatched his towel from the drying line and quickly folded it. After setting it in place on the wound, he took Nick's limp hands and managed to interlace the fingers and squeeze them together to make them hold.

"Nick? Can you hear me?"

Nick made a sound in his throat like the croakin of a rusted hinge.

"I'm gonna git you more comf'ter'ble! Just hang on!"

Nate bobbed up in the front window to check the yard and saw that a man had stepped out of the shade of the barn as he shooed away the horses from the bay. Not wanting to harm the animals, Nate aimed low at the man's boot and fired. A high squeal followed, and the man hopped back into the barn on one foot, cursing all the way.

Crouching low, Nate crept to his bunk, grabbed a box of .44-.40s and tossed them to the floor next to Nick. Then he hurried to Nick's bed, pulled off the mattress, and dragged it across the floor, laying it out beside his friend. Getting on his knees, Nate set the rifle on the floor, bent low, and worked his hands under Nick's torso. With a straining grunt, Nate rolled him onto the mattress face up. Nick grimaced and shut his eyes so tightly that a sunburst of lines fanned across his temples and disappeared under his dark curly hair.

Nate's jaws clenched like a vise as he looked into Nick's face. The familiar look of his friend was steadily taking on the mask of death. Nate looked down at himself. The sleeves of his shirt were streaked with blood. In the turning process, he had discovered half a dozen more gunshot wounds in Nick's torso, several in his legs, and two in his left arm.

After wiping his hands on his trousers, Nate reloaded

the Winchester and stuffed his vest pocket with cartridges. Then he made the rounds again to each window. Still, no one out there was willing to approach the cabin. Returning to the front window, he peered out at the barn and saw the hat with the shining band still lying in the snow. Now he was certain as to the owner of that hat.

"Dixie Brooks," Nate whispered. "The Texas Kid."

All the memories of the troubles Nate had endured with Brooks washed over him like a bucket of foul water. Dixie was one part of Texas that Nate had been glad to leave behind. What he could not understand was why Dixie was in the northern Wyoming Territory with an army of men trying to kill everyone in the KC cabin.

Even as Nate watched out the shattered window, someone threw a lasso that encircled the hat. In small jerks, the rope started the hat moving over the snow toward the barn. Nate brought up the Winchester and took careful aim. When he squeezed off the shot, the dark hat slid backward on the snow several feet, and the silver band came apart into half a dozen pieces. He cocked the rifle and waited for Dixie to stick his head out to curse the shooter. But nothing happened. Nate swung his aim to the barn's corner and fired into its pine siding, hoping to splinter the wood and gouge his way through to Dixie.

"God damn you, Champion!" came a faceless scream. "I damn-well kilt yore friend, and b'fore this day is done I'm gonna kill you, too!"

The fierce screech in Dixie's threat was a sound Nate would have recognized anywhere. He cocked the rifle and fired again into the corner of the barn.

"*Shit!*" Dixie squealed, his voice so high it sounded like a woman's.

Nate ran the circuit again, checking from each window. Because there was no activity in any direction, Nate figured they were planning something big. If they rushed him, he knew, they might suffer a few losses, but he could be dead within seconds of their attack. Even with his pending death in mind, Nate felt a sharp pang of anger. He was out here by himself, where all these men could kill him without any witnesses who could tell the truth to the world.

When he reached his bunk, he pulled down the leather book from the shelf and sat, laying the rifle beside him. Opening to the page where the pencil marked his place, he began writing on an unmarked sheet.

April 9, 1892

> *Me and Nick was getting breakfast when the attack took place. Two men here with us—Old Ben Jones and Billy Walker. The old man went after water and did not come back. His friend went out to see what was the matter and he did not come back. Nick started out and I told him to look out, that I thought that there was someone at the stable and maybe would not let Ben and Billy come back. Nick is shot, but not dead yet. He is awful sick. I must go and wait on him.*

Setting the book aside, Nate picked up his rifle and walked quietly to the front window. He saw no activity. When he turned to a gargling sound behind him, he saw that Nick's lips were moving, trying to form a word. Nate propped the rifle against the wall, hurried to Nick in a crouch, and dropped to his hands and knees. Leaning down, he placed his ear close to Nick's mouth.

"What is it, Nick?"

"Wah...dah," Nick whispered in a raspy breath. The word came to Nate like a wisp of steam rising from a sunbaked rock after a rain.

"I'll git you some," Nate promised.

As he brought a full canteen from the basin, Nate heard a man's voice at a distance to the south. "God-dammit! He's just one man! I want you men to rush the cabin *now*! Blast the son of a bitch out of there!"

Setting down the canteen, Nate picked up the rifle and ran to the back window. Peeking out from the side, he saw no attack coming. Instead, he heard a man's deep-throated reply in a drawling voice.

"*You* can rush 'im if you wont to. *I* seen 'im shoot!"

Hurrying back to the front room, Nate traded rifle for canteen and knelt. He lifted Nick's head an inch or two and carefully trickled water into his mouth. When Nick tried to swallow, he convulsed into a fit of coughing that brought a foam of red bubbles to his lips. When the racking ceased, Nick opened his eyes and looked at Nate as if he were telegraphing a silent message. *Looks like this is it for me.* Then Nick's moist eyes closed, and he seemed to concentrate on breathing. Nate bunched up some of the blanket on which Nick lay, making a makeshift pillow. Then he gently lowered Nick's head.

"I hit a few of 'em," Nate told his friend, "but I cain't kill 'em all. There's too many of 'em. But if they give up an' leave, I'll git you some help just as fast as I can ride." He watched Nick's labored breathing. The towel was now solid red, heavy with blood. Nick's fingers remained inter-locked over the compress. "You wonna try some water again?"

Nick made no response other than to suck in air and blow a few small pink bubbles that lingered on his lips.

For the next three quarters of an hour, nothing happened. Nate made continuous circuits to all the windows until, finally, he saw a group of men move into a flanking position on the hillside south of the cabin. Their only cover was a few junipers and a scattering of small boulders spread about the lower section of the hill. One man walked brazenly in the open, strutting down the slope with a pistol in his hand as if he were directing the troops. He began barking orders and pointing with the gun toward each place he expected a man to dig in.

"Who is this duck?" Nate mumbled to himself.

The "duck" was pear-shaped and chubby, dressed in the kind of natty, hunting outfit that the English cattlemen sometimes wore to ensure their image as outdoorsmen. On his short stubby legs, he wore tall, lace-up boots that reached just below his knees, where his trousers ballooned around his upper legs. His bloated head was topped by a tan Homburg with a stiff, jaunty brim that curled sharply at each side like a tight smirk. Though Nate had never met the man, he judged this poser to be "the Major"...Frank Wolcott...the Carbon County baron who had tried to drive Sumner Beach from his claim on the Sweetwater.

When the "duck" walked casually toward a stand of aspens near the road, he pocketed his revolver and swung his arms in a casual way, like a man out on his own touring the countryside just to see what there was to see. Because he never looked toward the cabin, Nate knew that the man was flaunting his power and cool courage for all the others to witness. It was as if he were daring Nate to shoot.

"I'll oblige you," Nate whispered.

Taking a step back from the window, he cocked back the hammer of the Winchester and snugged the stock into his shoulder. Over the sights of the rifle, he followed the man's progress and then eased his aim slightly ahead of his target as he began a slow squeeze on the trigger. Just before the gun roared and kicked back, Nate saw the man stumble. Through the smoke that filled the window frame, Nate watched the man get control of his balance and then look down at himself to examine the front of his hunting coat. Enraged, he stood facing the cabin with his gloved hands knotted into fists at his sides. He began screaming to his men to fire at will.

Nate readied for a second shot, but someone jumped out from the trees and pulled the fool to safety. Nate dropped low and scuttled into the front room as a barrage of gunfire peppered the cabin on all sides. Pieces of glass and wood flew through the air like a tornado picking up debris. Nick opened his mouth and tried to speak, but the sound of the fusillade drowned his efforts. Tiny pieces of reflecting glass shone all over his body. The bombardment went on as if it might never end.

Crawling to his bunk, Nate grabbed his book and leaned his back into the bedframe to write.

> *It is now about two hours since the first shot. Nick is still alive; they are still shooting and are all around the house. There is bullets coming in like hail. Them fellows is in such shape I can't get at them. They are shooting from the stable and river and back of the house.*

After another minute, when the shooting tapered off, Nate got to his feet but remained squatting. Setting the book on the bed, he crab-walked to Nick and began plucking away the sharp slivers of glass lying on his face.

"I'll git a blanket to cover you," Nate said. He hesitated to listen for Nick's breathing and saw a rare peacefulness settle over his friend's face. Nick's chest no longer rose and fell. There were no bubbles on his lips. Nate pressed his fingertips into the hollow of Nick's throat and waited, feeling for a pulse. There was none. Nate drew in a deep breath and then exhaled a long sigh. Very gently, he probed with two fingertips for Nick's eyelids and lowered over his unseeing eyes.

"So long, you big, Missouri cowboy. I reckon it won't be long b'fore I see you again."

Crawling to the bunk where Billy had slept, Nate pulled off the blanket and brought it back to Nick. He could not quite cover Nick's entire body, so he chose to hide the face and let the boots be exposed. Rising up to a crouch, he peered over the ripped-up sill and saw black smoke billowing out of the bay of the barn. He felt his heart squeeze down like a tightened knot in a hemp rope, and then relief flooded over him when he saw Dakah trotting with four other horses across the bridge and on up the main road toward Buffalo.

Returning to his bunk, Nate sat on the floor and continued writing.

Nick is dead, he died about 9 o'clock. I see a smoke down at the stable. I think maybe they have fired it. I don't think they intend to let me get away this time.

Chapter Thirty

For the next hour, Nate made the rounds, checking to see if anyone had worked his way closer to the cabin. He also hoped to catch someone with his guard down. Someone he could put down with a bullet and keep the invaders on edge and reluctant to attack. But nothing seemed to change out there, and no shots were fired.

He had expected to see the barn go up in flames, but that did not happen either. Nate guessed that the fire he had seen earlier was to keep men warm. Dixie's hat still sat in the snow, and now, as he watched, a rope was thrown over it again. When someone tugged on the rope, the loop slipped under the hat and disengaged. After being drawn in behind the barn, the rope was tossed out again with the same results.

Suspecting this was a ploy to hold his attention, Nate ran to the back window and saw four men rise up from their hiding places on the hill. Running in a crouch they started across the open ground midway down the slope behind the cabin. Nate leveled the Winchester and fired, and, as soon as he saw these men turn and retreat, he hurried back to the front window. Several men had started his way from the barn, but when they saw his movement in the window, they turned and retraced their tracks in the snow, running and bumping into one another like a panicked flock of chickens. Nate held his fire, not knowing if Old Ben and Billy were being held as prisoners in the dark bay of the barn.

After one more circuit around all the windows, Nate settled on his bunk and opened the leather book again.

> *It is now about noon. There has been someone at the stable throwing a rope out and dragging it back. I guess it is to draw me out. I wish that duck would get out farther so I can get a shot at him. I don't know what they have done with them two fellows that staid here last night. I could sure use them now. I wish there was enough here with me so we could watch all sides at once. They may fool around until I get off a good shot at the right person. Then maybe they will leave.*

For the next hour, Nate made the rounds. An occasional potshot cracked a window frame or buried into one of the plank walls. Once, a bullet came through the front window, ricocheted off the wood stove, and knocked Nick's metal coffee cup off the table and into the fireplace, where it rang against the mortared rocks like a horseshoe hitting a ringer.

Nate chose his shots with economy, knowing that his supply of ammunition was dwindling. When he peered out the front window, a flash of light caught his eye in the dark bay of the barn. A small flame hovered before a man's face as he lighted a cigarette. There was only an instant to peruse the man before a cloud of smoke obscured his face and the flame went out, but Nate was more than half sure that he seen the visage of Frank Canton.

Voices yelled out from the west end of the yard, and soon the rattle of a wagon could be heard out on the road from Hole in the Wall. Nate crossed to the west window and knelt between the bunks in time to see a buckboard hurry past the cabin headed for the bridge.

"Stop that damned wagon!" someone screamed from the barn.

Nate crept to the front door, unlatched it, and opened it less than an inch. Through the crack he saw six or seven men running through the cottonwoods, trying to reach the bridge before the wagon could. Three other men already stood in the road before the bridge, waving their arms and trying to hail the driver to a stop.

The man holding the reins did not heed their warning. Snapping the ribbons, he coaxed his horses into a full-out gallop and hunkered down to make himself less of a target. Nate thought better of opening the door wider to shoot, so he closed it, set the lock, and sidled to the north window. Just as he peered out, gunfire erupted as the cluster of men emptied their revolvers at the fleeing wagon.

Nate took aim at one of the shooters but hesitated when a horseman came up behind them on the road and demanded they cease fire. One of the men on foot pointed his gun at the lone rider and barked a command. Nate recognized the surly voice of the man on the ground. It was Mike Shonsey. At first, it looked like the new arrival would surrender to Shonsey. Raising his hands to the height of his shoulders, he pulled back on the reins and slowed his horse. Then as Shonsey started to cross in front of the horse, the rider kicked his mount into an explosive acceleration, knocking Shonsey into the brush beside the road.

The group of gunmen opened fire at the lone rider, who attached to the side of his horse Comanche-style and made good his escape. Nate aimed at Shonsey and fired and saw the skirt of his overcoat jerk. Right away, the group scattered in every direction, leaving the road empty. Shonsey moved in a lively manner and ducked under the bridge. Nate cursed himself for missing his target, but held his aim on the bridge, hoping that Shonsey would try to peek out above the bank.

"Show yore ugly face, you damned snake," he mumbled aloud.

Across the river, men were yelling and bustling about, getting to their horses in the cottonwoods. A party of the invaders gave chase, taking after the wagon and disappearing up the road in a cloud of dust.

"Whoever you are," Nate whispered to the two travelers who had stumbled into his mare's nest. "Go an' git me some damned help."

For the moment, it seemed like all the enemy's attention was focused on the two interlopers. One man stepped from the bay of the barn, cupped his hand beside his mouth, and yelled to the men hiding near the bridge. A second man emerged from the shadows, took a grip on the other's arm, and began pulling him back into safety. That second man's hat was pulled low, but Nate believed him to be Frank Canton. He took aim and fired just as the two men were swallowed by the shade of the barn's interior. When the smoke cleared, all appeared quiet and unmoving at the barn. From far up the road came sporadic gunfire that grew more distant until the shots could barely be heard.

After checking all the windows, Nate sat on his bunk to write.

It's about 3 o'clock now. There was a man in a buckboard and one on horseback that just passed. My attackers fired on them as they went by. I don't know if they killed them or not. I seen lots of men come out on

*horses on the other side of the river and take after them. I
shot at some men in the stable just now, don't know if I
got any or not. I must go and look out again.*

On this round, Nate tried to get a feel for how many
men he was up against, so that he could compare that
number to his supply of ammunition. If he could hold out
until dark, he might have a chance of living past this day.
He still had seen no activity in the ravine just southeast of
the cabin. He figured that route would be his best bet for
escape. Once he was down in the gully, he stood a chance
of slipping away into the night like a coyote.

His armory was well-stocked. He had his Colt's pistol
and Winchester, both in .44 caliber. He had three and a
half boxes of cartridges remaining for these. And there
was the .36 caliber carbine that his attackers had left
behind at Hole in the Wall. Two boxes of shells for that
one. Nick's pistol was a .45, and his cartridge belt held a
full set of "teeth." Nick's saddle rifle was an old Spencer
lever-action, which also took .45. Nate looked at the bunks
that Old Ben and Billy had used. The banjo and the fiddle
were stored away in their battered cases, lying on top of
the beds. But they had brought in no hardware, so Nate
presumed their weapons were in the barn.

All the guns were laid out on various bunks, and
ammunition boxes were emptied onto the bed covers for
easy access. Standing next to the front window, he
listened for gunshots in the distance, but there were none
to be heard. Instead, he heard men arguing inside the
barn. When he felt a large lump under his boot, he looked
down to see a fist-sized piece of quartz that had broken
free from the hearth during the last barrage of shooting.
Leaning down, he picked up the rough stone and held it in
his hand. He could not help but think about the old gypsy
woman and her crystal.

"Go! Go while you can," she had said. *"If you wait too long, dere iss nowhere to run."*

Nate crossed to the fireplace and laid the rock on the hearth. After adding a log to the fire, he returned to his bed and sat to write.

> *It don't look as if there is much show of my getting away. On each side of the house I count about a dozen men. One is Mike Shonsey. Another one looks like Frank Canton. I don't know for sure whether it is or not.*

A gunshot went off from the north, and the bullet came through the front window and tore through the pipe above the wood stove just below its right-angle bend to pass through the window. More guns fired in a more or less haphazard pattern. Laying down the pencil, Nate carried the Winchester and peered out of each window, in case these shots signaled the beginning of an attack. When he cycled back to his bunk, he sat and opened the book again.

> *I hope they did not catch them fellows, that run across the bridge heading for town. They are shooting at the house now. If I had a pair of field glasses I believe I would know some of those men. I hear them coming back from up the road. I've got to look out.*

The sound that Nate had heard on the road was the invaders hauling back the wagon they had chased. There were no animals harnessed to the traces. Instead, two men towed the wagon by rope behind their horses. He watched them approach the bridge until the gunfire at the cabin escalated to a frenzy of flying lead. At this point, it would have been suicide to try and peek out the window.

When the bullets stopped flying, Nate cracked open

the door and saw the lead end of the wagon tongue angled to the ground behind the barn. Then came the loud *thwack!* of an axe blade sinking into wood. What followed was a telling sound: the heavy *clank!* of metal striking metal and the *crackle* of wood fibers splitting apart. Nate thought about the stack of pitch pine fence posts piled in the last stall of the barn. And there was dry hay in the shallow loft. Closing his eyes, Nate felt a chill run the length of his body.

"They're gonna burn me out," he whispered to the empty room.

> *Well they have just got through shelling the house like hail. I heard them splitting wood. I guess they are going to fire the house tonight. I think I will make a break when night comes. If alive.*

For the next hour, the chopping and splitting and banging of a steel wedge went on without a pause. From the front window, Nate watched a knot of men gather at the front of the wagon and push it around the blind side of the barn until it barely extended beyond the corner. The bed of the wagon was filled with four feet of alternating layers of split wood and hay. Nate could hear the men hiding behind the pyre arguing and snapping at one another, but eventually the mass of combustibles began to trundle toward him.

A steady rain of gunfire was laid down to keep Nate away from the window. He cracked open the front door, but he had no reasonable shot. From the barn came a single rifle shot that splintered the edge of the door. Then a dozen guns opened up from the cottonwoods, a barrage that hammered the door. Nate closed and latched it. All he could do now was listen to the rolling pyre as it trundled across the yard toward the cabin. It may as well have been the Grim Reaper come to collect his soul.

Kneeling by his bunk, Nate made a quick entry in his book.

> *Shooting again. They aim to fire the house. It's not night yet. I can't see that I've got a prayer if I try and make my run in daylight.*

The north window darkened when the wagon pressed up against the front wall. With the wind coming out the north, Nate smelled the sharp, antiseptic scent of split pine enter the room. Then came a hammering sound, a sledge pounding on wood. Before Nate saw any flames, an acrid, black smoke began to seep through the shot-out window. Nate grabbed the iron poker from the hearth and tried pushing the wagon away, but it would not give. He realized then that the pounding must have been someone driving a wood stake into the ground where the wagon tongue bit into the dirt.

The burlap curtains were the first items to ignite inside the cabin. Nate pulled them down with the poker and stamped them with his boots, but he soon realized that the curtains were the least of his problems. A thick tongue of flames poured through the open window frame and arched upward toward the rafters. Darting to the door, he opened it just enough to see if his attackers were getting bolder now. Not a soul was in sight.

He knew they had no reason to risk being shot now. All they had to do was wait and let the fire drive him outside, where he would be the main feature of a shooting gallery.

"Come on out, Champion!" a voice yelled from behind the barn. Nate recognized Dixie Brooks's Texas twang. "The party's out here, an' we're all a-waitin' on you!"

Nate locked the door and started moving all guns and ammunition to the back of the room. Then he took down Dory's perforated painting and propped it beside the hearth. The flames consumed the front wall around the window, and already the roof was afire. Even though the flames were above him, the heat was horrific.

The wind pushed flames around the northeast corner of the cabin, and the east wall caught quickly. A stratum of dark smoke was trapped under the roof, and it hung over the room like a roiling thundercloud.

Sitting on his bunk, Nate opened the book and hurriedly scratched two quick sentences.

The house is all fired. Goodbye to all my friends, if I never see you again.

Looking down at the paper, he knew he was seeing his last written words in this life. He scribbled his name across the bottom of the page. When he closed the leather book in his lap, he stared at the painting of the horse on the cover. Shutting his eyes tightly, he spoke aloud, his voice just a murmur beneath the crackling of the flames.

"Reckon I'll be seein' you purty soon."

Within minutes, the fire had consumed the entire front wall. The northern half of the roof was ablaze. When the heat became unbearable in the front room, Nate carried the Winchester and his Colt's into the back storage. Then he went back for the painting, the book, and a box of .44 shells.

Sitting on the floor and leaning into the back of the hearth, he loaded both weapons to full capacity. The fire in the front room had built to a steady roar. Apparently, the roof had burned away enough to allow the smoke to escape. Only a small layer of smoke had accumulated in the storage room, but the air was foul with the stench of all that was burning.

Nate lay down on the wood planks trying to suck up some fresh air through the floorboards. Each time he drew in a breath, he could taste the freedom of the range, but he felt irrevocably distant from all that open country, as if the Powder River Basin had already forgotten him.

Chapter Thirty-One

Lying prone behind the hearth, Nate closed his eyes to the sting in the air, and a memory floated up from his past. Lying on the flat, midstream stone that parted the waters of Brushy Creek back home in Texas. There, on his belly, he had taken a series of deep breaths to fill his lungs before taking the plunge to meet Billy Hill's breath-holding challenge. Dory had been there, standing on the rock in her bare feet, her long blonde hair hanging below her shoulders, her light-blue dress shining in the sunlight. Nate remembered her brown doe-eyes fixed on him as if she were about to experience the ordeal with him.

"Dory," he whispered into the floor.

Flames pushed into the entrance of the storage room, and within seconds the heat intensified, making the air that he breathed seem to blister the wet tissue inside his mouth, nose, and throat. Leaning against the wall opposite the door to the front room, Dory's painting burst into flames. Reacting by instinct, Nate rushed to it as if he might somehow save it. The canvas burned so aggressively that Nate stopped his hand from grabbing it. Instead, he picked up the book and retreated. The leather was so hot on his fingers that he shifted the book to his belly and cradled it with the sleeves of his work shirt. Dropping the book, he unlatched the back door and cracked it just enough to see that the wind was pushing a torrent of thick, black smoke across the backyard and on toward the hill south of the cabin.

Leaving the door slightly ajar, he knelt to the book, opened the cover, and began tearing out the pages three and four at a time. When he had ripped out all but the words he had written today, he stuffed the book under his vest and down into the waistband of his trousers.

Once it was secure, he flattened himself to the floor and cupped his hands around his mouth to siphon up fresh air from below the cabin. The heat of the book pressing against his abdomen made him think of the night he had danced with Dory on the floor of the Masonic Hall in Round Rock. Her lithe body had attached to his, face to face. Their shared warmth like a melding of souls.

Nate got to his knees, turned at the waist, and threw the torn pages into the flames that still engulfed the painting. He watched the papers burst into a bright, white blaze —a flame within a flame. The skin on his face and hands stung as if he, himself, were about to ignite.

After pulling off his boots, he took the Colt's in his right hand and the Winchester in his left, pushed the door aside with the barrel of the pistol, and dashed out of the burning building into the smoke-filled yard. The relief from the heat was immediate, but the air was choked with caustic, black smoke, and he could not take a breath. He ran southeast for the ravine, sprinting like a spooked deer, but holding back just enough to remain upright, as the blinding smoke was disorienting to his sense of balance.

At first, no one seemed to know he had sprung free. No shots were fired. Then when he neared the periphery of the thick smoke, someone yelled from the bluffs off to his right.

"There he goes!"

Two shots were fired from the base of the hill, where there was good cover in the brush. The bullets tore through the air so close to Nate that he felt their wind brush him like the quick stroke of a feather. Then the shooting became general from three directions, and angry lead seemed to fly on every side of him. Speed was his asset, he knew, and now he gave it everything he had. By some miracle, he had not been hit.

He chanced a breath, and, though it stung his throat, he felt his lungs somewhat replenished. On the next breath, the results were better, and he felt his hopes rise as he made out the dark brush that grew inside the ravine. Flying across the yard, his legs running on the explosive power of survival, he aimed for a small gap in the bushes at the lip of the gully.

As he gathered himself for a slide down the bank of the ravine, he spotted two men kneeling at the bottom. Before they could shoulder their rifles to shoot, Nate veered right and hoped to find another open entry where no men were stationed. But, as soon he turned, two men suddenly blocked his way...a couple of cowhands by their dress...strangers...one as big as a bear and the other stooped and cautious. Both men leveled rifles at Nate, and he pulled off a fast shot with the Colt's, aiming at the bigger of the two men. Thinking he had hit the man, Nate started cocking the pistol to shoot his companion, but before he could bring the hammer to full cock, the big man fired, the sound deafening and the muzzle flash a blink of bright yellow. Nate's left arm spasmed and a searing pain shot through him as if he'd been struck by lightning. The rifle fell from his numbed hand and clattered to the ground, but with his right hand he completed the cocking of his pistol and swung the barrel up to point at the smaller man.

The next gunshot shocked Nate to the core, stealing from him all control of his body. This surrender of will was immediate and complete. It was less a dying than a transformation, as if he had been delivered into a hidden world that had always existed around him...but only now was it made available to his senses. More gunshots fired around him, and he felt their impact without feeling their sting. He was collapsing backward, and yet he knew he need not reach back to cushion his fall. He sensed that he was falling through some kind of expanded space that would provide no place for him to land.

He was not aware of closing his eyes, but he must have. When he opened them, he saw that the sky was no longer the arched vault of blue that served as a ceiling to the world. There was a new depth to it now, as if a great curtain had opened above to reveal an endlessness that no mortal could ever understand.

"Dory—" he tried to say, forming her name on his lips and breathing the word into the world he was leaving behind. He was vaguely aware of voices next to him, but they seemed spoken from another plane of existence...a place to which he was no longer privy.

"Damned toughest man I ever fought!"

"Helluva shot, too! This ol' boy wouldn' quit!"

"How the hell'd he stay in there so long? I figured he was burnt alive!"

"By God, if I had fifty men like *him*, I could whip the whole goddammed state of Wyoming!"

Nate left these voices to their own meaningless illusion of life, closed his eyes, and listened to Dory breathing his name into his ear. Then he went very still and continued falling away from the crowd of men staring down at him. As he fell, he knew that he was leaving everything behind him, forever...and that none of it mattered.

None of it.

Epilogue and Author's Note

This telling of Nate Champion's story is, technically speaking, written in the third person, yet it embodies the viewpoint of a first-person account, a literary device I call "first via third" person. A typical third-person narrative uses an omniscient voice to explain the larger picture that surrounds its protagonist. This can include the thoughts of secondary characters, the unseen events unfolding outside of the lead character's range of vision, and the machinations that are stirring up trouble "offstage."

By employing the "first via third" point of view, this author intentionally allows the reader to experience the events of Nate's life through *Nate's* eyes only, with no more information than that to which Nate was privy.

Nate Champion did *not* know that the Wyoming Stock Growers Association had secretly formed an "army of extermination" comprised of the powerful cattle barons of Wyoming and of Texan mercenaries, who were hired simply for their willingness to kill for money. This army was comprised of more than fifty men.

The WSGA barons had bestowed upon themselves

the "moral right" to use brutal force to ensure that the vast free-range pasturage of Wyoming would be available *only* to them. These elite businessmen had enjoyed this privilege for years. Why should they allow it to change?

Their plan was both audacious and heinous. After assassinating Jim Averell, Ella Watson, Tom Waggoner, John Tisdale, and Ranger Jones, they decided to invade the seat of Johnson County. There they planned to murder Sheriff Angus, the county commissioners, hostile newspaper editors, a few lawyers, and anyone else who posed a threat to the domination of the free range by the wealthy cattlemen. Frank Canton, one of their primary foot soldiers, carried in his pocket a "blacklist" of Johnson County citizens, who were to be executed in cold blood. Seventy people's names were on that list.

The power of the WSGA extended to the governor, who was complicit with the invaders. To aid and abet their criminal attack, he issued a proclamation: that no local militia or National Guard could interfere with the insurgent army's actions. But the big cattlemen's influence reached farther than the territorial boundaries. Senators Carey and Warren, both WSGA members and owners of large cattle ranches in the Powder River Basin, manipulated the president of the United States—Benjamin Harrison—into believing that all Wyoming cattle raisers who were not members of the WSGA were rustlers, plain and simple. They spread this canard throughout Washington, D.C., so that, if federal troops should be called into action, the small cattle ranchers would be targeted as the "enemies of the state."

The top brass of the powerful Union Pacific Railroad worked in secret alliance with the cattle barons, utilizing covert "midnight runs" to deliver the attackers and their mounts to Casper. From there, the invaders traveled by horseback through a grueling snowstorm into the Powder River country.

The formation of this "vigilante army" in Wyoming was a blatant act of insurrection. It violated state and federal laws and defied the Constitutional rights of American citizens. This monstrous collapse into anarchy—engineered by Wyoming's business elite—was made possible, in part, by the remoteness of the town of Buffalo and its further isolation when the invaders cut all telegraph lines running out of town. The covert operation came as a complete surprise to all the small ranch owners and citizens of Buffalo...just as it did to Nate Champion on the morning of April 9, 1892.

The invaders' approach route into Buffalo was abruptly modified when Mike Shonsey intercepted them to inform "Major" Wolcott that Nate Champion and a group of "rustlers" were holed up at the KC Ranch, where Shonsey had just spent a night with the enemy. Shonsey reported that these "outlaws" could be easily overtaken in their cabin.

When Wolcott made the decision to kill Nate Champion before attacking Buffalo, he believed he could demoralize the opposition ranchers, who looked up to Champion and had recently voted him in as head foreman for a new livestock association. At the same time, Wolcott knew that he would be eliminating the primary witness for the prosecution in Joe Elliott's trial for attempted murder. In making this decision to veer off for the KC Ranch, Wolcott not only faced a resistance he could never have predicted, but he also doomed the entire WSGA plan to take over Johnson County.

Nate knew none of this. When he awoke on the morning of his last day, he could not have had an inkling about the nightmare about to come his way. No doubt, his mind was on the day's chores.

After Nate was killed, a large group of the invaders gathered around his body. There was a common theme to the quiet conversations that mingled together at that death site. Every man present knew that he was standing over the corpse of a brave man who would not quit the fight. When the Texan killers learned that Nate, himself, had come from Texas, a pall of remorse fell over a portion of the crowd. If it is possible for hardened killed to feel regret, it must have happened that day.

Sam Clover, a *Chicago Herald* reporter, who accompanied the invaders, found the book under Nate's vest. The cover showed a bullet hole large enough to be probed by a woman's little finger. Blood had soaked through the hole, leaving a singed ring of crimson on each page like a royal seal pressed into the paper. Clover privately read the diary and then showed it to Frank Wolcott—the man who had spoken over Nate's corpse, saying "If I had fifty men like *him*, I could whip the whole goddammed state of Wyoming."

Wolcott called out to his men to be quiet. Then he proceeded to read Nate's last words aloud for all to hear. As he read, the crowd of killers remained dead silent. There was not a man in that audience who did not then know to respect Nate Champion. Except, perhaps, for Mike Shonsey, who, probably, listened to the recitation with varying degrees of gloating, resentment, and envy... and Dixie Brooks, "The Texas Kid," who had fired the first shot at Nick Ray and likely felt only regret that it had not been he who had fired the fatal shot at Nate Champion.

When the reading of the diary was complete, Wolcott handed Nate's pencil to Clover and then tore a blank page from the book. "Write a warning to others of his kind and pin it to his chest." He pushed the book onto the newspaperman and briskly walked away. Clover printed two words on the paper using all capital letters. He scratched the pencil repeatedly over each letter to darken the message into bold type. Then he pinned it in place on Nate's vest using a short, stiff piece of baling wire that one of the Texans retrieved from the barn.

THIEVES BEWARE! the note read—a misnomer of insult that bore no applicability to Nate Champion.

The diary was published the next week in the *Chicago Herald,* but not as a tribute to a courageous man making a noble last stand. Instead, it was meant as a warning—a prophecy to other "rustlers," should they continue their criminal ways.

The reader is encouraged to leaf back through the last three chapters of this book to reread all the italicized passages from Nate Champion's journal. These were his words...with the exception of two minor edits made by the author to clarify Nate's intention for the benefit of the reader.

The humble, thirty-four-year-old cowhand from Texas wrote not a single, self-serving phrase or made any effort to elevate himself to the status of heroism or bravery. He made no mention of running outside into a chaotic storm of gunfire to drag his wounded friend inside to safety. Nor does he describe his efficiency as a one-man force holding off a blood-thirsty mob of fifty. The fact that he was able to write a clear-headed account of the attack while awaiting his sure death says volumes about the kind of man Nate Champion was.

After a celebratory meal upwind of the smoldering ruins of the KC cabin, Wolcott and his army of invaders started north to continue their march to Buffalo. At the Western Union Beef Company, where Shonsey was foreman, they obtained fresh horses and pushed on. Then, after a two-hour rest at Fred Hesse's ranch, they rode on to the TA Ranch, where they set up camp and slept. Here, they were fourteen miles south of Buffalo, just a day's ride from their destination, where the mass killings would begin.

Unknown to all present at the KC siege, the wagoner and lone horseman, who had run through the gauntlet of shooters at the bridge and escaped, were two friends of Nate's. Jack Flagg's stepson, Alonzo, drove the wagon and whipped his team into a gallop when he sensed trouble. Following behind him was Jack, himself, on horseback. The two of them had set out from home and were on their way into Buffalo when they stumbled into the hornets' nest at the KC.

One of the horses harnessed to the wagon was hit by a bullet and began to weaken. Jack caught up and signaled to the boy to stop, for Jack's rifle lay in the wagon bed. When the pursuers came within sight, they saw Flagg standing behind the wagon, his rifle held diagonally across his body like a sentry on guard duty, his legs spread to show that he would not retreat. The group of pursuers foolishly fired off a dozen rounds from their pistols at 1,000 yards, but they would not approach within the deadly range of Flagg's rifle.

Alonzo cut the unwounded horse from the traces and mounted bareback. Then, stepfather and stepson hurried on to Buffalo to report what they had seen. The wagon they left behind, however, would play a major role in the demise of Nate Champion. This was the vehicle that the invaders converted into a "go-devil" to approach the KC cabin with a load of fuel to burn Nate out of his fortress.

Sheriff Angus was not in Buffalo when Flagg dashed into town with the news of the battle going on at the KC. In fact, Angus had received word of the fight from a rancher who lived four miles from the KC and had heard the continuous volley of distant gunfire. By the time Angus and his small posse reached the KC, the invaders were gone. Angus found the gruesome remains of Nick

Ray's incinerated body and the bullet-riddled corpse of Nate Champion with the ludicrous note pinned to his chest. Angus headed back to Buffalo in a hurry to get more men.

When the citizens learned of the death of Nate Champion and his friend, they grabbed their weapons and eagerly joined Angus's posse that eventually swelled to over 400 men. This new "army" located the invaders at the TA Ranch, surrounded them, and turned the tables by laying siege to Wolcott's gang of killers. Many shots were fired but to little effect on either side.

A WSGA rider broke through the sheriff's encirclement and got off a wire (on the recently repaired lines) to the governor, who in turn sent a late-night telegram to President Harrison, who was awakened by his staff with the urgent message.

Mr. President, the telegram began, *an insurrection exists in Johnson County, in the State of Wyoming, in the immediate vicinity of Fort McKinney, against the government of said state.*

This false claim duped the president into ordering troops from Fort McKinney to protect Wolcott and his invaders. This farcical version of "the cavalry coming to the rescue" resulted in ending the siege at the TA Ranch. Wolcott went through the pretense of surrendering by handing over all weapons to the army, which then escorted the invaders to the fort for their protection.

Eventually, the legal wheel began to roll, and arraignments were scheduled for the WSGA leaders who engineered the attempted takeover of Johnson County. Outside newspapers were swayed by the association to slant coverage of the story against Nate Champion and the other small-operation cattlemen, but there were enough honest citizens in Buffalo who would not allow the truth to be covered up. They demanded justice through the court system. But it was not to be.

Old Ben Jones and Billy Walker, both of whom would have been star witnesses in prosecuting the invaders, were jailed in another county for their protection, but both men mysteriously vanished. Later, it was discovered that the WSGA had generously recompensed the two witnesses for their losses in the cabin fire and then, after presenting them with graphic threats, escorted the two trappers onto a train traveling east, where they could not be extradited to testify in a Wyoming courtroom.

Even with so much uproar over the WSGA's arrogant and criminal methods, its political power remained formidable, extending even into the judicial system. Every case that brought a WSGA member to trial was dismissed. Including Joe Elliott's.

In 1894, two years after Nate Champion's murder, Asa Mercer, a successful editor with an illustrious background, published a book that told the true story of the Johnson County War: *The Banditti of the Plains, or the Cattlemen's Invasion of Wyoming in 1892*. This tell-all book was immediately suppressed by court injunction. Wagonloads of Mercer's books were impounded and stored in a basement prior to destroying them in a bonfire. The WSGA, it would seem, had developed a theme of burning up the enemy.

One night before the scheduled fire, however, a few hundred copies were stolen from said basement and spirited away in a wagon to Colorado, where many were secretly distributed to select owners for future exposure. The WSGA agents were relentless in tracking down as many of these "rescued" books as possible. Having such a book in one's possession contained high risks. Being caught with Mercer's book threatened one's life, property, and family.

Even when copies of *The Banditti of the Plains* were given homes on the shelves of the University of Wyoming and the State Library of Wyoming, these books quietly disappeared. And if they did, miraculously, happen to reappear, pages were missing, their telltale remnants showing where someone had ripped the pages from the spine.

Mercer was jailed for publishing his book. The printing plates were destroyed. He was charged with sending obscene material through the mail. In his mid-fifties at the time of the invasion, Mercer lived another two decades after his persecution by the rich and powerful cattlemen, but he never recovered from his losses.

In 1893, Mike Shonsey killed Dudley Champion in a gunfight near Lusk, Wyoming. The truth behind Dudley's death has never been sorted out due to conflicting stories. Shonsey became a family man and lived to the age of 87, when he died a nonviolent death in Iowa.

Martin Tisdale, a.k.a. Al Allison, left Wyoming under a shadow of shame after mishandling funds of his late half brother John's estate and denying John's wife and children their proper share of inheritance. He was killed in a gunfight in Glasgow, Montana in 1894.

Kate Tisdale survived the death of her husband, John, and the swindling scheme of her brother-in-law by opening a restaurant in Buffalo. At the age of 60, she died in a hospital bed in Johnson County in 1923.

Fred Hesse fled Wyoming after the invasion, but two years later he dared to return to operate his ranch. He was generally despised by all citizens, even receiving death threats and seeing his children bullied. In 1900, three of his young children died of scarlet fever, and this loss tended to soften the public's animosity toward him. He died in 1929 and was buried in the same cemetery where John Tisdale's body lay.

For fear of retribution for his part in the invasion, Frank Canton left Wyoming never to return. He went on to continue his career as a lawman in Alaska, Texas, and Oklahoma. Throughout his latter life, he molded his own history and shaped his character to his liking. He even enjoyed a certain amount of celebrity. The former outlaw, whose real name was Joe Horner, died of cancer in 1927 at the age of 78.

Ben Champion, little brother to Nate and Dudley, lived until 1929, when a heart attack took him "across the river" at age 69.

Did the invaders truly believe they were in the right? They said they did. But theirs was the voice of rationalization...and greed...and fear. They epitomized everything flawed in the human psyche and utilized one of the oldest persuasions of history: brutal violence. Perhaps the nineteenth century cattle barons of Wyoming affirmed the words of D.H. Lawrence when he wrote:

*"The essential American soul is hard, isolate, stoic, and a killer. It has never yet melted."**

One of the most remarkable pieces of this story is that Nate Champion—by fighting off his enemies for eight hours, enduring a blistering house fire, and finally succumbing to the inescapable fate of being shot down by overwhelming odds—never knew that he alone had saved the town of Buffalo, Wyoming from a horrible massacre. If someone could have whispered this news into Nate's ear as he lay dying, perhaps this story might be a kinder one to hold in our memory.

In the end, it must be said that Nate Champion did not sacrifice himself for his neighbors. Instead, he defended himself as best he could and fought valiantly simply because of the man that he was. Still, it is hard not to label him as a true American hero, one whose name ought to be remembered for all time.

A Look at A Last Serenade for Billy Bonney

Billy Bonney

A Novel on Billy the Kid

In this novel of America's most celebrated outlaw, Spur Award-Winning Author Mark Warren sheds light on the human side of Billy the Kid—and reveals the intimate stories of the lesser-known players in his legendary life of crime.

When John Blessing, composer and Santa Fe journalist, is assigned to report on a jailed prisoner who calls himself "William H. Bonney," what begins as a formal interview, evolves into an unexpected relationship and a self-examination of John's own cultured, city values.

After Billy the Kid's death, John embarks on a journey to find Billy's comrades and acquaintances—those who loved the Kid... and those who despised him. Was Billy Bonney a cold-blooded killer without a conscience, or was he a victim of the machinations of corrupt politicians in "the Santa Fe Ring?"

Ride along with John Blessing as he unravels one of Western history's most fascinating enigmas by diving into the lives of the influential people who helped shape Billy the Kid's life.

AVAILABLE NOW

About the Author

Mark Warren teaches nature classes and primitive survival skills at Medicine Bow, his nationally renowned wilderness school in the Southern Appalachians. His Wyatt Earp: An American Odyssey trilogy was honored by WWA's Spur Awards, The Historical Novel Society, and the 2020 Will Rogers Medallion Awards.

Mark is a 2022 Georgia Author of the Year recipient for his book *Song of the Horseman*, and his short story, "The Cowboy, The Librarian and The Broomsman," is a Will Rogers Medallion Award winner.

His other books include *Two Winters in a Tipi, Indigo Heaven, The Westering Trail Travesties, Secrets of the Forest, Indigo Heaven, A Last Serenade for Billy Bonney, Last of the Pistoleers, A Tale Twice Told*, and *Moon of the White Tears*.

With gratitude to the
researchers who dug up the
history of the Johnson
County War:

Wyoming Range War by John W. Davis, University of Oklahoma
Press 2010

The Johnson County War by Bill O'Neal, Eakin Press 2004

War on the Powder River by Helena Huntington Smith, University of
Nebraska Press 1967

The Banditti of the Plains by Asa Mercer, University of Oklahoma
Press 1954

Made in the USA
Middletown, DE
09 September 2024